The

Vintage

Book of

International

Lesbian

Fiction

The Vintage Book of International Lesbian Fiction

edited and with an introduction by

NAOMI HOLOCH AND JOAN NESTLE

Vintage Books
A Division of Random House, Inc.
New York

To all those who struggle for human rights.

A VINTAGE ORIGINAL

Copyright © 1999 by Naomi Holoch and Joan Nestle

All rights reserved under International and Pan-American
Copyright Conventions. Published in the United States
by Vintage Books, a division of Random House, Inc.,
New York, and simultaneously in Canada by Random House
of Canada Limited, Toronto.

Grateful acknowledgment is made to Warner Bros. Publications U.S. Inc. for
permission to reprint, in the story "Aphrodite's Vision," an excerpt from
"Wouldn't It Be Loverly" by Alan Jay Lerner and Frederick Loewe, copyright © 1956 (Renewed) by Alan Jay Lerner and Frederick Loewe, Chappell
& Co. owner of publication and allied rights throughout the world. All rights
reserved. Reprinted by permission of Warner Bros. Publications U.S. Inc.,
Miami, FL 33014.

Pages 345-348 constitute an extension of this copyright page.

Vintage Books and colophon are registered trademarks of Random House, Inc.

Library of Congress Cataloging-in-Publication Data
The vintage book of international lesbian fiction / edited and with an
introduction by Naomi Holoch and Joan Nestle.
p.   cm.
Includes bibliographical references.
ISBN-13: 978-0-679-75952-2
ISBN-10: 0-679-75952-2
1. Fiction—Women authors.   2. Lesbians' writings.   3. Lesbians—
Fiction.   4. Fiction—20th century.   5. Fiction—Women authors—
Translations into English.   6. Fiction—20th century—Translations
into English.   7. Lesbians' writings—Translations into English.
I. Holoch, Naomi.   II. Nestle, Joan, 1940–   .
PN6120.92.W65V56   1999
808.83'0086'643—dc21   98-32138
CIP

Book design by Jo Anne Metsch

www.vintagebooks.com

146684614

Esta noche, entre todos los normales,
te invito a cruzar el puente.
Nos mirarán con curiosidad—estas dos muchachas—
y quizás, si somos lo suficientemente sabias,
discretas y sutiles
perdonen nuestra subversión
sin necesidad de llamar al médico
al comisario político o al cura.

Tonight, among all the normal people
I invite you to cross the bridge.
They'll be curious about us—these two girls—
and perhaps, if we are wise,
secretive and subtle enough
they will forgive our subversion
without calling in the doctor
the commissar or the priest.

—CRISTINA PERI ROSSI

Please keep asking about us. Ask about the lesbians. Ask for us by name—my name, the names of others. Remind them that we exist, that we're here and we're not going away.

—RITA ARAUZ,
lesbian–feminist activist
from Nicaragua

Contents

Introduction

—An Egyptian wife is greeted by mysterious forces at work in her new home.

—An Irish woman travels through time in search of a wronged maiden.

—A teacher in Spain locks herself up in her grandmother's house with her young Colombian lover.

—A woman moves through the night streets of apartheid-torn South Africa of the 1950s in quest of passion.

Representing the work of thirty-four writers from twenty-seven different countries, *The Vintage Book of International Lesbian Fiction* offers the reader an entry into a diversity of remarkable lives and imaginations. Growing out of vastly different personal and cultural backgrounds, ranging from straightforward story-telling to more experimental forms, the stories reflect an international lesbian sensibility. Desire and longing—for home, for language, for women's bodies, for safety, for freedom—thread their way through these tales.

Because of its international scope as well as its subject matter, this collection has at its heart the challenge of translation: translation in the literal sense, since so many of these stories first appeared in a language other than English, but also in the figurative sense as the reader moves from culture to culture, from coded to clear meaning, following the expression of desire in all its nuances. Issues of translation are often central to the stories themselves as author and character search for a way to express or "translate" experiences and emotions into words where words are lacking. In the selection by the Norwegian writer Gerd Brantenberg, the young narrator, arriving in Scotland, faces not only the frustrating difficulties of applying her classroom knowledge of English to "real life," but discovers as well layers of meaning of words in her own language, layers which serve as a bridge to intimacy and self-awareness. In the story "My World of the Unknown" by the Egyptian writer Alifa Rifaat, a woman's sexuality is embodied symbolically, in the form of a seductive, womanly snake. While the protagonist struggles to understand the meaning of this serpent in her life, the Western reader must redefine a familiar sexual symbol in a totally new way. Such stories as these, which are shaped by and express so many different cultural nuances, carry the reader to new territories and often to different ways of reading, as language and lives are revealed to hold fresh and unexpected significance.

Steeped in a sense of place, many of these stories offer the reader an unusual perspective on national regions. The sun-drenched streets of Cyprus, the luxuriant garden of a provincial French town, the intimate afternoons in a small Italian fishing village, the plazas and ancient ruins of Mexico all come alive, imbued with a special sensuality. These vivid settings both incorporate and reveal the intense longings and daily rituals that mold the lives of the women represented here.

If place, words, and symbols take on new and sometimes mysterious meanings, one word emerges as particularly elusive. As we searched for "lesbian" texts, it became clear to us that the word only had meaning in particular cultures—that is, in the West. Originally referring to inhabitants of the Greek island of

Lesbos, the word disappears from common usage along with Sappho's texts, which were burned by the Catholic church in the 1300s. In the subsequent centuries, the term *lesbian* had little official existence except for a brief appearance as the name of a particularly flexible form of a mason's ruler. The word re-emerged in the late nineteenth century in the West as a label for a woman engaged in a sexual relationship with another woman—that is, in a socially, legally, and psychologically stigmatized act. Thus, for better or for worse, Western lesbian writers of the twentieth century have been given a category of identification that is not common to much of the rest of the world.

While the word *lesbian* is not global in its use and significance, it is clear, as these stories show, that emotional and sexual intimacies between women do indeed exist throughout the world. Although most of the authors included here write out of a constant connection to a lesbian sense of self, a few extremely powerful works in this volume, deeply rooted in specific cultures and embodying lesbian themes, were written by authors who do not define themselves as lesbian. Indeed, such terminology would not even be meaningful to an author such as Alifa Rifaat. The excerpt from the novel *Red Azalea* by the Chinese author Anchee Min, who is not a lesbian, gives a complex and moving portrait of a relationship between two women living through the Cultural Revolution in China during the late sixties. Struggling to survive the demands of grueling physical labor, a young woman finds herself drawn to the strong presence of her female commander. As these stories suggest, the world of non-Western lesbian literature is often less constrained by categories and definitions, exploring what the Indian writer Ginu Kamani calls the "fluid sensualities" of the non-Western world.

Such fluidity does of course appear in Western writing as well. *Letters to Marina* by Dacia Maraini from Italy reminds us of the rich possibilities of experience that may be opened once authors of any sensual persuasion are comfortable moving across sexual boundaries in their creation of characters and exploration of themes. The French lesbian writer Violette Leduc pushes the boundaries in other directions as she depicts the passionate sensuality of a young girl expressing her love for her grandmother, and a young schoolmate's intense need for physical freedom.

For many of our writers, the power of history is as strong as the power of desire. The three stories from South Africa offer an historical perspective on both how a public lesbian community fared during the height of apartheid and how personal commitment to political change enters a lesbian bedroom. For the Lebanese author Etel Adnan, moments of lesbian connection are absorbed into the suffering of Beirut. The rise of Nazism looms menacingly in the militaristic world of the German writer Christa Winsloe. It lives, too, as a painful memory in the work of the Israeli writer Gila Svirsky. The dislocation of exile and return is dramatized in "Waters" by the Cuban author Achy Obejas.

Caught up in the violence of history in the making, a number of the authors in this collection are writing from within the daily catastrophes of national upheavals. The contemporary Slovenian writer and lesbian activist Suzana Tratnik writes in a fevered voice that suggests both the desperation of war and of erotic attachment. Yasmin Tambiah contemplates her place as a lesbian and a writer in Sri Lanka, a country torn by ethnic civil war. The worldwide crisis of AIDS—an upheaval that has no national boundaries—invades Berlin in Karen-Susan Fessel's story "Lost Faces."

Like many of the characters in these stories, the authors represented here fight to maintain their integrity of desire in the face of history. Their stories suggest that women's desire— particularly for one another—can challenge boundaries and national identities from within. Makeda Silvera, born in Jamaica, describes the obstacles and conflicts faced by a "third world" author in her story "Her Head a Village." In an imaginary dialogue between the villagers and the author, Silvera poses the challenges that many international lesbian writers face. The villagers demand that she:

> "Write about women in houses without electricity."
> "Write about the dangers of living in a police state."
> "Write about Third World issues."
> "Write about . . . about . . . "
> "Stick to the real issues that face Black women writers." They reprimand her: "Your sexuality is your personal business. We don't want to hear about it."
> They accused her of enjoying the luxury of being a lesbian in a decaying society, of forgetting about their problems.

But the villagers' voice is also very much the voice of the author. Silvera's story "Caribbean Chameleon," which is included in this volume, explodes with tension as a Caribbean woman arrives in Canada, her place of work and exile, and reaches the breaking point on an immigration line. Such varied and often conflicting identities vying for living space within one imagination may well be one of the hallmarks of the lesbian sensibility. Many of the stories in this collection are infused with the energy necessary to balance such a vigorous, often unruly, and sometimes maddening internal population.

Like Silvera, who tells her story by breaking up language to reflect her narrator's crisis, several other contributors use innovative narrative forms that both incorporate and transform national literary traditions: the Uruguayan Peri Rossi often works with surreal allegories, reminiscent of such Latin American writers as the Argentinean Luis Borges. Marguerite Yourcenar, who is well known for rewriting both history and classical myth, creates a new universe for the mythic figure of Sappho. A pioneering voice in French-Canadian feminist literary theory, Nicole Brossard, represented in this collection by an excerpt from her novel *Mauve Desert,* invents a unique structure to tell her story. Finally, Maureen Duffy puts a new twist on the Joycean technique of stream of consciousness.

The Vintage Book of International Lesbian Fiction is marked by firsts: An excerpt from Anna Blaman's pioneer work, *Lonely Adventure,* often referred to as the Dutch *Well of Loneliness,* is published here in an English translation for the first time. The same is true for the contemporary French writer Mireille Best, the German author Karen-Susan Fessel, the Slovenian author Suzana Tratnik, and the French-Canadian writer Jeanne d'Arc Jutras. Another kind of first is the inclusion of the Cuban writer María Eugenia Alegría Nuñez. To include her work, both the writer and the editors had to overcome a series of obstacles such as the American embargo and the lack of direct telephone and mail contact.

Many of the voices that meet here for the first time would not have reached us without the ground-breaking work of international lesbian and gay civil rights organizations. Because these organizations have fought for lesbian visibility and acceptance, the 1990s have seen an emergence of a dynamic international lesbian writers' community that is of both artistic and political importance.

Mary Dorcey, a longtime member of the Irish feminist and gay liberation movements, captures the sense of possibilities arising out of such work in her story "A Noise from the Woodshed." We see her characters going about their lives: making love on a riverbank, repairing leaky gutters, and finding surprise allies where they least expect it. Like the river that runs through the story, Dorcey's prose sparkles with hope. Gina Schein, an

Australian writer, draws on a similar kind of energy in her story "Minnie Gets Married." Echoing a young world filled with irreverent pioneers, Schein humorously turns a stately and conventional moment on its head.

Children with their innocence and enthusiasm bring another dimension to this energy of resistance. In Christa Winsloe's novel, a young girl follows her passionate attraction for a teacher, despite the rigid and punishing rules that threaten to break her spirit. Violette Leduc gives a portrait of an endangered youthful energy that almost springs from the page. Dionne Brand's children turn a rural classroom into a theater of joyous curiosity. And finally, the Maori writer Ngahuia Te Awekotuku follows her adolescent character as she experiences both the power of her own lust and the abuses of the adult world. Taken as whole, these images of young girls prefigure the adult lesbian woman who is marked by a refusal to submit to the mutilating social forces that would confine her.

Writing about childhood is emblematic of the need to keep the past alive. For the lesbian writer, as for any marginalized artist, documenting the past and imagining a future takes a particular kind of stubborn courage. As Monique Wittig, the French lesbian feminist author, has written in her influential book, *Les Guérillères:* "You say there are no words to describe this time, you say it does not exist. But remember. Make an effort to remember. Or failing that, invent." Without a past—remembered or invented—the present lacks meaning and the future is unimaginable. By exploring the unspoken and creating a bridge between memory and hope, the stories contained herein respond to the urgency of Wittig's call to break history's hold on women's imagination.

Both the fiction and the editorial comments represented here necessarily reflect only a part of the story. We are sure that in the future, the boundaries formed by the covers of this book will be expanded—there is so much more to be done, so many worlds that remain unspoken. Yet we hope this collection and the writers in it will contribute to the realization of a compelling dream: in the words of the Spanish author Esther Tusquets, "The old dream of seeing art, love, and revolution joined."

The

Vintage

Book of

International

Lesbian

Fiction

Mary Dorcey

In "A Noise from the Woodshed" (1989), the Irish-born writer Mary Dorcey captures, as she describes it, the "fertile chaos" that accompanies the balancing act as women go about the business of living "the practical, the emotional, the political, and the sensual" all at the same time. An internationally recognized poet, short-story writer, and novelist, Dorcey continues to be an influential voice in the development of the Irish feminist and lesbian movement. We have chosen this story to open the collection because it depicts both in its form and content the rush of possibilities open to women when they leave the well-worn path of social expectations far behind. Irish to its bones and yet international in its depiction of the worldwide communities of politically active lesbians and other concerned women, "A Noise from the Woodshed" is a story of hope—sensual, resilient hope.

from A NOISE FROM THE WOODSHED

So it was one of those days, it might have been the third or the fourth or some other day entirely but one of those days anyway. You were up on a ladder fixing a leaking gutter, and she was at the bottom holding the middle rung to keep it steady and passing you up hammers and nails and putty and saws and books and photographs and anything else you might need, and she was

3

explaining to you her problems as a painter—an artistic painter, let it be known, and you were listening, and saying, every now and again, such useful, empathetic things about wall painting and ceiling painting and floor painting and things undreamed of by Michelangelo and in between times, as she handed up the hammer and the putty and the photographs of the one before and the one before her, of her aunt and her sister and one of her brothers—the better one—she was telling you about her mother, about the problem she was making for herself by leaving her unphoned for as long as it was taking to tell you about the problem, and what with going up and down rungs for inspiration and consolation and slices of Bavarian cheesecake—her sister's recipe, for bites and embraces, it was surprising how much of the gutter got fixed. And then the cat came along, or two or three: an uncle, a grandniece, and a half sister, and they walked along the roof, two paws on the slates, the other two in the gutter, which is the only way a cat knows to walk along a sloping roof, unless at the very crest of it which, in this occasion what with hammer and nails and ladders and photographs, was far beyond reach. Get down, Uncle Ivor, she said, or Bluebell or Poppy or whoever it was, and it might have been any one of a number too awful to contemplate (so you didn't) not to mention the damn dog. It's as well we're not painting it, she said, and it was, because on other occasions when she had been, one or other, two or four (cats) not to mention the damn dog—and you didn't—had ambled along and done their cat thing and the paw trail led over and in, up stairs and down to your lady's chamber in blotches of scarlet and mediterranean blue. And when the goats devoured the ivy and the hens laid eggs in the chimney, you laughed and went on working, and the phone rang unanswered and the letters lay unposted and you forgot them and old quarrels—for already you had had them—old quarrels when she behaved like her father, whose behavior she hated, or you behaved like your mother, a thing you feared was slowly creeping up on you infecting small gestures and phrases. Not that your mother's hereditary taint was the worst taint you could imagine. Oh no very much indeed, no. After all, you might have resembled your brother, the wrong brother. Or you rehashed or revived older quarrels of other lovers and times, who had left their stain like cat paws in the wet paint of an earlier heart.

Indeed it was as well you were only fixing the gutters, because on other days, lovers and mothers aside, when you were making the dinner, or adding a bit to the symphony, saving the whale, or lazy beds dug for potatoes (and no beds have ever been lazier, what with the sun shining that way on the bare skin of her back, and the spade being heavier in your hands than any spade before it, and the wood warm and piercing your hands with little splinters of desire—oh desire among the lazy beds getting lazier) and potatoes you know, contrary to common opinion, being the most fragile of vegetables, easily bruised or spoilt, and she said, yes you've told me before, very often before, and you had, of course, because a good potato is hard to find, even in a country where thousands died for the want of them, and you feel for potatoes and cherish their delicacy: flowery and open and butter melting thick and yellow in their whiteness. And you were putting in these potatoes, hanging out the sheets or some such, and she was reading to you passages from a notorious and much slandered feminist philosopher whose words were many and startling and interwoven and made your head spin (spinning being just one of her favorite words and a much sought after trade, had you known it), which was all fine and well, this weaving, except that it did not get the washing done. And then you dropped a sheet in the mud and had to drag it inside and start all over again with the cats climbing in the sink to chase the suds, and the hens flying in the window, and why hadn't you by this time got a washing machine, other women have, and if you want that kind of life why don't you go back to the suburbs where you came from, and if only you had held the sheet in the first place, and who is it who always complains about not finding time for feminist philosophers, yes but not when we're hanging up sheets in a northeast wind. It was beds we were digging, beds you fool, have you forgotten beds for fragile potatoes easily bruised, ah, easily bruised yes, and in the sun too, don't you remember what you said about sun on the back? Ah yes, beds it was, you're right, lazy beds and laying out the lazy beds and digging in the spuds, and with that you left the suds overflowing the sink and followed the cat trail of scarlet and mediterranean blue upstairs to the loft that was Cleo's until she needed more space. Given any excuse, this is what happens, which explains the gutters leaking, the sheets unwashed, the mothers unwritten to, the whales unsaved, the cats running riot, the feminist philosophers unread—and if we don't support them she said, who will, I mean actually go out and buy the goddamn books, not just get them on loan from friends?

And it was one of those days and it led to one of those nights and more of those mornings.

And that was long before you noticed the noise from the woodshed. A startling and disturbing noise that might have been many things or one. Do you hear that noise, she asked, looking up from the list of power stations for the nuclear family you were compiling at the kitchen table. And you looked up, and you did hear, and you both wondered if it had just begun or if it might have been going on for days, perhaps since you came, being so busy with lists and laundry and things in between, you might well not have noticed anything going on. There had been other noises before, of course, she said, mostly of an animal or vegetable origin: the time she found the bird, for instance, bald and featherless, that might have been a newborn blown from its nest, or an adult struck by disease, and she fed it mashed catfood in case it was a newborn that should have been eating regurgitated worms; then there was the vagrant goose escaped from a poultry farm where it failed to lay its golden egg; and the blue whale, or dogfish, or was it a seal, someone had brought up from the beach for saving; and the fox you caught raiding the garbage you had forgotten to leave out: bags and bags of black plastic refuse, foul rotting rubbish that had been on the way to the dump the morning Cleo decided she had had enough of the loft and took off on her Yamaha for somewhere more spacious. This Cleo, you were tempted to say, sounds a hard act to follow, more literal than metaphoric. Yes, she said, as if you had said it, which after all you very well might have—impossible to follow, even when you knew where she was going, but she had beautiful eyes, an amazing way with whales, and no woman could write a better symphony, another week and we'd have had it finished. In that case, you said, we had better get the rubber gloves, anxious to put the day on a more solid footing, you thought (more metaphoric than literal—your mind growing helplessly lateral, it should have thought boots—and would shortly), in case it's the garbage again or a goose or a dog or a seal making free with it. But the gloves, when you found them, were punctured—and who was it who was forever borrowing them for the garden so that when you came to do the washing they let in jets of scalding soapy water—and it couldn't all be blamed on the cats, inquisitive and temperamental as they were (not to mention the dog)—do you hear them on the roof this instant? And you did, and she said, don't bother with that now, it's the other noise we have to deal with. Out you went then, armed only with two odd rubber gloves, a sweeping brush, and one pair of wellingtons, and thank goodness once more for the discovery of rubber, for you might soon be up to your knees in decaying refuse, as she had been before, alone, lonely, and lovelorn: knowing where to look but having promised not to; a chase or a search of any kind being the one thing a claustrophobic could not take. As you knew, having known something of claustrophobia yourself. Out you went.

When you got to the woodshed you paused, stopped in your tracks, because the noise had stopped and you didn't know where it had gone. You would have paused anyway, not being sure what you might find and putting off the evil hour of angry geese or dead foxes, And then she opened the door, because you couldn't go on standing there forever, and it was what you had come for after all, and in the light from the door you saw a big red sleeping bag laid out on the straw, and in the next moment you saw the two heads at the top of it, one dark and one fair, and then the heads came up fully, and you saw the shoulders and one breast of two women, one black, one white though brown skinned, young, of unidentifiable class and culture, these things being impossible to define from bare skin and bone. Oh it's you, she said, which meant nothing to you. Yes, they said, it's us— and they said it together, as if they were used to saying things together. We heard the noise, she said. Yes, that was us, they said. We should have known, she said, I mean recognized it, knowing you were coming back. And of course you should have too and now that she said it you did—recognize the sound. It wasn't, after all, for the want of hearing it. But then other people are different, especially if you haven't even heard them speaking or weeping or singing, and anyone can make a mistake about these things, and you had. But now you knew. And from their voices talking now you also knew they were from the continent of North America. And she told you she had met them before and invited them to stay anytime. She had seen them in the hardware store or was it the haberdashers? and spotted them. There are always women being spotted this way and other women going around spotting—it is one of the things you have come to expect. How did you know, they had said to her. Oh I don't know, I just spotted you somehow. After that they had come to stay, Janette and Janelle from the U.S.A., and they wanted to sleep in the open in their big red sleeping bag under the stars, and, well, she said, there's always the woodshed if it rains. She remembered that now. They were on an asylum visit from the city where they worked in a women's refuge for battered women and raped women and women who had been molested as children and children who had been molested before they ever got to be women. And they needed a holiday from it—a vacation, as they said, though not speaking together, speaking separately now that they had grown used to the light and your faces. And there were four breasts now above the sleeping bag, full fleshed and dark skinned, and three arms, the last arm belonging to the woman with short red hair under the sleeping bag still. And they had slept out under the sky for three nights, needing the night and the stars and no noise but their own, or a bird's or an animal's or a leaf's or a stone's, or whatever it is that makes all the racket in the country when everyone says—how quiet it is—how do you stand the silence?

And after three days of this they had gone off or on, the way visitors do, especially women from the United States of America who have come to see Europe, or find their sanity, or escape it, after five years working with molested and battered women to whom they listen and listen and say very little, trying hard not to say all the things they want to, for this is non-directive counseling and it is listening without directing, which is almost impossible with all this pain that is so familiar and known in your bones. And so they listen and learn, learn more than they ever wanted to learn, and keep silent until the time somebody says— listen you need a break—five years is too long for anyone to listen without a break. And so they stop listening for a while, and go off to find Europe, and find the haberdashers, or was it the

grocers? which is where she spotted them, and invited them
home to sleep in the woodshed, or out under the stars, at least
until the rain came, which was five days ago, but she hadn't
noticed, being so caught up with your life since crossing the
river. Well, she said, we're glad it's you and not a badger or rat or
fox, or some other hapless creature, and this is certainly no day
for the garbage. Certainly not, they said, it's a day for the river
(for they had crossed it too, the same one, or another, but they
certainly had crossed a river). Indeed it is—why don't you come?
Well we're kind of okay here, they said, speaking together. Okay
so, she said, and there's always the loft if the rain gets cold—it's
not quite finished of course, we were just getting round to the
roof the day Cleo left. Fine, they said, we're real good with roofs
and, being women from the North American continent, they
probably were, being real good with all making and fixing and
getting acts together and quite undiscourageable, which was
something to say in this climate of rain and rivers and cats walking through the gutters so that you could not get at the roof to
mend it even when you started. And another thing, she said, in
that case, no doubt thinking of the windows. And you could see
that there was enough to keep them going for weeks, and they
had weeks to keep going, they said, and no better place to spend
them, and there was always the loft. They said they would
remember if the rain got cold and then the three arms joined
the other arm under the red sleeping bag, and you closed the
door and walked back up the path. And you said, thank the
mother it wasn't the garbage, this is no day for going to the
dump. No, she said, it's a day for going anywhere else, almost
anywhere else; shall we go and leave the gutter and the hens and
the list of power stations for the nuclear family and the letters to
your mother and the feminist philosophers. This is no day for
philosophy. But, you said, if we interpret philosophy as meaning
love of wisdom, or life, this is just the day it is for, and why not

dump it all and go and philosophize by the river? Ah, the river. And, anyhow, you said, now that there were Janelle and Janette from the United States making it in the woodshed, and when they got tired or thirsty or hungry or too hot or cold, they were bound to come out—sometime anyway—more or less, and then they could help with the symphony and the goats—and don't go through all that again please, she said, and you did not but definitely, when it came to feminist philosophy, it was mostly written by women from the American continent, she had to agree and if they would not read it, who would? and that was bound to be some sort of help. Too many bounds, she said, in this conversation, almost as bad as ifs and buts, but she saw your point and agreed with you. And that was a weight off your mind, which was tired of weights and bounds and wanted to go boundless, the weight off your feet by the river, any river.

Alright, she said, but first, she said, we should go into town and buy some stuff to finish the loft: some wood and nails and hammers and saws and, anyway, you never knew who you might meet in the hardware store, it being some time since she had been in being so preoccupied with your life outside it. Alright, you said, but remember, no spotting, whoever you spot, the loft and the woodshed being temporarily spoken for.

And on the way you collected a bottle of wine and your flute and she took her knapsack and fiddle. It was a day for the old tunes, walking arm in arm down the road till you came to a stream, sitting down together, love, and who knows, you might even hear the nightingale sing. Or at least a blackcap, its melodious song commonly mistaken, or a whitethroat or stonechat. And into the car you got, putting out the hens and some hydrangea plants waiting to be planted, or they might have been rhododendron, or even azalea, that should have been waiting in the woodshed but could not be now. And as the morning was hot, the sun hot on the windscreen, on your cheek, on your

neck, on your arms, as you drove, and dazzling her eyes so that
she put on her shades, as she called them, that made her sultry
and unknown and glamorous, which she was anyway, and the
only woman you knew with such an extraordinary collection of
household trappings, not to mention garden and farmhouse.
And you said, I think this turn on the left is the fastest road to
the river, and it might have been, and it was not only the heat of
the sun on your neck that was making you sweat: a lovely light
sweet earthy sweat unlike horses or ladies, the latter who only
glow. And you were glowing too, though no lady. And she knew
the way to the river even better than you, and no wonder, having carried how many others across it, you did not ask, though
of course you had asked before, and even considered counting,
but now the number escaped you, if you had ever established it,
and in no time at all you saw the water winding dark and wide
and orange, frothing creamy white at its edges and around the
snarl of black polished wood hazel, or yew or sycamore, which
had fallen across it, forming a dam so that it was deeper and
darker on the other side, deep enough for swimming or bathing
as ladies would say. And will we, she said, and took off her
clothes (being no lady) which were not many; fewer than the
first day when the weather was cooler. And you said, this is
where it all began, or some of it, the best part of it, do you
remember? There's no hurry, she said, no hurry at all, we have
all we need: the wood and the hammer and food enough for
four, and we can start on the loft tomorrow, or the next day, or
whenever the rain gets cold. And you lay down on the bank, the
grass tickling your face, and she said, do you remember, and
how could you not, with so little to distract you, and so much
the same, only better now that there had been talk and quarrels
and reconciliation and forgetting and fixing things that should
have been fixed long ago, now that she knew you looked just
like your mother and not at all like your father, and now that she

knew you had your sister's voice, and you knew the names of the ones before and had read old letters and had looked at the photographs, and now that the symphony was almost finished, and a start made on the book, and the Nubian goats milked. It was better, substance and texture, shading and tone being added to what had seemed beyond improvement but was not because now it was better even than before. Do you remember, she said, the first day and you did, you loved remembering the feel of her flanks as she carried you over, her strong back under your thighs and you urging her on, smelling the jasmine smell of her hair and promising yourself to get serious—oh so serious. And have you talked yet about women getting serious and all that it leads to?—looking into each other's eyes and taking one another seriously, seeing one another whole and entire not as stopgaps, mediators, sympathizers, that long lasting, tasting, touching look that is one of the best things going, and if it happens to be at the side of a river when birds are starting up in the fields surprised by you—larks, you think they are, who spin in the sky with such glorious larkful spinning, up in the air like that and a cuckoo— yes a cuckoo calls that cuckoo way from across the heather, a place so distant you can hardly imagine and yet so clear—so heartstillingly, sound breakingly clear, it comes that call, and who will not answer? Falling into the grass then, the wild red poppies, the cowslips, the speedwell speeding blue all around, waiting all around, the long supple green tassled grass: falling into it two women tired from the business of making a living, a loving, making each day a new living, tired from the business of standing up to be counted—and oh they are counting—never stop—and who started all that business anyway?—tired of counting, two women fall into the cowslips and the lark rises and the gutters wait for another day and philosophy waits and the potatoes lie lazy for another day.

And it was another of those days. And more and more

women are having them—days that is—snatched from drought and the torrents of life. More and more women riding about footloose, tongue loose, and fancy free, crossing the river when they come to it: the deep, rushing tide, keeping their heads and well above water and gaining the bank; they lie down where the grass lies green and growing in wait all round, lie down where the yellow iris waves in wait, the wild poppies blow, and a cuckoo—yes, it was unmistakably from over the heather—a cuckoo calls.

Makeda Silvera

In "Caribbean Chameleon" (1994), from her collection Her Head a Village, the Jamaican-born Makeda Silvera makes use of the fragmentation of language and structure to embody the ultimate loss of home and self. Influenced by the strong, independent women of her childhood, Silvera has used her fiction to penetrate the shrouds of silence that surround the dispossessed, whether they be the "man royals" and "sodomites" of her early memories or a woman struggling against loss of home and self as in the following story. Editor of the ground-breaking Pieces of My Heart: A Lesbian of Colour Anthology, Silvera is one of the many exciting voices exploring the complexities of lesbian culture in the Caribbean. Now living in Canada, Silvera uses "Caribbean Chameleon" to depict a clash of two worlds.

CARIBBEAN CHAMELEON

YARD. Xamaica. Jamdown. Jah Mek Ya. Ja. Airport. Gunman, mule, don, cowboy, domestic, refugee, tourist, migrant, farmworker, musician, political exile, business exile, economic exile, cultural exile, dreadlocks, locks-woman, fashion-dread, press-head, extension hair, higgler.

Leaving the Caribbean for the North Star.

Tourist with straw baskets, suntan, skin peeling, rum-filled stomach, tang of jerk pork Boston-style. Lignum vitae carvings, calabash gourds, a piece of black coral, earrings out of coconut shell. Not to forget the tonic juices to restore nature—strongback, front-end-lifter, and put-it-back. A little ganja, lambsbread, marijuana, senseh, collie weed, healing herbs, mushrooms; you can get anything, no problem, as long as there are U.S. dollars.

Dried sorrel, fried sprat, bottles of white rum, mangoes, gungo peas, coconut cakes, scalled ackee, cerasee bush, and single Bible. Reggae on cassette tapes.

Travelers dressed to kill.

Woman in red frock, red shoes, red extension hair, black skin.

Dreadlocks, Clarke's shoes, red, green, and gold tam, smoking on last spliff.

Cowboy in felt cap, dark glasses, nuff cargo round neck to weigh down a plane.

Woman in black polka dot pantsuit. Black winter boots high up to knees, drinking one last coconut water.

Tourist drinking one last Red Stripe beer inna sun hot.

Leaving the Caribbean for the North Star.

Back to work, to winter, snow, frostbite.

Theater, live at the airport. Older woman bawling, young bwoy whining and pulling at woman in red frock. "Ah soon come, ah only going for a week. Yuh bawling like me dead."

"Forward to di Babylon lights," utters dreadlocks in Clarke's shoes.

"Cho, a tru certain tings why ah don't shot you. Yuh a push up life, yuh waan dead? Bumbo claat, watch weh yuh a go," cowboy demand.

"I was in di line before you," answer woman in polka dot pantsuit.

"So wha? Yuh want to beat me?" bulldoze cowboy.

"No, but ah only asserting mi rights."

"Cho, gal, a fight yuh want? Mi will box yuh down. Mi a di baddest man around. Step aside."

"Gwan bad man, gwan before di plane lef you."

JA customs officer has eyes deep in passport, behind desk, trying to figure out whether dis is a banana boat passport or what.

"Well praise the Lord for a nice holiday, tomorrow back to work." Woman in black polka dot pantsuit talking to herself.

"Ah, a well-spent vacation. Why do they want to leave?" tourist wonders.

Airport personnel hard at work. Bag weigh too much. Too much clothes, too much food, too much herbs, too much souvenirs. Too much sun packed in suitcase and cardboard boxes.

Temper crackle in dis small island. Sufferation pon di land. Tribulation upon tribulation. Some cyaan tek di pressure. Chicken fat, pork fat fi dinner. Badmanism reign, rent a gun, like yuh rent a car. Gunshot a talk, cowboy, dons, police, and soldier tek over di streets. Woman have fi tek man fi idiot—learnt survival skills. Man tek woman fi meat—ole meat, young meat, sometimes ranstid.

Destination America. Destination Britain. Destination Europe. Destination Canada. Destination foreign land.

Fasten seat belt. Iron bird tek off. Fly over di Caribbean Sea. A site of Cuba, di Cayman Islands. Plane get cold. Goose bump rise. Blanket pull closer to skin.

Approaching the North Star. Atlantic Ocean, flying high over sea. Good-bye May Pen Cemetery, good-bye gunman, murderers step aside, good-bye dead dogs in gully, rapist, womanbeater, police, soldier, cowboy, Northcoast hustler, good-bye.

Fly higher, iron bird. Away. Good-bye.

Good-bye sunshine, warm salty sea, music with di heavy drum and bass. Good-bye mama, baby, little bwoy, good-bye, no tears, a jus' so. Wah fi do?

Woman in polka dot black pantsuit. Work tomorrow. Department clerk. Live-in domestic to work under North Star. Praying that in five years, no more kneeling to wash floor, no more scrubbing clothes, replace that with washing machine, vacuum cleaner. Lady in red to seek better life, telling Immigration is holiday. Send for little boy and older woman when life tek. Dreadlocks leaving the sunshine, collie weed, "just for a time, just for a time, Babylon force I," him tell himself. Cowboy cool, cowboy determine, "Foreign land, north light, fi me and you, anyone, land of opportunity, to buy di latest model gun, to slaughter di baddest bwoy."

Good-bye slave wage, stale food, ranstid meat, tear-up clothes, rag man, tun' cornmeal, dry dust.

Music soft, no heavy drum and bass. Missing home already. Complimentary drink sweet, though, another Chivas on the rocks, another Courvoisier, cyaan buy dem a Jamdown. Plane get colder. Drinks warm up body.

Woman in black polka dot pantsuit close eyes, shut out her job in di North Star. Walk baby in pram. No matter what weather. Snow high. Shovel it. Walk dog. Feed the baby. Feed the mother. Feed the father. Clean up after. Wash the clothes. Iron some. Fold up the towels and sheets. Vacuum the carpet. Polish the silver, All in the name of a honest day's work.

Plane fly low. North Star light pretty, shining all over di land. Immigration. Line long. Which one to enter. Woman or man. White or Asian. Black or white.

"Where have you been?" "Where have you been?" "How long was your stay?" "Purpose of your visit?" Tourist, white, safe every time, unless foolish to take a little collie weed, a little spliff. Woman in red pass through, safe, can't touch it. Dreadlocks just coming to play music at stage show, no rush to live here, in a Babylon. Safe. Cowboy visiting mother, polite, nice smile, dress good, stamp in book, gwan through. "Three weeks you say?" Safe. Woman in black polka dot pantsuit. "Where you been to?" "Jamaica." "Reason?" "Vacation." "Vacation? Family?" "No. I stay in a hotel." "Why a hotel?" "What yuh mean, sir?" "Why a hotel if you were born there?" "Because, sir, I go on a vacation. What yuh saying, sir? Black people can't tek vacation in dem own homeland?" "What items did you bring back?" "Two bottles of rum, sir, di legal amount, fry fish and cerasee bush for tea." Officer slap ink stamp in the passport. Conveyer belt. Round and round. Lady in black polka dot pantsuit pick up luggage. Show stamped card. Over there. Same questions. "How long were you out of the country?" "Two weeks." "Purpose?" "Vacation, mam." "Where did you stay?" "Kingston, mam." "Did you stay with family?" "No mam, I visit dem, but I stay in a hotel." Suspicion. "Hotel?" "Yes mam." "Take off your glasses, please." Officer look lady in black polka dot pantsuit up and down. "What date did you leave Canada for Jamaica?" Woman in black polka dot pantsuit start breathing hard. "I have me landed papers right here." "Open your suitcase, please." Suitcase get search. Hand luggage search. Handbag search. Sweat running down woman black face. Line long behind her. Officer call for body search. Woman in black polka dot pantsuit trembling. Head start itch. Line longer. Black and white in line. Woman in black polka dot pantsuit sweating with embarrassment.

North Star cold. But sweat running down her face. Line behind long-long. People tired of waiting. Impatient wid her, not wid di Immigration woman. "What you looking for, mam?" Question to hands searching. Ripping through suitcase. Disorder among di sorrel. Rum. Fruits. Fry fish. Routine, routine. Passenger behind getting vex wid her. Too much waiting. Lady in black polka dot pantsuit try to calm nerves. Think bout work. Up at 5 A.M. Feed di baby. Walk di dog. Put out garbage. Cook di breakfast. Clean di house. . . . Anyting . . . to take away dis pain. Dis shame. But not even dat can take it away. "What you looking for? WHAT YOU LOOKING FOR?" Woman in black polka dot pantsuit gone mad. Something take control of her. Black polka dot woman speaking in tongues. Dis woman gone, gone crazy. Tongue-tie. Tongue knot up. Tongue gone wild. "WHAT YOU LOOKING FOR? Yes, look for IT, you will never find IT. Yes, I carry through drugs all di time. But you will never find it. Where I hide it no Immigration officer can find it. Is dat what yuh want to hear?" Woman in black polka dot pantsuit talking loud. Black people, Jamaican people in line behind. Dem close eyes. Look other way. Dem shame. Black polka dot woman nah get no support. Hands with authority. Hands heavy with rage. Tear away at suitcase. Throw up dirty drawers. Trying to find drugs. Only an extra bottle of white rum. Polka dot woman mad like rass. Madwoman tek over. Officer frighten like hell. Don't understand di talking of tongues. Call for a body search in locked room. Black polka dot woman don't wait. Tear off shirt. Tear off jacket. Tear off pants. Polka dot woman reach for bra. For drawers. Officer shout for Royal Canadian Mounted Police to take madwoman away. "TAKE HER AWAY. TAKE HER AWAY." Take this wild savage. Monster. Jungle beast. "AWAY. Arrest her for indecent exposure." Woman in black polka dot pantsuit foam at the mouth. Hair standing high. Head-wrap drop off. Eyes vacant. Open wide. Sister. Brother. Cousin. Mother. Aunt. Father. Grandparent. Look the other way.

Jesus Christ. Pure confusion at Pearson International Airport. The cock crowing once, twice.

Mireille Best

"Stéphanie's Book" ("Le Livre de Stéphanie"), by the French writer Mireille Best, makes its first English appearance in the excerpt below. Published in France in 1980, the story reflects both the progress made and the ground that remains to be covered before women can freely choose to commit themselves to other women. In a lively, direct style filled with quirky humor—even omitting punctuation in some places—Best captures the poignant subtleties of "ordinary" existence while illuminating the complex forces shaping individual choices. Born into a working-class family in Le Havre, Best now lives in the south of France with her life partner, Jo.

In the following pages, the narrator, a married woman with two sons, is "liberated" for a few days from family life and obligations, free to spend time with Stéphanie, her youngest son's teacher who has become her friend.

from STÉPHANIE'S BOOK

ELL Stéphanie says here you are single   It's time to take advantage of it   We could celebrate my new name   We could . . . I let her unweave an endless carpet of possibilities on which I am afraid to tread. Because while Bernard is in Marseilles and the kids at their grandma's who lives on the way— Oh! said Bernard, they'll only skip school for a day and a half. . . . Anyway, they are not doing anything anymore. . . . —I had promised myself I would do my spring cleaning. I even took Friday off to have three full days with the weekend. If I listen to my beautiful mermaid, all is lost. . . . Three days to put things away, worries Stéphanie, that's how you can't find anything any-more! What about us going to the beach.

—At this hour?

—But Stéphanie says, at this hour it's more beautiful There is no one, and it's still warm.

Three days' vacation Stéphanie says Take it or leave it. And in a big gesture of her arms that hit the roof of the car, her wrist still tied up in the strap of her gym bag, she recites: The first night They went to the ocean to baptize Stéphanie The water was dark and the sky clear and the sand white under the moon. . . . Suddenly serious, she nestles her hands in mine. Don't be a chicken. . . . Say yes to me We may never be able to do this again.

I notice that it's still daytime and to see the moon we'll have to wait a little while longer. And so what Stéphanie says, and taking her hands away from mine, she gently turns the ignition key. The engine submits with a sigh. Me too. This is kidnapping.

Indeed Stéphanie says whose eyes suddenly light up like a room where you just opened the blinds.

I haven't even prepared my meal for tonight. . . .

Shush! Stéphanie says Tonight we don't eat, we drink.

Stéphanie's studio resembles her. It has Indian hangings with mellow tones, wicker chairs that are warmed by pinkish beige sheepskins thrown on them, small cushions piled up haphazardly on the floor. . . .

Leaning out the window we watch the evening unfold for a long time, and the silence around us spreads like a puddle of water that overflows endlessly.

It's incredible how nice the weather is Stéphanie sighs finally. Then I turn toward the inside of the apartment full of ashtrays filled with cigarette butts, books spread all over the place, records askew on the shelves, notebooks piled on a table. . . . There's a roll of drawing paper on the bed and a slipper all alone in the middle of the rug. This is a mess, isn't it, Stéphanie says. If I had known that I was going to kidnap you tonight I would have made some order But this is irreparable. She picks up the slipper, which her fingers fold and unfold mechanically. Her breath, curiously, is short. I . . . I'm not used to having people who keep their house in order Don't stand there like this Andrée you hear You make me shy. Sit down. Don't stay there like a signpost.

I feel like I've lost my sense of direction since I have nothing to do and I sit down obediently. And of course, Stéphanie says, you chose the wrong one. I feel the strength of the armchair with my back and hips. What's "wrong" with it, I wonder. That's not it, Stéphanie says. I was imagining you in the other one I've never seen reality tie so many knots as it has with you. It's upsetting Stéphanie says as she turns on the lamps, whose slightly myopic luminosity dilutes itself in what's left of the day. . . .

Stéphanie is a bit strange at times.

Fleetingly, I struggle against that kind of vertigo that grabs you in some dreams where everything seems normal but where something is out of place and you wonder with some anxiety what it is, because it might be you.

And Stéphanie laughs in my face with something pathetic, which I may be inventing because absolutely nothing comes across in the words that she says. Don't mind what I'm saying I'm silly.

It may be because of this theatrical gesture that she uses to hold her hands out to me But I understand very well that it is to abolish the distances and I confiscate the slipper that she hasn't stopped torturing and that she held out to me with her hands.

I put the slipper on its original carpet. I take her hands, little and cold, in mine, and following her hands that I am holding, she bends toward me against the light and I hurry to say that I'm going to die of thirst if she doesn't do something about it right away.

With Stéphanie's laughter finally bursting out, several pounds of atmosphere jump out the window.

We shouldn't become depressed Stéphanie says as she goes to the kitchen to get some ice cubes. While the evening draws the sky like a watercolor. A sky with a liquid transparency that becomes paler and paler and spills over.

I'm trying to remember when the last time was that I was able to stay like this to watch the twilight while someone was preparing something for me to drink or eat. Maybe at the maternity hospital twelve years ago, when I held Pitou's little head and felt his little silky hair slightly humid with sweat Under my hand a tiny heartbeat was going through his clothes and I was falling asleep against my warm baby not yet dissociated from my own body To me Inside me Around me Like Grandma's chest when I was so little. . . . The young nurse dressed in blue has come in The baby must sleep As if I had never had a baby before As if this kid didn't sleep better on his mother's body than on a cold mattress And took my kid away. You must go to sleep now Grandma would say and she'd gently pull me away from her and the cold would tear apart our warmth that had joined us together just a moment earlier I don't want to go! The same revolt The same primal scream of the flesh that is separated The same distress, each time And to say nothing because you're grown up and reasonable and that to grow up is to learn to shiver alone.

Whenever Didier or Pitou, screaming and stamping with rage for a whim, would finally stretch their arms out to me, I could not refuse shelter Bernard would shrug his shoulders and mumble some things that were very relevant about child-rearing And

I would have bitten him. Because when you are faced with a sign of distress, you don't oppose it by reasoning You run You hurry. To learn to live Bernard said. . . . You must have neither a heart nor a belly to witness this succession of little agonies endured in indifference without a reaction.

I caught you Stéphanie says

Doing what, my God

Escaping through the window.

And she comes toward me loaded with enough little snacks to feed an army I make a gesture to help her out, but she interrupts it with a move of her knee You be quiet or I'll throw everything on the floor. Under the threat, I remain still. Praying that she'll manage to save the bottles at least.

A torrent of pots cans little packages flows from her arms onto the table with not too much noise and without breaking anything. Two bottles of champagne still remain in her arms.

But, Stéphanie . . .

That's all I have, Stéphanie says I hope that you like champagne at least.

But, Stéphanie, this is totally unreasonable. . . . She spreads her arms, finally free, in a sign of powerlessness. I thought we were going to see the sea. . . . Yes, Stéphanie says, but I am hungry. And thirsty Especially thirsty.

Everything is so complicated Stéphanie says. . . .

You're not helping me. . . .

I help her to strip off the cellophane wrap from the packages of cookies. You're doing it on purpose, Stéphanie says severely Andrée are you REALLY doing it on purpose!

I smile at her angry locks of hair where the light from the lamps put copper reflections as the window is getting darker.

Everything is bathed in a soft light like the kind you see in restaurants where I never go anymore. It's a secret celebration and I have nothing, nothing to do but stretch my arms and legs with a sigh of comfort while a tender saxophone begins confiding in stereo. Finally a human music Music and not the kind of noise that my sons' "awesome" singers make so loudly. . . .

You like it? Stéphanie says squatting within arm's reach in front of the turntable. I put my hand on her curls They are warm and silky And her head leans slightly to better feel the caress or to follow it like Grandma's dog used to do. I've never seen a dog so sweet He used to roll his big eyes to try to see me over the bumps of his eyebrows My big boxer all in all My Sweet One overflowing with love for humankind. Bernard never wanted a dog It sheds its hair It drools It's unhealthy for the children What do we do with it when we go away on vacation Especially at Mother's place It has to pee all the time It's not happy in an apartment It brings trouble with the neighbors It means extra work It eats the cushions and the legs of the furniture It scratches the wallpaper It stinks It climbs on the beds. . . .

I knew it Stéphanie says Finally some human feelings You were doing it on purpose, weren't you. Only partly, Stéphanie. I'm not used to friends who are like Sweet One and the pony from the fair I'm not used to having girlfriends just for me Who have a celebration just for me. And who talk to me Stéphanie above the champagne that will get warm in its bucket that's too small Who talk to me with words that have a meaning of their own. As if we were somewhere else in another galaxy Who smile at me with eyes that make bubbles. . . .

I'm a married woman Stéphanie. A mother A part of a whole with whom people can only speak a collective language, that's to say null. You don't confide to just anyone. We speak from couple to couple From family to family From group to group. A language for all, Readings For All . . . Nothing for anyone anymore. So you lose the habit, even without noticing it Like you lose the habit of stretching your legs and of waiting to be served. I am thirsty too, Stéphanie.

I got up to put one of the two bottles back in the fridge. Can't you sit still for five minutes Stéphanie says.

She uncorks the bottle of champagne very well.—I cannot stand people who let the cork jump to the ceiling and who spill the foam on the table.—

This way, Stéphanie says, everything will be easier, you'll see.

To simplicity, Stéphanie says raising her glass. To the sea To springtime, which is almost over To friendship To the difficulty of moving forward when you've lost your crutches. . . .

To thirst. To thirst Especially when you're scared to death and you don't know what to say in order to be neither too far apart nor too close.

That's it, I say. To panic thirst.

You don't resemble your life Stéphanie says.

She had already told me that before While she was putting her shorts on in the dressing room at the gym and what do you do in life! I work for an accountant Does the accountant pay you well Oh! Just barely above minimum wage. That is disgusting Stéphanie says that is really disgusting, after ten years! Why do you take it. O Stéphanie from another planet . . . Kindly I explained to her about the number of unemployed people in the county The files that the boss gets from his drawer to show me when he feels that I'm too quarrelsome, as if it were totally by chance. There are currently thirty-four, Stéphanie, thirty-four letters from unemployed boys and girls who are ready to take my place for even less money. All younger than I am, with diplomas that I don't have. Tell them we have no opening AT THE MOMENT Andrée, would you. And Andrée swallows her anger and politely tells the candidates that there is nothing at the moment Some of them insist You must give them several polite refusals. The accountant signs the letter with a little sigh.

And what if you prepared for the exams Stéphanie says. Yes. But I'm too old to work in administration. Yes. But I can't, my husband. And with the children on top of it, no, I can't do it. I understand Stéphanie says She smiles at me Takes my hand quickly and lets go of it She says You don't resemble your life.

No, maybe not yet But I resemble it more and more It surrounds me And I struggle less and less. . . . Finally one must let go to have peace It's too much struggle to assert that you exist Too much struggle to resist the daily grind the worries the tiredness Too much struggle to manage to read a single book. . . . I feel I'm becoming more and more stupid.

I still haven't read your book, you know

You don't like it?

Oh I do No time It's silly to say this but there's always a catastrophe or an emergency as soon as I take it out of its drawer So I don't touch it anymore It's been weeks now. . . . Maybe tomorrow I'll have time to read it.

Mañana será otro día Stéphanie says Tomorrow is another day Let's make today last.

Drink Stéphanie says whose eyes are making more and more bubbles Whose curls are rolling tighter and tighter Whose lips with no makeup are taking on color as if by transparency and are moving with so much life that you feel like touching them.

But you don't touch people's lips These are things you just don't do when you have all your reason You can touch the hand that's allowed but not the mouth To hold the waist, yes, but not the breast To put a kiss on the cheek, yes, but not in the neck, you just don't do that. One can caress other people's children's hair but not their husbands' hair A real traffic code And everyone knows about all these invisible rules And you wonder why it's so hard for me to live with my hands behind my back Even with the children now that they are grown up Even with Bernard because for him it's the beginning of a path with a precise destination and he hasn't felt like it for quite a while now. Or quickly, skipping the steps in between But as far as I am concerned, I do like the steps in between And then afterward you must let him sleep what's wrong with you tomorrow I must get up. . . . And also I want a dog A dog that belongs to me a sweet and demanding dog and tomorrow I'll go to choose one while Bernard is gone The children will be enthusiastic and I know Bernard won't be able to put it outside A puppy can melt any heart.

What are you thinking about Stéphanie says. Quick, quick, no thinking. Too late you've already thought about it.

I say I was thinking about the fear of gestures I was thinking that I want a dog. . . .

About what Stéphanie says.

About . . . the mouth of a pony.

You are a strange girl Stéphanie says Even stranger when you are drunk. Eat You shouldn't drink without eating It's not my intention to give you a hangover.

She smokes seriously and her eyes on me don't quiver any more than quiet water You could think that she's listening to who knows what Maybe the music But there is no more music.

It's funny don't you think to be here with you at this impossible hour. . . .

What time is it by the way.

What does it matter Stéphanie says.

We munched and drank some more while a black singer was wrapping a melody around my neck that was alternately raspy and airy Stéphanie went to get the other bottle, which she opened in the discreet way that I like But what is it that I don't like in Stéphanie And I think I might have moaned that it was less and less reasonable, but from far away, from the bottom of a slightly whirling comfort From the bottom of the sheepskin that smelled like a warm animal From the bottom of the chiaroscuro light diffused by the lamps where Stéphanie was dancing.

She danced alone two or three beats, then she stopped, came to throw her laughter at me almost on my mouth Are you dancing?

I think I won't remember how. . . . Come, Stéphanie says, I can dance very well when I am slightly drunk Otherwise I cannot I'm afraid.

Afraid of what?

You don't understand a thing Stéphanie says. For example, see, I had a lot of things to tell you that I couldn't tell you in the dressing room of the gym. . . . Are you coming or not. Don't be so stiff Stéphanie says It only the two of us let go. . . . It's been years since I have danced, you know Stéphanie. What did you want to tell me. I don't remember Stéphanie says, I lost everything. It's just like these little notes of paper that you put in your pocket after scribbling fantastic things on them: either you lose them completely or you find them and the text is half illegible and it doesn't really say anything about your genius. So you throw them away. One should talk when the spark comes out, otherwise it's too late.

She blows an imaginary match close to my neck and I navigate in an iridescent fog Luckily the slow dance is very slow and Stéphanie's slightly tight body protects me against vertigo.

A spark that is blown out is sad.

The essential stays Stéphanie says whose naked forearms are resting on my shoulders The essential, she says, is the atmosphere that shivers around certain persons. Around you Stéphanie says. You understand?

Maybe, yes, I don't know. . . .

It surely has to do with waves Stéphanie says If you insist on a scientific explanation. She laughs and in the upset of her laughter I distinguish clearly her warm little breast against my breast. The fleeting desire to hold tighter To snuggle. It's true that she dances well, Stéphanie. While she is trying to clarify what she means with a tiny forefinger that caresses my eyebrows.

The world is motionless Stéphanie says. And then someone appears Someone who seems to be totally ordinary And suddenly the scenery vibrates around her. A harmony is established You're happy to live.

It's a love story I say.

If you want Stéphanie says Everything is a love story anyway. I received you full force Like a landscape Like a sunset Like a melody Don't start laughing Stéphanie says Not now.

I was not laughing. I don't really know where I am anymore. The last beat of the slow dance saves me in extremis from a curious acquiescence that had been sneaking in without my feeling it. A feeling that all's well In its place Must have been like this forever.... A feeling that the silence now reduces to pieces. Stéphanie lets go of me suddenly and catches her breath as if she had just swallowed some water.

Come on Stéphanie says. This time we are going to see the sea. But I decline I'm really in no state to drive. Too bad Stéphanie says We'll go tomorrow in the daytime You must also know how to do ordinary things. And this bottle Stéphanie says we should finish it Since we're almost done with it.

I must go home Stéphanie It's very late....

Very early Stéphanie corrects It's a nightingale really mixed with a lark. But if you can't drive to go see the sea I don't see how you could go home without killing yourself. I'll hang myself around your neck, I'll roll myself around your legs, I'll tie you up with the cords from the curtains, but I won't let you go!

Drink Stéphanie says. Then we'll break the glasses and we'll go to sleep. There is room for two in this bed. I'll make myself tiny And if I bother you I'll sleep on the carpet Like a little dog. Do you still want a little dog?

Absolutely.

We'll go choose it tomorrow Stéphanie says sitting cross-legged at my feet and throwing her head back to smile at me.

So I stretch my hand toward her warm curls. You were saying very nice things earlier on the quivering of the atmosphere.

Too late Stéphanie says The quivering has changed into an earthquake You can't describe an earthquake You should've asked me questions before the last glass of champagne. It's going to have a bad ending Stéphanie says, if we don't go to bed immediately.

So I let go of her curls to put my hand on her mouth A simple and obvious gesture and you wonder why you torture yourself for trifles. Under my fingers her lips shiver like the pony's but smaller and softer She closes her eyes the way you turn off the light.

I must have slept After I remember soft movements around the open bed An Indian cotton shirt that I put on as pyjamas and that is a bit too small for me.

A vague bewilderment at being there   The image of Stéphanie's body, naked like only a blond's body can be in the light But maybe I dreamed it because I was already sleeping Stéphanie's voice, slightly out of breath A voice that breathes between words Very high above my face and yet I feel its breath I roll toward a warm light Indian cloth, which welcomes me.

A little three-note melody wakes me up from a silly dream in which I was walking toward the waves.

Waves of very light curly hair stroking my legs my thighs. My hands dive into it because it's soft and a ray of light brightens up the horizon. Then I stroke the mouth of the pony who starts singing on three notes.

A sunbeam falls down obliquely into my slightly opened eyes. A surprisingly thin arm comes across this ray of sunlight and passes above my head. I follow it with my eyes. I see the finger resting on one of the small clock's switches. The little melody stops in the middle of the second note. The arm smells of vanilla.

I open my eyes completely.

Stéphanie's clear gaze. Slightly veiled under a jumble of hair. Like a sunrise when the spring hasn't yet arrived definitely.

Or maybe the mist is in my own eyes.

Stéphanie smiles silently.

Holds her hand out to me, palm up, across the bed.

I put my hand on this hand, which is opened like a gift to say good morning.

And I squeeze it, it's so soft and it nestles in the palm of my hand.

I close my eyes on its warmth.

I become nothing but my hand in Stéphanie's hand.

When I open my eyes again, after an eternity of well-being, Stéphanie is still smiling amid the waterfall of her curls.

I have to go to school Stéphanie says.

Stay still Stéphanie says I am going to prepare breakfast.

I nestle in her place where some of her warmth and the scent of vanilla still linger.

My eyes are closed very tightly in order to be like a little kid again.

And I go back to my dream in progress It's made of waves and warm hair I am so deeply into it that the voice calling me, a voice with air moving around the words, must insist for me to come out of the dream and it's my turn to come out of my dream, limp like a sea anemone that lets the currents move her and that gets stranded.

There is also the smell of coffee and I cannot resist it. A coffee that I have not prepared. That is steaming hot and waiting for me on the little table.

Good morning Stéphanie says.

You look funny in this outfit Stéphanie says.

Automatically, I pull the sides of the wrinkled Indian shirt tightly against the top of my thighs.

Stéphanie's laughter brightens the radiant morning that starts to warm up the window even more.

I adore you Stéphanie says, but I also like hot coffee.

I stagger from the bed to the armchair feeling deeply happy and exhausted.

Are you cold? Stéphanie says.

Oh no. I feel so good it's incredible.

I dive into the coffee with my slice of buttered bread. It has never been like this since the time I left Mamie's home.

I tell Stéphanie that I'm regressing into childhood and also that she's going to be late for school if we start to chat.

Between two sips of coffee she explains what I must do with the key after my shower if I absolutely want to go home.

And if you clean up this house before you go, I won't talk to you anymore.

Stéphanie is whistling in the shower. Her whistling and the water stop at the same time.

Stéphanie puts her clothes on, her curls are in order, her skin still slightly damp, her school satchel in her hand. Much more like a schoolgirl than a teacher. And she gives me a strong kiss somewhere between neck and cheek. And the contact of her skin is already so familiar to me that it shocks me.

Please Stéphanie says. Please, come back. . . .

And it's really if I want to, and these aren't empty words, I understood perfectly well.

Because of the dog Stéphanie says. If you still want a dog. We'll have to go pick one out.

At four-thirty Stéphanie says, do you want to?

I want to. I want everything: the dog and Stéphanie. And I barely wonder by what bizarre alchemy these two unconnected elements have become inseparable. I think I have a slight headache.

I say yes to Stéphanie's smile and to the wind made by the closing door.

Translated by Janine Ricouart

Cristina Peri Rossi

These two tales by the Uruguayan writer Cristina Peri Rossi represent a narrative voice very different from others in this collection. A respected lesbian-feminist writer in Latin America and Europe, Peri Rossi was forced into exile from her country in 1972 and now lives in Spain. The collection Forbidden Passion *(Una pasión prohibida: 1986), from which these tales are drawn, combines satire, the surreal, parable, and fable; the stories bear witness to the centrality of desire in human existence. Human beings, says Peri Rossi in her introduction, are "arrows shot out in time and space to catch the impossible." In the first selection, frustration over the human condition is such that it turns the Final Reckoning on its head. In the second selection, the creative spirit—marginalized or exiled—is embodied in a mysterious female voice whose persistence testifies to the tenacity of art and the human need for expression however solitary the setting, however "unheard" the song.*

FINAL JUDGMENT

THE morning newspapers didn't announce an eclipse, and the forecast promised good weather, clear skies, and little humidity; thus, in principle, there was no reasonable explanation for the presence of a large violet cloud advancing sluggishly toward the mountain like an unseemly presence, an unplanned indiscretion of the sky.

He wasn't willing to hasten his step—no matter that the soft breeze of September might become a wind, as it seemed quite ready to do—because he was a man of solid principles, moderate political ideas, and strong convictions; anyway, those leaves that were now whirling around his head were a subversion of September's order, and he decided not to pay them any attention. Nor was he willing to consider the purple color that the mountain had taken on, completely out of place if one takes into account the early hour of the day in which he was setting off, with measured pace, to his work in a bank office on one of the central streets of the city.

But this wasn't all. When he got to the corner—a cross street full of store windows where his profile blurred like a sort of faraway mannequin—he felt a drop of rain on his nose, and he noted that a middle-aged lady who was going by in the opposite direction opened her umbrella like a medieval dome. It seemed humiliating to him.

And if this weren't enough, the vendor at the newsstand where he always bought his paper greeted him hurriedly, unfolding over the newspapers and magazines a piece of plastic that fluttered in the wind like a trapped butterfly. "What strange weather!" he felt the obligation to say as he took money from his pocket to buy the newspaper.

He saw indistinct women's forms under dark yellow raincoats. What he hated most about the brusque disappearance of the sun was that it altered, even confused conventional notions of time. In truth, the gray sky that was opening up now like a circus tent could be that of the early morning or midafternoon, and he detested uncertainties, confusions, vacillations.

He had to quicken his step against his will, which he considered a small personal indignity. It seemed that life was full of ordeals and disagreements impossible to repair.

The violet cloud spread out like an ink stain and covered the sky. The air had acquired a Prussian blue tone, and he was happy that this expression came into his head because in the uncertainty of this morning that seemed like an afternoon, it summoned up a sense of order even if it was a military order. But Prussia had gotten lost somewhere, sometime.

Then he heard the booming of thunder, hollow and charged with electricity, like an iceberg suddenly breaking up. He shuddered. Ever since he was a boy he couldn't keep from trembling violently whenever he heard that trombone in the sky. He was going to send a letter to the Meteorological Center. It wasn't acceptable for them to make this kind of error in the weather forecast. Didn't he pay taxes regularly? Didn't he go to work every day, arrive punctually, and never take time off?

The second roar of thunder, even more spectacular than the first, caught him just as he was quickening his step to cross the street, and it boomed like a large building falling to pieces. Then a crash that he couldn't identify made him raise his head. It hadn't begun to rain consistently yet, but red and yellow lightning drew winding rivers in the sky like lines on the maps one got in school. These lightning flashes divided the sky in two, and the dark clouds parted like curtains rising on a stage. Behind them the landscape just coming into view was more serene (he seemed to pick out a small blue area, pure and with amber-colored borders). The sky appeared to open up, submissive, to make way for another sky. And if everything was harsh, churned up, damp, and electric in the superficial sky (the one closer to his eyes), the other, the one that appeared behind, was tame, radiated a harmonious light, and, especially, was not a noisy, but rather a silent sky. It evoked the religious cards of his childhood, with their apocalyptic landscapes, lilac-colored clouds, and light beams that went through mountains. Everything that he had rejected as childish in his maturity returned in this naïve vision like a joke in bad taste: it was the exact place where the old man reconciles himself with the boy. And he couldn't stop looking; for a period of time that he could never determine, he remained absolutely still, as if he had surprisingly lost the ability to move, and he thought that if anyone walked by at that moment (but now the street was strangely deserted; most probably the bad weather had cleared it out), he or she could have perfectly well taken him for a statue.

Then suddenly in the great opening in the sky, like a stage curtain going up, he saw God make his appearance. He didn't come down or make any movement; He simply appeared among the clouds, only His head, and both looked at each other for a moment.

Everything was motionless around him: he observed that the trees on the street were floating, the cars lay immobile, a sepulchral silence reigned on the street (you could only hear the rhythmic sounds of the traffic lights changing), the passersby had disappeared, and the lilac light of the buildings made them seem to float like houses suddenly turned into boats, and he into Noah. Surprisingly, he wasn't nervous; he felt comforted and at the same time vaguely disappointed. Comforted, because with everything resembling the religious cards of his childhood, a certain part of his uncertainty disappeared; and disappointed, because he couldn't stop thinking that, whatever else it meant, this vision was naïve.

Finally they found themselves face to face. This seemed to be the most important moment in his life, and everything since his birth brought him to this instant, this revelation, this culmination.

He tried to move but felt as if something or someone, without effort, were restraining him.

Then he spotted other people inside their houses, also motionless just as he was: speechless dark shadows, immobilized forever in the moment of lifting a fork to their mouths, opening a door, petting the cat, reading the paper, writing a letter. Like mechanical dolls suddenly halted by some flaw in the works or frozen by a child's wish. Even more, he thought that from the beginning, in the clear dawn of time when things were first named, everything had led to this in some mysterious but steady, obscure, and inescapable way. Everything: Napoleon and the Seven Infantes of Lara, the Medicis and Charlemagne, Etruscan cemeteries, Teutonic orders and slips of the tongue, paintings by Murillo, Hesiod and films by Chaplin, women who die in childbirth, the swans on the Wansee and the drawings by Utamaro, the Second World War, the music of Wagner and the martyrdom of Ursula, the October Revolution, the student rebellion in Córdova and the opera *Evita,* haiku, the Beatles and Eleanor of Aquitaine. Everything led to this, through the enigmatic paths that the short span of human life could never grasp, but that now were revealed in all their inevitability.

He was a cautious man, and the last day couldn't take him by surprise. He had remembered the biblical verse that told the just man to prepare himself for the great event; he didn't have anything to lose because he hadn't held on to anything, and the trumpets of Jericho, thunderclaps though they were, resounded in his ears like the echo of ancient music. He had awaited this day anxiously, but also humbly and with meekness, because no one should be so proud as to expect to be selected for the last day. He had prepared himself silently, without harboring any ideas about rights in the matter, and now he had his opportunity.

Finally they found themselves face to face. He dug around in his pockets. Time had stopped, frozen like water in a lake. While he was digging around in his pockets, he made a gesture to God, asking Him to wait. What could an instant mean when it comes to all eternity?

From the inner pocket of his jacket he took out some type-written pages (he was a meticulous man), and putting on his glasses (he suffered from a slight farsightedness) he began to read God a list of charges that for fifty years had accumulated against Him, impartially, like an anonymous investigator who has followed a suspect without His ever knowing.

Translated by Mary Jane Treachy

SINGING IN THE DESERT

THE fact that she sings in the desert shouldn't surprise anybody since many people have done so since the beginning of time, when everything was sand (and also sky) and the oceans were frozen over.

We know that they sang in the desert, but we didn't listen to them, so we could say that up to a certain point they sang for themselves, although, in principle, this was not the purpose of their song.

Since we didn't hear them, we could also doubt that they ever sang at all; nevertheless we are sure that their voices rise or rose above the desert sands with the same kind of certainty that allows us to affirm that the earth is round without our having seen its shape, or that it rotates around the sun without our having any proof that we are moving. It's this kind of conviction that makes us suppose that they have sung in the desert even though we haven't heard them. Because song is one of the things that people do, and deserts really do exist.

She sings in a low voice. The sands are white and the sky yellow. She is sitting on a small dune with her eyes closed, and the dust covers her neck, eyelashes, and lips, from which a wisp of voice escapes like a sweet liquor onto the parched land. She sings without anyone listening, in spite of which we are certain that she is singing or that she has sung at one time.

Surely the wisp of her voice gets lost almost immediately in the motionless yellow space that surrounds her. And the sun, voraciously sucking the few drops of water up from a nearby lake, furiously drinks up the notes of her song. She doesn't stop singing nor does she sing louder; she keeps singing in the middle of the white sands and the pyramids of salt that arise like temples to a blind and dull-witted god. The sands, which have devoured more than one camel and its rider, hide the notes of her song. But the next day (or the next night, because although we can't hear it we can imagine that she also sings under the dark sky in the solitude of the desert), she lifts up her voice once more. Such persistence shouldn't surprise anybody for it seems somewhat intrinsic to song and sometimes intrinsic to the desert. So much so that it would be difficult for us to imagine a desert without a woman stationed on a sand dune, singing without being listened to.

We don't know the nature of the song although we are convinced that the song exists. When she comes down to the city (because she's not always in the desert; sometimes she participates in our city life and performs the conventional acts that we have been repeating ever since we were born), we accept her like just another inhabitant because, in truth, nothing distinguishes her from the rest of us except the fact that she sings in the desert, and we can forget this since nobody hears her. When she disappears again, we suppose that she has returned to the desert and that in the middle of the white sands and the sky like an ocean she lifts up her voice, elevating her song which like a drop of water dropped from space, is swallowed up by the dune.

Translated by Mary Jane Treachy

Shani Mootoo

Shani Mootoo, an Indo-Trinidadian-Canadian writer, portrays a sexual need that challenges the domestic confinement of women in her story "Lemon Scent" (1993). Enriched by the layers of her cultural legacies, Mootoo's fiction makes possible new disclosures of women's intimacies. Over fifty years ago, another Indian feminist, Ismat Chugtai, published a short story entitled "The Quilt" (1941) depicting a disturbing sexual encounter between an upper-class Indian wife and a young servant woman. As a result, she was charged with obscenity by the British authorities. In this contemporary story, Mootoo, who now lives in Vancouver, returns to the portrait of a wife who, without the protection of class privilege, pursues pleasure in the face of danger.

LEMON SCENT

I. PAISLEYS IN THE SPACES BETWEEN

HER pale brown hands, skin fine and smooth like brushed silk, clutch an oval silver tray against her yellow sari in the area of her navel, indenting lightly. I look down at her offering—faintly wrinkled reddish-black prunes. Careful not to linger to contemplate the shape of the hands, the impeccably manicured shiny-shell-pink fingernails, I concentrate, instead, on spaces between

43

the score of healthy-looking prunes slit slightly and stuffed plump with peanut butter, the slits sealed over with firm pink icing. The spaces between the prunes reveal a white, linen-textured paper doily embossed with low-relief paisleys.

The outer edge of her oval tray brushes against the area of my navel. Above the tray there is a heat growing, filling the space between her and me, and the smell of her cologne on fire thickens to fill up the space. I trace paisleys in the spaces between the prunes with my eyes.

I am careful not to imagine the warm smell of her skin, behind her ears, on the back of her neck. Grasping the tray tightly with her right hand, she obscures my paisleys with her left, fills my view with her hand. Between thumb and middle finger she picks up a prune. Her forefinger guides it from behind up toward my mouth.

I am careful not to look into her eyes.

A little shaft of light glimmers off the band of her gold wedding ring as it catches the light from another room. As her hand reaches my mouth I look over her shoulder to the other room. Her husband stands leaning against a wall sipping his drink, chatting with his friends. I barely open my mouth and her cologne rushes against the back of my throat. Her fingers touch my lips. My tongue flits against her forefinger. The heat and smell of her cologne, like a pounding surf, fill up my mind.

I am careful not to linger.

2. THE GESTURE OF DEEP CONCERN

He looks out the kitchen window with the phone pressed to his ear. Down the hill from that side of his house run miles and miles of undeveloped forested land—wild samaan, giant ferns, ginger lilies, bird-of-paradise bushes, and palm trees, all meshed in suffocating philodendron vines—meeting the sea in the distance.

He doesn't really see what he is staring at. Level with his eyes is the horizon line where the faint sliver of white sea butts against the white sky.

His voice is distant, fading in and out of the bad telephone connection. His edges are softened with a gesture of deep concern.

". . . has everything she could ever want but . . . I don't understand . . . is sulking, her depression again, you know . . . I am going out for some drinks with the guys from work tonight, so please come over. Spend the evening with her. . . . I'll be back late, very late. Spend the night. Lately she only ever laughs when she is with you. . . . I can count on you, can't I. . . . ? I don't want her to be unhappy. . . ."

He pauses, breathing in faint traces of his wife's lemon-scented cologne that linger around the mouthpiece of the phone. Reaching across meandering miles of rough country roads, the line's crackling ceases long enough for him to utter a sacred masked warning: "I must not lose her."

He hangs up the telephone, shoves his cold hands into the back pockets of his blue jeans, and absently looks out the window across the rolling green lawn, dotted here and there with lone hibiscus and croton that his wife conscientiously tends, to the wire and concrete fence that surrounds his property.

He stops at the door of their bedroom before entering and anxiously watches her, his prized exquisite accomplishment, envy of his men friends, huddled in a lifeless puddle on the bed. Standing in the doorway he is not fully at ease informing her that soon he will be leaving and that he has invited Anita over to keep her company for the evening.

An image of Anita and his wife talking intently and at length, almost shyly, at a party recently, comes to his mind. She seems to sizzle with life in Anita's presence. He hopes that his gesture will charm her to him. He sees her chest flutter. Her breathing quickens noticeably.

She uncurls herself and slowly emerges from the bed. He walks over to her and reaches hopefully for her waist, but she glides in and out of his fingers before he can pull her toward him. Knots of fear are beginning to cramp his stomach. Gradually his eyes harden, redden with anger.

Sitting on the edge of the bed, pulling the heavy gray-and-red sports socks, twisting and shoving his feet into graying leather running shoes, he glances up at her every few seconds.

At her dresser she stands leaning in toward the mirror, brushing her long, wavy black hair until it fluffs out light and full around her face and down her back. He has the impression that she is brushing out her hair more thoroughly than usual. He watches her face in the mirror, hoping that she will look over at his pleading face. Without taking her eyes away from her face in the mirror, she offers him a cup of tea before he leaves, but he can feel that her intention to make it is weak and unwilling.

From his stillness in the room, she knows that he is watching her as she readies herself for Anita's visit. Nervously she rambles, saying that if it rains the eaves on the roof will overflow because they need to be cleared of the leaves shedding from the poui tree in the backyard. He does not answer.

He watches her shake the bottle of lemon cologne into her hand. She rubs both hands together lightly, quickly dabs behind her ears and pats her neck, running her hands down onto her chest, the palms of her hands brushing her breasts. She pours more cologne into her hand and rubs it on the small mound of her stomach, massaging it. When she turns to walk over to her closet he gets up and crosses over to the dresser to brush his hair. Looking straight into the mirror at his own reflection, he says more loudly than is necessary, "I'm really glad that you have such a good friend in Anita."

She pulls a dress so forcefully off its hanger that the hanger springs away, snapping off the metal rod and clanging to the wooden floor. He continues, "I wonder why she isn't yet married. She is a bit of a tomboy . . . not exactly appealing to a man. Do you think she is attractive?"

With her face still facing the open closet, she manages to pull up the zipper on the back of her dress by herself. He walks over to her and puts his hands on her waist. He turns her around and cups her face with his hand. With half a grin, as if cautioning her, he adds, "You know, she might be one of those types who likes only women."

He drops one hand to his side and with the other he grabs her face along her thin sharp jawline and pulls her face up to his. Uncured sharp lemon scent settles bitterly on the back of his tongue. With his lips almost against hers he whispers, "If I ever find out that you two have slept together I will kill you both."

He presses his opened mouth onto hers, pulling her lower lip into his mouth briefly. He smooths back the hair from her face, turns, and leaves.

3. UNDER THE SAMAAN TREE

The dry clay earth is creamy brown, like their bodies. Underneath them a thick wool blanket, lime green, like the long thin leaves of the bird-of-paradise surrounding them, softens the ground. Their clothing is concealed in a straw bag a shade lighter than the earth. Like a fan, the edges of the densely broad-brimmed samaan dip and sway overhead, evaporating the fine beads of sweat off their bodies as fast as they form.

Kamini props herself up on her stomach and reaches a hand out to part a couple of branches of the bird-of-paradise, so that she can glimpse the house a little way off in the distance. She can see the back of the house, the top of the back stairs outside the kitchen, where she often stands looking over in this direction (One can only find this spot if one knows where to look—

behind the fence, down the steep hill with tall razor grass, a little beyond the edge of the forest to the vined, spreading samaan. From the house one can see only the top of the tree, nesting ground of hundreds of noisy parakeets.) Just behind that is where they lie.

After making love, she always parts the branches and pensively looks over to the house.

She feels Anita's palm touching her, feeling her damp skin, the shape of her arched back, fingertips skirting her bony shoulder blades. Looking at the fenced-off house in the distance, she is unable to respond like she had minutes ago to the slightest coming together of their skins. Anita sits up slightly, beginning a firmer rubbing, a more intent massaging. Kamini knows that Anita has sensed her worry.

Even though there is no one in the forest to hear them, Anita whispers, "What's happening?"

Kamini lets go of the branches, which spring back up, blocking out the house and the hill. Looking into the wall of bush she remains silent. The fermenting smell of rotting wild fruit floats over them in a wave of a cooling breeze, sharp and sweet. Anita turns to lie on her stomach and puts her arm around Kamini's back.

"What's wrong, what's going on?"

Kamini looks down at the dusty clay earth just beyond the blanket. Reddish brown leafcutter ants with young, bright-green leaves in their mouths, hovering over their heads like umbrellas, march in single file back and forth over the cool ground. Black ants scurry erratically, frantically. She looks at them but does not really see them.

"He says that he'll kill us both if he ever finds out about us."

"What! Both? What do you mean? What made him suspect?"

"I don't know."

"What did you say to him?"

"Nothing."

"Do you know what made him say that? Do you think he means it?"

"I don't know. I don't know why he suspects. He just does."

Anita turns over and flops her back down; her head hits the blanket with an exaggerated thud. She clasps her hands on top of her stomach and forcefully expels a combined breath and the word "Fuck!"

Kamini looks down at Anita's face, which is oddly bright, a smile taking shape on it. "What are you smiling about?"

Anita unclasps her hands and reaches up to touch Kamini's cheek.

"He's always so arrogantly flattered that those men he works with and parties with would like to have you, and so cocksure of himself that they never could. And now he's worried about me!" She grins shyly, which makes her look much younger than she is, and stares up into Kamini's face. "I just sort of like the idea that he's jealous of me, squirming about whether he has you or I do. He's probably right this minute anxiously wondering if we're somewhere making love."

"It's not something to joke about, Nita. I don't think he is joking. He would kill us if he found us together, you know! I'm really frightened that he might come looking for us."

"Does he suspect about this place?"

"I don't think so."

Anita extends her arm on the blanket, an invitation Kamini accepts, resting her forehead down on Anita's shoulder. They lie still for several seconds, then Anita pulls Kamini to rest on top of her. Their chests, stomachs, and thighs are still damp. Their bodies become slippery with sweat, but gentle breezes cool them in the shade of the big tree. The branches of the samaan shift and part to reveal a thin, pale blue sky. Anita looks up distractedly, trying to catch the blue. She turns her head and whispers into

Kamini's ear, "Kam, I have to ask you something. Did you sleep with him last night?"

Kamini is still.

"Tell me Kam, did you? When was the last time you slept with him?"

Kamini lifts her head and, without looking at Anita, turns to face the bird-of-paradise bush. Anita is spurred on by Kamini's silence.

"Kami, you slept with him last night, didn't you?"

"No."

"Well, when was the last time . . . ? You did, I can tell that you did. God! I can't stand the thought of him touching you, kissing you, going and coming inside of you. How could you!"

Kamini pulls away, off onto the blanket, stiffening her body.

"What's wrong with you?" Her voice drops, sounds defeated. "I am his wife, you know! What am I supposed to do? Say no all the time? I am married to him. I can't always say no every time he wants to make love. . . ."

Anita, hearing her sadness, tugs at her to pull her closer. Her eyes are full of tears, and Anita sits up and says coyly, "You and I make love. He and you have sex, and even once a year is too often for my liking."

"Cut it out. You make me feel as if I'm sleeping around. If I keep saying no, no, no to him, he will suspect even more strongly. You don't know him! I wouldn't put it past him to . . ."

Anita reaches out and touches Kamini's lips with hers, taking in the smell of skin, lips, mouth. She slides her lips around to Kamini's cheek and leaves them lightly resting there, her tongue anxious but holding back. The earthy smell of the forest, alive with decaying fruit, subsides for a moment as Anita feels herself suddenly awakening again to the familiar warm lemon scent, blunted by the evening heat, sharpened by the closeness of Anita's breath, hovering between their faces. Kamini feels Anita responding to her smell. She lies back onto the blanket as her lover's mouth follows hers. Her fingers take time curling over Anita's shoulders, drawing her closer down as she curves her pelvis up toward Anita's. She lets Anita nestle her body between her thighs.

Kamini glances up momentarily to the top branches of the darkening samaan, bristling with lime green parakeets beginning to land for the evening, ruffling themselves, hopping around, shifting their positions. Responding to Anita, she bends her knees and gradually slides her feet up on either side of Anita's body. The blue of the sky has turned warm yellowish white.

Marguerite Yourcenar

In her 1975 preface to Fires, *in which her re-imagined tale of Sappho appeared, the Belgian writer Marguerite Yourcenar describes the work as a "sequence of lyrical prose pieces connected by the notion of love." Born in Brussels in 1903, Yourcenar was the first woman to become a literary "immortal" when she was admitted to the Académie Française in 1981. A self-taught classical scholar, she lived a secluded life off the coast of Maine with her partner, translator, and collaborator, the American Grace Frick. She died in 1981, leaving behind her an acclaimed body of work, marked by its homoerotic themes. The following excerpt is a rare moment in the writer's work where the intricacies of lesbian desire are clearly visible.*

SAPPHO OR SUICIDE

Not to be loved anymore is to become invisible;
now you don't notice that I have a body.

Between us and death there is sometimes only the
width of one single person. Remove this person
and there would be only death.

How dull it would have been to be happy!

*I owe each of my tastes to the influence of chance friendships, as
though I could only accept the world from human hands. From
Hyacinth I have this liking of flowers, from Philip of travel, from
Celeste of medicine, from Alexis of laces. From you, why not a
predilection for death?*

have just seen, reflected in the mirrors of a theater box, a
woman called Sappho. She is pale as snow, as death, or as the
clear face of a woman who has leprosy. And since she wears
rouge to hide this whiteness, she looks like the corpse of a mur-
dered woman with a little of her own blood on her cheeks. To
shun daylight, her eyes recede from the arid lids, which no
longer shade them. Her long curls come out in tufts like forest
leaves falling under precocious storms; each day she tears out
new gray hairs, and soon there will be enough of these white
silken threads to weave her shroud. She weeps for her youth as if
for a woman who betrayed her, for her childhood as if for a little
girl she has lost. She is skinny; when she steps into her bath, she
turns away from the mirror, from the sight of her sad breasts. She
wanders from city to city with three big trunks full of false pearls
and bird wreckage. She is an acrobat, just as in ancient times she
was a poetess, because the particular shape of her lungs forces
her to choose a trade that is practiced in midair. In the circus at
night, under the devouring eyes of a mindless public, and in a
space encumbered with pulleys and masts, she fulfills her con-
tract; she is a star. Outside, upstaged by the luminous letters of
posters stuck to the wall, her body is part of that ghostly circle
currently in vogue that soars above the gray cities. She's a mag-
netic creature, too winged for the ground, too corporeal for the
sky, whose wax-rubbed feet have broken the pact that binds us
to the earth: Death waves her dizzy scarves but does not fluster

her. Naked, spangled with stars, from afar she looks like an athlete who won't admit being an angel lest his perilous leaps be underrated; from close up, draped in long robes that give her back her wings, she looks like a female impersonator. She alone knows that her chest holds a heart too heavy and too big to be lodged elsewhere than in a broad bosom: this weight, hidden at the bottom of a bone cage, gives each of her springs into the void the mortal taste of danger. Half eaten by this implacable tiger, she secretly tries to be the tamer of her heart. She was born on an island and that is already a beginning of solitude; then her profession intervened, forcing on her a sort of lofty isolation every night; fated to be a star, she lies on her stage board, half undressed, exposed to the winds of the abyss, and suffers from the lack of tenderness as from the lack of pillows. Men in her life have only been steps of a ladder she had to climb, often dirtying her feet. The director, the trombone player, the publicity agent all made her sick of waxed mustaches, cigars, liqueurs, striped ties, leather wallets—the exterior attributes of virility that make women dream. Only young women's bodies would still be soft enough, supple enough, fluid enough to let themselves be handled by this strong angel who would playfully pretend to drop them in midair. She can't hold them very long in this abstract space bordered on all sides by trapeze bars: quickly frightened by this geometry changing into wingbeats, all of them soon give up acting as her sky companion. She has to come down to earth, to their level, to share their ragged, patchy lives, so that affection ends up like a Saturday pass, a twenty-four-hour leave a sailor spends with easy women. Suffocating in these rooms no bigger than alcoves, she opens the door to the void with the hopeless gesture of a man forced, by love, to live among dolls. All women love one woman: they love themselves madly, consenting to find beauty only in the form of their own body. Sappho's eyes, farsighted in sorrow, looked farther away.

She expects of young women what self-adorning idolatrous coquettes expect of mirrors: a smile answering her trembling smile, until the breath from lips moving closer and closer obscures the reflection and clouds the crystal. Narcissus loves what he is. Sappho bitterly worships in her companions what she has not been. Poor, held in contempt, which is the other side of celebrity, and having only the perspectives of the abyss in stock, she caresses happiness on the bodies of her less threatened friends. The veils of communicants carrying their souls outside themselves make her dream of a brighter childhood than hers had been; when one has run out of illusions, one can still lend others a sinless childhood. The pallor of these girls awakens in her the almost unbelievable memory of virginity. In Gyrinno, she loved pride and lowered herself to kiss the girl's feet. Anactoria's love brought her the taste of French fries eaten by handfuls in amusement parks, of rides on the wooden horses of carousels, and brought her the sweet feel of straw, tickling the neck of the beautiful girl lying down in haystacks. In Attys, she loved misfortune. She met Attys in the center of a big city, asphyxiated by the breath of its crowds and by the fog of its river; her mouth still smelled of the ginger candy she had been chewing. Soot stains stuck to her cheeks shiny with tears: she was running on a bridge, wearing a coat of fake otter; her shoes had holes; her face like that of a young goat had a haggard sweetness. To explain why her lips were pinched and pale like the scar of an old wound, why her eyes looked like sick turquoises, Attys had three different stories that were after all only three aspects of the same misfortune: her boyfriend, whom she saw every Sunday, had left her because one evening she wouldn't let him caress her in a taxi; a girlfriend who let her sleep on the couch of her student room had turned her out, accusing her wrongly of trying to steal her fiancé's heart; and finally, her father beat her. Attys was afraid of everything: of ghosts, of

men, of the number 13, of the green eyes of cats. The hotel
dining room dazzled her like a temple where she felt obliged to
speak only in a whisper; the bathroom made her clap her hands
in amazement. Sappho spends the money she has saved for years
through suppleness and temerity for this whimsical girl. She
makes circus directors hire this mediocre artist who can only
juggle flower bouquets. With the regularity of change that is the
essence of life for nomadic artists and sad profligates, together
they tour the arenas and stages of all capitals. Each morning, in
the furnished rooms rented so that Attys will avoid the promis-
cuity of hotels full of too-rich clients, they mend their costumes
and the runs in their tight silk stockings. Sappho has nursed this
sick child so often, has so many times warded off men who
would tempt her, that her gloomy love imperceptibly takes on a
maternal cast, as though fifteen years of sterile voluptuousness
had produced this child. The young men in tuxedos met in the
halls of theater boxes all recall to Attys the friend whose repulsed
kisses she perhaps misses: Sappho has heard her talk so often of
Philip's beautiful silk shirts, of his blue cuff links, of the shelves
of pornographic albums decorating his room in Chelsea, that
she now has as clear a picture of this fastidiously dressed busi-
nessman as of the few lovers she couldn't avoid slipping into her
life. She stows him away absentmindedly among her worst
memories. Little by little, Attys' eyelids take on a lavender hue;
she gets letters at a post-office box and she tears them up after
reading them; she seems strangely well informed about the business trips that might make the young man run into them, by
chance, on their nomadic road. It is painful to Sappho not to be
able to give Attys anything more than a back room in life, and to
know that only fear keeps the little fragile head leaning on her
strong shoulder. Sappho, embittered by all the tears she had the
courage never to shed, realizes that all she can offer her friends is
a tender form of despair; her only excuse is to tell herself that

love, in all its forms, has nothing better to offer shy creatures, and were Attys to leave, she would not find more happiness somewhere else. One night Sappho, arms full of flowers picked for Attys, comes home later than usual. The concierge looks at her differently than she ordinarily does as she walks by; suddenly the spirals of the staircase look like serpent rings. Sappho notices that the milk carton is not in its usual place on the doormat; as soon as she is in the entrance hall, she smells the odor of cologne and blond tobacco. She notices in the kitchen the absence of an Attys busy frying tomatoes; in the bathroom the want of a young woman naked and playing with bathwater; in the bedroom the removal of an Attys ready to let herself be rocked. Facing the mirrors of the wide-open wardrobe, she weeps over the disappearance of the beloved girl's underwear. A blue cuff link lying on the floor reveals the cause of this departure, which Sappho stubbornly refuses to accept as final, afraid that it could kill her. Once again, she is trampling alone on city arenas, avidly scanning the theater boxes for a face her folly prefers to all bodies. After a few years, during one of her tours in the East, she learns that Philip is now director of a company that sells Oriental tobaccos; he has just been married to a rich and imposing woman who couldn't be Attys. Rumor has it that the girl has joined a dance company. Once again, Sappho makes the rounds of Middle East hotels; each doorman has his own way of being insolent, impudent, or servile; she checks out the pleasure spots where the smell of sweat poisons perfumes, the bars where an hour of stupor in alcohol and human heat leaves no more trace than a wet circle left by a glass on a black wooden table. She carries her search even as far as going to the Salvation Army, in the vain hope of finding Attys impoverished and ready to let herself be loved. In Istanbul, she happens to sit, every night, next to a casually dressed young man who passes himself off as an employee of a travel agency; his slightly dirty hand lazily holds

up the weight of his forehead. They exchange those banal words
that are often used between strangers as a bridge to love. He says
his name is Phaon, claims he is the son of a Greek woman from
Smyrna and of a sailor in the British fleet; once again, Sappho's
heart quickens when she hears the delightful accent so often
kissed on Attys' lips. Behind him stand memories of escape, of
poverty, and of dangers unrelated to wars and more secretly
connected to the laws of his own heart. He, too, seems to
belong to a threatened race, one that is allowed to exist through
a precarious and ever provisional permissiveness. Not having a
residence visa, this young man has his own difficulties; he's a
smuggler dealing in morphine, perhaps an agent of the secret
police; he lives in a world of secret meetings and passwords, a
world Sappho cannot penetrate. He doesn't need to tell her his
story to establish a fraternity of misfortune between them. She
tells him her sorrows; she goes on and on about Attys. He thinks
he has met her; he vaguely remembers seeing a naked girl jug-
gling flowers in a cabaret of Pera. He owns a little sailboat that
he uses on Sundays for outings on the Bosphorus; together they
go looking in all the sad cafés along the shore, in restaurants of
the island, in the modest boarding houses on the Asian coast that
poor foreigners live in. Seated at the stern, Sappho watches this
handsome male face, which is now her only human sun, waver
in the light of a lantern. She finds in his features certain traits
once loved in the runaway girl: the same pouting mouth that a
mysterious bee seems to have stung; the same little hard forehead under different hair that this time seemed to have been
dipped in honey; the same eyes looking like greenish turquoises
but framed by a tanned, rather than livid, face, so that the pale
brown-haired girl seems to have been simply the wax lost in
casting this bronze and golden god. Surprised, Sappho finds herself slowly preferring these shoulders rigid as trapeze bars, these
hands hardened by the contact of oars, this entire body holding

just enough feminine softness for her to love it. Lying down on the bottom of the boat, she yields to the new sensations of the floodwaters parted by this ferryman. Now she only mentions Attys to tell him that the lost girl looked like him but wasn't as handsome: Phaon accepts these compliments with a mocking but worried satisfaction. She tears up, in front of him, a letter in which Attys announces that she is coming back; she doesn't even bother to make out the return address. He watches her doing this with a faint smile on his trembling lips. For the first time, she neglects the discipline of her demanding profession, she interrupts the exercises that put every muscle under the control of the spirit; they dine together; and surprisingly, she eats a little too much. She only has a few days left with him in this city; her commitments have her soaring in other skies. Finally he consents to spend the last evening with her in the little apartment she rents near the port. She watches him come and go in the cluttered room, he is like a voice mingling clear and deep notes. Unsure of his moves, as though afraid of breaking fragile illusions, Phaon leans over the portraits of Attys for a better look. Sappho sits down on the Viennese sofa covered with Turkish embroideries; she presses her face in her hands like someone trying to erase memories. This woman who until now took upon herself the choice, the offer, the seduction, the protection of her more vulnerable girlfriends, relaxes and, falling, yields limply, at last, to the weight of her own sex and of her own heart. She is happy that, from now on, all she has to do with a lover is to make the gesture of acceptance. She listens to the young man prowl in the next room; there, the whiteness of a bed is sprawled like a hope remaining, in spite of everything, miraculously open; she hears him uncork flasks on the dresser, rummage in drawers with the ease of a housebreaker or a boyfriend who feels he is allowed everything. He opens the folding doors of the wardrobe, where, among a few ruffles left by Attys,

Sappho's dresses hang like women who have killed themselves.
Suddenly the ghostly shudder of a silken sound draws near like a
dangerous caress. She rises, turns around; the beloved creature
has wrapped himself in a robe Attys left behind: the thin silk
gauze worn on naked flesh accentuates the quasi-feminine
gracefulness of the dancer's long legs; relieved of its confining
men's clothing, this flexible body is almost a woman's body. This
Phaon, comfortable in his impersonation, is nothing more than
a stand-in for the beautiful absent nymph; once again, it's a girl
coming toward her with a crystal laugh. Distraught, Sappho runs
to the door to escape from this fleshly ghost who will only give
her the same sad kisses. Outside, she charges into the swell of
bodies and runs down the streets leading to the sea; they are littered with debris and garbage. She realizes that no encounter
holds her salvation, since, no matter where she goes, she runs
into Attys again. This overwhelming face blocks all openings but
those leading to death. Night falls like a weariness confusing her
memory; a little blood endures next to the sunset. Suddenly she
hears cymbals clashing as though fever hit them in her heart;
a long-standing habit has brought her back, unawares, to the
circus at the very hour when she struggles with the angel of
dizziness each night. For the last time, she is intoxicated by this
wild-beast odor that has been the odor of her life, by this music
like that of love, loud and discordant. A wardrobe woman lets
her into the dressing room, which she enters now as if condemned to death; she strips as if for God; she rubs white
makeup all over herself to become a ghost; she snaps the choker
of memory around her neck. An usher, dressed in black, arrives
to tell her that her hour has come; she climbs the rope ladder of
her celestial scaffold; she is fleeing skyward from the mockery of
believing that there had been a young man. She removes herself
from the yells of orange vendors, from the cutting laughter of

pink children, from the skirts of dancers, from the mesh of human nets. With one pull, she brings herself to the last support her will to die will allow: the trapeze bar swinging in midair transforms this creature, tired of being only half woman, into a bird; she glides, sea gull of her own abyss, hanging by one foot, under the gaze of a public that does not believe in tragedy. Her skill goes against her; no matter how she tries, she can't lose her balance; shady equestrian, Death has her vault the next trapeze. She climbs at last higher than the spotlights: spectators can no longer applaud her, since now they can't see her. Hanging on to the ropes that pull the canopy painted with stars, she can only continue to surpass herself by bursting through her sky. Under her, the ropes, the pulleys, the winches of her fate now mastered, squeak in the wind of dizziness; space leans and pitches as on a stormy sea; the star-filled firmament rocks between mast yards. From here, music is only a smooth swell washing over all memory. Her eyes no longer distinguish between red and green lights; blue spotlights, sweeping over the dark crowd, bring out, here and there, naked feminine shoulders that look like tender rocks. Hanging on to her death as to an overhanging ledge, Sappho looks for a place to fall and chooses a spot beyond the netting where the mesh will not hold her. Her own acrobatic performance occupies only half of the immense vague arena; in the other half, where seals and clowns carry on, nothing has been set up to prevent her from dying. Sappho dives, arms spread as if to grasp half of infinity; she leaves behind her only the swinging of a rope as proof of having left the sky. But those failing at life run the risk of missing their suicide. Her oblique fall is broken by a lamp shining like a blue jellyfish. Stunned but safe, she is thrown by the impact toward the netting that pulls and repulses the foamy light; the meshes give but do not yield under the weight of this statue fished out from the bottom of the sky. And soon roustabouts will only have to haul onto the sand this marble pale body streaming with sweat like a drowning woman pulled from the sea.

⌒

I will not kill myself. The dead are so quickly forgotten.

One can only raise happiness on a foundation of despair.
I think I will be able to start building.

Let no one be accused of my life.

It's not a question of suicide. It's only a question of beating a record.

Translated by Dori Katz and the author

Emma Donoghue

In "Looking for Petronilla" (1996), the Dublin-born writer Emma Donoghue re-creates and unifies disparate moments of Irish time as her narrator travels in quest of a wronged woman. Donoghue's fascination with history and the lesbian presence within it was amply demonstrated in her pioneering work Passions Between Women: British Lesbian Culture (1668–1801). *Both in her current work—a collection of fairy tales—and in her novels, which depict the early days of Ireland's lesbian-feminist movement, Donoghue uses mythic and real time to address issues of gender and social inequalities. In style as well as in content, this story exemplifies Donoghue's ability to seduce the reader into a world where all historical time is open to her characters.*

LOOKING FOR PETRONILLA

'VE been away too long.

The plane took me from London to Dublin in less than an hour. I would have come this way before if I had known how simple it was. When I first took the boat to England, vomiting up my whole self into the Irish Sea, I swore I'd never go back. But most promises wear out in the end. This plane trip was almost merry, clouds back-lit by champagne.

I bought it in honor of Petronilla. Since she couldn't be here today it seemed only fitting to toast her virtues in overpriced bubbly, ten thousand feet above the island she never left. The rented Volvo took me to Kilkenny with surprising speed. They've built craft shops on every corner and knocked down a lot of old houses. Kyteler's Inn is still there, though; its wooden lines stand firm against the swarm of tourists. There's an Alice's Restaurant in the cellar ("It's a kind of magic!" jokes the sign, catching the sunlight), and upstairs is called Nero's; how very suitable. What's your poison, traveler?

I stand at the bar and order a glass of the best red they have. I look around, waiting for the centuries to fall away, but my eyes lodge on the chintzy little tablecloths and chairs. I am so used to the twentieth century that it is almost impossible to imagine myself back to the fourteenth. Hard to believe that this round-bellied building was ever cold and damp, with one fire sighing and the smell of tallow flaring in the nostrils of visitors.

I peer at the wall, where a Disney hag pours cups of smoking brew for four little men with uneasy expressions. Perhaps they have noticed that their shoes, toes tied to their knees, are from the wrong country and century. I read through the five-line caption, which is a tribute to the powers of invention. Nothing worth losing my temper over. Why should anyone remember, anyway, except someone like me, whose business it is? There's been a lot of water under the bridge since 1324. History always becomes a cartoon, where it survives at all. Your best hope for a ride toward posterity is the bandwagon of folklore.

"Oldest house in Kilkenny, this is."

I accept the wineglass from the graying woman behind the bar. "So they say."

"You know the story?"

"Oh yes." I take a sip: not dry enough. I wonder what kind of hash this woman could make of the tale, but it hardly needs another telling. It is remarkable only for the gender of the protagonist. When a man kills his wife, he is a tortured rebel, *criminel de passion,* dusky Othello or bluff King Hal. When a woman kills her husband, she is never allowed to forget it. I stare at the drawing again. Alice Kyteler, four times widow in two dozen years, has evolved into a long-nailed monster, a Kilkenny Clytemnestra.

"Researching?"

My eyes swivel back to the bartender, who is polishing glasses with a Guinness tea towel. "Beg your pardon?"

"Doing a radio program or something? Family history?" she adds. Her hand has paused, knuckles yellow against the glass.

"More or less," I tell her, with a ghost of a smile.

"Very nice."

I glance back at the wall beside me, then at the others, weighted down with old maps and giant replica copper pots. No picture of Petronilla de Meath. I suppose I could ask the bartender, but I'm not sure my mouth could bear to form the words.

Why is it that almost nobody knows Petronilla's name, when she was much more remarkable than her mistress? No demon Dame Alice called up and bound with spells ever served her so faithfully. What interests me is not so much the mistress's evil, which seems after almost seven centuries to amount to no more than a banal footnote in the annals of war and treachery, but the maid's extraordinary ordinariness. How through thick and thin, sickness and sin, Masses read backward and Christian funerals Petronilla retained her sense of being a good servant, whatever that could mean in a house like this one. As if she had heard some fireside tale that ended with the tag *Whanne that yr mistresse sell here soule to Luciphere ond take a wisshe for to kille her lawfulle wedded husbandes, be you of gode cheere ond giff her al manere of aid for to brewe ye poysionne.*

"I love history, myself."

I turn on the bartender, who is rubbing at the lipsticked lip of a glass. "Why is that?"

Her blue eyes, behind her glasses, seem surprised by the question. "Well, it makes you feel more complete, doesn't it?" A pause. "Knowing where you're from."

"Does it?"

"Reminds you there's more to the whole business than your own little life." She gives me a wholly unmerited smile. "I like to think that no one ever really dies as long as their folks remember them."

"Perhaps they'd prefer to."

"Remember them?"

"Die."

"Oh. Oh I don't think so," says the woman, as if to reassure us both.

I ask to be directed to the Ladies; this seems the best excuse for poking around. For all the dark wood, most of these walls look new; these smooth beams have never had a sconce stuck in them. I hitch up my tights, careful not to tear them. I take off my heavy ring to wash my hands. My face looks back at me with a hint of defiance: no new lines today. On the wall, a Kondo-Vend machine offers me the Quality Range of Luxury Lubricated Sheath Contraceptives. I can tell I won't find what I'm looking for in Kyteler's Inn.

As I cross the narrow elbow of St. Kierán's Street, I find myself humming a tune, a very old one; I realize that it has been stuck in my head since Dublin. The words slide onto one another like water over worn rocks. Voice on anonymous voice, disciplined in melancholy resignation.

Quiconques veut d'amors joïr
Doit avoir foy et esperance

Such patience the singers had back then, giving every melancholic syllable its own line of music, a full half minute to a phrase, as if they had all the time in the world. Faith and hope is what the seeker after love must have. Faith to keep you longing, hope to relieve your despair.

The town has become a maze of gift shops and boutiques; I can't tell where anything used to be. As I step off a curb, a car roars by, inches from my handbag. LABHAIR GAEILGE says the bumper sticker, as if simple encouragement could set my tongue to talking the language I've long forgotten.

What was Petronilla's first name, I wonder? The one she knew herself by when she was a raw serving-maid who could speak only two tongues and both of them with a County Meath accent. When her hair still fell loose under her white coif, not yet having been tucked away as the mark of womanhood. When she came in a cart to Kilkenny, telling her beads, before her mistress renamed her for the saint whose day it was, the Roman Virgin who tended Peter. What went through the girl's head those first months, I wonder, as she ran to order: "Fetch my Venetian brocade, the rayed one you fool," and "Strap on my pattens if you would not have me wade through every puddle in town," and (in a low voice) "Have you fetched candles of beeswax for the ceremony?"

She was Dame Alice's loyal bondswoman from the start; she was a dagger thrown back and forward between those ruby-weighted hands. The first Sabbath made her retch in a corner, but she said nothing, told no one, never broke trust. The girl had no malice of her own, but her mistress's orders girded her like chain mail, and obedience made her brave.

The most inexplicable thing is that at no point in her imprisonment or trial did Petronilla try to run away. Did she keep hoping Dame Alice would return from England to burst the doors, with all the force of law or simply a click of her stained fingers? Or did the maid simply keep her garbled faith, offering herself as ransom for her vanished mistress, waiting on the pleasure of the dark master? Or, more likely, did some portion of her drugged conscience feel her execution to be a proper end to the story?

What is clear is that she was not one of the weeping, piteous victims who flock across the pages of history. She embraced her death as a final order. Does that make her mistress's betrayal better or worse? All the records have to say on the matter is that at the hour of her death, Petronilla declared that Dame Alice was the most powerful witch in the world.

I feel slightly faint. I am standing on a street corner with a slightly crazed expression. A small girl leaning against a lamppost watches me; she has a purple birthmark the shape of a kidney. "Lights changed ages ago, Mrs.," she points out.

I cross without answering her. I should be looking for the jail, but I can't face it yet. I wander up the hill, past Dunnes Stores, a stall selling local fudge, a poster inviting costumed revelers to a Quentin Tarantino Night.

St. Canice's seems almost small after the great cathedrals of England. Its walls are gray and serene; beside it, the round tower pencils the clouds. I look for the grave, but they must have moved it. Inside the church I finally stumble across the headstone, one of a dozen propped against the walls. With difficulty I make out the old French letters framing a fleur-de-lis cross. *Here lies José de Keteller,* they say. *Say thou who passest here a prayer.*

He came to this town in chain mail with a long sword, an old-style legitimate killer. Learned Gaelic, grew long mustaches, finally even rode without a saddle in the native way. A peaceful settler, shaping himself to the island fate had placed him on, José de Keteller was not to know how his name would be immortalized by his iron-willed daughter. Why is it so much worse to execute husbands than infidels, I wonder? Most of us are descended from killers, one way or another.

None of this is telling me anything I didn't already know, and my feet are beginning to ache. In the museum, I take my shoes off for a moment to stretch my feet on the smooth wooden floor. What a motley collection we have here: grisset and candle mold, cypress chest and footstool, a copy of a will specifying what a certain widow would inherit from her husband if she did not remarry or have carnal knowledge of any man willingly (this last bit makes me smile), and a deer skull with antlers six feet wide. On a dusty shelf I find huge metal tongs, for stamping ihs on holy wafers. My heart begins to thump again.

Downstairs in the bookshop, I calm myself with a collection of photographs of Irish lakes. The girl assesses me as a browser and turns back to the phone, demanding (in an accent that I haven't heard in a long time) to know who said she'd said she fancied that spotty eejit. I turn the pages, recognizing the heads of birds. I move on to the small history shelf, where I learn that the town's most famous witch was, in fact, framed.

"Alice Kyteler (possibly a misspelling of Kettle, a fairly common English surname)," I read in one hardback,

> was a victim of a combination of the worst excesses of fourteenth-century Christo-patriarchy. Threatening to men by virtue of her emotional and financial independence, this irrepressible bourgeoise, who always kept her maiden name through repeated widowhoods, aroused the hostility of avaricious relatives and a misogynistic Catholic establishment. As in so many other "witch trials," powerful men (both church and lay) projected their own unconscious fantasies of sexual/satanic perversion onto the blank canvas of a woman's life.

I can't help smiling: blank canvas my eye. There is a grain of truth there, of course: before she ever trafficked with darkness, the citizens of Kilkenny resented the Kyteler woman's fine house, bright gowns, every last ruby on her fingers. But that does not make her innocent.

The girl on the phone is eyeing me wearily. She is letting her friend speak now, the faraway voice winding down like clockwork.

How the twentieth century loves to issue general pardons. At this distance, it cannot distinguish the rare cases of serious evil from those of farmers' wives burnt by neighborly malice. Dame Alice should not be lumped in with the victims. She was the real thing. She could be said to have deserved the punishment she never got.

Unlike Petronilla, not mentioned in the historical analysis. Petronilla, who should have been set free when the whole sorry mess was concluded. Why could she not have been shaken out like a wide-eyed cat from a sack, to run across country and live some ordinary life?

It is too hot in here, all at once; too cosy, with a tub of Connemara Marble Worry Stones going cheap beside the till and remaindered Romance stacked high on a table between the symmetrical stares of Décor and Archaeology. I replace the books neatly and leave.

Outside it is cooler, at least; the edgy breeze of late afternoon fills the town. I walk along the main shopping street, wondering where the jail could have got to. A hamburger carton impales itself on my heel; I kick it off. My toes feel crushed; my head is beginning to pound. Anything could have been built on the site of Petronilla's last months: a hardware shop, a B&B, a public toilet. A jail is by nature anonymous; all it requires is four walls or a hole in the ground, a barred square of light if you're lucky.

I pause outside a pub offering Live Trad To-Nite, staring at the five bars just above ground level, the darkness behind them. All they hide is a cellar of beer barrels, but if I close my eyes I can almost see her pallid hands caressing the iron. Petronilla in the shadows, crouched in her dirty smock, once good linen, a present after her first year of service. A face like a drop of honey, looking out of a bedraggled wimple—unless they shamed her by leaving her head naked. Did her pale hair come down at last, escaping coif and cap and veil, falling back into girlhood?

I rest my palms against the pub's gray slate, ignoring the glances of passersby, and try to conjure up the rest of her. Would there be marks of torture, the telltale insignia on wrists and soles? Probably not; there would have been no need, since she seems to have told the whole story freely once her mistress had escaped to safety. Besides, they probably preferred to bring the girl unmarked to the stake, a perfect sacrifice to the fire-breathing dragon. Where would they have done it, I wonder—outside the jail, outside the city walls, or in the busy thoroughfare of the market square? Which supermarket sits on Petronilla's ashes now? Pressing my fingertips so hard against the cement that they turn gray, I ask every question I can think of. Was there anyone there that day who, remembering alms or a kind word or just the turn of her cheek, had enough mercy on her to add wet faggots to the kindling? Was there enough smoke to put her to sleep before flames licked the arches of her feet?

This is one of the times when I wish I still had the ability to cry. Petronilla is not here. There is nothing left. I don't know what I was hoping for, exactly: some sign of presence, some message scratched for me on the prison wall, some word from her walking ghost. I shut my eyes more tightly, but all I can hear is some inane pop song leaking from a taxi window. *Hold on,* the singer begs. *Every word I say is true. Hold on, I'll be coming back for you.*

I let go of the wall; the pads of my fingers are scored and pockmarked. As I stare at them they plump into their usual shape. The daily miracle, the return to the same healthy flesh. How long must it go on?

I stride back to my car, through a crocodile of French school-children; in the carpark, I have some difficulty remembering what color I rented. Automatically I fasten my seat belt. I have never tried to kill myself; I am afraid to discover that it would not work. I shrug off my shoes and lean my head back on the padded rest. What on earth am I doing here?

My ring is cutting into my finger; I pull it off and stare at it. Rubies to stave off disease; this is my last one. Once in Birmingham someone tried to mug me, and I cracked his nose with this ring.

Time has not absolved me of anything. The clothes have been transformed, the name is different—I change it every fifty years or so—but the face in the rearview mirror is the same. And in almost seven centuries of exile I have not managed to forget Petronilla.

It's almost funny, isn't it? One would think that a woman who in her esoteric researches had stumbled across the secret of immortality would feel free. Exhausted by life's repetitions, yes, starved for fresh food, tormented by the bargain she made, but in some sense free. To wander, at least, to move, to leave behind the quarrels of mortals. I never expected to be so haunted by one face that I would have to make my way back to Kilkenny.

More than any husband or lover or child; more than anyone I have hurt since I went into exile; more than anyone I left without warning (when they wondered why I was not aging) or killed with my bare hands (when they deserved it). Petronilla's is the only death I still regret. Leaving her behind was the worst thing I have ever done.

I did no harm to my first husband, the richest moneylender in town; I bore him a son and fed him tidbits on his deathbed. As for my second, in my grandmother's time I could have followed the old ways and left him after a year and a day, but under Common Law I was his for life, to stamp his mark on. I bent under his weight like a reed, and in the pool of humiliation I brushed against my power. He was sick already—the beatings were getting feebler—but the poison sped him on. My third . . . yes, I remember. I dispatched him in a night, after I caught him in the linen cupboard ripping the skirt off Petronilla. The night before his funeral I dropped his heart in the River Nore.

As for my fourth, John le Poer, he was a loving man who shut his ears to the rumors circulating about me. But by then, you must understand, I had signed with my own blood, and the sacrifice was called for. His hair came out in handfuls when I brushed it at night; his nails began to bend backward. Petronilla never claimed to understand the rituals, but she knew that whatever Dame Alice said had to happen. When John, made suspicious at last by the gossip of my dead husbands' disinherited children, talked to Bishop Ledrede, it was my faithful maid, my flawless echo, who repeated to me every word they had said. When my husband wrenched the key from my belt and burst into my room, finding and forcing open the padlocked boxes, I kept one curious eye on Petronilla. She wept because the story was almost over, but she showed no shame.

I was charged along with eleven accomplices, most of whom barely knew me to see. The seven charges told of dogs torn limb from limb and scattered at crossroads, fornication with Ethiopian hobgoblins, and a dead baby's flesh boiled in a robber's skull. The grease I used to keep my face soft was listed as a sorcerous ointment for the staff on which I flew across Kilkenny town by night. Bishop Ledrede was widely read and had a vivid imagination. He was not to know that power is composed of simple elements, once you have stumbled across it.

Ledrede did not do it for the money his spiritual court could hope to confiscate; like myself, he was motivated by wrath and glory. And so, when I had indicted him for defamation and sailed to England with all my jewels, when my son William had agreed to pay for the reroofing of St. Canice's as a penance, and when the other accused accomplices had melted into the night, then the bishop focused his gaze on Petronilla. She was all he had left.

It was not that I could not have brought her with me, torn her out of prison somehow; I simply never thought to. That is my crime; that in the urgency of my flight, full of the sense of my own devilish importance, I did not even condemn my maid deliberately, but carelessly, as I might have said, "Pick up that sarsenet gown."

I have had plenty of time to think of her since. In almost seven centuries of wandering I can make an informed comparison: I have met no one who loved so well or was so betrayed. She was not a natural killer: she ground poisons together out of mute loyalty, and what purer motive is there than that?

It is so long since I killed, I have almost forgotten how. It is not worth risking nowadays. They lock you up, take down what you say, and never put an end to it. Oh Petronilla, how I envy your death. Not the manner of it, the pain and squalor, but its definition. How it took you by the hand and led you away before your bursting youth could dwindle.

Unless I am casting a web of glamor over the story to lessen my guilt? But that's not how it works. My envy and my guilt pin each other down. Petronilla's, short and powerless, is the life I did not lead, and cannot lead no matter how long I drag on, and will never fully understand. Petronilla's exultant face I cannot leave behind me. She follows behind, just out of view, and all the rippling voices are hers.

Quiconques veut d'amors joïr
Doit avoir foy et esperance

Having had faith and hope enough to last her short lifetime, did it come down to love in the end? Was that what she feasted on, among the rats in Kilkenny jail? How could I be loved by such as her?

For all my sheer elastic skin, I am a hollow woman. My ribs are an empty cauldron now; my breath couldn't put out a candle.

I start the car. My one faith is that I will find some trace of Petronilla. My one hope is that she will teach me how to die. My one love now, the only one whose face I can remember. There, around some corner, she burns, she burns.

Sylvia Molloy

One of the most important lesbian novels to date in Latin American literature is Certificate of Absence (En breve cárcel) *(1981) by the Argentine author Sylvia Molloy. Reflecting the fusion of Latin America and Europe that is characteristically Argentinean, Molloy writes with an intensely psychological focus. In this novel, a woman alone in a room attempts to write her way out of the confines of the past and present, a process that paradoxically threatens to strip the future bare. Molloy, a critic as well as a novelist, has done extensive work on Latin American women's writing and on the construction of sexualities. A striking aspect of the novel excerpted here is the fundamental yet neutral presence of lesbian relationships, a structure through which issues of memory, desire, loss, and exile express themselves. In this passage, the narrator struggles against the current of early memories and family ties and the impending loss of her lover, Renata, whose inability to understand the narrator's native language underscores the lost intimacies of childhood.*

from CERTIFICATE OF ABSENCE

HY is it difficult to speak of her mother, her sister—Isabel and Clara—when she speaks fearlessly of other women? In one of the versions she foresaw for this story she would have spoken a great deal of her sister. She does not know exactly in what way: she would have wanted to keep her in the margin, regulating her appearances in the story and keeping her in childhood where she remembers her best. She would keep the Clara she whipped for looking so blond, the Clara whose tiny pubis she saw in the bathtub, the Clara who played dolls with her, but few other images. However, there are also dreams: Clara comes back to her often at night. More than once, when sleeping next to Renata, she awoke with a start near dawn and could not return to sleep. She had said something out loud, something Renata did not understand. How could she understand it? She had just spoken to her sister in a language that Renata did not speak, calling Clara's name. Renata quite rightly turned over and went back to sleep, while she was left with fragments that slowly dissolved. Someday she will rescue those fragments. She feels tempted to do so tonight.

Once more she spends peaceful, almost sleepless hours, haunted by a precise, reedy music that plays over and over. It was a strange, exhausting day. She spent it with Renata and realized once more that she loves her. She also realized that their meetings had changed and lacked their former violence. It is clear now that they speak two different languages. They will never come together in this story, which started out with hope, then turned to fury, and even now is changing. Tonight she accepts, or almost accepts, the idea of parting with Renata, foreseeing the end of the road: because of her mistakes, or Renata's, it does not lead anywhere. Before the final good-bye, which she is already planning, she knows there will be painful moments. She believes she has the strength to survive them: they will be tests, ordeals. She does not want to guess at the pain and the difficulty and write about them, since she will have to live through them in any case. That is why she seeks refuge in her sister's blurry figure. Clara calls to her, the Clara to whom she now knows she always wanted to make love.

She writes of her with sadness. She sees so little of her sister, perhaps will not see her again. There is something in Clara against which she must defend herself. Tonight, unable to sleep, she suddenly remembers Clara's insomnia as an adolescent, the nights she refused to turn out the light. She also remembers her listlessness. Clara at eighteen would spend hours lying in bed, saying she needed nothing, wanted nothing. On those occasions she was only able to hold Clara's hand. She loved her dearly but could not stand that image of surrender: she had seen it before, in their mother, when she told her daughters she wished she would never wake up. In spite of the insistent images that return to haunt her, she knows she must save herself. And yet, there is something about Clara that makes her want to protect her, wherever, whenever, despite all her fears.

Tonight she remembers Clara for something she prized in her father, in her Aunt Sara: her sense of humor. If that is Clara's best feature, why not guard it? She would like to recover the complicitous language she and Clara shared, the private fantasies they built together, and, most of all, the laughter she needs so badly. What she really misses today, more than Clara's sense of humor, is that irrepressible laughter that bound them together as children. She remembers how, at meals, their faces puffing up and their eyes watering, they winked at each other in silent agreement. They would hold back their laughter until the others left the table. Once alone, they were free to finish the meal at their leisure, picking a section of tangerine, a peeled grape, eating some grated apple. (She still has one of her mother's apple graters, shaped like a fish.) It was then that their laughter exploded. They noisily spat out the peeled grapes, which they used as missiles, trying to see who could shoot the farthest, who could hit the target.

———

News has just reached her that the house where she grew up has been sold. She will not see it again. Better said: she will not return to it again in her writing, as she has done up to now, peopling it from a distance. In her mind she goes through it in detail as if it were a dead body, as she looked at the dead bodies of her father and her aunt, as one day—hopefully not too near at hand—she will look at her mother's dead body, like an untidy heap of bones that has finally lost the appearance of a whole.

She remembers the first time she saw that house, a few months after her sister was born. She herself was about four. Her father had to go over some papers with the former owners before they moved and took her along. She remembers a dining room full of people for tea, as it would so often be later, full of other people. She was given a cup of weak tea and a dry cookie she crumbled up, knowing she would not be able to swallow it. She looked at the dining room fireplace, telling herself that this was her new home. An old woman presided at a table she remembers as huge; she also recalls many other children, lots of noise. All of a sudden, as the family began to disband, the old woman changed places and sat down next to her. She talked to her, making her forget the cookie she could not eat. She took her outside to the front yard and showed her a jasmine bush, asking her to take care of it for her. But she did not take care of it; she was four years old and did not know how to take care of plants. She did, however, go look at it regularly, until one day that spindly jasmine, which probably would never have done well anyway, suddenly disappeared. Had it grown, it would now reach the balcony of the room where she and her sister slept and might even touch the window of their parents' room. Jasmine: there are so many kinds. For childhood the star jasmine, with little flowers, like the one she should have taken care of, or the other one that covered the shed in the backyard where she and

Clara kept their toys. For later in life, the Arabian jasmine, with fleshy white flowers that always die gloriously. There are also the others, which most people do not know now. They have sky-blue flowers, barely scented (that is their defect) and the best name of all: jasmines from heaven. They used to twine around a privet hedge in her yard, next to the wild plum.

Like the old woman, she would like to entrust something, she does not know what, to the new owners of that house where she will not set foot again. She had left things behind there, even habits—like the one of avoiding the creaking floorboard between her bed and her sister's—which will be lost when the house turns into a new home. How could she ask someone not to fix the latch on the shutters in her room so that her window would always remain half-open, reassuring her every morning with a show of light? Or tell them that, near a spigot, by some ever-greens, lies her dog, who struggled against poison throughout a long night and was buried by the gardener? Or warn them about a wild oleander, also at the back of the yard next to the toy shed, the leaves of which, pronounced deadly by their mother, made her and Clara sick one Saturday afternoon? Taking advantage of the fact that the kitchen was deserted after lunch, they had con-cocted a tonic, the virtues of which she has forgotten, made of vinegar, honey, and the forbidden leaves, which they called Delta Tonic. Memories like this one strike her as puny, pathetic; she has lost the place that would hold them together, and in time her memory will lose them too.

Is there something she should have done in that house and did not do? Something that will return to haunt her as it did this afternoon when she lay down to sleep, sated by an incoherent past? She dreamed twice of herself by the sea, at the end of the summer. On both occasions, she felt dissatisfied, with the sensa-tion of having missed something very close at hand. She had not gone into the water that awaited her, and now it was too late and she had to start on her trip back. Was that an image of her childhood? If so, it does not surprise her: she still needs water, is always thirsty. There is something still lacking; if not, why write, as she does, mostly about unhappiness? Why write of the solitary ceremonies in which she took pleasure, the games she played facing a mirror, facing her sister? Childhoods, as someone has said, are always hellish and have naught to keep but little rotting souls and a small sleep.

She must tear herself away from her childhood: dwelling on it strikes her now as a vain habit. If she has not recorded moments of shared happiness from those days, it is because they did not exist, or perhaps because she did not know how to recognize them. Enough: to try to recover the past, falling into the temptation to remember incidents so as to later read them in a different way, is a useless task, just as it is useless to ask someone else to interpret them for her. For example, she sees herself in the bathroom when she was about eight, sitting on the toilet. In the narrow space between two tiles on the wall, between the toilet and the washstand, there are two nails: on one of them hangs a brass ring with a pink ribbon, on the other a brass ring with a blue ribbon. She knows that as soon as she finishes she must take the ring with the pink ribbon to her parents' room and put it in a small crystal bowl (now in her possession) on her mother's dresser. Clara had to do the same with the blue ribbon. That was how they communicated their message. It was a wordless ceremony, an indirect way of reporting a performance established by their mother, which sometimes turned into a contest: who would take the ribbon first? The few times she has referred to that ritual, in the presence of others, she has met with negative reactions: she and Clara were being denied any kind of direct contact with their bodies. That may be true; she does not know, and it does not particularly matter. What she does know and does remember is the pleasure of translating. That which her body had expelled became a ring (which she thought was gold), a silk ribbon, and an old crystal bowl. She also remembers (and this still strikes her as important) that she never wanted the pink ribbon, but always the blue one. She would have done the unthinkable to be the one to take the blue ribbon and leave it in her mother's bowl.

She, her mother, her sister: so distant from one another. What happened to all three of them, women with ravaged features, almost robbed of their faces? Ultimately, the ones who did have faces, in life as in death, were her father and Aunt Sara. Theirs were faces meant to last—or is she imagining the faces she saw in the caskets so as to preserve in the past what she cannot preserve in the present? She does not see herself as having a face of her own, nor does she see Clara that way. As for her mother, she can only see her dead. Then her mother will really match the image she always remembers of her. Just as when she was young, before Clara was born, she will have very smooth, yet very strong skin. She will gather up her braids behind her ears and do her mouth like a little red heart. She will have very fine hands, those hands she has always wanted to kiss. She will have very delicate feet, feet she entrusts only to her shoemaker, just as she entrusts her hands only to her glovemaker. She will wear a turban and have pearls around her neck; she will carry a flat red purse under her arm and will pull on her black gloves after touching her daughter's face to bid her good night. She will smell of a perfume that, as a child, she could not stand, but which she knew her father liked. Despite all of this—she will tell her mother in the casket—why was there so little said between us, how could we fight so often? Perhaps she will say this to her mother soon, while she is still alive, although she pictures herself saying it after her death, when her mother can no longer disarm her.

She had forgotten to mention her mother's profile. She will see it, already slightly sunken, when her mother is dead. It is the haughtiest profile she has ever seen and she cannot forget it.

She is writing in the dark. When she speaks of her mother and of her sister (not when she speaks of Vera, or Renata) her eyes blur. Thinking of the two of them, so far away, she immediately sinks (she cannot find a better word) into the memories she has of each. There is absolutely no passion, just a need to become one with her mother and sister, to lose herself in them. In her dreams she often gives them food. This comes like a sudden revelation: why does she feel she must feed them, why must she protect them? Why must she eat her father's dry hand, in a recurring dream, so that her mother will not see it? She dreams of a restaurant in Paris, on the rue du Roi de Sicile, to be precise. She is taking her mother and her sister there, but once they arrive, the restaurant has disappeared. The three of them are starving and she is incapable of finding the place where one eats so well. Again, she dreams of the two of them: she has promised them an outing, almost an underground exploration of the city between two secret points very distant from each other. When she gets to a door, almost hidden between two old buildings, where the journey is to start, she cannot open it. As a guide she is evidently of little use. There is something, she tells herself, something in these dreams and in many others like them, dreams that have her continuously leading her mother and sister through cities—Antwerp, Paris, Rome, Buenos Aires—without knowing where she is going. In all of them there is a secret point she never finds.

She has had to mention the names of cities. This troubles her, but they are after all part of her dreams. She now decides to give places—all her places—their name. The snowy city where she met Renata and spied on Vera again is Buffalo, New York. The city where she met up again with Renata and Vera is Paris. The city where she grew up—and where she would grow up again, given the choice—is the city of Buenos Aires.

She has pointed out clues and now feels at peace. She is aware, however, that she has fallen into these tardy revelations so as not to go on facing those feminine presences, to protect herself from them. Suddenly they descend on her, like fearsome divinities, and all she can say is: "I summoned you here." And more modestly: "I wanted all of you—mother, sister, lovers—to be here, I live only in you."

Translated by Daniel Balderson

Dale Gunthorp

Drawing on her experience as a young adult in the strife-torn South Africa of the 1960s, Dale Gunthorp creates a tale of passion against a background of bias in her short story "Gypsophila" (1990). South African–born Gunthorp, now living in London, is a journalist in third world issues who turned to lesbian fiction when Britain's Parliament banned the "promotion of homosexuality" in 1988. In its opening scenes, "Gypsophila" evokes the apartheid-restricted lesbian and gay bar life of Johannesburg. At the heart of the story, however, is the pursuit of a lesbian relationship that carries the narrator through late-night streets, where the obstacles to her journey are both historical and personal.

GYPSOPHILA

I didn't bring the stuff into the house. My lover came home with it, great swaths, collapsing armfuls of tiny white flowers threaded on gray. She crammed it into a jug, gave it water, put it on the table in this silent room. And I stand in the doorway looking at hundreds of points of light shimmering like remote stars: gypsophila.

How odd these connections are, things yoked by one private history. Or even a nonhistory, by something that, in Johannesburg's winter more than twenty years ago, didn't happen. I hadn't meant to give her gypsophila. A bottle of wine would have been more appropriate, certainly more useful to me, already stiff with nerves. But although I had thought about the evening all week, nothing practical had presented itself, nothing so sensible as: should I take her champagne, a book, chocolates, flowers (proper flowers, not something that was only just not a weed)?

She hadn't given much scope for planning, come to think of it. She had barely described the way to her flat after "Come and have a bite to eat at my place, say next Wednesday, eightish." I didn't hear what she was saying at first, there was such a din in the bar, such a din in my head.

It was Johannesburg's only regular gay bar in those days, and not even a proper bar. It was the Pro, a slit of a place in a drab modern hotel, where actors hung out after the theater. Since the law excluded women from real bars, drinks were brought in from the kitchen and it had the legal status of a "lounge." Since apartheid was a fact of life, only the ponciest of African queens, only the butchest of Indian dykes could appear—noncitizens acceptable, in this underworld that was deviant but uncourageous, so long as they were no more than bedding material. They brought the total numbers to about twenty. Perhaps the Pro had only come by its label of gay bar because Beatrice was there every night. At about ten, he, a rugby-forward-sized Boer[1] well into his fifties, would arrive on stiletto sandals, or wearing pendulous earrings, always with carrots in a little wicker basket—and he joked and teased, sang dirty songs, and drank hugely until closing.

1 Boer: literally, a farmer; in the English slang of the time, an Afrikaner peasant

I was also there every night. To feed this habit, I had taken a flat around the corner. I was twenty-one and alone. I had had a lover at school and later languished after various stony-hearted women, but I wasn't looking for a lover, though I thought constantly of love. I was looking, I suppose, for sex. I thought I was searching for meaning.

Sometimes women came in, in twos or fours, and, whatever I was looking for, I would look at them. They had bleached short hair lacquered into duck's-asses unyielding as metal, masses of lilac or green shadow around eyes ringed with black, mouths dry with nicotine and no lipstick. They laughed with Beatrice and the queens, but not with me. They prodded one another with the toes of their long, pointed boots and smiled lazily at one another, till the blood was bursting against the walls of my temples.

Some spoke in English, in loud, classy, colonial voices. From these I learned who was cheating on whom, what BMs[2] were secretly camp; who was on the run from Priscilla, doing a Dora,[3] or knocking off the most gorgeous bird.

Others sat in tight huddles. From them I pulled at threads of darker-toned talk, in Afrikaans. Occasionally, these close women would break out to twit Beatrice (fellow Afrikaner, fellow pervert, but farther down the line) in nervy music-hall English. Sometimes, as they got drunker, their voices and fists would rise in fury against the world. There was Evonnie of a powerful musculature who, after a few drinks, would challenge Beatrice to arm wrestling and lose with very bad grace. Sarie and Sannie would arrive incensed at their boss and leave incensed with each other. Petronella displayed jagged lines on her wrists, carved, she said, with shards of milk bottles. Some-

2 "BM": a straight; literally "bloody moron"
3 "Priscilla": the police; "doing a Dora": staging a heavy drama

times their rage spilled over: one or two would be bundled into taxis by the management, and a wave of relief would roll through the bar. And Beatrice, shaking his earrings till they chimed like bells, would say: "We, the Boers, the Lord's Chosen People: we are not couth."

I didn't stare at the English Barbie dolls, but nobody seemed to mind or notice how hard I peered at these women whose stories were engraved on their faces. Discretion is not an option for Daughters of the Volk guilty of the only unnameable vice of an ethic obsessed with vice. I was also repelled by them, and for the same reason. It was many years and many failures later that I learned not to be shocked by people who flaunted, like a colonel's ribboned medals, their mutilated psyches.

Weeks passed. The men were kind, but I wasn't looking for their barbed companionship. I wanted to join the women but couldn't make the move. If, in the lavatory, someone smiled, I would rush out blushing, my hands still wet and my hair uncombed. These were my people, but I was not theirs. Their clammed unhappy world was my world, and it terrified me. Like a child who could not swim sitting on the edge of a swimming pool, I watched and envied their sport and tried to nerve myself to plunge into an element that seemed bottomless and unsupporting as the deep blue of outer space.

Then one night the moment to plunge chose itself. Diana came in, with three dykes—two bleached duck's-asses, one delicate-featured Indian woman. Like everyone else, they wore tight pants and swirled their cigarette holders. Their talk was directed inward. But Diana's eyes, great pools of gray, gazed idly around the bar and encountered mine. She held my look for a second, then, with a nod, turned back to her friends.

Champion eavesdropper that I was, I soon picked up their conversation. Though her talk was laced with all the slang I was still learning to push past my lips, she was talking about subjects it was surely not proper to raise in the Pro. In a measured public voice, she was complaining about the pay and working conditions of black actors. She wasn't saying anything clever or witty. She had no suggestions about what anyone could do about it. She was embarrassing the only African there, a pretty young man wearing a coral necklace, perhaps ruining for him a few hours of fantasy, reminding him that the oppressed have a duty to be angry. But I wanted to hear more, and to know her. I wanted to look through those clear gray eyes that could see into our ghetto with its spider-encrusted wires and also into other people's iron ghettos: see beyond.

I didn't have the boldness to break in to her talk (which at her table was being met with yawning indifference). I just sat there and willed her to do something.

She did. She went up to the bar. I emptied my glass at a gulp and followed.

She ordered; I ordered; she half turned toward me: "That accent of yours? You're not from Johannesburg."

I nodded.

"Ghastly place, Jo'berg."

I was suddenly shy. Perhaps I grinned.

She was studying my face: "You're from?"

"Natal. The sugarcane country."

There was a pause. Soon she would nod again and move off. I had watched too long; my tongue was tangled in my thoughts. I trawled for it. Out gushed, in an awful tweety-pie voice: "Black canecutters have even worse working conditions than black actors."

"I'm sure they do." Her eyes wandered to my table, took in the plastic handbag and grubby white nylon gloves, then settled beyond, on the Tretchikov print, the one then to be found in every other public place and living room, of a rose flung down beside a dustbin. She sighed.

"You shouldn't be drinking alone, if you're taking brandy and water," she said. "Come and join us."

Beatrice, perched on his usual stool at the bar, had been watching this scene with raised eyebrows. As I turned to follow Diana, he grabbed my ponytail. "Don't give in so quick, darling." His forearm locked against my throat. "Patience, girlie. You're only a virgin lover once; hold out for the best bid."

At times I'd been grateful for Beatrice's jokes; though they unnerved me, they reminded me that I existed. But tonight he was low company, and I wriggled free.

"Or if you must do it"—he reached into his basket and handed me a limp bunch of carrots—"take me too. I adore lettie ladies. All that delicious squishy boneless juicy slurping—like oysters making love."

Diana's gray eyes turned to steel. "Drop dead, you overfed capon."

"Oh gorgeous." Beatrice's vast body shriveled like an oyster squirted with lemon. "Tongue like a whip on this diesel dyke. I'll sit so quiet in the corner. I'll let you gag me to suppress my cries of ecstasy."

Diana's arm now wrapped my shoulder as she led me away, and I knew that Beatrice had done me a favor.

I don't remember what she said, what I said, what the dykes said. Only that there was a burn on my shoulder where her hand had rested; that what she did say was wiser, subtler, and funnier than anything ever said before; that her eyes took in the entire world; that in the center of their gray deepening to black hovered something unfathomable. She was certainly nice to me, bowing her head to ask if I wanted a cigarette, if I had a job, if I missed my mother, if I lodged nearby, if there were poisonous snakes in the sugarcane. I said yes to all these things.

Then, "Have a bite at my place," to which I also said yes.

They pulled on their leather jackets and left before closing time, roaring off on two Lambrettas, one of the dykes with her arms tight around Diana's ribs, and I watched them vanish into the cold neon-pointed night.

In the seven intervening deserts of nights, Diana didn't come into the bar. But Beatrice's interest in me blossomed and, in the absence of Diana, I was again grateful for his friendship. "Come sit on my knee, girlie," he would say, "and hear Auntie's warning about the slings and arrows of outrageous fortune. Beware, my lovely. Beware of women, but most of all beware of brickies."[4] The two outsiders now in huddle as exclusive as anybody's, he told me how, in the early hours, he would be haunting the metal halls of the railway station in search of brickies. Most nights he picked up one or two. I don't know if he offered them carrots. Sometimes he chose badly—or perhaps too accurately—and ended up in hospital. Occasionally he got a policeman by mistake and ended up in the prison hospital instead. "Let Auntie's ruined complexion," he would say, "be a lesson to you of the perils of crawling outside the laager,"[5] and his crumpled face, brandy-scented sweat and grease oozing from its open pores, would bear down on mine. "You, little meisietjie,[6] you still have a choice. Let Mama pick you a husband and buckle down to it. Do as Auntie says and you'll get a garden with a swimming pool in it. You can spend your days there, dreaming about lettie ladies over your G&T."

And then: "Mama will make it one of those men who grows fat when he gives up rugby; an army chappie, say, thick as two short planks, a bloke who talks in grunts. He won't pry into your soul; he won't notice if you do your nails while he's screwing you."

4 "Brickie": rough trade, literally a bricklayer
5 "laager": armed enclosure of ox wagons
6 "meisietjie": little-little girl

Beatrice's two great hands, nails earthstained as hooves, would cradle mine. Sometimes he tutted over my nails, bitten to the quick. "Oh poor little claws. Why do women destroy their few weapons? Sharpen them, my angel, like a cat. Then you can teach your soldier to be a good boy. But Mama must choose right. Tell her Auntie Beatrice will advise."

The thought of Beatrice and my mother talking, even being in the same room, was so shocking that I laughed hard for minutes.

Beatrice, who had been repulsive to me, whom I had feared because I could never tell when he was mocking me, became, in those seven nights, my best friend. He poured his accumulated despair into my ears. He came to my flat, and we slept in the one bed, chaste as nuns. We bumped across town to his smallholding, to see neat rows of winter vegetables and the filthy shack in which he cooked and occasionally washed and bedded his houseboy and his brickies. We drank a lot of brandy together, and I found the sensation of workdays wobbly with hangover disturbingly pleasurable: they distanced me from the granite edifice of work. I grew able to treat the heap of papers on my desk with indifference. Official faces that used to burn into my consciousness faded to ashes. I didn't eat much, though I had an endless supply of carrots, but got through a pack and a half of untipped Lucky Strikes every day. And the dark and dangerous world he sketched and that I now found myself entering became increasingly fascinating. If I had read Genet, or Colette, if I had read anything at all outside of the syllabus for the Natal Senior Certificate examination or the boneless novels in the public library, I would have been able to define this excitement. Definitionless, I poured all those feelings into the image of a woman with wandering gray eyes.

I devoured every scrap of information about Diana. She came from Cape Town. She believed in God and tore strips off people who teased her about it. She was a theater set designer. The three women with her were freelances, employed by her for one production, a musical based on a story by Alan Paton. She liked spy thrillers. Her lover had gone off to Nyasaland with a liquor-shop owner. She designed her shirts and had them made up by an Indian tailor. She lived alone in Doringbos, a formerly mixed-race area whitened by a Group Areas Act.[7] Doringbos was now largely occupied by white railway workers, who had taken over the houses of the evicted colored families. Beatrice didn't much like Diana. "She's cold, sweetheart, and a snob, like all cold women."

All this, even the horrible place she lived, increased her glamor. This was a woman who could unseal the doors of a mind, and she had asked me to dinner.

On Tuesday night, Beatrice, enticingly discouraging, bid me a lugubrious farewell. He warned me that Diana tended to go on about things; if she did, I was to launch into song with "You ain't nothing but a hound dog," since Diana loathed pop music. He was sure Diana wasn't the sort who would ask vulgar questions about butch or femme, but if the subject came up, I was to say that I was absolutely brilliant at both. Then he advised Listerine for the breath and silk knickers for the ass and gave me a bunch of carrots to take as an offering.

I didn't follow his advice. Wednesday was so crammed with deciding whether or not to wear a bra, what opening remarks to make (and how to get from them to an exploration of psyches), what to do if she fed me soft eggs or bloody steak (things that turn my stomach over) that I forgot Beatrice's carrots rotting in the sink. I didn't question, either, what I knew I wanted to do: to go to Doringbos on foot—only some three miles, but

7 An apartheid law excluding blacks from any parts of town worth living in

absolutely not to be done in a city where every night the streets were emptied of citizens by apartheid's pass laws.[8]

It was only when I set out across the tsotsi-infested[9] streets of Hillbrow, nerving myself to pass from there through the unlit pool of Berea to Doringbos, where there might still be children playing rounders among the parked cars, that it came to me. I had no offering. Between a beer hall and a filling station huddled a little florist's shop, its frontage a mist of gypsophila. The night was cold, and the wet streaks that ran from the flower buckets to the gutter glistened with the threat of ice. The smell of vegetation mingled with hops and petrol. I would bring to Diana that musky gray-greenness, armfuls of lace over which her eyes could wander. Inside, there were roses, red, pink, and yellow; there were bold, theatrical strelitzias; yard-long gladioli and canna lilies; there were gray and purple proteas—rolled-up hedgehogs, the national flower. Outside, in the cold, gypsophila stars trembled.

I went in. "How much is the gypsophila?"

His voice was terse: "The baby's breath? Really? You want those weeds, left over from a First Communion at that Roman place up the road?"

I did.

He sighed. "God strike me, dametjie,[10] if I lie to you: it was a First Communion for a bunch of kaffirs. Really, man, all dressed up in white, carrying prayer books and candles!"

Oh, my countrymen! Depression familiar as sin clouded the pretty little shop.

"You don't want them? Well, they're clean. I hosed them down. Say twenty cents a bunch."

---

8 Under the pass laws blacks needed a permit to be outside the townships or bantustans and could be arrested if they didn't go back to these ghettos after working hours
9 "tsotsi": out-of-school youths who mug and rob
10 "dametjie": Afrikaans for "little lady"

Not possible; they were too cheap.

He misread my hesitation. "Aag man, just take the lot."

No need to panic. No need to run. The shop was no more horrible than the rest of the world. I looked round for alternatives. Roses—too intimate; strelitzias—ugly; gladioli—common; what? I picked up a protea, two, three. Perhaps they were all right. No scent, no velvet texture, no glow, but they were handsome. And she came from the Cape, where proteas grow on the mountainsides. And they were suitably expensive. They would do. On the way out, I paused again at the gypsophila. Why not? I took as much as I could carry and made up an unlikely bouquet of delicate white points with the three woody desert heads of proteas in the center.

No inconspicuous passage through Berea was now possible; I was lit by a constellation of gypsophila. One curb crawler I escaped by dropping into the vestibule of some flats; another followed for several blocks, waving a ten-rand note out his window, but fortunately not getting out of his car. The third didn't proposition but drove behind at walking pace, hissing insults about low white women. He seemed to be on his way to Doringbos. Perhaps his daughters were just then playing rounders in the street. I walked fast, stopping only to answer the greeting of two black streetboys strumming a guitar made from a paraffin can. They admired the flowers. They were protection for a few minutes, and they didn't find it odd that there should be a lone white woman on the street after dark. I gave them a few cents, which they rolled up in tattered handkerchiefs and stuffed into their shorts. Perhaps that night, if the police didn't pick them up, they would sleep curled round central heating vents.

In Doringbos, there were smells of frying boerewors[11] and the yells of children fighting inside the carcasses of wrecked cars. I

---

11 "boerewors": coarse beef sausage

found Diana's place, a tall, dark house with sash windows, pressed against the cliff that separated Doringbos from Highlands. Years later, I lived in a house like that in Muswell Hill in London and found it as Gothic and forbidding even though it was on top of the cliff.

I checked my watch. Arrived early, and safe. I took a stroll to the corner and back. I shouldn't have walked of course. I should have confessed that I had no car and asked Diana to pick me up. Would I ask her to drive me back? Would I have to go back? Perhaps we would talk all night about this city, about this country, and perhaps she would say it could be saved. But perhaps she would lecture me, as she'd lectured her friends at the Pro, but about the foolishness of walking the streets of Johannesburg. If she did, could I say that one tried to make something right by acting as if it were? To Beatrice, to whom nothing and everything was ludicrous, I could have said that I walked because I wanted to strip down, come dressed only in my soul. Could I approximate, say to Diana that I had wanted to endure some ordeal because there was nothing real that was not plucked from the jaws of a shark? Could I say that I chose to walk in search of the knowledge of good and evil?—not the desiccated wisdom of the catechism but of the living tree, living serpent. What Diana would have made of these observations, I do not know. To me, my shadow looping about me in the car lights, every thought that came was divine revelation. For all that, when once more I faced the shut door, I decided to let her think I'd come in a taxi.

The gypsophila bundle behind my back, I rang the bell. After a long time, the peephole darkened, and the door opened on a colored woman hauling on a dressing gown.

"You're for Diana?"

She had recognized me as a lesbian as quickly as I had recognized her as black and therefore living in the house illegally.

Perhaps she was Diana's friend; perhaps they were all revolutionaries. My heard leaped with excitement. "Yes, may I come in?"

"The flat round the back." She gestured.

"Thank you very much. Thank you very . . ." The door had shut.

With a light heart, I trotted round past the dustbins, stopping to note how the gypsophila reflected the big African moon. The colored woman didn't look like a theater person; she was curt, almost arrogant; could she be a member of Umkhonto we Siswe[12] in hiding? If I could walk the streets of Johannesburg at night, couldn't I become a runner for them? Would Diana initiate me?

Even in winter, when it doesn't rain for months, the place, overhung as it was by the cliff, smelled damp, vegetable, tumescent with new life. I felt my way for the last few steps till helped by a light from somewhere inside. The door was open.

"Hello." I carried the flowers high before me. "Hello, hello, Diana." A white-painted hall, a living room crammed with books and one of those new reel-to-reel tape recorders, a glimpse of a neat bedroom with a Basuto blanket serving as counterpane. A beautiful place in the midst of the awfulness of Doringbos. "Diana?"

In the kitchen, an African woman was ironing sheets. "The missus is working," she said in a tired voice. "It's the dress rehearsal next week."

"She's expecting me."

"You want to wait?"

I did. I sat on soft chairs and hard chairs. I explored the flat. I looked at my watch. I walked to the road. The curtains were

12 "Umkhonto we Siswe": Spear of the Nation, the military wing of the ANC, then committed to a program of sabotage against state infrastructure

drawn upstairs. The children had gone. I walked back. I searched the shelves in vain for banned books. I looked at my watch again. It hadn't stopped. I examined the tape recorder but didn't dare to try it. I walked back to the road again. I listened to the iron bumping. I tried not to think it peculiar that a revolutionary should have a maid, and one who called her "missus." I helped myself to a glass of water. I failed to get a conversation going with the maid.

At nine she said she was going and wanted to lock up. "That's okay," I said. "I'll be off then." I put the flowers in the butler's sink, fluffing out the gypsophilia. "Goodnight," I said, and left.

Her keys jangled. How did she get home, or did she, too, squat illegally on the premises? I walked. I didn't think about the maid; I didn't even thing about Diana. All I wanted was to smash my fist into the gob of every curb crawler.

But I didn't go home. I went to the Pro. "Oh, you appalling creature," shrieked Beatrice, "what on earth are you doing here?"

I put my arms around his enormous chest.

"D'you know what you've done to me, you dreadful woman? You've ruined my best fantasy—of taking creamcakes to you and Diana in bed." I had my face flat against Beatrice's egg-stained shirt and was sobbing.

"Oh sweetheart," he said, dropping cigarette ash in my hair. "If you only knew how much I love women who can still cry. Now I'm crying too, and it's utterly delicious. In my next life, they're gonna have to let me be born a lesbian."

I don't know how I got home that night. I was certainly very drunk.

I didn't go to the bar the next evening. If I was too sick to go to work, I was too sick for that. I cleaned the flat, though it was already very clean. There was no way out. Diana had forgotten. My odyssey was a very small show when there were dress

rehearsals. I took off my clothes to look at myself in the mirror
and saw one of twenty million bodies bred in a poisoned soil. If
I could be allowed no inner life, perhaps at least I could pledge
this body to freedom, fight and follow the leaders—Mandela,
Sisulu, Mbeki, Slovo[13]—follow them to prison. I had lived two
decades in the world of apartheid and done nothing to change
the ugliness. I'd hardly thought about it except as a reflection of
my own discontent. Perhaps the revolution would not be too
proud to accept a lesbian. I looked at my mirror image again: I
had thought Diana might like that little triangle of dark hair. I
ran my fingers through it, and it sprang back into curls, so gutsy,
even on me, someone with head hair as straight and lifeless as
nylon thread. I looked harder still at the mirror and flexed my
skimpy biceps. If fate was going to deny me love, I could at least
demand drama. I'd join the revolution as a kamikaze bomber.
The eyes in the mirror welled up with the rich sense of tragedy.

The doorbell screeched. The peephole showed Diana. I scut-
tled off to scrub my face and find some clothes.

"Beatrice sent me." She came in grumpily. "Why did you
rush away like that last night? Couldn't you wait a few minutes?
There was a lot of traffic." She stood with her hands in her
pockets. Her eyes were fixed on the blackened window. She did
not bow, elegantly, from the neck. Her leather jacket was but-
toned tight across her breast.

We were on her Lambretta, charging through Hillbrow,
Berea; we flashed past the two streetboys; we swung round the
cliff to Doringbos. We were parked deep into the hedge, with
the scooter triple-locked against the attentions of children. We
felt our way round to the back. She was banging pans in the
kitchen, throwing together a meal. It seemed very probable that

13 Nelson Mandela, Walter Sisulu, Thabo Mbeki, Joe Slovo, and many others had
recently been sentenced at the Rivonia Trial

I would sleep that night under the Basuto blanket and equally probable that I would be very nervous and wholly inadequate.

She kept breaking off to answer the phone: people wanting changes made to the backdrop, a door to hang the other way, different lighting at the end of the overture. Nothing about Umkhonto.

I didn't take any phone messages; I didn't lift pans starting to burn in the kitchen. I was feeling the rugged sepals of the proteas, thrust into a thick brown earthenware jug. They hadn't opened any further, but then they unravel very slowly. Proteas last for weeks—forever, if you like dried flowers. There was no sign of the gypsophila.

Perhaps the seeds of this brilliant constellation of gypsophila were scattered in the same Big Bang that made the other, older galaxy, I thought, as I stood in the doorway of a room in London, looking at flowers brought home by my lover, more than twenty years later.

Many things have scattered. Even apartheid has fragmented. A new order prevails, which prescribes equality for blacks, queers, and all the other persecuted people. I hope the young man in the coral necklace has found a better refuge than the Pro, but law alone does not bring liberation. The black gays and the white gays have no common language until they reach under the blanket, and Johannesburg's gay bars have exchanged fear of the police for a greater fear of tsotsis. Now London jostles with exiles, among them Diana, among them me, and here we have found a world where we can be human. Beatrice didn't escape; nor, I suppose, did the Afrikaans dykes. Perhaps they still drink at some anonymous club, whispering fearfully of the unknown that follows the brutal and doomed order that had given them, and me, a gangster protection. The world has widened, but they were not on an ascending curve, and the new freedom is not for them. Perhaps they live with ferocious dogs behind high walls; perhaps they are old and ill, or mad; perhaps they are dead.

Certainly many things have died. But there is still the Roman church where gypsophila flowered at First Communion ceremonies. The white people have abandoned it for their exclusive chapels in the suburbs and all the prayer books there are held in black hands. Would Diana remember that church? Would she remember if I asked her what became of that other First Communion gypsophila, if she gave it to the maid?

Karen Williams

Karen Williams, who describes herself as a nomadic black South African dyke, is the author of the second selection representing South Africa in this collection. "They Came at Dawn," published in The Invisible Ghetto (1993), the first anthology of lesbian and gay writing to emerge from South Africa, takes us into the heart of the battle against apartheid and its terrifying consequences. Williams's story powerfully underlines the intensity and dangers of a liberation struggle that impacted on all battles for survival, including the freedom of self-expression.

THEY CAME AT DAWN

HE air was rancid with tear gas that morning. Empty bullet cartridges mingled with dust, blood, and the fog and winter rain. Shadows of what a few moments ago were living, marching people now stalked over the flats and shantytowns with the industrial smog blown by the southeaster. The Mountain was rallying her children. Propaganda pages blew ahead, paving the way for the shadows, and dust to follow. Soon the pages too had to succumb to the fate of lying wet, stuck to the road, with the Casspir and Buffel tracks erasing The Word.

It was all revolution: all war.

The banging on the door that set the windows rattling was neither unfamiliar nor unexpected. Yet they were afraid. Sara and Michael looked at each other alarmed, before Michael scurried to the back door hoping to get away. There was no time for good-byes. Petrified, Sara waited for the jackboot that would bolt out the door to shock her to her senses. She wondered whether they would use handcuffs or just beat her senseless and drag her limp body to the gaping van. Where would she wake up?

"Sara. Fuckin' hell! Open the door!" It was Kherry's hoarse, insistently urgent whisper.

It wasn't the police. She'd better go and call Michael back inside.

"Sara!"

"Coming, wait!" Sara jumped from one foot to another, unsure whether to go and get Michael first, but instead she rushed to the door. With her fingers slipping and missing the lock, she clumsily opened the door and bundled a wet and frustrated Kherry in.

"Wait," Sara ordered and ran to the backyard to get Michael, her steps thudding over the ghastly pause that cloaked the neighborhood. The round rattle of machine-gun fire was heard in the far distance.

Sara didn't know whether to burst out laughing at the pitifully comical picture Michael cut, stuck there in the wire fence, trying to vault out of the backyard. (When had he become so worn and haggard, so spindly?)

"Michael . . ." The soft whisper froze him, and his frightened, beady eyes seemed shocked in their sockets as they looked at Sara, as if to say: It's all right if you told. There was no chance for me to run anyway.

"It's okay, Michael—it's only Kherry."

His body went limp and he fell to the ground as the tension

snapped. "Shot by a sniper," thought Sara, looking at him closely. No—only nerves.

"Michael!" Kherry exclaimed in disbelief when he and Sara walked through the door. "I thought the police had . . ."

"No, they haven't got me. They've got a fat chance too. I've done nothing wrong."

"I heard that they picked up all the leaders and just about everyone they could think of, last night," Sara said. "Then shot like hell again this morning. Ai, this fuckin' state." She shook her head and sighed.

"They looking for you too?" Michael asked Kherry. And then his head jerked, for somewhere there was a slight sound.

"No." Michael and Sara stood looking at her expectantly, so she felt compelled to add: "My mother kicked me out."

"God, today of all days," Sara muttered to herself.

"Politics?"

"Yes. No," Kherry added immediately. She paused and looked at them directly. "I'm lesbian," she announced as boldly as she had to her mother earlier that morning. She had said it with much pride to counter the revulsion in her mother's mind. But now she closed her eyes and waited for the bullets her friends would aim at her to rain down.

"This is all we need! Jesus, Kherry!" The irritability in Michael's voice couldn't disguise the minefield of nerves triggered at the mere sound of the automatic kettle switching itself off.

"Have you got other clothes and things with you?" Sara asked, as if all this was nothing new to her.

Michael got up, loudly scraping the chair along the floor as he stormed out. Then he strode to the toilet, entered it, and banged the door behind him. He flushed the toilet immediately, out of anger at another of Kherry's "little problems."

"All I have is this money," Kherry said to Sara, digging her hands into her anorak and presenting a crumpled five-rand note between her fingers.

Marta, Kherry's grandmother, had thrust the note into her granddaughter's hand as Kherry stormed out of the house. Her eyes brimming with tears. Marta said, *"Djy's altyd in my gebede, Poplap. Ko ienige tyd dat djy iets nodig het. Ek sallie djou ma se ie."* ("You are always in my prayers, my darling. Come any time that you need something—I won't tell your mother.")

And with that she squeezed Kherry's hand as if to seal her promise. That was probably the last of her grandmother's rent money, Kherry realized as the bus stopped at the roadblock to be searched by the police.

"Don't worry, you can stay here as long as you like," Sara reassured her later that night as they all sat in the dark huddled over their coffee mugs.

"Michael," Kherry said. She was waiting for him to comment, for he had been ignoring her all day.

"Kherry," he spat out. "Just pull yourself together." His hand was sharply cutting the air in an attempt to emphasize his words. "Just . . ." He paused, now in the passageway, searching for words. "Just—come—right."

Kherry and Sara looked down at their coffee, embarrassed, just as they did even later when Michael suddenly jumped up in the middle of listening to Coltrane and bellowed "Fuck you!" at Kherry. Then he frogmarched himself back to the toilet and again flushed the toilet after banging the door behind him.

Kherry sat there, listening to Coltrane, remembering her discoveries with Michelle—love, and the denial of a truth. In the end not even the promise of togetherness could save them.

Sometimes it was easy outside, in the days when they got long, friendly stares and conspiratorial smiles from the white women in the road. The ones with short hair. But the outside also crept in, making it difficult to swallow. For it was as if they had thought all the letters of the alphabet could compensate for the not-enoughs of elsewhere. Not enough rent money; not enough to eat; not enough love to stop two young black girls from feeling so blindly, and so very alone.

Then word got around and it got around fast. Michelle was given two days to vacate her apartment. The landlady had classified her as "funny people."

"Perhaps it's because you're single," Kherry tried to explain as Michelle threw the contents of her cupboard into boxes.

"They're always suspicious of young women—they think that all we do is have loud parties and bring men home!" This was Michelle, no longer able to hide the remnants of the last city she had fled from.

"Perhaps it's because you're always asking her to repair that leak in the bathroom," Kherry said, trying to sound jovial.

"Perhaps it's because I'm a dyke," said Michelle, her voice restrained, as she tried to control herself.

And then she was gone, to another city.

The police came at dawn all beefy and sweaty. And Michael was found and taken away. The women were beaten up and then warned.

Nobody knows what they've done with Michael—but it's rumored, these days, that tenth floors are not the safest places to be.

Cynthia Price

The third and final selection from South Africa, "Lesbian Bedrooms" (1996) by Cynthia Price, offers the reader a brief literary moment of respite as Price creates a space of everyday lesbian living. With the constitutional end of apartheid has come a critical step toward curtailing another oppression: South Africa today stands as the first country in the world to have as part of its constitution the guarantee of equality before the law for its lesbian and gay citizens. Price, who lives with her two children and her partner of fourteen years in the coastal town of Kwa Zulu Natal, South Africa, presents in this first-time published story a vision of "normalcy," embodying the hope of a new national vision.

LESBIAN BEDROOMS

WHAT do lesbians do in their bedrooms?

They wake in the morning and stretch. They say nasty words to their alarm clocks and curse about having to go to work *again*. On weekend mornings they lie in with their cats and dogs and children, trying not to spill their tea when the family get restless.

They glance disappointedly at the mirror, which shows another gray hair, the lines starting to creep beneath the eyes, and the disappearing waistline. They put on makeup, mutter over a laddered stocking, and scratch under the bed for a missing shoe.

They dispense aspirin and warm soup when one of them is feverish with flu and tiptoe around the bedroom when someone has a sore head from too much wine the night before. They offer sympathy and a shoulder to cry on when the day has been rough. They collapse onto the bed at the end of the day and fall asleep without taking off their shoes.

They vacuum fluff from under the bed, fluff the duvet covers, and stack newly ironed, warm-smelling clothes in the cupboards. They sort the underwear into separate shelves so there will be no mixups in the hurried rush of mornings' dressings. They sort the shoes into pairs and know that they won't stay that way for long. They discuss what color the new curtains will be and when they will be able to fit them into the already tightly squeezed budget.

They relax on a Sunday afternoon with the sun sifting through the curtains, listening to the sounds of a neighbor mowing his lawn in the distance, and feel guilty that their own grass needs a cut. They argue about whose turn it is to get up and make the tea—"I made the lunch, it's your turn to put the kettle on!" They both offer to cook the supper tonight.

They talk about future plans and they dream together. They read books, play cards, do crosswords, listen to music. They keep each other warm in winter and fight over the blankets. In summer they swat mosquitoes and ask each other if the window is open and "Are you sure you switched the stove off at the wall?" They nudge each other to roll over and "Stop that damn snoring! How the hell am I supposed to sleep?" They lie awake at night and wonder why it's so damned quiet—"Is she still breathing?"

Then there are those private intimate moments shared only between the two of them, not for public viewing, discussion, or curiosity. Moments that will always remain intimate and private.

Alifa Rifaat

In "My World of the Unknown" (1983), the Egyptian writer Alifa Rifaat explores the realm of female passion using themes and imagery that remind the reader of how culturally bound our "universal" symbols may be. Born in 1930 into a conservative middle-class Egyptian family, Rifaat received little formal education. Paralleling the narrator in this story, she married at an early age and accompanied her husband in assignments as a provincial government worker. Drawing attention because of their subject matter, her short stories break the long silence surrounding middle-class Egyptian women who live according to traditional roles while harboring other selves. Independent of western feminism, Rifaat finds a way to portray the complexity and mystery of female desire.

MY WORLD OF THE UNKNOWN

THERE are many mysteries in life, unseen powers in the universe, worlds other than our own, hidden links and radiations that draw creatures together and whose effect is interacting. They may merge or be incompatible, and perhaps the day will come when science will find a method for connecting up these worlds in the same way as it has made it possible to voyage to other planets. Who knows?

Yet one of these other worlds I have explored; I have lived in it and been linked with its creatures through the bond of love. I used to pass with amazing speed between this tangible world of ours and another invisible earth, mixing in the two worlds, on one and the same day, as though living it twice over. When entering into the world of my love and being summoned and yielding to its call, no one around me would be aware of what was happening to me. All that occurred was that I would be overcome by something resembling a state of languor and would go off into a semi-sleep. Nothing about me would change except that I would become very silent and withdrawn, though I am normally a person who is talkative and eager to go out into the world of people. I would yearn to be on my own, would long for the moment of surrender as I prepared myself for answering the call.

Love had its beginning when an order came through for my husband to be transferred to a quiet country town and, being too busy with his work, delegated to me the task of going to this town to choose suitable accommodation prior to his taking up the new appointment. He cabled one of his subordinates named Kamil and asked him to meet me at the station and to assist me.

I took the early morning train. The images of a dream I had had that night came to me as I looked out at the vast fields and gauged the distances between the towns through which the train passed and reckoned how far it was between the new town in which we were fated to live and beloved Cairo.

The images of the dream kept reappearing to me, forcing themselves upon my mind: images of a small white house surrounded by a garden with bushes bearing yellow flowers, a house lying on the edge of a broad canal in which were swans and tall sailing boats. I kept on wondering at my dream and trying to analyze it. Perhaps it was some secret wish I had had, or maybe the echo of some image that my unconscious had stored up and was chewing over.

As the train arrived at its destination, I awoke from my thoughts. I found Kamil awaiting me. We set out in his car, passing through the local *souk*. I gazed at the mounds of fruit with delight, chatting away happily with Kamil. When we emerged from the *souk* we found ourselves on the bank of the Mansûra canal, a canal on which swans swam and sailing boats moved to and fro. I kept staring at them with uneasy longing. Kamil directed the driver to the residential buildings the governorate had put up for housing government employees. While gazing at the opposite bank a large boat with a great fluttering sail glided past. Behind it could be seen a white house that had a garden with trees with yellow flowers and that lay on its own amidst vast fields. I shouted out in confusion, overcome by the feeling that I had been here before.

"Go to that house," I called to the driver. Kamil leapt up, objecting vehemently: "No, no—no one lives in that house. The best thing is to go to the employees' buildings."

I shouted insistently, like someone hypnotized: "I must have a look at that house." "All right," he said. "You won't like it, though—it's old and needs repairing." Giving in to my wish, he ordered the driver to make his way there.

At the garden door we found a young woman, spare and of fair complexion. A fat child with ragged clothes encircled her neck with his burly legs. In a strange silence, she stood as though nailed to the ground, barring the door with her hands and looking at us with doltish inquiry.

I took a sweet from my bag and handed it to the boy. He snatched it eagerly, tightening his grip on her neck with his pudgy, mud-bespattered feet so that her face became flushed from his high-spirited embrace. A half smile showed on her tightly closed lips. Taking courage, I addressed her in a friendly tone: "I'd like to see over this house." She braced her hands resolutely against the door. "No," she said quite simply. I turned helplessly to Kamil, who went up to her and pushed her violently in the chest so that she staggered back. "Don't you realize," he shouted at her, "that this is the director's wife? Off with you!"

Lowering her head so that the child all but slipped from her, she walked off dejectedly to the canal bank, where she lay down on the ground, put the child on her lap, and rested her head in her hands in silent submission.

Moved by pity, I remonstrated: "There's no reason to be so rough, Mr. Kamil. Who is the woman?" "Some madwoman," he said with a shrug of his shoulders, "who's a stranger to the town. Out of kindness the owner of this house put her in charge of it until someone should come along to live in it."

With increased interest I said: "Will he be asking a high rent for it?" "Not at all," he said with an enigmatic smile. "He'd welcome anyone taking it over. There are no restrictions and the rent is modest—no more than four pounds."

I was beside myself with joy. Who in these days can find somewhere to live for such an amount? I rushed through the door into the house with Kamil behind me and went over the rooms: five spacious rooms with wooden floors, with a pleasant hall, modern lavatory, and a beautifully roomy kitchen with a large veranda overlooking vast pistachio-green fields of generously watered rice. A breeze, limpid and cool, blew, playing with the tips of the crop and making the delicate leaves move in continuous dancing waves.

I went back to the first room with its spacious veranda overlooking the road and revealing the other bank of the canal where, along its strand, extended the houses of the town. Kamil pointed out to me a building facing the house on the other side. "That's where we work," he said, "and behind it is where the children's schools are."

"Thanks be to God," I said joyfully. "It means that everything is within easy reach of this house—and the *souk*'s nearby too." "Yes," he said, "and the fishermen will knock at your door to show you the fresh fish they've caught in their nets. But the house needs painting and redoing, also there are all sorts of rumors about it—the people around here believe in djinn and spirits."

"This house is going to be my home," I said with determination. "Its low rent will make up for whatever we may have to spend on redoing it. You'll see what this house will look like when I get the garden arranged. As for the story about djinn and spirits, just leave them to us—we're more spirited than them."

We laughed at my joke as we left the house. On my way to the station we agreed about the repairs that needed doing to the house. Directly I reached Cairo I cabled my husband to send the furniture from the town we had been living in, specifying a suitable date to fit in with the completion of the repairs and the house being ready for occupation.

On the date fixed I once again set off and found that all my wishes had been carried out and that the house was pleasantly spruce with its rooms painted a cheerful orange tint, the floors well polished, and the garden tidied up and made into small flowerbeds.

I took possession of the keys and Kamil went off to attend to his business, having put a chair on the front veranda for me to sit on while I awaited the arrival of the furniture van. I stretched out contentedly in the chair and gazed at the two banks with their towering trees like two rows of guards between which passed the boats with their lofty sails, while around them glided

a male swan heading a flotilla of females. Halfway across the
canal he turned and flirted with them, one after the other, like a
sultan amidst his harem.

Relaxed, I closed my eyes. I projected myself into the future
and pictured to myself the enjoyment I would have in this house
after it had been put in order and the garden fixed up. I awoke to
the touch of clammy fingers shaking me by the shoulders.

I started and found myself staring at the fair-complexioned
woman with her child squatting on her shoulders as she stood
erect in front of me staring at me in silence. "What do you want?"
I said to her sharply. "How did you get in?" "I got in with this,"
she said simply, revealing a key between her fingers.

I snatched the key from her hand as I loudly rebuked her:
"Give it here. We have rented the house and you have no right to
come into it like this." "I have a lot of other keys," she answered
briefly. "And what," I said to her, "do you want of this house?"
"I want to stay on in it and for you to go," she said. I laughed in
amazement at her words as I asked myself: Is she really mad?
Finally I said impatiently: "Listen here, I'm not leaving here and
you're not entering this house unless I wish it. My husband is
coming with the children, and the furniture is on the way. He'll
be arriving in a little while and we'll be living here for such a
period of time as my husband is required to work in this town."

She looked at me in a daze. For a long time she was silent,
then she said: "All right, your husband will stay with me and
you can go." Despite my utter astonishment I felt pity for her.
"I'll allow you to stay on with us for the little boy's sake," I said
to her gently, "until you find yourself another place. If you'd like
to help me with the housework I'll pay you what you ask."

Shaking her head, she said with strange emphasis: "I'm not a
servant. I'm Aneesa." "You're not staying here," I said to her
coldly, rising to my feet. Collecting all my courage and emulat-
ing Kamil's determination when he rebuked her, I began push-

ing her in the chest as I caught hold of the young boy's hand. "Get out of here and don't come near this house," I shouted at her. "Let me have all the keys. I'll not let go of your child till you've given them all to me."

With a set face that did not flicker she put her hand to her bosom and took out a ring on which were several keys, which she dropped into my hand. I released my grip on the young boy. Supporting him on her shoulders, she started to leave. Regretting my harshness, I took out several piastres from my bag and placed them in the boy's hand. With the same silence and stiffness she wrested the piastres from the boy's hand and gave them back to me. Then she went straight out. Bolting the door this time, I sat down, tense and upset, to wait.

My husband arrived, then the furniture, and for several days I occupied myself with putting the house in order. My husband was busy with his work and the children occupied themselves with making new friends and I completely forgot about Aneesa, that is until my husband returned one night wringing his hands with fury: "This woman Aneesa, can you imagine that since we came to live in this house she's been hanging around it every night. Tonight she was so crazy she blocked my way and suggested I should send you off so that she might live with me. The woman's gone completely off her head about this house and I'm afraid she might do something to the children or assault you."

Joking with him and masking the jealousy that raged within me, I said: "And what is there for you to get angry about? She's a fair and attractive enough woman—a blessing brought to your very doorstep!" With a sneer he took up the telephone, muttering: "May God look after her!"

He contacted the police and asked them to come and take her away. When I heard the sound of the police van coming I ran to the window and saw them taking her off. The poor woman did not resist, did not object, but submitted with a gentle sadness that as usual with her aroused one's pity. Yet, when she saw me standing in tears and watching her, she turned to me and, pointing to the wall of the house, called out: "I'll leave her to you." "Who?" I shouted. "Who, Aneesa?" Once again pointing at the bottom of the house, she said: "Her."

The van took her off and I spent a sleepless night. No sooner did day come than I hurried to the garden to examine my plants and to walk round the house and carefully inspect its walls. All I found were some cracks, the house being old, and I laughed at the frivolous thought that came to me: Could, for example, there be jewels buried here, as told in fairy tales?

Who could "she" be? What was the secret of this house? Who was Aneesa and was she really mad? Where were she and her son living? So great did my concern for Aneesa become that I began pressing my husband with questions until he brought me news of her. The police had learnt that she was the wife of a well-to-do teacher living in a nearby town. One night he had caught her in an act of infidelity, and in fear she had fled with her son and had settled here, no one knowing why she had betaken herself to this particular house. However, the owner of the house had been good enough to allow her to put up in it until someone should come to live in it, while some kind person had intervened on her behalf to have her name included among those receiving monthly allowances from the Ministry of Social Affairs. There were many rumors that cast doubt upon her conduct: people passing by her house at night would hear her conversing with unknown persons. Her madness took the form of a predilection for silence and isolation from people during the daytime as she wandered about in a dream world. After the police had persuaded them to take her in to safeguard the good repute of her family, she was returned to her relatives.

The days passed and the story of Aneesa was lost in oblivion. Winter came and with it heavy downpours of rain. The vegetation in my garden flourished, though the castor-oil plants withered and their yellow flowers fell. I came to find pleasure in sitting out on the kitchen veranda looking at my flowers and vegetables and enjoying the belts of sunbeams that lay between the clouds and lavished my veranda with warmth and light.

One sunny morning my attention was drawn to the limb of a nearby tree whose branches curved up gracefully despite its having dried up and its dark bark being cracked. My gaze was attracted by something twisting and turning along the tip of a branch: bands of yellow and others of red, intermingled with bands of black, were creeping forward. It was a long, smooth tube, at its end a small striped head with two bright, wary eyes.

The snake curled round on itself in spiral rings, then tautened its body and moved forward. The sight gripped me; I felt terror turning my blood cold and freezing my limbs.

My senses were numbed, my soul intoxicated with a strange elation at the exciting beauty of the snake. I was rooted to the spot, wavering between two thoughts that contended in my mind at one and the same time: should I snatch up some implement from the kitchen and kill the snake, or should I enjoy the rare moment of beauty that had been afforded me?

As though the snake had read what was passing through my mind, it raised its head, tilting it to right and left in thrilling coquetry. Then, by means of two tiny fangs like pearls, and a golden tongue like a twig of arak wood, it smiled at me and fastened its eyes on mine in one fleeting, commanding glance. The thought of killing left me. I felt a current, a radiation from its eyes that penetrated to my heart, ordering me to stay where I was. A warning against continuing to sit out there in front of it surged inside me, but my attraction to it paralyzed my limbs and

I did not move. I kept on watching it, utterly entranced and captivated. Like a bashful virgin being lavished with compliments, it
tried to conceal its pride in its beauty, and, having made certain
of captivating its lover, the snake coyly twisted round and gently,
gracefully glided away until swallowed up by a crack in the wall.
Could the snake be the "she" that Aneesa had referred to on the
day of her departure?

At last I rose from my place, overwhelmed by the feeling that
I was on the brink of a new world, a new destiny, or rather, if
you wish, the threshold of a new love. I threw myself onto the
bed in a dreamlike state, unaware of the passage of time. No
sooner, though, did I hear my husband's voice and the children
with their clatter as they returned at noon than I regained my
sense of being a human being, wary and frightened about itself,
determined about the existence and continuance of its species.
Without intending to I called out: "A snake—there's a snake in
the house."

My husband took up the telephone and some men came and
searched the house. I pointed out to them the crack into which
the snake had disappeared, though racked with a feeling of remorse
at being guilty of betrayal. For here I was denouncing the beloved,
inviting people against it after it had felt safe with me.

The men found no trace of the snake. They burned some
wormwood and fumigated the hole but without result. Then
my husband summoned Sheikh Farid, sheikh of the Rifa'iyya
order in the town, who went on chanting verses from the Koran
as he tapped the ground with his stick. He then asked to speak to
me alone and said:

"Madam, the sovereign of the house has sought you out and
what you saw is no snake. Rather it is one of the monarchs of
the earth—may God make your words pleasant to them—who
has appeared to you in the form of a snake. Here in this house
there are many holes of snakes, but they are of the nonpoison-

ous kind. They inhabit houses and go and come as they please. What you saw, though, is something else."

"I don't believe a word of it," I said, stupefied. "This is nonsense. I know that the djinn are creatures that actually exist, but they are not in touch with our world, there is no contact between them and the world of humans."

With an enigmatic smile he said: "My child, the Prophet went out to them and read the Koran to them in their country. Some of them are virtuous and some of them are Muslims, and how do you know there is no contact between us and them? Let your prayer be 'O Lord, increase me in knowledge' and do not be nervous. Your purity of spirit, your translucence of soul have opened to you doors that will take you to other worlds known only to their Creator. Do not be afraid. Even if you should find her one night sleeping in your bed, do not be alarmed but talk to her with all politeness and friendliness."

"That's enough of all that, Sheikh Farid. Thank you," I said, alarmed, and he left us.

We went on discussing the matter. "Let's be practical," suggested my husband, "and stop all the cracks at the bottom of the outside walls and put wire mesh over the windows, also plant wormwood all round the garden fence."

We set about putting into effect what we had agreed. I, though, no longer dared to go out onto the verandas. I neglected my garden and stopped wandering about in it. Generally I would spend my free time in bed. I changed to being someone who liked to sit around lazily and was disinclined to mix with people; those diversions and recreations that previously used to tempt me no longer gave me any pleasure. All I wanted was to stretch myself out and drowse. In bewilderment I asked myself: Could it be that I was in love? But how could I love a snake? Or could she really be one of the daughters of the monarchs of the djinn? I would awake from my musings to find that I had been wandering in my thoughts and recalling to mind how magnificent she was. And what is the secret of her beauty? I would ask myself. Was it that I was fascinated by her multicolored, supple body? Or was it that I had been dazzled by that intelligent, commanding way she had of looking at me? Or could it be the sleek way she had of gliding along, so excitingly dangerous, that had captivated me?

Excitingly dangerous! No doubt it was this excitement that had stirred my feelings and awakened my love, for did they not make films to excite and frighten? There was no doubt but that the secret of my passion for her, my preoccupation with her, was due to the excitement that had aroused, through intense fear, desire within myself; an excitement that was sufficiently strong to drive the blood hotly through my veins whenever the memory of her came to me, thrusting the blood in bursts that made my heart beat wildly, my limbs limp. And so, throwing myself down in a pleasurable state of torpor, my craving for her would be awakened and I would wish for her coil-like touch, her graceful gliding motion.

And yet I fell to wondering how union could come about, how craving be quenched, the delights of the body be realized between a woman and a snake. And did she, I wondered, love me and want me as I loved her? An idea would obtrude itself upon me sometimes: did Cleopatra, the very legend of love, have sexual intercourse with her serpent after having given up sleeping with men, having wearied of amorous adventures with them so that her sated instincts were no longer moved other than by the excitement of fear, her senses no longer aroused other than by bites from a snake? And the last of her lovers had been a viper that had destroyed her.

I came to live in a state of continuous torment, for a strange feeling of longing scorched my body and rent my senses, while my circumstances obliged me to carry out the duties and responsibilities that had been placed on me as the wife of a man who occupied an important position in the small town, he and his family being objects of attention and his house a Kaaba for those seeking favors; also as a mother who must look after her children and concern herself with every detail of their lives so as to exercise control over them; there was also the house and its chores, this house that was inhabited by the mysterious lover who lived in a world other than mine. How, I wondered, was union between us to be achieved? Was wishing for this love a sin or was there nothing to reproach myself about?

And as my self-questioning increased so did my yearning, my curiosity, my desire. Was the snake from the world of reptiles or from the djinn? When would the meeting be? Was she, I wondered, aware of me and would she return out of pity for my consuming passion?

One stormy morning with the rain pouring down so hard that I could hear the drops rattling on the windowpane, I lit the stove and lay down in bed between the covers seeking refuge from an agonizing trembling that racked my yearning body, which, ablaze with unquenchable desire, called out for relief.

I heard a faint rustling sound coming from the corner of the wall right beside my bed. I looked down and kept my eyes fixed on one of the holes in the wall, which I found was slowly, very slowly, expanding. Closing my eyes, my heart raced with joy and my body throbbed with mounting desire as there dawned in me the hope of an encounter. I lay back in submission to what was to be. No longer did I care whether love was coming from the world of reptiles or from that of the djinn, sovereigns of the world. Even were this love to mean my destruction, my desire for it was greater.

I heard a hissing noise that drew nearer, then it changed to a gentle whispering in my ear, calling to me: "I am love, O enchantress. I showed you my home in your sleep; I called you to my kingdom when your soul was dozing on the horizon of dreams, so come, my sweet beloved, come and let us explore the depths of the azure sea of pleasure. There, in the chamber of coral, amidst cool, shady rocks where reigns deep, restful silence lies our bed, lined with soft, bright green damask, inlaid with pearls newly wrenched from their shells. Come, let me sleep with you as I have slept with beautiful women and have given them bliss. Come, let me prise out your pearl from its shell that I may polish it and bring forth its splendor. Come to where no one will find us, where no one will see us, for the eyes of swimming creatures are innocent and will not heed what we do nor understand what we say. Down there lies repose, lies a cure for all your yearnings and ills. Come, without fear or dread, for no creature will reach us in our hidden world, and only the eye of God alone will see us; He alone will know what we are about and He will watch over us."

I began to be intoxicated by the soft musical whisperings. I felt her cool and soft and smooth, her coldness producing a painful convulsion in my body and hurting me to the point of terror. I felt her as she slipped between the covers, then her two tiny fangs, like two pearls, began to caress my body; arriving at my thighs, the golden tongue, like an arak twig, inserted its pronged tip between them and began sipping and exhaling; sipping the poisons of my desire and exhaling the nectar of my ecstasy, till my whole body tingled and started to shake in sharp, painful, rapturous spasms—and all the while the tenderest of words were whispered to me as I confided to her all my longings.

At last the cool touch withdrew, leaving me exhausted. I went into a deep slumber to awake at noon full of energy, all of me a joyful burgeoning to life. Curiosity and a desire to know who it was seized me again. I looked at the corner of the wall and found that the hole was wide open. Once again I was overcome by fear.

I pointed out the crack to my husband, unable to utter, although terror had once again awakened in me passionate desire. My husband filled up the crack with cement and went to sleep.

Morning came and everyone went out. I finished my housework and began roaming around the rooms in boredom, battling against the desire to surrender myself to sleep. I sat in the hallway and suddenly she appeared before me, gentle as an angel, white as day, softly undulating and flexing herself, calling to me in her bewitching whisper: "Bride of mine, I called you and brought you to my home. I have wedded you, so there is no sin in our love, nothing to reproach yourself about. I am the guardian of the house, and I hold sway over the snakes and vipers that inhabit it, so come and I shall show you where they live. Have no fear so long as we are together. You and I are in accord. Bring a container with water and I shall place my fingers over your hand and we shall recite together some verses from the Koran, then we shall sprinkle it in the places from which they emerge and shall thus close the doors on them, and it shall be a pact between us that your hands will not do harm to them."

"Then you are one of the monarchs of the djinn?" I asked eagerly. "Why do you not bring me treasures and riches as we hear about in fables when a human takes as sister her companion among the djinn?"

She laughed at my words, shaking her golden hair, which was like dazzling threads of light. She whispered to me, coquettishly: "How greedy is mankind! Are not the pleasures of the body enough? Were I to come to you with wealth we would both die consumed by fire."

"No, no," I called out in alarm. "God forbid that I should ask for unlawful wealth. I merely asked it of you as a test, that it might be positive proof that I am not imagining things and living in dreams."

She said: "And do intelligent humans have to have something

tangible as evidence? By God, do you not believe in His ability to create worlds and living beings? Do you not know that you have an existence in worlds other than that of matter and the transitory? Fine, since you ask for proof, come close to me and my caresses will put vitality back into your limbs. You will retain your youth. I shall give you abiding youth and the delights of love—and they are more precious than wealth in the world of man. How many fortunes have women spent in quest of them? As for me I shall feed from the poisons of your desire, the exhalations of your burning passion, for that is my nourishment and through it I live."

"I thought that your union with me was for love, not for nourishment and the perpetuation of youth and vigor," I said in amazement.

"And is sex anything but food for the body and an interaction in union and love?" she said. "Is it not this that makes human beings happy and is the secret of feeling joy and elation?"

She stretched out her radiant hand to my body, passing over it like the sun's rays and discharging into it warmth and a sensation of languor.

"I am ill," I said. "I am ill. I am ill," I kept repeating. When he heard me my husband brought the doctor, who said: "High blood pressure, heart trouble, nervous depression." Having prescribed various medicaments he left. The stupidity of doctors! My doctor did not know that he was describing the symptoms of love, did not even know it was from love I was suffering. Yet I knew my illness and the secret of my cure. I showed my husband the enlarged hole in the wall and once again he stopped it up. We then carried the bed to another corner.

After some days had passed I found another hole alongside my bed. My beloved came and whispered to me: "Why are you so coy and flee from me, my bride? Is it fear of your being rebuffed or is it from aversion? Are you not happy with our being together? Why do you want for us to be apart?"

"I am in agony," I whispered back. "Your love is so intense and the desire to enjoy you so consuming. I am frightened I shall feel that I am tumbling down into a bottomless pit and being destroyed."

"My beloved," she said. "I shall only appear to you in beauty's most immaculate form."

"But it is natural for you to be a man," I said in a precipitate outburst, "seeing that you are so determined to have a love affair with me."

"Perfect beauty is to be found only in women," she said, "so yield to me and I shall let you taste undreamed-of happiness; I shall guide you to worlds possessed of such beauty as you have never imagined."

She stretched out her fingers to caress me, while her delicate mouth sucked in the poisons of my desire and exhaled the nectar of my ecstasy, carrying me off into a trance of delicious happiness.

After that we began the most pleasurable of love affairs, wandering together in worlds and living on horizons of dazzling beauty, a world fashioned of jewels, a world whose every moment was radiant with light and formed a thousand shapes, a thousand colors.

As for the opening in the wall, I no longer took any notice. I no longer complained of feeling ill; in fact there burned within me abounding vitality. Sometimes I would bring a handful of wormwood and, by way of jest, would stop up the crack, just as the beloved teases her lover and closes the window in his face that, ablaze with desire for her, he may hasten to the door. After that I would sit for a long time and enjoy watching the wormwood powder being scattered in spiral rings by unseen puffs of wind. Then I would throw myself down on the bed and wait.

For months I immersed myself in my world, no longer calcu-
lating time or counting the days, until one morning my husband
went out on the veranda lying behind our favored wall alongside
the bed. After a while I heard him utter a cry of alarm. We all
hurried out to find him holding a stick, with a black, ugly snake
almost two meters long lying at his feet.

I cried out with sorrow whose claws clutched at my heart so
that it began to beat wildly. With crazed fury I shouted at my husband: "Why have you broken the pact and killed it? What harm
has it done?" How cruel is man! He lets no creature live in peace.

I spent the night sorrowful and apprehensive. My lover came
to me and embraced me more passionately than ever. I whispered to her imploringly: "Be kind, beloved. Are you angry
with me or sad because of me?"

"It is farewell," she said. "You have broken the pact and have
betrayed one of my subjects, so you must both depart from this
house, for only love lives in it."

In the morning I packed up so that we might move to one of
the employees' buildings, leaving the house in which I had
learnt of love and enjoyed incomparable pleasures.

I still live in memory and in hope. I crave for the house and
miss my secret love. Who knows, perhaps one day my beloved
will call me. Who really knows?

Translated by Denys Johnson-Davies

Yasmin V. Tambiah

The work of Yasmin V. Tambiah from Sri Lanka represents a unique contribution to this volume. Having spent several years in North America, the author returns to a country torn by ongoing civil war and finds herself experiencing a series of exiles. Although not a work of fiction, the pieces (1988–1991) pose many of the questions that shape this collection. How does a lesbian writer sustain herself in the face of complex and contradictory national histories and personal choices? In what ways does language both confine and allow for expression of the imagination? Through the use of vivid detail coupled with analytical language that here takes on an immediacy far removed from academic musings, Tambiah gives voice to crucial struggles that reach beyond national frontiers.

THE CIVIL WAR

September 1984: Three months since I returned to Sri Lanka with an American college degree. The civil war has spilled beyond the Northern Province. Metal gates to my parents' house still bear the dents of rock-throwing mobs. There are ax marks on the wooden doors. New plaster hides a ceiling charred by a burning tire. Embattled elsewhere I relive the horror of July 1983 through my siblings' eyes. It is difficult to articulate the deep loss within, the negation of familiar fictions, the awareness that exile in one's own country is even less bearable than at a distance. It is a loss compounded by my family's fear.

February 1985: Carrying the national ID card is mandatory. It will protect me from arbitrary arrest, they say. But the civil war has spilled beyond the Northern Province. Authorities have collapsed many identities into a Tamil last name. The card does not attest that I am also Sinhalese, speak no Tamil, and dream in English. It is silent on conflicting loyalties and the struggle to recover myself from colonialisms. I am reduced to someone else's definition, terrorized into keeping boundaries I neither constructed nor consented to.

December 1985: Exile. Four months in North America. White graduate classmates are puzzled that a twentieth-century South Asian might share the experiences of a Medieval Jew. Their imagination stops at my brown skin. There has always been a civil war beyond the Northern Province. Those at risk cannot afford ignorance. I have learnt to recognize the languages of domination and gather a community of resistance for a dangerous journey toward necessary transformations.

1988–1990

SANDALWOOD

s i step through the door your scent meets me, mingling intimately with incense burnt for Devis. Enclosed by your strong brown arms, bangles tinkling their welcome, i taste melted jaggery on your lips, sea salt within. In your eyes i forget time, collapse space. Your well-ordered apartment outside washington d.c. transforms into dense lush jungle heady with araliya, jasmine, magnolia, sandalwood. My fingers sink into moist soil rich with life. Rounded, like the elephant yogini we celebrate, you claim me. Familiar endearments roll off your tongue teasing nipples dark as your own. Fierce, passionate, protective, reflections dancing where our Kalis meet, you bring me home.

I am no longer cracked earth hidden between asphalt sidewalks in north america waiting for the monsoon that comes only in my dreams to drench, heal, close fissures through which i bleed. Your firm knowing touch re-members sensations grown distant . . . tired limbs massaged, face caressed, head stroked to lessen pain, to calm a restless spirit. That touch you cook with, food we both know, grew up on, still eat making do with american substitutes and precious imports. Tastes of jeera, koththamalli, pepper, star anise blend easily on your fingers. You name us "rasam and rice sisters," "ovaltine dykes," laughing, voice concepts made alien here. Dravidian warrior, friend, lover, you bring me home.

1990

TRANSL(ITER)ATION I

ow does the decolonizing tongue move? Speak, erupt, disrupt? Does it roll words, familiar-tasting yet illegitimate? Singlish. Tamilian english. English with an "educated" sri lankan accent. South asian english. From approbation of whiteness to defining destinations. From exoticized other to subject self. From exile to return.

It is risky to say my lover tastes of jaggery, to write that we reflect Kali in our lovemaking, to refuse translation of cultural specificities, transliteration with asterisked explanations, decontextualized descriptions, dislocated selves. It dares the privileged to leap chasms of imagination, rejects their referents, refuses voyeurism. It presumes an audience familiar with these requisites, engaged, like me, in returning. But this return is not comfortable, not guaranteed. Decolonization is not about coming back to unchanged fictions. I do not defy translation to recover the world of my fathers. In the dialect(ic)s of nationalism, there is no room for me.

How then does this decolonizing self speak?

With old concepts reworked to reflect realities of turbulence, to mouth visions of the dead, to secure spaces where the silenced may find voice. With new ideas birthed at subverted boundaries, in erotic constellations, outrageous dreams. With expressions from many places, unfragmented; accessing many identities, self-named. With wisdom of many wanderings, inscribing home.

1990

TRANSL(ITER)ATION II

(for Aruna and Giti)

HERE I come from, to roll my tongue talking sex is to blaspheme against the "pure" woman, the essential sri lankan. To be sexual, even by myself, is deviant, pollution by western values. Some south asian progressives claim we were comfortably erotic before british victorianisms permeated our psychic and somatic languages. But they too would erase a woman inscribing herself without the phallus. In such a text where do I locate my desire? How do I grasp the apsara-princesses of Sigiriya? Or dark Tara with her full rounded breasts, firm-swelling stomach, exquisite long fingers that play with me in my dreams?

Here, in the united states, to roll my tongue talking sex is heretical. I mean, where north atlantic inhabitants control the discourse on eros, a south asian lesbian is a contradiction in terms.[1] Erotic. Exceptional. But can she kiss, make fierce love? Things some south asian lesbians wonder even about one another. So effective the circumscriptions we must transform violently to acknowledge verities that predate vedic domestications and white colonizers, to comprehend the undivided feminine. Creatrix-warrior-lover-devourer. Self-referent. Self-revering.[2]

To talk sex as a south asian lesbian decolonizing myself is to communicate eros dangerously. Tracing my lover's inky-purple lips my tongue speaks an old power, serpent's fire. Raging passion and passionate rage flow from the same source. Knowledge to rend imprisoning fictions, articulate forbidden truths, consume with desire. Tara needs no mediation, no translation. Wisdoms that arm and pleasure me on the treacherous journey home.

1990–1991

1 My thanks to V. K. Aruna for this concept.
2 I am indebted to Giti Thadani for these insights.

Dionne Brand

The Trinidadian-born fiction writer, poet, and filmmaker Dionne Brand celebrates the playfulness of young lust in her story "Madame Alaird's Breasts." A resident of Toronto, Canada, for over twenty years, Brand is part of a flourishing Caribbean Canadian lesbian writers community. In this story, taken from her collection Sans Souci *(1989), Brand uses the classroom and language learning as a site for sexual curiosity, normalizing young girls' fascination with a mature woman's body. Her characters' joyous energy as they innocently focus on their well-endowed teacher gains a new dimension when juxtaposed to the Trinidadian immigration act that forbids homosexual women and men from entering the country.*

MADAME ALAIRD'S BREASTS

MADAME Alaird was our French mistress. "*Bonjour, mes enfants,*" she would say on entering the classroom, then walk heavily toward her desk. Madame Alaird walked heavily because of her bosom, which was massive above her thin waist. As she walked her breasts tipped her entire body forward. She was not tall, neither was she short, but her bosom made her look quite impressive and imposing and, when she entered our form room, her voice resonated through her breasts, deep and rich and Black,

"*Bonjour, mes enfants.*"

We, Form 3A, sing-songed back, "Bonjour, Ma-dame A-lai-air-d," smirking as we watched her tipping heavily to her desk. We loved Madame Alaird's breasts. All through the conjugation of verbs—*aller, acheter, appeler,* and *écouter*—we watched her breasts as she rested them on top of her desk, the bodice of her dress holding them snugly, her deep breathing on the *eu* sounds making them descend into their warm cave and rise to take air. We imitated her voice but our *eu*'s sounded like shrill flutes, sharpened by the excitement of Madame Alaird's breasts.

We discussed Madame Alaird's breasts on the way home every Tuesday and Thursday, because French was every Tuesday and Thursday at 10:00 A.M. They weren't like Miss Henry's breasts. We would never notice Miss Henry's breasts anyway because we hated needlework and sewing. Miss Henry was our needlework and sewing mistress.

Madame Alaird wasn't fat. She wasn't thin either, but her breasts were huge and round and firm. Every Tuesday and Thursday, we looked forward to having Madame Alaird's breasts to gawk at, all of French period. Madame Alaird wore gold-rimmed bifocals, which meant that she could not see very well, even though she peered over her bifocals pointedly in the direction of snickers or other rude noises during her teaching. But this was merely form; we doubted whether she could see us.

Madame Alaird's breasts were like pillows, deep purple ones, just like Madame Alaird's full lips as she expressed the personal pronouns.

"*Je-u, tu-ooo, ell-lle, no-o-us. Mes enfants, encore. . . .*"

"*No-o-us, vo-uus, ell-lles,*" which we deliberately mispronounced to have Madame Alaird say them over. Madame Alaird's breasts gave us imagination beyond our years or possibilities, of burgundy velvet rooms with big-legged women and rum and calypso music. Next to Madame Alaird's breasts, we loved Madame Alaird's lips. They made water spring to our mouths just like when the skin bursts eating a purple fat mammy sipote fruit. Every Tuesday and Thursday after school, bookbags and feet dragging, we'd discuss Madame Alaird's breasts.

"But you see Madame Alaird breasts!"

"Girl, you ever see how she just rest them on the table!"

"I wonder how they feel?"

"You think I go have breasts like Madame Alaird?"

Giggles.

"But Madame Alaird have more breasts than anybody I know."

"She must be does be tired carrying them, eh!"

Giggles, doubled over in laughter, near the pharmacy. Then past the boys' college.

"And you don't see how they sticking out in front like that when she walk is like she falling over! Qui! Bon jieu!"

"But Madame Alaird ain't playing she have breast, oui!"

"And girl she know French, eh?"

"Madame Alaird must be could feed the whole world with them breasts, yes!"

Giggles reaching into belly laughs near Carib Street in chorus, *"BONJOUR, MES ENFANTS!"* rounding our lips on the *bonjour,* like Madame Alaird's kiss.

Madame Alaird was almost naked as far as we were concerned. It did not matter that she was always fully clothed. She was almost puritan in her style. Usually she wore brogues and ordinary clothing. Madame was not a snazzy dresser, but on speech day and other special occasions, she put on tan heels, stockings seamed up the back, a close-fitting beige dress with perhaps a little lace at the bosom, and her gold-rimmed bifocals hung from their gold string around her neck, resting on her breasts. Madame Alaird was beautiful. The bifocals didn't mean that Madame Alaird was old. She wasn't young either. She was what we called a full woman.

We heard that Madame Alaird had children. Heard, as adolescents hear, through self-composition. We got few glimpses of Madame Alaird's life, which is why we made up most of it. Once, we saw her husband come to pick her up after school. He drove an old sedate-looking dark green Hillman, and he was slim and short and quiet-looking with gold-rimmed peepers, like Madame Alaird's.

"But woii! Madame Alaird husband skinny, eh?!"

"It must be something when Madame Alaird sit down on him!"

That Tuesday or Thursday Madame Alaird's husband added fuel to the fire of Madame Alaird's breasts.

"He must be does have a nice time in Madame Alaird breast, oui."

"Madame Alaird must be feel sorry for him, that is why."

Madame Alaird went through a gloomy period where often the hem of her skirt hung and she wore a dark green dress with the collar frayed. We were very concerned because the period lasted a very long time and we knew that the other teachers and the headmistress were looking at her suspiciously. Among them, Madame Alaird stood out. They were not as pretty as she, though she wasn't *pretty,* for she was not a small woman, but she was as rosy as they were dry. In this time, she was absentminded in class and didn't look at us, but looked at her desk and took us up sternly in our conjugations. Her breasts, hidden in dark green knit, were disappointing.

We were protective of Madame Alaird. In the wooden and musty paper smell of our thirteen-year-old girl lives, in the stifling, uniformed, Presbyterian hush of our days, in the bone and stick of our youngness, Madame Alaird was a vision, a promise of the dark-red fleshiness of real life.

"Madame Alaird looking like she catching trouble, eh?"

"But why she looking so bad?"

"It must be she husband, oui!"

"Madame Alaird don't need he."

"Is true! Madame Alaird could feed a country! How she could need he?"

"So he have Madame Alaird catching hell, or what?"

"Cheuupss! You don't see he could use a beating!"

"But Madame Alaird could beat he up easy, easy, you know!"

"You ain't see how the head teacher watching she?"

"Hmmm!"

And so it went for months until, unaccountably, her mood changed. Unaccountably, because we were not privy to Madame Alaird's life and could only see glimpses, outward and filtered, of what might be happening in it. But our stories seemed to make sense. And we saw her breasts. The only real secret that we knew about her life. Anyway, Madame Alaird was back to herself and we lapped our tongues over her breasts once again, on Tuesday and Thursdays.

"Girl! Alaird looking good again, eh."

"She must be send that old husband packing."

"She must be get a new 'thing.'"

"You ain't see how she dress up nice, nice, woi!!"

We were jealous of Madame Alaird's husband and vexed with him for no reason at all. We even watched him cut-eyed when he came to pick her up from school.

"She must be find a new 'thing'! Oui foo!"

"Madame Alaird ain't playing she nice, non!"

So the talk about Madame Alaird's breasts went, for months and months, until we were so glad to see Madame Alaird's breasts again that we cooked up a treat to please her. The vogue that month was rubber spiders and snakes, which we used to sneak up on one another and send down the boney backs of our still breastless bodices.

Our renewed obsession with Madame Alaird's breasts, our passion for their snug bounciness, their warm purpleness, their juicy fruitedness, had us giggling and whispering every time she walked down the hall and into Form 3A, our class. Madame Alaird's breasts drove us to extremes. She was delighted with our conjugations, rapturous about our attentiveness. Her *Bonjour, mes enfants* were more fleshy and sonorous, her *ue*'s and *ou*'s more voluptuous and dark-honeyed. We glowed at her and rivaled one another to be her favorite.

The plan was cooked up to place a rubber snake on Madame Alaird's chair, so that when she sat down she would jump up in fright. We had the idea that Madame Alaird would laugh at this trick and it would put us on even more familiar terms with her. So, that Tuesday, we put the plan in motion and stood in excited silence as Madame Alaird entered and tipped heavily toward her chair, a deeper, more sensuous than ever *Bonjour, mes enfants* pushing out of her full, purple lips. All of us burst out, shaking with laughter as Madame Alaird sat, jumped up, uttered a muffled yell, all at the same time. Then standing, looked severely at us—we, doubled over in uncontrollable laughter—she resounded, in English,

"When you are all ready to apologize, I shall be in the office. I shall not enter this class again until you do!" and strode out of the door.

After the apology, made in our forty-voiced, flutey girls' chorus, after our class mistress ordered it, Madame Alaird returned and was distant. This did not stop our irreverence about Madame Alaird's breasts. We ignored the pangs of conscience (those of us who had any) about upsetting her and rolled out laughing, for days after. Lustful and unrepentent.

"You ain't see how Madame Alaird jump up!"

"Woi! Madame Alaird breasts just fly up in the air and bounce back down."

"Oui fooo! Bon Jieu! Was like she had wings."

"Madame Alaird ain't playing she have breasts, non!"

"Bon Jieu oiii!"

In her classes, we lowered our eyes to the burgundy velvet rooms of her beautiful breasts, like penitents.

Violette Leduc

L'Asphyxie *(1946), the first novel by the French writer Violette Leduc (1907–1972) and excerpted here, was championed by Simone de Beauvoir and acclaimed by leading French writers, though commercial success did not follow. Constructed in a series of short narratives, the work is unified by the point of view of a young girl who records her own attempts and those of others around her to live their often idiosyncratic lives in a small northern French town, not unlike the city of Arras where Leduc grew up. A controversial writer, Leduc experienced the punishing effect of censorship firsthand when she was obliged to cut a section from the first volume of her autobiography that chronicled an explicitly sexual relationship between two schoolgirls. In the pages appearing here, the energy of young female lives is also linked to forms of mutilation, while the dizzying intensity of their lives—and Leduc's language—militates against those forces that confine and define female experience.*

from L'ASPHYXIE

I was stretched out at the edge of the field, my school bag swollen with useless things at my feet. . . .

She ran by herself, but I didn't let her out of my sight. I was following her game attentively.

She was running blissfully behind a butterfly. It had her breathing hard. It even had her in a sweat. She hadn't let go of her school bag. She was going at a gallop. Her glasses didn't budge. . . . She existed only for the butterfly. It existed only for the pleasure of the flight. She galloped on, then staggered, then galloped again, tracing with her legs the whims of the butterfly. . . . An about-face and it began to climb. I saw two violet petals that quivered in the breeze. A breeze that was a delight against the skin. Then I tried to look at the sun. It was impossible. I shut my eyes. I heard the comings and goings of little summer creatures. A hornet took a sudden interest in me. A hen, its work done, began to stutter its satisfaction. Farther away, a novice bugler blew sounds that broke apart before ending. . . . They fanned the plain with their chilly resonance. . . .

She was coming near. She was going on with her stupid race. Her glasses seemed more solemn than their owner. She bumped into me. Drops of sweat slipped down my back. I realized that I had lost it. I shivered.

"Stop, Mandine!"

I was catapulted into a world where it no longer existed. The heat drew taut like an archer's bow. The burnt grass was not comforting. The plain offered itself up endlessly to the sun. It was hostile to she who wanted to create soothing hopes, for I longed to find it right away, on this plain that hid nothing. . . .

Her circle completed, she ran in front of me.

"Stop, Mandine! I lost it!"

She stopped. She looked at me over her glasses, turning herself into an old woman. That very morning, she had admired it, had fondled it. She knew exactly what I was talking about.

"Mandine, what am I going to do?"

But she too was possessed by an absence. Held in the grips of the desire to possess it, this absent thing. . . .

She hunted violently in her satchel. Then she remembered me.

"You've got my sympathy, you poor thing. . . ."

I dropped the subject, letting her look for what she wanted. I didn't dare return to my nonchalant stance. Ants were searching for provisions under the grass. If only I could enlist in that colony of slaves. . . . She had found the box. She pulled it out and struck the last match on it. In that midday light that cut through everything, the small fearful flame evoked pity. Mandine didn't look at it. Yet it lasted.

She pricked the box again and again with a needle. She was creating the prison and the tomb of the absent one. Her concentration was incredible. Between her lips, her tongue appeared like a large crimson bud. And you could hear her peculiar breathing because the midday plain, all absorbed in this heat of catastrophe, had left room only for us. . . .

Her actions were making her hot. Her cheeks were aflame, her bangs were sticking to her forehead, her eyes full of lust. Her face was becoming interesting. I felt sorry for her.

"You can't catch it, Mandine. It's gone."

She closed her satchel. She stared at me, mean because of her craving.

"It'll be back. I'll get it!"

The butterfly flew over us, innocently. She didn't see it. As for me, I would have happily exchanged my skin for those two wings that would perhaps collapse in the box, against the oblong body that would die without having to justify itself as I would for what I had lost. . . . Quietly, with no roll of the drums, anguish would soon fall on me, massive as a rock. . . .

"Mandine, tell me what I'm going to do. . . ."

She had it. Her right hand had gulped up the butterfly. She tightened her fist. All her strength flowed into her fist. Her face took on subtlety. Her thick, orderly eyelashes flickered, revealing what Mandine didn't want to reveal: intense pleasure. Her nostrils made small hollows. Her smile, as fleeting as a bubble, nestled in the corners of her mouth. Mandine, an eagle who seized its prey in silence.

She could no longer keep it to herself. "Get up! Come on, get up!"

Standing, I had to bear the weight of my anguish. I refused to really think about what I had lost. . . .

Mandine was against me, glued to me. Her fist rose up to my chin with the slowness of a censer. She loosened her fingers avariciously. With her left hand, she seized a wing that believed itself to be free. She waved it from the tips of her fingers, like an acrobat who raises another by the strength of his wrist. But it was only a conjuror's trick in cruelty. I saw the mark of her nails in the palm of her hand. I also saw that the butterfly had left a little of its magical dust. . . . She continued to wave it and send her sugary young girl's breath against my neck.

"Let it go, Mandine!"

". . ."

She moved it back and forth in front of me, assessing my distress. She pulled away from me, spun around with it, her arm outstretched. She was dizzying the butterfly and herself.

"Let it go, Mandine!"

". . ."

With her free hand, she opened the box, imprisoned the butterfly, and shook the box every which way. She was voraciousness itself. She wanted more. She listened. It was beating against the walls. Its sad little taps did nothing to oppress its jailor. Satisfied, she stored the box in her school bag. Order had returned. I was left with the single-minded intelligence of the smartest girl in the class. Now she could think about what I had lost.

"You left it in the cloak room. First though, we'll look here."

She ran across the plain of Mons, but I knew that she was looking for another butterfly, that she still lusted after pleasure.

A few scattered drops fell here and there. Although meager, the rain calmed the heat and us as well. It tricked my thoughts and, as the fat drops cooled the back of my legs, I believed I would find it. . . .

I stood up and ran behind her. I tripped several times in the holes left by horses' hooves: the cavalry came to exercise on this plain. I also tripped over the grocer's clerk. I knew him by sight. He was stretched out on a young woman. They each had a daisy between their lips, chewing on the stems. They seemed dissatisfied, uncomfortable, undecided, short of breath. They were breathing hard and the flowers moved forward and back. The whole picture lacked elegance. I circled them like a timid dog. He shifted his position. I fled.

Mandine was waiting for me.

"I didn't find it, but I've got an idea."

"Tell it to me!"

She kept it to herself. It had stopped raining. There was no way to push away the weight of the heat. The clouds had formed a coalition. She took my hand and set us off in a wild gallop toward the school that we had left an hour before. The sun was regaining the upper hand. A few pearl gray veils to tear through. . . . We were running, but the heat of hell was at our backs. Mandine was only herself when she was running. She told me we would find it. The caretaker would hold it out to me from between the bars of the gate. I listened avidly to this weaver of hopes. If I were to wear glasses as tightly fitted as hers, everything would go better. . . .

The caretaker was snoring, the door of his office partly open. In the empty building, it was a death rattle which was growing. . . .

We had yelled, we had stamped our feet. He had deigned to put aside his sleep to inspect the cloak room and grumble that he hadn't seen it.

Destroyed, I sat down on the front steps of the school. I imagined my return home, the blood in my veins had practically come to a standstill. I would have exchanged my skin for a caretaker's so that I could look for what I had lost, asleep on my feet, utterly indifferent. But I needed to think like Mandine: *It will turn up, I'll find it.* I would check every house, every closet in the city. Once I had it under my arm, I would give it to my friend. She would take it to my house. I wouldn't go home. I would live in a toolshed. I would eat peas and raw carrots. . . . These sterile ramblings didn't help me to reach a decision. The sun was hiding. The heat was turning into an ambush. It oppressed the earth. A procession of stealthy clouds glided by slowly, a trail of cataclysms on a tight rein.

Then the man from rue de Foulons suddenly appeared. He spoke to Mandine:

"What's the matter with that child?"

"She lost her umbrella."

He continued on his way, reassured, in a hurry, released.

The weather was arranging itself for the stage. On the façades of the buildings, it was theatrical. The clouds followed us in a fury. Mandine had led me off in another wild gallop. She was taking me back to my house. We would find it there. I was ready to believe anything.

Our school bags beat wildly against our sides. Children, dogs, and old people watched us. Mandine had been born to run. Her glasses too. She looked like a top student who had thrown propriety to the winds. . . .

We arrived.

I could see Grandmother from a distance. She was chatting with the neighborhood dwarf lady. She gave me an affectionate wave. I didn't return it, paralyzed by remorse that her state of ignorance set off in me. Her gesture became as simpleminded as that of the young peasants who wave at the express train that flies through the countryside. . . . I didn't rush toward her. I belonged to that complicitous sky, to those sullen clouds, to the façade of our house that was bathed in such an appropriate light, to that cherry tree which was being taunted by the wind. . . . I belonged to the thing I had lost.

"I've changed my mind. I'll leave you here, you poor thing. I'm not going in. I'd be late. We've got that geography assignment. . . ."

The race was suffocating Mandine's heart.

Standing still, she was once again the well-behaved pupil made of marble.

"Don't leave me. Stay for one minute. Just one little minute!"

Through her glasses, she understood that at that moment I had no one but her. I was calling out to her for help.

She came in. The weather was growing dramatic. The sky was blaspheming with its color. Stretching out your hand, you could feel heat settle on your finger tips.

As for me, I no longer had any blood in my veins.

Our house was an oasis. The coolness intimidated us. We walked on tiptoe. Up in her room, my mother was singing: *I simply met you and you did nothing to try to make me love you.* She was practicing in front of her mirror. She never grew tired of herself. Above us, on the ceiling, you could hear her rehearsing the movements of an elegant woman out for a walk.

Mandine coughed loudly to announce our arrival. I was more of a stranger here than she was.

"Who's there?" my mother asked.

I didn't dare answer.

"It's us," went on Mandine, who wasn't acquainted with the cold blue eye.

She came down in light shoes. She reached the step that groaned. I was rambling again: I will live in a shed, I'll eat peas and raw carrots. . . . Then she was with us.

Mandine admired her and didn't understand why I was afraid to go home to a such an attractive mother.

"So you've brought her back?"

She took on a soft voice, boneless and vague. It disgusted me. Mandine found it pleasant. Between the two of them, I was the dunce.

She realized it. "Where did you put your umbrella?"

The mask fell away. Mandine took flight.

Time shivered. Finally, the storm was moving in.

She was waiting for my answer. She looked at what was happening to the sky.

"I'm waiting!"

I threw my answer at her.

"I lost it."

She listened to me but she refused to believe me.

"Where did you put your umbrella?"

It was becoming serious. I fiddled with another answer.

"I don't know. I lost it."

Emotion made me hoarse.

"You don't know where you lost it, you little beast?"

She had thrown herself at me. It was the beginning of deliverance. The catastrophe was finally being born. I had pulled it out of myself. To have it there was a relief. Anguish would soon be packing up its bags. I heard a grandiose orchestra full of cymbals and gongs traveling ominously from one end of the horizon to the other.

At this point, her hands were screaming at me. It was soothing. But the weather was becoming agitated. The light, growing weak, had rolled itself up into a ball. I didn't say anything, I didn't do anything. She flung an inferno of words into the middle of the room.

"To think that I'm killing myself for that. She's going to land us in the street. A brand new umbrella. The finest one in the whole city. That creature doesn't deserve half of what's done for her. Anybody else would dump her at the orphanage. She's got no feelings, no guts. Numbskull! A real numbskull!"

She was shaking me by the shoulders, by the arms. She jerked me forward, then backward. She threw me on my side. With every gesture, she sent me to the orphanage, but she didn't let go of my arm. . . .

The first bolt of lightning brought some relief to the room.

I hadn't put down my satchel: it was all I had. She tore it from my arm. It fell. I cried out.

"Are you going to shut up? She'll do anything for attention, this kid. If the neighbors hear you, you're going to get it. . . ."

She was roaring at me.

My pencil box fell open and everything inside scattered across the floor. This little chaos annoyed her more. I tried to pick the things up. She grabbed my wrists.

"If you move, I'll beat the living daylights out of you."

A nasty rain stabbed at the earth.

She let go of me. From a distance, her gaze destroyed my face. Her features took on greater definition. Anger highlighted her bone structure.

She had me under surveillance. She didn't ask for any explanation. She didn't have the time for that. She closed the window that had no curtains.

"This time, you're going to get it. Get over here!"

I went. She was waiting, as peacefully as a police commissioner who's toying with abominations. . . .

She began her same task over again. She kept saying words, words, words, and I died in between each one. Or, in the spaces between the words, I became the worst of assassins: the imaginary assassin.

I fell at her feet, my cheek resting on the tip of her patent leather shoes.

"Don't touch me, you idiot. . . ."

My cheek drew comfort from the smooth tile.

A passionate rain was falling. In the gutters, the water was exulting.

She had lifted me up by the lapels of my dress, rather than stooping to my height. I became her own personal scoundrel.

"Tell me what happened. If you don't . . ."

"Stop it!"

"She'd be the death of you, this one would. . . ."

The orchestra made up of cymbals and gongs was circling the house. In between our cries, you could hear a whole rumble of arguments from the sky.

"To think that I'm making myself sick for that!"

I was responsible for her agitation.

"Stop!"

Finally, my tears reached a decision.

She made me turn and twist like our little lilac bush at the end of the garden, caught in the storm. I bent over and straightened up in time to the movements of the plant. My tears were everywhere, like the drops of water falling from the lilac leaves in the form of a heart. . . . I was exhausted. She who receives the blows suffers in addition the infernal fatigue of the one who delivers them.

The orchestra of cymbals and gongs was no longer a ribbon stretched across the horizon. It was in front of us, all-powerful with explosions that resembled imprecations, arguments that lashed at our ears. . . .

I didn't dare look at her. She might have been disheveled. . . .

We were attending a tournament of lightning bolts. In the roof gutters, it was an orgy.

I didn't see the lilacs straighten up. I no longer saw anything at all. Her task was timeless. The downpour became eternal. Light was hanging by a thread. . . . Then sorrow took me in hand. It was a sap that circulated inside me like the water in the gutters. . . . I forgot my mother and myself by crying for both of us with all my strength. I was swollen with sorrow.

I was being born once again.

Something else had escaped. A ray of new light illuminated the corner cupboard. The orchestra of cymbals and gongs was on its last legs. The storm was already falling to pieces.

Grandmother arrived in the company of the fresh air.

Had I forgotten about her? No, but in the worst moments, I didn't think about her. When she would come in one door, bad things would leave by the other. . . . That day nothing could stop my mother. She was still shaking me. Grandmother separated us. Consternation ran over her face, her skin like an exposed nerve. Her sadness was too big for her.

Looking at me, she apologized. "I was waiting for the end of the storm. We were writing down the recipe for rabbit pâté. . . ."

My mother shrugged.

"Do you know what this numbskull did?"

"No. I just got here."

"She went and lost her umbrella. Don't you think she should be hanged?"

I stared at Grandmother. I waited. My tears were flowing and were not noticed.

"You buy her things that are too fancy for her age. You're going to make her sick. Go lie down. You're going out for lunch. . . . You look awful."

This song of common sense rose up like a stream of water from a fountain. It covered me in light. Grandmother understood. My mother was looking at me, her face inscrutable.

"Are you telling me that she's not crazy, and are you telling me that she has feelings. . . ."

The bell rang.

"I'm not here for anyone," my mother said, exasperated.

"What if it's him?"

"I'll meet him downtown."

It was him.

"I'm going upstairs to dress. I'm getting out of here. This place disgusts me. . . ."

She slammed the door, telling my grandmother that the chicken was burning in the oven.

Grandmother opened the window.

"The lilac bush is broken."

"How do you know?"

I showed her my little finger. I loved her. I didn't tell her everything.

"You'd better look at the chicken." I wasn't hungry but I was afraid of another explosion. . . .

She was taking her time.

"Tell me where it hurts."

"Let's not talk about it."

I didn't tell her everything. Neither did she. There was restraint between us. It was almost perfect. She ran her hands over me anyway. I said no everywhere.

"I don't think things are going well with him. It's because of that. . . . She's not getting what she wants. . . ."

During the storm, I had thus served as a double for the man who would not give in.

"I'm going to take care of the bird. . . ."

It was true that the smell from the kitchen was demanding attention. Alone, I picked up my pencil box. It seemed to belong to a past world. I wasn't listening to the end of the storm, which was dragging itself away. In the corner by the cupboard, there was a large pool of light. I was becoming feverish the way one does before leaving on a trip. . . . Grandmother came back.

"You'll go back to school at three o'clock. When she's gone, we'll eat whatever you want outside."

". . ."

"Pull your chair closer."

We turned our back on the garden. She said that we'd take advantage of it later. For the moment, we listened, we took deep breaths. Scoured, the sky was a tapestry woven with the songs of birds. One of them was holding its little service at the edge of a tree trunk. . . . The convalescent sun warmed the back of our necks. I pressed my cheek against her shoulder covered in shiny black cotton. I rested my hand on her worn-out woman's knee. Time flowed like milk.

She appeared and disappeared. She had rearranged her face. She was pleased with herself.

"You're sitting in a draft."

She slammed the door. That's what we were waiting for.

We could allow ourselves anything. I took Grandmother by the hand.

"Promise me that you'll go along with me."

"Promise me that you're all right."

She was my savior and my companion. I led her into the garden. Her hand trusted mine. I led her to the shed. I took out the tools and told her to wait for me. I came back with a chair. She settled into her kingdom. I had turned several flower pots upside down. I rested her feet on them. This way, she wouldn't get wet if another storm drenched our vegetables. . . .

I saw the strawberries that were arching their backs like a cat under the curve of the leaves. I picked a lot of them. I sliced some bread, I crushed the fruit on the bread. I sprinkled some sugar and arranged the slices on a fancy plate. Holding it, I ran.

"If you break it, we're finished!"

But happiness isn't clumsy.

We ate looking at the garden. It looked worn out. As for the earth, the storm had made it plump. It was spilling over onto the teary-eyed lettuce. Two newborn worms decorated a cabbage. The green peas and their leaves looked like a carefully destroyed forest. The stalks of the onions were prostrate. The shallots' braided stems were crawling in the mud. Invincible, the thyme, safe and sound, tickled our sense of smell.

We quenched our thirst with clusters of currants.

It wasn't enough.

The garden path was lined on each side with rose bushes. Their red flowers would still be in bloom on All Saints' Day. At the height of a frost, while the grass in the lanes was begging for pity, the thorny leaves would fight on. . . . Today, I saw drops of brightness on the roses. The rain had tired them out a little.

"Will you let me do what I want?"

"Yes."

"Completely?"

"Yes."

Before beginning, I kissed her: I threw myself into an adventure.

"Come back quickly."

She followed me with her eyes. I was as light as a feather. . . . First I picked the biggest flower. I held it like an altar candle. I was careful to give it to her with its shining drops of rain still on it. She looked at it and rested it on her lap.

"Put it on, Grandma!"

"I'm too old. . . ."

I thought she was younger than the whole world, but I didn't know how to tell her.

I picked them with the same fierceness that would grip me when I stole alfalfa for our rabbits. . . . I left only the saddest. I

had placed them in my petticoat in order not to soil my dress. I
prepared my move. I managed to throw them all at once into the
hollow that she had readied between her knees.

We bent down at the same time. I rubbed my face against the
petals. All she did was lean her head on mine. From under this
tender protection, I breathed in the perfume that threaded its
way deep inside me. The sparkling wetness refreshed my lips, my
eyelids, the lobes of my ears. . . . My idea exploded.

"Let's run away, Grandma."

She didn't say no. Her breath full of illness fanned my hair.

"Someone's at the door!"

"Go open it! I can't move with all this. . . ."

She called after me. "Ask who's there."

It was the neighborhood dwarf.

Grandmother had closed the door to the shed and arranged
the flowers on the ground. She was protecting our kingdom.

"I came to tell you that my rabbit pâté is in the oven. If you
want to take a look. . . ."

"Not really," Grandmother answered, perhaps thinking of our
impossible escape.

"You seem strange. . . . It's true that storms affect people of
our age. . . ."

The dwarf denied the idea of her own with grotesque
coquettishness.

"You're not saying a word. It's clear that the storm has upset
you."

Grandmother was contemplating the ballet being performed
by the laundry that was drying, dancing, supplicating in our
neighbors' garden.

"Grandma, she's talking to you."

Would the dwarf give birth to yet another sentence belonging to the world of women?

"... I was thinking about the most beautiful day of my life. ..."

"Tell us about it," pleaded the dwarf. "Was it a long time ago?"

"Today."

"You're not going to try to make me believe that a recipe for rabbit pâté will have been the best day. ..."

The dwarf wavered between frustration and pride. "It's true that a recipe like this can't be found just anywhere."

"I had forgotten it," my grandmother confessed.

I didn't know what to do with myself. The tiny woman remained still. Time grew thin. Grandmother was dreaming and was keeping nothing back. I didn't understand that I had transfigured her.

"Today, I have been completely fulfilled. ..."

"You're raving. ... You're too old for. ..."

"Today I have no age."

The dwarf stamped her foot.

"You're getting on my nerves with your mysteries."

Our happiness inspired me. "We picked these for you."

She kissed me. Her soft mustache made me gag.

"You emptied your garden for me?"

"Your recipe was worth it," my grandmother added, finally giving me a hand.

"... Flowers. This is the first time it's happened to me. ..."

I looked at her face, transformed by a secondhand gift. I had just sown happiness everywhere.

"I have to run. I can smell the pâté from here."

The dwarf carried away the flowers. She looked like a florist's assistant setting off to make a delivery in town.

We went back inside. Memories simmered in the room. The cherry cupboard was radiant, an example to follow. I thought about school. Grandmother said she would come wait for me when it was over.

On the way, I avoided the Mons plain. In the sky, in the air, there were only peaceful victories. Awnings threw their shade on the sleepy stores. The afternoon was resting on its laurels.

I was questioned. I said that I had had to pick up medication for the dwarf. I didn't see Mandine. Was the "one little minute" I had asked for responsible for her absence? The thought didn't disturb me in the least. Another pupil had been put in my place.

"You, the twins, move apart. She'll sit between you. . . . You'll keep an eye on her. . . ."

I settled down between my two police agents. I was in equilibrium like a clock between two candle sticks. One shined with intelligence and effort, the other with an extraordinary gift for drawing. We were reviewing the Crusades. I simply crossed my arms across my chest. The brunette noted my red eyes. She pressed herself against me. She didn't ask me anything but made horrible faces to cheer me up. When she stopped, she followed the effect of her remedy on my face.

"You've just dropped down six places," the teacher announced.

It was a matter of indifference to me, since I was roaming through other worlds. . . .

The blond twin, with her face like a poem, her clear, moonlit skin, was better behaved. The historic dates that came from her lovely lips disgusted me even more. . . .

The brunette had turned a visiting card over on her book. While the teacher wrote on the board, she drew. She didn't hold her pencil as we did. She didn't suck on it. She used it for quick, catlike scratches. Those jolts, those stormy gusts of lines created an elegant lady whose feet were smaller than an accent mark. At times, the pencil skipped over the page with fervor, at times it slipped into the pleats of the skirt only to reappear impassioned.

She turned the background into velvet with an intense blue and
put the card in my pocket. I was overwhelmed, as my grandmother had been. I saw clouds made of fluffed-up egg whites.
Chubby-cheeked, fringed with a paler froth, they recalled a
band of young boys off on an escapade in the sky. If only I could
offer her that on a visiting card! I was able to thank her out loud,
under cover of the chorus braying historical dates. . . .

"Who goes by Mandine's house?"

I raised a finger.

"You'll go ask for news."

"Why?"

"Why? You want to know why? You're not going."

Another girl raised her hand.

We went out. Not a single student to give me information.
They were running off to kill time with art lessons. . . . Grandmother wasn't there. The caretaker was supervising everyone as
they left.

"Excuse me, sir?"

He turned his back to me.

"Can you tell me what happened to Mandine?"

"Oh, that girl! . . . She was always running for no reason.
Now she's learned her lesson."

Grandmother was coming.

"I have to go, sir. Tell me what happened to her."

"You're giving me orders? Don't bother me, I'm working."

"I'll tell you," said Grandmother.

She had brought our afternoon snack in a closed basket.

— "What happened was she was run over. They may be able to
save her leg. . . ."

Stupefied, I became stupid. "She won't be able to run anymore?"

"Don't ask questions like that. . . ."

It was the one and only question for Mandine. We were headed toward the Rhonelle Gardens.

"We'll think of her as we walk," said my grandmother, who, being late, had put her hat on crooked, an old nest of shining straw.

I held the basket. She carried my school bag under her arm.

Translated by Naomi Holoch

Anchee Min

Anchee Min's Red Azalea *(1994) is a unique exploration of homoerotic relationships between women in modern-day China. Born in Shanghai in 1957, Min was sent to a labor collective, where she was discovered by talent scouts and recruited to work as a movie actress at the Shanghai film studio. She came to the United States in 1984 with the help of the actress Joan Chen. Min's writing is not only an historical breakthrough but a powerful testimony to the complex confluence of desire, culture, and history. Written in an often stark, always compelling language, the novel tells the story of a young woman sent from Shanghai to work on a near-barren farm during the turbulent Cultural Revolution. Amid the paranoia, Red Guards, mandates, and misinformation of the time, the narrator finds herself drawn to her female commander.*

from RED AZALEA

As the daylight faded, I found myself at the farm's brick factory. Thousands of ready-to-bake bricks were laid out in patterns. Some stacks were eight feet high, some leaning as if about to fall, and some had already fallen. I could hear the echo of my own steps. The place had the feel of ancient ruins.

One day there was another sound among the bricks, like the noise of an erhu, a two-stringed banjo. I picked out the melody—

"Liang and Zhu"—from a banned opera; my grandmother used to hum it. Liang and Zhu were two ancient lovers who committed suicide because of their unpermitted love. The music now playing described how the two lovers were transformed into butterflies and met in the spring again. It surprised me to hear someone on the farm able to play it with such skill.

I followed the sound. It stopped. I heard steps. A shadow ducked by the next lane. I tailed it and found the erhu on a brick stool. I looked around. No one. Wind whistled through the patterned bricks. I bent over to pick up the instrument, when my eyes were suddenly covered by a pair of hands from behind.

I tried to remove the hands. Fingers combatted. The hands were forceful. I asked, Who is this? and there was no reply. I reached back to tickle. The body behind me giggled. A hot breath on my neck. Yan? I cried out.

She stood in front of me, smiling. She held the erhu. You, was it you? You play erhu? I looked at her. She nodded, did not say anything. Though I still could not make my mind connect the image of the commander with the erhu player, I felt a sudden joy. The joy of a longing need met. A lonely feeling shared and turned into inspiration. In my mind, I saw peach-colored petals descend like snow and bleach the landscape. Distant valleys and hills melted into one. Everything wrapped in purity.

She sat down on the stool and motioned me to sit next to her. She kept smiling and said nothing. I wanted to tell her that I had not known she played erhu, to tell her how beautifully she played, but I was afraid to speak.

She picked up the erhu and the bow, retuned the strings, bent her head toward the instrument, and closed her eyes. Taking a deep breath, she stroked the instrument with the bow—she started to play "The River."

The music became a surging river in my head. I could hear it run through seas and mountains, urged on by the winds and clouds, tumbling over cliffs and waterfalls, gathered by rocks and streaming into the ocean. I was taken by her as she was taken by the music. I felt her true self through the erhu. I was awakened. By her. In a strange land, faced by a self I had not gotten to know and the self I was surprised, yet so glad, to meet.

Her fingers ran up and down the strings, creating sounds like rain dropping on banana leaves. Then her fingers stopped, and she held her breath. Her fingertips touched and then stayed on the string. The bow pulled. A thread of notes was born, telling of an untold bitterness. Slowly, she vibrated the string. Fingers dipped out sad syllables. She stroked the bow after a pause. The notes were violent. She raised her head, eyes closed and chin tilted up. The image before me became fragmented: the Party secretary, the heroine, the murderer, and the beautiful erhu player. . . .

She played "Horse Racing," "The Red Army Brother is Coming Back," and finally "Liang and Zhu" again.

We talked. A conversation I had never before had. We told each other our life stories. In our eagerness to express ourselves we overlapped each other's sentences.

She said her parents were textile workers. Her mother had been honored as a Glory Mother in the fifties for producing nine children. Yan was the eighth. The family lived in the Long Peace district of Shanghai, where they shared one wood-framed room and shared a well with twenty other families. They had no toilet, only a nightstool. It was her responsibility to take the nightstool to a public sewage depot every morning and clean the stool. I told her that we lived in better conditions. We had a toilet, though we shared it with two other families, fourteen people. She said, Oh yes, I can imagine your morning traffic. We laughed.

I asked where she had learned to play erhu. She said her parents were fans of folk music. It was her family tradition that each member had to master at least one instrument. Everyone in her family had a specialty, in lute, erhu, sheng with reed pipes, and trumpet. She was a thin girl when she was young, so she chose to learn erhu. She identified with its vertical lines. Her parents saved money and bought her the instrument for her tenth birthday. The family invited a retired erhu player to dinner every weekend and asked him to drop a few comments on the erhu. The family hoped that Yan would one day become a famous erhu player.

She was fifteen years old when the Cultural Revolution began in 1966. She joined the Red Guards and marched to Beijing to be inspected by Chairman Mao at Tienanmen Square. As the youngest Red Guard representative, she was invited to watch an opera, newly created by Madam Mao, Jiang Qing, at the People's Great Hall. She liked the three-inch-wide belts the performers were wearing. She traded her best collection of Mao buttons for a belt. She showed me her belt. It was made of real leather and had a copper buckle. It was designed by Comrade Jiang Qing, my heroine, she said. Have you read Mao's books? she asked. Yes, I did, I said, all of them. She said, That's wonderful, because that's what I did too. I memorized the Little Red Book and know every quotation song.

I told her that I was a Red Guard since elementary school, my experience much less glorious than hers, though I would not be fooled about how much one knew about Mao quotation songs. She smiled and asked me to give her a test. I asked if she could tell where I sang.

The Party runs its life by good policies. . . .

Page seven, second paragraph! she said.

If the broom doesn't come, the garbage won't automatically go away. . . .

Page ten, first paragraph!

We came from the countryside. . . .

Page a hundred forty-six, third paragraph!

The world is yours. . . .

Page two hundred sixty-three, first paragraph!

Studying Chairman Mao's works, we must learn to be effi-
cient. We should apply his teachings to our problems to ensure a
fast result. . . .

She joined my singing.

As when we erect a bamboo stick in the sunshine, we see the
shadow right away. . . .

Where are we? I shouted.

Vice Chairman Lin Biao's Preface for Mao Quotations, second edition! she shouted back, and we laughed, so happily.

. . .

I wrote to my parents in Shanghai. I told them about the Party
secretary, Commander Yan. I said we were very good friends.
She was a fair boss. She was like a big tree with crowded
branches and lush foliage, and I enjoyed the cool air sitting
under her. This was as far as I could go in explaining myself. I
told my mother the farm was fine and I was fine. I mentioned
that some of my roommates' parents had made visits, although
the farm was not worth the trip.

My mother came instead of writing back. I was in the middle
of spraying chemicals. Orchid told me that my mother had
arrived. I did not believe her. She pointed to a lady coated in
dust standing on the path. Now tell me I was lying, she said. I
took off the chemical container and walked toward my mother.
Mom, I said, who told you to come? Mother smiled and said, A
mother can always find her child. I kneeled down to take off her
shoes. Her feet were swollen. I poured her a bowl of water. She
asked how heavy the fungicide-chemical container was. Sixty

pounds, I said. Mother said, Your back is soaked. I said, I know. Mother said, It's good that you work hard. I told her that I was the platoon leader.

Mother said she was proud. I said I was glad. She said she did not bring anything because Blooming had just graduated from the middle school and was assigned to a professional boarding school. Her Shanghai resident number was also taken away. We have no money to buy her a new blanket; she still uses the one you left. It's good to be frugal, don't you think? Mother said. What about Coral? I asked. Will she be assigned to a factory? Mother nodded and said she had been praying for that to happen. But it's hard to say. Mother shook her head. Coral is afraid of leaving. The school people said that if she showed a physical disability, her chances of staying in Shanghai would be much better. Coral did not go to see a doctor while she was having serious dysentery. She was trying to destroy her intestine to claim disability. That was stupid, but we were not able to stop her. A lot of youths in the neighborhood are doing the same thing; they are scared to be assigned to the farms. Coral is very unhappy. She said she had never asked to be born, she said that to my face. My child said that to my face.

I placed Mother in Yan's bed that night. I wanted to talk to my mother but instead fell asleep the minute my head hit the pillow. The next morning Mother said she'd better leave. She said that I should not feel sorry for myself. It shows weakness. And her presence might have increased my weakness and that was not her intention in being here. She should not be here to make my soldiers' homesickness worse. I could not say that I was not feeling weak. I could not say my behavior would not influence the others. I wanted to cry in my mother's arms, but I was an adult since the age of five. She must see me be strong. Or she would not survive. She depended on me. I asked if she would

like me to give her a tour of the farm. She said she had seen
enough. The salty bare land was enough. She said it was time for
her to go back.

Mother did not ask about Yan, about whose bed she had slept
in the previous night. I wished she had. I wished I could tell her
some of my real life. But Mother did not ask. I knew Yan's title
of Party secretary was the reason. Mother was afraid of Party
secretaries. She was a victim of every one of them. She ran away
before I introduced Yan.

Mother refused to allow me to accompany her to the farm's
bus station. She was insistent. She walked away by herself in the
dust. Despite Lu's objection to a few hours' absence, I went to
follow my mother through the cotton field. For three miles she
didn't take a rest. She was walking away from what she had
seen—the land, the daughters of Shanghai, the prison. She ran
away like a child. I watched her while she waited for the bus. She
looked older than her age: my mother was forty-three but
looked sixty or older.

When the bus carried Mother away, I ran into the cotton
fields. I exhausted myself and lay down flat on my back. I cried
and called Yan's name.

The day she was expected back, I walked miles to greet her.
When her tractor appeared at a crossroad, my heart was about to
jump out of my mouth. She jumped off and ran toward me. Her
scarf blew off. The tractor drove on. Standing before me, she
was so handsome in her uniform.

Did you see him? I asked, picking up her scarf and giving it
back to her. Leopard? She smiled taking the scarf. And? I said.
She asked me not to mention Leopard's name anymore in our
conversation. It's all over and it never happened. I asked what
happened. She said, Nothing. We didn't know each other. We
were strangers as before. Was he there? I was persistent. Yes, he

was. Did you talk? Yes, we said hello. What else? What what else? We read our companies' reports, and that was all.

She did not look hurt. Her lovesickness was gone. She said, Our great leader Chairman Mao teaches us, "A proletarian must liberate himself first to liberate the world." She scraped my nose. I said, You smell of soap. She said she had a bath at the head-quarters. It was their special treat to branch Party secretaries. She had something important to tell me. She said she would be leaving the company soon.

I closed my eyes and relaxed in her arms. We lay quietly for a long time. Now I wish you were a man, I said. She said she knew that. She held me tighter. I listened to the sound of her heart pounding. We pretended that we were not sad. We were brave.

She had told me that she was assigned to a remote company, Company Thirty. They need a Party secretary and commander to lead eight hundred youths. Why you? Why not Lu? It's an order, she said to me. I don't belong to myself. I asked whether the new company was very far. She said she was afraid so. I asked about the land condition there. She said it was horrible, the same as here, in fact worse, because it was closer to the sea. I asked if she wanted to go there. She said she had no confidence in con-quering that land. She said she did not know how she had become so afraid. She said she did not want to leave me. She smiled sadly and recited a saying: "When the guest leaves, the tea will soon get cold." I said my cup of tea would never get cold.

Lu turned the light off early. The company had had a long day reaping the rice. The snoring in the room was rising and falling. I was watching the moonlight when Yan's hands tenderly touched my face. Her hands soothed my neck and shoulders. She said she must bear the pain of leaving me. Tears welled up in my eyes. I thought of Little Green and the bookish man. Their joy and the price they paid. I wept. Yan held me. She said she could not stop herself. Her thirst was dreadful.

She covered us with blankets. We breathed each other's breath. She pulled my hands to touch her chest. She caressed me, trembling herself. She murmured that she wished she could tell me how happy I made her feel. I asked if to her I was Leopard. She enveloped me in her arms. She said there never was a Leopard. It was I who created Leopard. I said it was an assignment given by her. She said, You did a very good job. I asked if we knew what we were doing. She said she knew nothing but the Little Red Book. I asked how the quotation applied to the situation. She recited, "One learns to fight the war by fighting the war."

I said I could not see her because my tears kept welling up. She whispered, Forget about my departure for now. I said I could not. She said, I want you to obey me. You always did good when you obeyed me. She licked my tears and said this was how she was going to remember us.

I moved my hands slowly through her shirt. She pulled my fingers to unbutton her bra. The buttons were tight, five of them. Finally, the last one came off. The moment I touched her breasts, I felt a sweet shock. My heart beat disorderly. A wild horse broke off its reins. She whispered something I could not hear. She was melting snow. I did not know what role I was playing anymore: her imagined man or myself. I was drawn to her. The horse kept running wild. I went where the sun rose. Her lips were the color of a tomato. There was a gale mixed with thunder inside of me. I was spellbound by desire. I wanted to be touched. Her hands skimmed my breasts. My mind maddened. My senses cheered frantically in a raging fire. I begged her to hold me tight. I heard a little voice rising in the back of my head demanding me to stop. As I hesitated, she caught my lips and kissed me fervently. The little voice disappeared. I lost myself in the caresses.

Gerd Brantenberg

This selection from Norway, an excerpt from the novel Four Winds *(1989) by the contemporary lesbian-feminist writer Gerd Brantenberg, presents a narrator, Inger, who embodies the profound changes that have occurred since the publication of Ebba Haslund's pioneering work, in the 1950s. In this excerpt, Inger, an eighteen-year-old lesbian, is on her way to Edinburgh, Scotland, to work as a maid. Here, the problem of language faced by Inger is a complex metaphor for crossed boundaries, for lost homes and newly acquired freedoms. Set in northern Europe of the 1960s,* Four Winds, *the final book in a three-volume semi-autobiographical series, portrays a growing passion, a loving but tormented family, and the beginnings of the Scandinavian gay liberation movement.*

from FOUR WINDS

6. ABERDEEN ROAD

I n the bar on the M/S *Blenheim* was a charming Danish woman who was at least thirty. She had fair, curly hair in a casual style, a cigarette holder, and slender silk-stockinged legs, one placed impertinently over the other on the bar stool. On the whole it was simply a matter of bad luck that she hadn't ended up in Hollywood, but instead she had a ruined marriage behind her; she told her whole life history to a young girl on the stool beside her. Straight to the point. The girl also told selected portions of her own: it was clear she'd led a trouble-free life so far. For her part, the girl marveled over how older people can tell the most horrible things to a perfect stranger, but she felt like she'd ended up in the middle of a world adventure already. The bartender poured drinks, and the woman treated. Everything was exciting. But then they neared Horten. Already here the boat was beginning to make some slow sideways movements, back and forth, that made her incapable of following the story of how the lady's ex-husband had tipped over the table on Christmas Eve—with roast pork and everything, she couldn't catch all the details of the menu. "Have a whiskey, honey! It's good for the waves!" the lady said, and the girl believed her. She downed whiskey and drank toasts with the lady, who by now was in the middle of an attempted strangling off the Atlantic coast, and as they rounded Færder Lighthouse, there was only one possibility in the whole world. The toilet.

Inger didn't see anything more of her fellow passengers until she stood, dazed and chilled, in a large, gray hall on Tyne Commission Quay a day and a half later.

The new country was flat and gray with unending railroad tracks, chimneys, tiny lawns with laundry hanging out to dry, and a dark, flat sky above. And suddenly the sea opened up. "Berwick!" called the conductor with rolled r's unlike any English she'd ever heard before, and that's how it was with everyone who said anything. It was as if they had the language inside their mouths; it wasn't supposed to be pronounced clearly! The in*dus*trial revolution.

She walked toward the gate at Waverley Station with the neck of her guitar leading the way. She'd checked the rest of her luggage. Seventeen pieces in all. Why'd she have to bring along her guitar? It seemed completely out of place. A guitar is always out of place until it ends up in your lap at a party. Here there was nothing to indicate a party. A mob of people all hurrying along under the roof of an enormous train station.

"Are you Inger?"

A completely strange lady with gray hair, tweed suit, and large, nervous eyes had suddenly stopped her with this question. Inger had a sudden desire to answer "No" and go home right then. She'd never seen complete strangers before. In Fredrikstad there were no completely strange people. Even the ones you'd never seen before, you had seen. Inger stared at her in terror and hostility. I don't have anything to do with this lady. "Yes," she said, intensely unhappy.

"Is this all your luggage?" the lady asked, still in English. But unlike the others she'd heard, she spoke clearly. "No, it . . . *blirsendt-med-reisegods* . . . it, it, it . . . comes, I mean . . . it."

Where was her English?

"Will it be sent separately?" the lady inquired. "Yes," Inger nodded so hard that her head practically came unhinged, in order to make up for the English she'd studied passionately for seven years and always gotten A's in. Mrs. Mayfield took her bag and marched on brisk half-high heels three steps ahead of her in the direction of the taxi stand.

The taxi drove up a hill away from the station and came immediately up into the city. A castle partially obscured by fog rose toward them. They turned to the right into a horde of burgundy-colored buses with white roofs, everything on the wrong side of the street. "This is Princes Street!" She said it as if it were the most famous street in the world. Inger saw it all through a perfectly nightmarish glow. "This is the Scott Monument." She pointed at a dark sort of Eiffel Tower towering up. "Did you have a good trip?"

"No," Inger replied. "I was . . . was . . . *sjøsyk.*"

"Were you seasick?"

This was dreadful. Her mouth just wouldn't cooperate! And the workers in the coal mines during the industrial revolution in Anglo-American Reader I, II, and III had never been seasick. They had been the subject of the Iron Law of Wages. That wages tend to fall to the lowest level that the most desperate man will accept. Should she say that?

They drove up hill and down on perfectly straight streets, the houses got smaller, they lay in endless rows, in pairs, and all the doors were open. They were green. With a number above. They stopped in front of one with the number 6. They'd arrived! She had reached her goal. Mrs. Mayfield seized her bag and marched ahead of her up the little garden path. Inger had never seen a drearier house.

A chilly and slightly cloying smell confronted her when she came in. She looked in at a long hallway and a staircase. Mrs. Mayfield stopped at the end of the hall; Inger followed her. "Inger, this is your room." And she stood there staring into a closet.

There she saw: a narrow, dark-brown chest of drawers, two straight-back chairs, a bed with a gray-green blanket, and a margarine crate for a nightstand. Through the window she looked out at a wall where there were two gray garbage cans. The land of her dreams, the Edinburgh of her fantasies, sank down inside her and disappeared in the depths of her soul. A year! she thought.

A year?

She was placed behind a mound of mashed potatoes. Now they were to eat "lunch." In the middle of a smell she had never had in her nose before. The family was sitting around the kitchen table. Sheila stared directly at her from across the table with eyes as big as saucers. She gestured with her fork while she talked at breakneck speed with her mother. "Bt wht kn yu du?" she said. Here they had learned all this time that "but" is pronounced "baht" and not "boot," and then it was only "bt." She listened, fascinated. Of all the remarkable things she had seen in this short time Sheila was the most remarkable. She had a prominent mouth, which was red, and small freckles on a nose that was a little bit flat over the root and didn't look the least bit like any of her classmates who'd stood on the steps of the Phoenix.

Adam was small and picked at his food, and Sheila teased him. Glen was tall and skinny in a military-colored shirt and ate without saying a word. The smell was coming from him. "Eat your food, Adam!" Mrs. Mayfield yelled. "Just wait till your daddy gets home!" The daddy, and the one called Duncan, weren't home. They were at the office and at school, respectively. Mrs. Mayfield addressed her son exclusively in the form of threats. Whatever would happen when his father got home was clearly big and terrible. But he continued to pick anyway. "Mummy?" he said, "This meat is rotten." The little mouth was obviously full of imagination. Mrs. Mayfield exploded. "Adam!" she bellowed. "What do you think Inger thinks of you?"

As if she were doing anything of the kind—having an opinion about his potato eating! "She's not eating either," Adam said. Inger's mashed potatoes were now becoming the center of attention. Crushed, she stared down into the potatoey landscape. The North Sea undulated through her now, the first time in two days that she was no longer in motion. Not since Rakel Jonassen's blood pudding in seventh grade home ec class had she felt so wretched.

A disgrace. Here she arrived at a strange house, eighteen years old. And the first thing she did was to not eat up her mashed potatoes. But the alternative was to throw up all over her new family. Mrs. Mayfield removed the potatoes with an expression of disapproval. "H!" she heard clearly. Glen put on some bicycle clips with odd staccato movements. "Cheerio!" he called and disappeared out the door. It was the first thing he'd said. Sheila donned a helmet. Then she disappeared on the motorbike with the same strange word for good-bye. Up to Edinburgh University. She sent Inger a quick glance before she disappeared. Maybe she can't stand me, Inger thought suddenly. Such things happened. You could look at a face for half a second and know that you couldn't stand the person. In that case I'm certainly not going to stand her either.

The first thing Inger did in her new job as maid was to burn a hole in some rubber gloves. She was supposed to put them on to remove a red-hot grate in the stove in the kitchen so that she could rake out the old embers and pour on more coal. This was supposed to be done with the poker, not with your hands. But who had ever heard of a poker? Inger didn't even know what it was called in Norwegian, and she was certainly not interested in finding out either. But there was a definite possibility it was called an *ildrake*. At any rate she'd burned a hole, and her forefinger hurt like hell. Mrs. Mayfield stared at the result. "They were brand new!" she exclaimed. The burned finger didn't interest her in the slightest. "Do you know what?" she continued in a threatening way. "We've had eight girls in this house, and none of them have wrecked more than *three* things in a whole year. How is it going to go with you when you already start wrecking things on your first day? If you wreck more than three things, you'll have to pay for them yourself."

"Wreck" was *ødelegge*. She didn't know what the word for *salve* was. She just stood there smarting.

At six o'clock in the evening supper was to be eaten in the living room. It faced the street, and through the windows you could look out at all the other gray houses, in pairs, mirror images, just like this one. Mrs. Mayfield couldn't stand her next-door neighbors. They had dogs.

The supper table was set—large, dark brown, and polished—with blue-flowered cups and plates on a trolley next to the table. The trolley. "Inger, come here!" Inger was not used to tables.

Papa would usually eat his dinner standing—with his plate on top of the refrigerator. Mrs. Mayfield showed her how she should put one and a half teaspoons of sugar in the teacups on the trolley, and three spoonfuls in Daddy's cup. Daddy's cup was twice as large as the others and rounder. She looked at it with all the jealousy and irritation it deserved. "How much do you eat for supper?" Mrs. Mayfield inquired. What kind of food? Don't I just help myself? I eat until I am full. Five pieces of rye-krisp with cheese, thanks. And a cola. "Ah . . . I . . . maehhh . . . what?" she said. "Well, Sheila and I eat three half slices of toast for supper and two half slices for breakfast." Inger thought that sounded like much too little. "I will . . . eat . . . yes . . . that . . . thank you, yes, too," she said. "And you can have butter on one of the slices, and margarine on the other two, and if you have jam, you can't have butter, too," Mrs. Mayfield said. "A ha," Inger said. "'A ha' is very bad language in this country, Inger." "A ha? . . . I mean . . . is it that?" "It certainly is." "But, but." "You do want to learn to speak properly, don't you?" "Yes," Inger replied, and missed the Norwegian word *jo,* which she needed to answer a negative. A kind of *jo*-hole appeared. Now she would have to learn to say "yes" through the *jo*-hole.

Daddy Mayfield arrived home. With bowler hat and vest and gold watch and long, contented steps across the floor, he stretched out his hands toward her before he even got through the door. "Aaaaaaaah!" he said. "Here's our new Norwegian girl!" She liked him immediately. He gripped her hand warmly and sat down at the end of the table. "And has she had a good trip?" he asked, to Mrs. Mayfield. "She was seasick, poor thing," says Mrs. Mayfield, to Mr. Mayfield. Then she looked over at Inger. "Isn't that so, Inger?" "Yes," said Inger through her *jo*-hole.

Mrs. Mayfield doled out fried ends of sausage and bacon from her end of the table and passed them around. Toast wasn't the only thing on the menu. Daddy interrogated his family one by one. What had they done today? They only spoke when he addressed them. Finally he drummed his fingers on the tabletop. Little Adam hopped down from his chair, ran over to a cupboard in the corner, and took out a can. Then he dug out a chocolate biscuit. He ran over to his father with it—with great bashfulness and much squirming. Then he darted back to his mother.

Daddy Mayfield slowly chewed the biscuit in front of the family. It was a chocolate biscuit wrapped in red paper and foil with a tiny jack of clubs diagonally across. Inger used all her strength to keep from looking at the biscuit. Envy crept in from the top of her head to the bottoms of her feet. The biscuit was called "Clubs." Daddy chewed on. No one else got one.

"Well," said Mrs. Mayfield to Inger after they had cleared the table and done the dishes. "You are here as a daughter of the house. That means that the same rules apply to you as they do to Sheila, so I might just as well acquaint you with them right now. You must be home at half past ten at the latest during the week and ten o'clock on Sundays. You must wash your clothes once a week, and you're not allowed to go to the International Club, and you're not allowed to go out with Negroes."

We'll see about that, thought Inger. She doesn't know who she has in her house.

THE LANGUAGE AND THE GIRL

If Inger had known beforehand how awful it was to go abroad, she never would have gone. But now she was here. Abroad one had to vacuum on three stories—with "the sweeper" and "the Hoover," respectively. She surveyed them with deep contempt the first morning when Mrs. Mayfield hauled them out of a broom closet under the stairs. Mrs. Mayfield had a small, round, and distinctly low-sitting rear end. The sweeper was a yellow thingamajig with roller-thingies underneath. The Hoover was a vacuum cleaner with a brown bag along the handle. I'm leaving, thought Inger. She was also given the "mopper." The mopper was a long handle with a bristle at the end, the type that until now she had only seen in the movies. So she had labored under the misconception that the tool was a joke. Marilyn Monroe dusting her pink telephone.

There were lots of things she'd thought were a joke that now turned out not to be. She stood in the drawing room upstairs and was filled with a dizzying boredom at the thought of the year ahead of her. The only thing that helped her were the Fredrikstad eyes. They were in the ceiling and in the walls and everywhere and followed her with unbelieving looks. Then they immediately died laughing.

"Don't you have an apron?" Mrs. Mayfield said. Inger stared stupidly at her. The Fredrikstad eyes eagerly followed along.

"An *apron?!*" Mrs. Mayfield repeated more loudly, as if the very sound of the word indicated its meaning. The appalling fact dawned simultaneously on her and the entire population of Fredrikstad: she'd gone out into the world without an apron!

"Dust the house every day," Mrs. Mayfield said. Dust, dust, dust. Dust! If only she could see it! But everywhere she saw nothing but bright, shining surfaces. She was to use the Hoover upstairs on Monday, the sweeper downstairs, the sweeper upstairs on Tuesday, the Hoover downstairs, and the sweeper and the Hoover and the Hoover and the sweeper. But in the attic (a room concealed by a closet door one flight up) she was only to use the sweeper, because the cord on the Hoover wasn't long enough to reach up here.

She always knew what date it was. It was one day less until the day she was going home. She missed Mama and Papa. The longing sank down inside her like something heavy and unbelievable as soon as she was alone in her room. They weren't there. She

wanted to go to them and tell them everything. They were waiting. And then they weren't waiting. She couldn't go to them.
For the first time in her life there was no living room to go into
where Mama and Papa were sitting.

From one day to the next she was reduced to a nobody. It
would've been much better for everyone concerned if she'd had
a little more training in this. But she had no experience as a
nobody. There she had stood with her diploma. She knew that
Hargreaves had invented the spinning jenny in 1764, she knew
what a turnpike road was and that England and Scotland were
united in The Act of Union in 1707. But she had no idea what a
clothespin was called in English. Or a faucet. Or a garbage can.
And in point of truth, that was all she had use for when she came.

She dusted the twelve bannister posts from upstairs to downstairs, and it was especially in these posts that infinity lay. From
now on my value lies in my ability to remove dust, she thought.
What a waste! What a waste of me!

She looked up in amazement. She'd thought her first English
thought.

Rosenkål was called Brussels sprouts. Who would have dreamed
that? Cauliflower was also funny. The "caul" came before the
flower. She'd come to learn the language. And already after three
weeks she had learned a large number of new words and expressions. She knew now that a *klesklype* was called a "clothes peg,"
søppelbøtte a "pig pail," and she knew that an *utslagsvask* was
called a "sink"—and every Friday the ash bucket was set out on
the sidewalk to be emptied, and this was called "to put the
bucket out" (not "to put out the bucket"), and *vannkran* was
called a "tap," *komfyren* was called the "cooker," *rødbeter* were
called "beetroot," and the Hoover and the sweeper, and the
sweeper and the Hoover, do the drawing room, do the fireplace,
do the potatoes, do, do, do, put, put, put, put the garbage out,
put it there, the silver goes in the dining room, thank you Inger,

but more than all these things, and beyond them, and from the first moment in this new country, she'd heard one expression, and this expression was: It's not suitable.

It's not suitable. She knew what it meant, and it wasn't because this expression wasn't used in Norway, didn't frequently march triumphantly in all its oppressiveness through Nygaards-gata, but nothing that was said in the small-town gossip there by the mouth of the river could measure up to the reprimanding and eternal expression: It's not suitable.

Adam came. He said: "Why, Mummy?" He asked Why about everything, like all children on earth, and his constant protests were a great comfort. "Why do I have to eat up my food, and why is the sky blue?" Mummy heard Adam's questions, and she said, "Because *I* say so. Now, don't be a nuisance! That's the way it is. Wait till your Daddy comes home. Now don't argue. It's not suitable."

Inger learned. She was learning English so fast that it made her head spin. And it sent shivers down her spine.

Glen was sitting there eating. The smell didn't come from him. It was the gas. She knew that now. She just associated it with him. He shouted his messages across the table: "Bread, please! Tea, please!" with a wavering look, and a blush washed over his face. This boy was not like other boys. He never looked his father in the eyes. In the evenings he'd sit sewing on an enor-mous needlework project. "What's it going to be?" Inger asked. "A rug!" he shouted despairingly into the fireplace. Then he didn't say any more. Inger soon realized that he was backward. That's what it was called if someone acted like that in Fredrik-stad. "He's nervous" was all Mrs. Mayfield said. It was not to be discussed. That wouldn't be suitable. Every morning he ate breakfast by himself in the kitchen, because he went to work early. Inger met him every morning on her way to the coal bin. "Where do you work?" she asked. "In Bruntsfield Park!" he

answered. But he was a little calmer now. When his father spoke
to him his entire face was aflame.

Sheila dashed in. "I'm fed up with this house. Hell's bloody
teeth." Entertaining expressions poured out of her mouth. Hell's
bloody teeth. Inger laughed enthusiastically. "Stop it, Sheila. It's
not suitable," Mrs. Mayfield said. But Inger thought it was
awfully suitable. She suddenly needed Sheila to like her face. It
was no use that she'd decided from the start that she wasn't going
to like Sheila one whit more than Sheila liked her. She liked her.
She saw her. She stuck her head with its crash helmet and
slightly prominent mouth through the door. She had on long,
green stretch pants, or a dark plaid skirt, and a multicolored
striped scarf from Edinburgh University behind her. The colors
indicated the college. She flung the crash helmet onto the table
with a bang.

"Oh bloody hell! I'll freeze to death on that bike one of these
days. Look at these legs! They're all purple!" Inger wanted to
answer. She was burning to answer: "No wonder your legs turn
purple when you drive that bike in silk stockings!" But the sentence hit a dead end at the expression "No wonder." Strange
how you could need such a little expression so much. And she
suddenly realized that no matter how many English words she
might manage to heap up in her mouth, it'd be so clumsy and
would take so long that the joke would collapse. She had to face
the horrible fact: she was incapable of making her laugh.

Getting girls to laugh at school during recess, boys to howl
over their desktops—that had been life's greatest and most natural pleasure, in the middle of a life where otherwise you were
too fat or had no luck with boys. And there she stood, with "No
wonder" like a clump of cold mashed potatoes in her throat.

But Sheila didn't let that bother her. She was always full of
ideas and was almost always in a good mood, and she was one of
those people who could keep a conversation going indefinitely,

asking lots of questions, which she answered herself, you didn't have to contribute a thing. She was tall with reddish curls that she rolled up on curlers every evening, and she had these large, merry, yellow-brown tinderbox eyes that looked straight at Inger, and she said: "Oh, Inger! You're lucky! You get so many letters! You get letters every single day. I never get any!" And Inger said: "That's because I write them."

This was her first decent, witty reply. She was proud and happy. Sheila answered: "Well, then. No wonder you get them."

No wonder! That was how you said it! No wonder! Never again would she be stumped by "No wonder." No wonder, you could say. No wonder.

This was a wonder.

Sheila's words ran incessantly through her head. When she wasn't there, Inger still heard her. It was a remarkable phenomenon, and she looked forward—to the daughter of the house coming home.

It took some time before she realized that was what she was doing. That she was actually doing it all the time. And when the daughter of the house *was* home, she was simply and unexpectedly happy.

One afternoon Sheila couldn't find her gloves. Inger saw them on the desk and made throwing motions to her, because she was standing in the other end of the kitchen, but since she couldn't think of the right English word for throw, she shouted *"Fakk!"*

Sheila got just as red as she had when Inger had handed her the sanitary napkins the week before. "You must NEVER say that when Mummy is listening, Inger! It's not suitable." "But what's wrong?" "That word!" *"Faak?"* "Oh, stop it!" "But it's Norwegian! . . . it means . . . to, to, to receive!" "Well it means something entirely different in English." "But what does it mean?" "It means to sleep with someone," Sheila said.

Finally Inger understood that what she had stood there shout-

ing was nothing less than to fuck. "Fuck!" she had yelled, innocently. "So what do you say?" she asked. "Catch!" "Oh, *ja,*" said
Inger, "you should hear what the past tense of that word sounds
like in Norwegian." "Caught?" Sheila said. "Yes," said Inger,
laughing. "But what does it mean? What? What? Don't stand
there making fun of me." "It means to . . . to . . . to . . . ," Inger
said. How could you translate *kåt? Kåt* was *kåt* and nothing but
kåt. "It means to . . . *want* to sleep with someone," Inger said.

Now they both laughed. Stood there not going anywhere.
Sheila threw off her jacket. "Ish! I don't feel like going to the
university this afternoon. Let's have some dirty words! What is
'fuck' in Norwegian?" Inger said the word, and Sheila repeated
it. It sounded comical in an English mouth. "It's a swear word in
English. Fuck off." "Not in Norwegian. You don't fuck off
unless you are really fucking off." "What's bloody?" "*Blodig.* But
we don't swear with that, either." "But aren't there any dirty
words in Norwegian then?" "Sure there are. *Faen i helvete!*"
"*Faen i helvete,*" repeated Sheila. "What does that mean?" "The
devil in hell."

Now they got around to sexual organs. But when they got to
the female ones they got quiet. Sheila didn't want to say the English ones, and Inger didn't want to say the Norwegian ones.
Fitte, thought Inger. Cunt, thought Sheila. And they were quiet.

This—the most wonderful place on the whole body, where
all life began, had—on both sides of the North Sea—the worst
and most unmentionable name of all. Here there was no difference. The other things you could and couldn't say were ridicu-
lously different in the two languages. But here they merged into
a single gigantic linguistic disgrace. Cunt and *fitte.*

The two girls looked at each other. They'd been through
everything. And here they stood. They looked down. Then they
whispered their words. Sheila and Inger whispered the names of

their sexual organs. For that was the worst thing that could be said, so it was amazing that it had any sound at all. And the strange thing was that the word that wasn't their own country's word, they could easily say out loud, without scruples and disgrace.

And this was how Inger managed to hold out at 6, Aberdeen Road.

Translated by Margaret Hayford O'Leary

Esther Tusquets

In her novel The Same Sea as Every Summer (El mismo mar de todos los veranos, _1978), which is excerpted here, the Spanish writer Esther Tusquets creates a complex portrait of a sexual relationship between a university professor and one of her female students. Born in Barcelona in 1936, Tusquets is one of the most influential feminist writers in contemporary Spain. Although the novel appeared at a time that encouraged more liberal attitudes toward homosexuality and women's rights, it nevertheless created controversy, given the primacy and explicitness of its lesbian content. These excerpts evoke the life of a previous student generation as seen through the eyes of an older woman in search of remembered vigor; her liaison with a young Colombian woman, Clara, draws her into the passion of the "New World."_

from THE SAME SEA AS EVERY SUMMER

am behind the desk—definitely on the other side—on the platform, and just by stretching out my hand, I can touch the blackboard at my back. And a little farther, between the blackboard and the first of the high windows, a relief map of Spain. Greens and ochers attenuated by the dust of a thousand years. I didn't believe that they still made this type of map, although it is very possible that it is the same one from back then, useless and forever forgotten between the blackboard and the first window, because the strange thing about my return this October—this time on the other side of the desk and on the platform—is not the things that have changed, the uncontrollable outrage of time, of so many years, of almost thirty years—I returned to the university after almost thirty years and everything was, of course, very different!—the surprising thing, the incredibly strange thing, is that here—as in the shadowy well of the library—almost nothing has changed. You wake after centuries with the prescribed words already on the tip of your tongue: "Where am I? What does all this mean?" You are ready to glance around with astonished wonder, but the glance of astonished wonder happens by itself, only in this story what produces it is that you are in the same place and among the same objects as when you went to sleep, because in the Enchanted Forest everything has slept while you slept for the very same one hundred years, everything has slept under the influence of a good fairy so that you won't feel uncomfortable when you awaken. The same benches of dark wood, with inscriptions patiently carved during the drowsiness of the classes—some, many, have probably been added, but surely those from my time are still there, unharmed by possible new coats of paint—the same tender, wavering green behind the panes of the high windows—you don't hear, but you can see the murmur of the trees in the plaza, and just seeing those branches moving up there, it is as if all the warmth of spring were brashly seeping into the still-cold, dark classroom: it was on mornings like these, in the Mays of exam time, when spring murmured outside and inside it was still the worst of winter, mornings in which we were already at the classroom door, about to enter the library or the seminar room, it was on mornings like this one when we would suddenly decide that the very essence of human freedom, the fullness of an existence in which our truest essence was rooted, consisted of something as simple as going out into the street and walking down to the sea (the Ramblas were like a big, green, purring cat, the tip of its tail submerged in the sea), and if we all had not gotten out of bed when the alarm rang, had not dressed and breakfasted quickly (to be there at nine on the dot), had not run the risk of running into the chubby little priest in the hall who supposedly taught us Greek or Latin, because we escaped from class minutes, seconds before the arrival of the teacher (now I am on the other side of the desk, on that grotesque and worm-eaten platform that will fall down any day now, and perhaps I don't recognize the faces of the boys and girls who probably sneaked off toward spring right next to me as I was coming inside and going against the current into winter), if we had not known that there were only three four fifteen days to go before exams and there still remained ten fifteen twenty all the lessons to study, perhaps walking out into the street and down to the sea (first filling our mouths with the taste of a thousand strawberries submerged in whipped cream) would not have assumed that character of a gratuitous, free, almost perfect act, and I believe that in part it was the expression, the words that we liked so much, because cutting class and walking down to the sea sounded good, and at that time, perhaps more than at any other moment in our lives, our performance was influenced by the magic of words and we enjoyed playing our roles as we loudly and disdainfully pushed our way along the shadowy walk, interrupting each other, overdoing poses that we had just learned, often poorly learned at the movies or from books, we acted out an impossible *House of Troy* for the old people who—like the attendant in the library— would look at us reprovingly from their benches, for the women that we almost knocked down on our way and who puffed and snorted like aggressive whales behind their children and their shopping carts, and this was definitely a performance in their honor (young insolent students who cut class and walked down to the sea), then more than ever obliged to present an image, to turn ourselves into a show, to live by words, as if being young did not by chance entail, as it always had and I imagine still does today—because they don't seem so different to me, however much they smoke grass, make love freely—freely?—wear blue jeans and haven't read, don't even know what *The House of Troy* is—lying hours on end in dark rooms behind locked doors, sick from smoking, from literature, from this lethal May air, our bodies limp, restless, and exhausted, struggling clumsily in the sadness and in the anguish that had been pursuing us since adolescence—or perhaps, as in my case, since childhood—and which now, on the verge of disappearing, or at least becoming transformed or toned down, reached its final paroxysm and seemed on the verge of destroying us, poor victims of the greatness and servitude of being only seventeen years old, because among ourselves, in rooms overflowing with smoke and the strumming of guitars, between the cheese sandwiches still associated with our childhood and the Cuba libres of our newfound freedom, we admitted that we were alone and sad and frightened, infinitely bereft of support and direction, but on the street, and especially on the Ramblas, and above all during exam time, if we walked down to the sea, we felt obliged to present this noisy, violent, somewhat irresponsible and insolent image, this image that was brought out in us and then rejected by those unsmiling old people sitting on the benches, the whale women behind their children and baskets. The same benches of dark wood, the same tender, wavering green behind the tall monastic windows, the same platform, worm-eaten and threatened with collapse even then, the same long old desk—as old then as it is now—the same relief map of Spain. All a bit grimy. Worn, grimy, dusty. Cold. Today I feel an urge to go up to the map and run my fingertips carefully along the peaks of the mountain ranges, submerge them in the river basins: if not for this, what is

the purpose of this absurd map, lost forever in a university classroom where geography has never even been taught? But since I
am on the other side of the desk and on the platform—the fact
that I don't really know why or what the devil I am doing here is
another story—since I definitely can no longer fill my mouth
with a thousand strawberries with whipped cream at the farmers' market, because strawberries are almost nonexistent this
year in my insipid city, and where there used to be stands, a sin-
ister supermarket opened a short time ago, since I can't walk
down to the sea, because I have lost my companions and spring
and even the desire to do so, it will be better for me to stay very,
very still at my place, talking to them about something—as soon
as they finish filling out the cards with a few questions that I gave
them simply because I didn't know how to begin today—without giving them an opportunity to take me, now that I have
almost finished the course, for a half-crazy person. In mid-May,
with the trees waving their tallest branches behind the high
monastic windows, with all the murmuring and the stifling sensations of spring in the wide plaza, with the parks more obscene
than ever as the luxuriant new leaves burst forth, with all paths
open to the sea—I wonder if the Colombian girl could be walking along one of them now, or if she is under the magnolia in a
flowering garden, or sitting with the idiots who stayed behind
and are toiling over the cards—it seems absurd to be installed on
the other side of the desk, on the platform, absurd to be here
this morning. But it seems even stranger that they—I repeat that
I don't think they are all that different from us, although they
wear sweaters and blue jeans, have their hair curled or long, their
cigarettes or joints (that certainly has changed) permanently
lit—hand the cards to me one after the other with great seriousness, return to their places, and sit down in silence, their eyes
fixed on me—not on the tall branches—while I began to talk to
them about Ariosto.

. . .

I have finished the repertoire of my stories—although it is only
a feeling, since the stories are almost infinite—I have the feeling,
then, of having finished the repertoire of my stories, stories that
are almost always very similar, and that I renew, revive, and
repeat in the face of each possibility of love, as if loving were
only finding the best of pretexts to recall, or perhaps to invent,
to take dusty old memories out of the closet, to open the costume trunk and to put on the costume of ancient sorrows—at
bottom the same, single sadness—the costume of innumerable,
renewed periods of loneliness that constitute a life, before an un-
tried and perhaps—oh, miracle of love—even remotely interested onlooker, as if loving is a pretext for offering this precious
image of myself once again—you are exaggerating, says Clara,
you aren't so narcissistic—yes, Clara, I am so narcissistic, although
quite possibly I don't even like this image, which I nourish and
spoil, as my father spoiled and tended his image to the end, his
image of a weak-willed, tired man, a bit cynical and perfectly
capable of aesthetic infamies—quite possibly I don't even like
this image of myself—for offering this image in a sad mating ritual that, unlike those associated with many species of fish and
birds, is much grayer and infinitely less showy, and I have already
put on and taken off all my feathers, with their crests and
plumes, I have fluttered my translucent fins and multicolored
tails in warm tropical seas, I have poured upon Clara the bitter-
sweet tide of memories, in the abysmal depths of my grottos—
Clara, the most attentive and exceptional of all my listeners,
because Clara isn't (I have never wanted to say this) one more in
a long line of lovers, and until Clara, absolutely no one came so
close to sharing and taking on my unrecoverable past, so close to
accompanying me in impossible, definitive loneliness—the bit-
tersweet tide of memories that still live, but that may never have

been the way I recall and tell them to her, I have related the fur-
thest, most intimate of my stories to her—except the one that I
have never told anyone until now, that I stubbornly refused to
discuss or comment with anyone, the poisonous one lying hidden in the deepest part of my marshes, throbbing and burning
like a wound that never heals, the story that expelled me, that
destroyed and nevertheless condemned me forever to my
labyrinths, and perhaps I have never told it to anyone, not even
to Clara, because I am incapable of reducing it to a story, of
putting in order and reducing to story form that lethal, interminable injury that in reality marked the end of all stories and
started a gray period consisting only of data, facts, and quotations—I have told my stories, I have put on and taken off my
costumes, I have exhausted all the recesses in my labyrinths and
grottos, and now I am at peace—or almost at peace—with the
ghosts of a past that I have lovingly reconstructed for Clara, or
for myself, taking advantage of the pretext that Clara offered
me, or perhaps I hoped that when I raised my past from the dead
once again, raised it at last for a different listener, it would die
once and for all, would stop wandering about like an unhappy,
sleepless specter, would rest in peace under the flowering
almond tree in the cemetery, because the ghosts are vanishing
and the past is collapsing around us gently and softly, leaving me
empty and calm, while, in this landscape of ruins and remains,
Clara—a laughing Clara who asks, when I finish the story of
Sofía, "Why are you telling me these things? What are you trying to frighten me with or what are you trying to warn me
about? About you? About myself? You know that I will risk it
anyway"—Clara flourishes and relaxes among the ruins; I see a
different Clara emerging in Grandmother's old house, through
which we seek each other and caress each other without respite,
but also without impatience or apprehension, with new, recently learned gentleness, everything surely imposed by this

smiling, expansive Clara who—having annihilated the ghosts of
a past—seems to have taken sure command, because there has
been no repeat of the desolately violent caresses of the first days,
as dreadful as the croak of sea birds lost inland on stormy afternoons, or of the tender brutality on that afternoon when Clara
came to the house and we made love in front of the dying
embers in the fireplace, because now days and nights blur into a
single act of infinitely protracted love, a love that Clara invents
for me second by second—she had to invent it, since neither she
nor I knew that it could even exist—a love devoid of programs
and goals, as tender and clumsy and delicious and wise as that of
two adolescents who might spend centuries engrossed in loving
each other, a love unacquainted with paroxysm or weakness—
there is no before or after—because where pleasure should cul-
minate and desire die, a subtle, voluptuous live ember always
remains, and even when we are both asleep, our bodies continue, rocking, cradling each other, entwined and seeking one
another, and we love each other in dreams or in an interminable
doze, although I don't know whether Clara has truly ever slept
in all these nights and all these days—she assures me that she
has—because when I wake up, there are her wide-open eyes
always spying on me, watching my sleep, her hands and her
mouth are there for me, initiating the caress, her legs ready to
encircle me, and the fact that I may feel sleepy or hungry at
times—that I could feel any other thing that isn't love—constitutes a touching but rather incomprehensible weakness for this
crazy adolescent, and she lets me sleep or brings me food with a
condescending, mocking expression of consent, as if acceding
to the necessities—so different from ours—of a small child or an
earthling who has fallen, poor thing, with all his dead weight
and limitations into a land of undines or Martians, and I am not
sure whether she has slept a single hour in the days and nights
that we have spent loving each other throughout the empty

house, even though, when I ask her, she may assure me that she has, and that only to stop me from bothering her and wasting my time on silly things, and only so I will devote myself entirely to the only important and, especially, the only real thing—loving each other—she hurriedly and indifferently swallows the fruit juices or big glasses of milk with honey that I prepare for her, and only in the face of my insistence does she finally consent to call out and order meat, eggs, bread—solid, disagreeable nourishment for the exclusive use of a famished earthling, because the undine will stubbornly continue living on milk and fruit juice, apparently more compatible with love—although the exterior world—all that remains outside the door of this house—should not exist, and step by step, Clara's will is turning Grandmother's old house into the impregnable castle of Sleeping Beauty, and her desire causes a dense, thick growth of hedge and underbrush to encircle the walls, where the aspirations and curiosity of any violator of our solitude will die; it turns this house by the sea into the monster's palace, in whose rooms and secret gardens the love of Beauty and the Beast triumphs (and now I know that we are both Beauty and we are both the Beast), where no one dares to interrupt or cross the bewitched fence where the white rosebush blooms, the palace inhabited only by invisible servants—I told the cleaning woman not to come these days and the dust is accumulating on the furniture, but it doesn't seem to matter either to Clara or to me—because when someone really feels "my loneliness begins two steps away from you," then the only solution is to wait for a thick wall, for an impenetrable forest to grow around the two lonelinesses magically fused into a single company, and there is nothing to do but wait for eternity to begin right now. And while Clara abolishes external reality with her constant, passionate insistence—if a reality really exists, if anything external could exist—while she keeps away this so-called world that exists on the other side of hedges and

walls and that is alien and perhaps hostile to us, while she bites
her nails and gloomily watches over my short, infrequent phone
calls to Mama and Guiomar—the indispensable ones to keep
them from coming to the house—calls in which I try to explain
that I wanted to stay here for a few days to recover from Grandmother's death or to clear up what they call my "problems with
Julio"—what could they understand by my problems with
Julio?—while she keeps the telephone off the hook for hours
and hours, and she tells Maite—when the poor woman finally
gets through—that I am not home or that I have died, and
watches the mailman pass by the garden fence with infinite dis-
trust—but Clara, Clara, who would think of writing to me
here?—while she gets rid of the shopkeeper and the cleaning
woman (who has finally come, surprised that we don't need her)
with feverish urgency, as if their mere presence on the threshold
already constitutes a danger, as if she had sniffed out a hidden
fire in some corner of the house and had to run and put it out,
and dismisses them, thrusting exorbitant tips into their hands,
though at other times she forgets to pay them—and they find
themselves on the street without an inkling of what is happening here—while she does all of this, she is meanwhile construct-
ing a different reality: a reality based on words, situated in an
unknown place in time and space—on the other side of the silk
cocoon in which she wraps me—because this is what Clara is
doing: weaving a silk cocoon around me—she is building an
impossible future for both of us, an improbable future that
opposes and prolongs my implausible, perpetually reinvented
past—which sleeps in peace at last under the flowering almonds—
a future to which we will both fly very soon, transformed into
radiant butterflies, a future that could as well be located in the
suburbs of Marseilles as in Colombian jungles, and which at
times seems to unfold in Paris or in New York or even in
Barcelona, but in which we are invariably together, endlessly

together, always loving each other and turning this love into a magic lever that can transform the world, because—Clara has decided—this exceptional love, this love that occurs only once every thousand years, can't end in ourselves, it must also embrace all oppressed people, all sad people, all people downtrodden unjustly, all the lonely people in the world, this love must be capable of carrying us up to unsuspected heights, it must finally lead us to transgress all limits, to violate all norms once and for all, and then to reinvent them, and I am afraid— terribly afraid—that in her fantasies, Clara imagines the two of us in guerrilla uniforms, which certainly wouldn't look bad on her, composing immortal sonnets or the definitive study on Ariosto—between armed raids and terrorist bombs—and caressing each other with caresses newly learned during the respite from combat—our hands still smelling of fresh ink and homemade gunpowder—the old dream of seeing art, love, and revolution joined.

Translated by Margaret E. W. Jones

Karen-Susan Fessel

In her story "Lost Faces" (1996)—translated here into English for the
first time—the German writer Karen-Susan Fessel depicts a contemporary time of love and loss. This story, like the excerpt from The Child
Manuela by Christa Winsloe, has at its creative heart a vision of catastrophe. For Winsloe, it was the encroaching presence of Nazism. For
Fessel, it is a nonhuman foe, an enemy that crosses national boundaries
unseen and unheard. Fessel, who has long been involved in the social
and publishing life of lesbian and gay Berlin, has chosen here to com-
memorate a community besieged by AIDS.

LOST FACES

HEN Erik died, I was lying under the hot sun of Portugal,
letting sand run through my toes, and arguing with Klara about
the origin of energy, or, more precisely, the origin of human
energy: was it by nature earthbound, or was it part of the universe? We could not agree: on the one hand, because we could
not manage to leap over the chasm between faith and knowledge; on the other hand, because we were simply too lazy. Our
argument trickled away into the Portuguese sand, and while
with languid gestures and half-shut eyes we tossed each other
one question or another, Erik died in a white room in the AIDS

section of a Berlin hospital, surrounded by tubes, medical appa-
ratus, vases of flowers, and Sonja.

In the evening, Klara and I would run home from the beach,
along barren salt fields. With every step that took us away from
the sea, the air grew warmer, the heat of the city streamed
against us, oppressing us from a distance; and when we plunged
into the narrow streets, our clothes once again stuck to our bodies. Later we sat in the mild night air, ate fish, drank wine, and in
that way celebrated the lingering decline of our love. At night,
in our stifling hotel room, beneath whose windows at about five
in the morning the street cleaners rattled their barrels, we made
love; after all, we had time, and nothing else to do.

At some time during those days, Janusz, many hundreds of
kilometers away, gathered up his courage and set out on his rusty
bike to ride, for the third time in two months, the long distance
from Kreuzberg to Moabit. He said later that he had already had
a premonition: but what use was that? Premonitions do prepare
you in advance, but they don't make anything easier, and when
Janusz opened the door and saw the other hollow-cheeked face
that had taken the place of Erik's, he was no better armed
against the pain that shot from his spine to his brain and down
again—or was it the other way around? He met Sonja on the
stairs; she held the bag with Erik's things, and Janusz took it
from her and carried it while they went to the exit together, past
the many faces marked by sickness; Janusz recognized most of
them, from other places, from other times, from another world.
He knew one of the nurses too, Sabine: Sabine, who every time
she finishes the five-week-long night shift on the AIDS ward
cannot sleep well. She has bad dreams, she says. She dreams of
the men whom she knows from other places, from places that I
too know. Bars, pubs, discos: places full of life, of life in community. Sabine says she sleeps badly because she always has to
think how all these men whose bony bodies she takes care of

daily, and puts to bed, and gives injections to—how all these
men will die soon and she has to think how many there have
been already, and that there are more and more, so that in
dreams she sees the pubs, the bars, and the discos emptied more
and more, till at last hardly anyone is left, only separate, isolated
figures and a preponderance of women.

In reality of course the pubs and bars are not emptying out;
on the contrary, there seem to be more and more bars and more
and more people in them, but just no longer the same people.
Sometimes when I sit on the stool way back in the corner of my
favorite bar, I discover the back of a head, a familiar shape; a
memory stirs and then I know whose face it belongs to—but
when at last I have a chance to glimpse the face, then it's a
strange one. The other face, the one I was thinking of, that one
is lost. I see lost faces everywhere, and the worst of it is that for
each face that I can remember, countless others come that I can
no longer picture. They are gone, I will never think of them
again, and yet I have known them, these lost faces.

In Adenauer Place as Klara, travel bag over her shoulder, disappeared around the corner, I already sensed that we were
through. Our pleasure in each other had dwindled; it was torn
like a delicate gold chain that one has only recently received as a
gift, hasn't got used to yet, and whose loss therefore is not especially painful. What else did I sense?

Nothing, really. I only wondered what might have happened
during my absence. When Janusz told me on the phone a few
hours later that Erik had died, a feeling of apathy overcame me. It
made me sad and weary, because this was not news, his death was
not an event; it was a process that had long, long been in motion,
and now this was the end. "Oh," I said dully, dull to the core.

We had lost Erik, he had lost the battle, the battle, his life.
Evenings, in the bar, on my stool, I looked around and studied

the people there. For which of them was Erik's face also now lost, a face that one had often seen and recognized and that now was lost. How many would now not think of him ever again? I did not know him well. From a face, he first became a whole person for me when he sat between Janusz and me in Janusz's kitchen and did not want to finish his salad because he was feeling bad again. Janusz took him home, and I stood in the kitchen and hesitated for a while to throw Erik's half-eaten salad into the garbage. It seemed strange to me, in some way unjust. It reminded me of all the salads that he would never again finish eating; in fact, it reminded me of everything that Erik would never eat again. But finally I threw away the rest of the salad.

Janusz went to the burial. Later he told me it had been dreadful, but also beautiful. Dreadful, because none of Erik's relatives appeared; instead, there were a large number of his friends and acquaintances, most of whom in the last weeks had not shown up at his sickbed. Stiff, looking embarrassed, they stood there, and when Sonja—Sonja, who had accompanied Erik from their youth to the very end—broke down in tears, they gathered around her, pitying and dismayed; they formed a circle of silence, and from this circle one or another hand stole out and was laid awkwardly on Sonja's shoulder. But how can one relieve suffering by the act of consoling? And how to relieve one's own bad conscience?

But, Janusz said, Erik's burial was beautiful because one could sense him in the resonant tones of the classical overtures that he had requested; in the three sentences from his journal that someone read in Sonja's place; in the waves of sorrow and remembrance that rolled back and forth among the mourners and was manifested by a sad smile, a hardly noticeable shake of the head. However, at the end, when all was over, the mourners stole away alone or in twos, wordless, without greetings, and even Janusz left by himself, hands in pockets, like a thief who has put his loot back into place so as to conceal his deed.

I met Klara a few weeks later; we went to a disco full to bursting with jolly, laughing men. Heat rose chokingly. Chests were bared, legs in leather rubbed against tight-fitting jeans. Do you feel this energy, said Klara, how it pulsates? This is a small model of universal energy in the purest form of its translation; how can you say that there's a difference between down here and up above, it's all one, isn't it.

I wedged myself between the dancers, threw myself among them and let myself be driven into a cauldron of aging youths and youthful death. I danced passionately, looked at the faces around me, here they were, they were dancing with me, wildly, full of strength still. And then I saw too the other, lost faces. I gathered them to myself one after the other. I danced, I danced the last dance, for Erik, the last dance, for we, I thought, we here below, we are still alive, so long as we dance we are still alive, and you, you live with us. And later I turned and saw Klara, her gaze in the distance, her eyes heavy, I saw sun and sand, from days gone by, a lost happiness, there will come a time when I shall no longer think of it; nevertheless, I did know it.

Translated by Nora Reed

María Eugenia Alegría Nuñez

Born in 1953, María Eugenia Alegría Nuñez, who now lives in the *Cuban seaside village of Varadero, holds a degree in classical philology and describes herself as "new to writing." She is currently working on a collection of short stories that, as she describes it, will focus on "obscure lives with unsuspected talents." This theme is exemplified in her story "The Girl Typist Who Worked for a Provincial Ministry of Culture," which is included here. In these pages, Alegría Nuñez creates a character who innocently subverts the suffocating worlds of bureaucratic constraints and academic pomposity with an irony reminiscent of that found in certain stories by the Uruguayan writer Mario Benedetti.*

THE GIRL TYPIST WHO WORKED FOR A PROVINCIAL MINISTRY OF CULTURE

HE page fell, and the typist never saw where. Completely mesmerized she goes about creating her inexhaustible world of words, between folding screens of paper and a thousand vegetable forms that creep along the colored mosaics, until they pile one version on top of the other in an inconceivable palimpsest of words never uttered but a thousand times heard that will become her work—enormous, endless, forged within the verbal wasteland that she is copying.

She shows the sun her solitude at midday. She drinks sweetened tea that sticks to the table, putting out incessant cigarettes. She had spent so many hours for so many years copying other people's writings that she began to mix her own words in with what she copied, and almost without wanting to or without thinking about it, a work of unexpected splendor was born. A work in which words spill over one another in battles where style decides the victory. Every transcript, every document or memo reaches its destination with unusual errata, words never before placed in that order, precise and brilliant like the rare light that makes them new, unexplored. Nobody knows where they come from, but everyone is thankful for that perfume in the midst of so much dryness.

One weary afternoon under the August sun, a bored and idle poet trapped in a girl typist's body began to collect all the tiresome pages with errata. When she collated them, she was surprised to discover a certain continuity. In obedience to a mysterious textual architecture, dazzling poems, stories, novels, and tales were composed, which were then trimmed down according to the flatness of what those lily white pages said, until only one novel emerged, rising up out of the union minutes, depositions, certificates, speeches, all that monotonous verbiage. It was an exceptional work, only comprehensible to initiates, those who not only knew the impenetrable lingo of official documents but also had the sensitivity to recognize interpolations. After years and years of typing so much verbal stupidity, the reading of the novel grew toward infinity. A new compilation and arrangement of all her office work during that period was necessary. The typist would put all that together carefully, with a few quick stylistic revisions, and from there her brilliant opus would emerge. It surged forth clean and beautiful, full of daring images that sprang from jumbled writings. Her first stories, her long poems that finally found their place in the composition of that one and only novel, created a narrative experience without precedent in the Spanish language. But the name of the author remained unknown. In spite of that notorious Cuban desire to honor individual accomplishments, plus the involvement of the secret services of the police and desperate attempts to track down the transcripts and documents that tumbled out from everywhere, authorship was never determined. Hundreds of girl typists put parts of their own lives and jobs into that tumultuous mass of paperwork circulating ceaselessly through the cultural bureaucracy.

The first interpreters of that body of literature tried hard to clear away what seemed to be pure rubbish. But when their work was practically finished, they doubted it had really been worthwhile. And feared that taking the typist's paragraphs and sentences out of the monotonous bureaucratic texts, was, in fact, some kind of terrible mutilation of that which had occasioned in the first place such a marvelous work. Because it was those very words of transcripts and documents, the endless repetition of the same expressions as in a bad popular song, that had given birth to the luminous ideas from which the typist's radiant poetry had sprung. She was definitely overwhelmed by the tedium but perhaps also bewitched by the rhythm of sentences repeated a thousand times, the same words empty of meaning, the wasted universe created by the colored mosaics, the folding screens of paper, familiar slogans, the incessant music of keys clicking in the office. Because we all know that the reproductive potential of words inundates everything. And when something is said or read or heard, it becomes real, takes on an existence of its own that rises above and finally imposes itself on our direct perception of things and people.

About that time, fierce literary discussions arose among critics until the problem was resolved into two schools, one of which demanded that the bureaucratic hogwash be expunged from the text like a diamond evolving out of carbon. That was called the Diamond School. The other school demanded textual integrity no matter how long the text turned out to be, which in some way vindicated the formality of bureaucratic lingo by recapturing its ritualistic function in society. That was the Ritual School. After many long and heated struggles in symposia, international conferences, and the academic press, the matter came to the attention of the international Spanish-speaking literary market, and several deluxe editions of the Diamond School were published that included the Complete Poetry, Stories, and Excerpts from the Novel with the impressive title of *A Light Shines in the Darkness.* On the other hand, the Ritual School broke all records worldwide with its publication of the Complete Works in sixty thousand volumes, where a select few could enjoy reading about everything that happened in official cultural circles in the Province of Matanzas from the 1970s to the 1990s. Finally all the typist's stories and poems, plus the long and marvelous novel, could be read in their entirety.

But the girl typist herself—sunk in a world of glasses of tea that stuck to tables, putting out incessant cigarettes, reading silly novelettes and watching soap operas—never knew of her anonymous fame, which spread all around the world to the glory of the word.

Translated by Lisa Davis

Ngahuia Te Awekotuku

Representing Aotearoa/New Zealand, Ngahuia Te Awekotuku, the Maori writer, describes herself as part of an extended family of weavers, orators, carvers, storytellers, and cross-dressers. In Tahuri *(1989), her first collection of short stories, Awekotuku portrays the experiences of a runaway Maori girl who, with her own home-grown audacity and cultural wisdom, takes on all the obstacles that threaten her journey to adulthood. The three stories here reflect several of the author's primary concerns: the power of the Maori earth itself and its mythical representations, the potential for violence against women, and the wonder of youthful lesbian lust.*

PARETIPUA

CAME out of the whare. Stood on the step, big and strong. Paretipua. Hair wrapped in a towel. From the bath, from the steam. Hair wrapped in a towel, dark dark blood dark red towel. Wrapped up. On top of her head. Paretipua. Came out of the whare.

Shoulders bare, and wide, and brown, deep color, glossy. Deep color too on her cheeks, on her face, on her chin.

Bright eyes flashing and sweet kind smile. Sweet kind smile and white white teeth. And fingernails, too.

Sweet kind smile, bright eyes flashing. Paretipua. Came out of the whare. Hair wrapped in a towel. Shoulders bare.

Across the Ruapeka, dawn glittering feebly through the steam.

Slowly, the sun rose; shadows crept like blots upon the water; tree branches twisted, and the raupo stretched and rustled, wiry thin. The woman paused at the doorway, welcoming the morning, herself stately as the sun. She balanced the heavy towel on her head, looked around, noticed her small niece, the quiet, queer one, setting the breakfast pots down near the ngawha. She smiled. At the little girl. At the promising, preening sun. She smiled.

Paretipua. Shoulders bare and wide and brown, deep color, glossy. Lifted her arms up. High, elbows high. Bent her head over. Head with hair wrapped in a towel. Dark dark blood dark red. Bent her head over, arms up. And fingernails, too. Paretipua.

Towel undone. Hair spilled out, black, black. Falling, falling. Falling down, falling. From shoulders bare and wide and brown. Black hair, black. Long. Thick. Long. Waves of black. Long hair, dyed muka ropes, dried by the sun.

Black, black. Waves of black. Falling, falling. Paretipua.

She flexed her shoulders, turned her neck, swung around, and the heaviness of her hair spilled almost to the step. The weight of it. Yet she could never cut it, not freely, this gift she wore like the finest cloak; it meant too much, for too many people. So instead, she enjoyed it. The wonder, the blackness, the weight. And the beauty. Steadying her feet, bending forward slightly, knees spread, hand clasping thighs, she tossed it to the sunlight, to the morning; a cloak, a fishing net, a cloud of lustrous black.

Waves of black. The wonder. Sparkling and shimmering, black, black, caught in the sunlight, water stars, shimmering and sparkling.

Water stars, made by the hair, caught in the sunlight, black, black.

Falling, falling. Sparkling and shimmering, water stars, water stars. Black, black. And water stars.

From the sunlight. From the morning.

From the shoulders bare and wide and brown. From the waves of black, black. The wonder. From the morning.

From her. Came out of the whare. From Paretipua.

OLD MAN TUNA

HE pulled the laces tight on her shoes, eyes scanning the riverbank. Vague shapes in the stream. Her brothers were still there—not quite waiting for her, but still there. That was the main thing. Although she wanted to, she didn't yelp with delight. She had promised to shut up and be quiet, so that she didn't scare away the fish. The fish, the fish. Much more important than her, a mere girl, who was just a nuisance anyway. Though she could have her uses. Maybe.

They were still ahead, but she could see them; large, dark shapes gliding through the shadows. Big guys. Milton was nineteen and had a motorbike and a pakeha girlfriend. He told spooky kehua stories that made your skin tingle and go all stiff like a dead chicken's, while his eyes got bigger and bigger and glowed like headlights. Scary and horrible. But Milton was fun too; he always brought home Cadbury Roses chocolates for his sister and Bailey's Irish Cream for the old lady, who loved him.

She hadn't met the girlfriend yet; plenty of time for that, he reckoned. His brother, Tuku, wasn't so sure. He was always thinking—never said much, read his books and looked out of the window most of the time. No motorbike for him; he had his sights set on a Citroën. Style. That was his secret, as he moved through the rustling bushes in his uncle's old swandri and Grandfather's frayed-out cords. Style, that's Tuku, graceful as a preening cat. Clutched in his left hand, the cold smoothness of an AFFCO meat hook. His eel gaff.

The moon was on her back, and pale light dripped feebly down between the weeping willow branches. They stopped. They were there—at the place; barely ten minutes walk from home. Too close, thought Whero.

"Here's fine." Milton lifted his rod and flexed it lovingly. "Got that big one last night, just about this spot. Let's try her out again, e bro?"

The younger brother nodded. Both men stretched, and shrugged, then set to fixing their gear.

Whero watched, squatting in a pool of darkness, her elbows wrapped around her knees. So much for her big outing with the boys. It was boring; even the place was wrong; if she climbed up a nearby tree, she could see the lights at home; if she really stretched her neck she could see right into the sitting room, past the lace curtains. And there would be Kuia, happily watching TV, blue haze flickering across her gentle face. Whero had hoped they'd walk for miles, all the way to the mouth of the river. What a bummer.

She stood up. Whispered. "Hey, Milt, can I go for a walk?"

Whirr, whirr, whirr went the reel. Whirr, zipzipzip. "Okay. Not too far."

"I won't. I'll just go down a little bit. Not far."

"When I whistle, you come back, girl." Zipzip, whirr.

"Yeah, I will." She glanced at Tuku, who was crouching like a river stone, absolutely still. Gaff at his side. String line between finger and thumb of right hand. He was at it again. Thinking.

She felt marvellous—free! Out in the night air! She danced quietly along the track, breathing in the darkness and faint moon-gleam, running her fingertips through a wall of flax. Paused as the track opened onto a scrubby bank. Dense grass fringed and dripped into the river; the water looked dark, a solid oily mass of black, punctured with melting globs of light. Out of the water, a raupo clump tufted shivering; some spines drooped sadly, streaming in a greasy line around an ancient log, which formed a ragged, festering bulk to the shore. Threatening, choked in a slime of thick weed.

Whero stopped. She knew this place—how different it looked at night! Worse even than in the daytime. Spooky. The water, so still. Where the Old Man Tuna lived, they said. Somewhere in that weed. In the willow stump. Or underneath the log. A Big One.

Yuk, she thought. Strained her ears. Whirr, whirr. Everything was normal, okay. If he whistled, she'd hear. If she shrieked, he'd hear. Both of them would. And her own favorite place, where she liked to be and doze and think, was close by, just a little bit farther along. Where the water trickled again.

Behind her, in the dark weeds, something moved. Broke the water, like a boneless ebony arm. It rose smoothly, gleaming, from the ooze. Then fell into it once more.

Her favorite place—a tree trunk. A wide, massive branch that reached over the river, it cradled her body and, with a sigh, she settled onto the nuggety bark. Her favorite place. She'd be there for hours, wiggling on her back, looking at the leaves change color, weekend after weekend, until they dropped off and the stark winter blue peered down; or else, straddling frontways, she'd gaze into the water, watching blossoms float by. And she'd dream; daydreams. Now, at last, she was here—at night! In the dark, in the shadows. By *herself.* She drank the cold of the night, breathed the chill air, turned onto the tree. And rested her cheek, and ear, on the silvery gray surface, listening to the tree's blood moving. She closed her eyes. Listened. To the tree, to the river trickle, to the sound of being free.

Whirr, whirr. No, whistle. Sound of air hissing through a gap in the front teeth. Milton. Close by, coming to her tree. Whero sat up, then relaxed. He was there, just in front of her, framed by a rustling stand of tall flax stems. Silently, he moved toward her. His jacket was unzipped, and the yellow flecks in his jersey glittered. He bent toward her, still whistling softly. One hand on her shoulder, pressing gently.

"Lie back."

Whero wasn't sure what was going on, but she did as she was told. Leaned into her tree, feeling safe in her favorite place. Milton nuzzled at her neck and was somehow planting something between her legs. It was his other hand, fumbling down there while he snorted in her ear. His bum was moving, slowly, softly, pushing against her. Whero squeaked, caught some of his hair in her mouth. Squeak. Then tried moving her own hips, pinned down by his weight. He stopped.

"Shuddup girl, don't move and then I'll finish."

It felt funny. She was aching inside, and he kept pushing against her. His mouth was half open and his eyes were shut, and his bristles scraped her chin. It was beginning to feel wrong. She started to struggle, weakly, in a halfhearted way, then decided to concentrate instead on the dappled shadows that played across his face, and the tree bark, and the flax stalks moving, and the moon on her back too. If she shut her eyes, she could listen to the music of the water, running across pebbles and stones and clumps in the stream, avoiding that other place; she let her mind drift away with the water. . . .

"Hey Milt! C'mere! Hurry up bro. I got it. I got the bugger.
C'mon e—"

Yells and excited shouts a few yards away. Tuku bagging a big
one.

"Hurry up e!"

Hands on his sister's trembling shoulders, Milton heaved himself up, turned, lifted his face, snorting. "What, man? What the
hell's the racket for?"

"Old Man Tuna. I got him. I got him!"

"What? Shit, you're having me on e"—in a split second, he
was gone.

They were by the heaving, weed-choked water, Tuku hauling
at the gaff, twisting his wrists, flat on his front, knees digging
into the track, feet somewhere firmly in the green wall behind
him. His older brother gripped the sugar bag, its flaccid mouth
gaping and ready. They waited for the writhing and thrashing to
die down; it seemed to go on forever. Whero looked on, not
saying a word, wishing she was somewhere else, but staying still,
being quiet. Wanting like hell to get away.

The tuna fought, tiring the two young men. It pulled, then
stopped, then pulled again.

Suddenly it was loose. The gaff hung slack in Tuku's hand.
Milton snarled. The girl sank far into the flax leaves, folded in
their slick wetness, waxy hard.

Old Man Tuna had got away again.

Milton cursed his brother and the fish. Tuku scrambled up,
brushed himself off. Feeling useless again; he'd never make a hero,
an action man. But he'd always look good. And he liked to think.
He really did. Angry, frustrated, they made their way back home.

"Hey, where's the girl?"

"E? Oh—I thought she was with you, e."

"Nah. Musta gone back already, e."

Slowly, murky sludge began to settle, blots of weed sitting

damp upon its surface. Whero crept out of the flax, close to the river, eyes focused on the half-sunken log. Everything was still, quiet again. She thought of her brother, what he had done. It had happened, that was for sure. Yes it had. She remembered.

She couldn't take her eyes off the log, the bank of twigs and leaves and other stuff rotting in its forks. Night black, midnight black, something seemed to be waiting. She took a step forward.

A thick length of darkness arched out of the weeds, curled and twisted around, spun on itself like a great whip, sleek and shining. It skimmed across the water, it filled every part of that small, sluggish hole. Then it heaved once more and was gone, plunging down into the mud.

WATCHING THE BIG GIRLS

HE loved watching the Big Girls. Especially when they were in front of the mirror, in the toilets. They jiggled and jostled, and pulled each other around, and flounced and combed and fluffed their hair, and then suddenly they would go very very still. Looking.

Looking at each other, but most of all, looking at themselves. Wow.

And if a Big Girl came in by herself, that was even better. Tahuri would quietly shrink into a corner, making herself as tiny as possible. So small that no one could hear her. But *she* could see *them!* It was exciting.

Her favorite Big Girl was Cassina. She should've been a boy, the old people said, named after Montecassino where her uncle was killed, long before she was born. Cassino. But that was a boy's name, they said. So here she was—Cassina, instead. And all the faraway, exotic, foreign, enchanting pictures that her name sounded to Tahuri were there—in her, in her eyes, and her hair, and her lips, and even her ears.

Cassina had beautiful ears, neatly tucked against the sides of her head, with finely rounded lobes. She wore stars on them; stars sometimes, and other times little gold circles that slept and slipped through the holes that Kuikui had drilled with a small hukere stick and muka thread. Ouch. She twirled them, her long Cutex scarlet nails bright in the gloss of her hair. Most of all, Tahuri liked the big gold circles—hoops they were. Gleaming and gilded, like the sun through smoke, or steam. But that was only on very special occasions, because the hoops were a secret that Cassina sneaked on when Kuikui and her mother, Karu, were not around. For some reason they didn't like the hoops at all, and they said so—but they never said why. They didn't like the fingernails, either, but made their stand on the hoops. This puzzled Tahuri, and made Cassina mad, but she wore them anyway. In sort of secret. Golden hoops and rich black curls that went all over the place, never ever sat in a decent beehive, but ballooned in fat black blossoms all over her head and swirled around her shoulders.

Cassina was beautiful. She'd bat her long, dense eyelashes, and "do" her dusky eyelids, and smile and sparkle at Tahuri, there in the corner by the rubbish tin. That was the neat thing about Cassina—she always noticed if her little cousin was there, and she always grinned at her, making Tahuri feel all warm and cosy inside.

Not like Trina. She was a witch, but somehow she had a lot of boyfriends with cars even; while Cassina got around with Heke, on his broken-down motorbike.

Trina was skinny, and white. Her legs and arms were the color of the old old sheets at the pa—creamy-ish, and dotted. Sometimes freckles surfaced on her nose in summer, and she hated that, cadging a huge flax hat from Kuikui "to preserve her complexion." Whatever that meant. She'd come into the wharepaku, usually alone, her long neck swanning into a deep plum beehive, shades of purple in the reddish brown, spangled stiff with lacquer. Trina would turn her head this way, then that; lean toward the mirror and dig carefully at the clotted spikes that ringed her slanted hazel-green eyes, muttering about mascara; check the line of pink around her pearly little teeth; take a sleek powder compact from her clutch purse and cover the offending specks upon her nose; examine her eyelids too; and then, with a satisfied sigh, she'd stand back and purr at herself. No ladders in the stockings. Good. Then, she'd turn once, twice, three times, on the balls of her white, slingback spike heels, and with a spring of stiff petticoats and frothing skirts, she was out the door. Without even a blink in Tahuri's eye.

Ben sometimes came in too, by herself. Bennie was special— she was different, and she was kind, too. Always had the Juicy Fruit or the PK chewing gum for little kids like Tahuri. She never looked quite right, though; her feet looked too big for her shoes, and her shoulders were as wide as Heke's. And her hair was cut funny, so it dropped like a dog's tail over her forehead and went straight down to a V at the back of her neck. Her clothes weren't very interesting either, really dry and colorless— purple shirt, black jerkin, and gray pleated skirt, which hung halfway down her densely muscled, rocklike calves. Bennie— called Penupenu by Kui—had the legs all right. But she just used them to jump and dance and run around with; she never ever shaved them, like Trina, so very fine threads occasionally caught the light on her shins, because she hated stockings too. Along with all that dangly stuff that held them up. Tahuri decided that Bennie would've made a really handsome boy—she never wore makeup, but her eyebrows were jet black and moved from fat to thin above her dark dark eyes, framed in a lace of thick eyelashes. No need for the mascara there. Her nose was medium, and her teeth were big and white, and her smile was huge when she smiled; ear to ear, and dimples puckered up, and her sallow skin would glow.

Bennie'd be luscious too, like Cassina, if she really tried, thought Tahuri. But Huhana was the one. She outshone them all, even Cassina. "Suzie," they called her in Wellington, but when she came home, she was Huhana, Cassina's big sister, a woman of the world. While Cassina was tall, Huhana was short, and while Cassina was dark, Huhana was even darker: a ripe, rich color like the polished oak piano the nuns had at school. Huhana wore fashions—her sister got the hoops from her—and when she came into the wharepaku, Tahuri gasped. Her eyes even popped. Wow. This was fashion.

Huhana had squeezed herself into a blood-red tight skirt that gripped her rounded hips and slid in a silken line down her thighs. Her legs nipped together at the knee, making her full bum swing as she walked, and her ankles curved like bows from her black patent leather stilettos. The same stuff, gleaming and brittle, encircled her waist, a tense band three inches wide, clipped together by a bright gilt buckle, set squarely beneath her blouse. Cut low, it was more of a bodice, with no shoulders or sleeves or anything like that. It was like a pari, without the straps—a stiff thing wrapped around the chest and back, covering the front, but showing a lot too. And Huhana was showing it for sure. The material was hard and black and grainy and turned over into a little fold at her titties, which rose and jiggled and heaved like lush chocolate jellies. Tahuri's fingers twitched at the sight; they looked so soft, she was dying to touch them! Wow!

Huhana beamed at her; carefully looked herself over, powdering down the shine on her face. She'd unclipped the buttons on her slithery black gloves, and they were folded back over her forearms, so her fingernails, lips, and skirt pulsed in the same hot color.

Tahuri was enchanted: she watched as Huhana caressed the frosty glitter knotted at her throat, sparkling on her earlobes; as she slicked her smooth french roll, stretched and straightened her stocking seams, and pulled off her shoes and wiggled her toes, and put them on again, for fashion. And with a wink of silver eyeshadow and arched brows at Tahuri, she was gone.

"That was Suzie from Wellington," the little girl murmured to herself.

Time passed, and Tahuri was still watching the Big Girls. And she was one herself, at last, but she couldn't primp and preen like the others—no way. Instead, she preferred to slouch, cool and silent, in the same corner, by the same rubbish tin, watching.

Reti reckoned she was a bit perverted, like her older sister Ben, who went away to Auckland and came back looking like Elvis. Tahuri thought that was okay and went looking for Penu, but missing seeing her; she only stayed one night, then shot back to the big smoke, her royal blue Lurex shirt flashing through the window of the bus. Her younger cousin snatched a quick look at the shirt and waved and waved, promising herself to get one too.

A Lurex shirt. Wow. Even better than the old black jersey she refused to take off, ever. Even at this creepy youth club dance, where all the big girls tittered while their parents and grandparents nodded, and the big boys flashed hungry eyes and razzed each other to ask a girl to jitterbug. And what came after the jitterbug?

Weddings and babies. Cassina with Heke and four little kids; Trina working in the draper's shop with a big puku, while her husband Lennie sold insurances, and Huhana now Mrs. O'Shea in Dublin, with twins and an Irish sailorman. Bennie was the luckiest of all—she drove a dry cleaning van and grew more muscles and didn't give a hoot about all that wedding stuff.

This made a lot of sense to Tahuri, so she stayed in the wharepaku, where none of the big boys could ask her to jitter-bug.

She checked the toilet paper, and the washbasins, and the floors. She sat on the rubbish tin and went out sometimes and got a drink, or had a dance with Reti, then back she came.

Always, when the Big Girls came parading by.

Watching the Big Girls. Loving them.

Dacia Maraini

In her novel Letters to Marina *(1981), Dacia Maraini, one of Italy's best-known contemporary women writers, brings together setting and character so that each progressively reveals the other. The narrator, having fled to a village to escape the mysteriously invasive powers of a female lover, addresses a series of letters to her while attempting to finish a long-overdue novel. Although not herself a lesbian, Maraini, in her work, reflects the importance of feminist liberation struggles in Italy, assuming the right of all women to shape their lives as they choose. This freedom infuses the pages of the novel excerpted here. With humor and an extraordinary talent for evoking a sense of place, Maraini follows her narrator in her "routine" interactions with the life of the village, creating a text that speaks eloquently of the vibrant inner life of a woman alone.*

from LETTERS TO MARINA

Dear Marina

A short time before I left Rome the porter gave me a parcel with a note. I recognised the handwriting immediately: those l's like buttonholes sewn in angry haste and the r's that get confused with those speedy flying n's. And your firm threatening signature M. The note read "Red Riding Hood has eaten the wolf" and even if you hadn't put your signature I would have known it was you.

Inside the parcel I found a pendant of black antique glass with a long teardrop to hang carefully round my tense white neck as a mark of my ingratitude. I've asked you so often not to send me presents. I don't want them. The last time I picked up that ring you gave me I could feel your breath in my ears like a ferocious dragon. I felt the flames reaching right down my throat. It isn't presents you're giving me but little magic signs to imprison me inside the charmed circle of your will. The black glass teardrop on my throat the small crown of bleeding thorns on my finger the green enamel serpent encircling my wrist—I am nothing but a plaster madonna hung with votive offerings that will stay there forever scintillating in the morning sunshine and in the evening lights as a memory of eternal promise.

Dear Marina

Another day of seclusion. Every morning I get up at half past seven. The alarm clock goes off but my eyes are open even before it starts to ring. My sleepy gaze rests on the gasometer that stands at the far end of the football ground to the right of the sea. I look to see whether the large gray cylinder has risen or gone down during the night. On the distant horizon to the north I can make out the fiery plumes of the oil refinery in the morning mist. When the wind blows toward the south the flat is permeated by the heavy sickly sweet smell of oil.

I get washed and dressed and go into the kitchen to make myself a cup of coffee. I hear my neighbor singing while she warms the milk for her boys. Later I hear her impetuously thumping the floor-cloth onto the floor as she drags it through the flat. The walls are made of paper and one can't avoid participating in the lives of one's neighbors. Signora Basilia has a loud hoarse voice and her tiny body is capable of the most incredible feats. Out of her minuscule belly she created and expelled two boys who weighed eleven pounds each at birth (she says with pride that "they tore my body apart like two bulls"). And while she does the housework she bellows forth in a great deep voice full of cavernous echoes that you'd think belonged to a woman ten times her size.

I eat and drink slowly while I try to imagine the fingernails of my characters. One can sometimes tell more from someone's fingers and nails than from their faces. Strange that with you I looked first at your feet rather than your hands. Perhaps it was because your cactus feet were so clearly visible beneath the table. From time to time you touched them as if you weren't quite sure of still finding them there all quiet and peaceful. After all feet talk like hands: yours told me that you were romantically and perversely in love with yourself.

After breakfast I go down to buy a paper and something for lunch—a thin slice of meat two tomatoes and a bunch of basil which I put in water in a glass jar to stand on the table where I work. I like to smell it while I'm writing.

The newsagent asks me "Are you on your own?" I don't quite understand what he's getting at—on my own? Without children or husband or mother or father or sisters? He gives me an equivocal fatherly look whose implication is that if I am alone here without a man and without a family he will protect me—at least that's how I interpret it. The first time my neighbor came to see me on the excuse that her children were asleep she too asked me, "Are you all by yourself?" and from then on her curiosity has grown daily. A woman on holiday alone must be hiding something: some sort of grief or unrequited love or illness. Who knows what secret sorrow it might be?

For a moment I thought of telling her: "I'm here to escape

from a girl who wants to gobble me up." But she wouldn't have understood. And anyway that's not the whole truth. I'm also here to write my book. And to escape from the temptation of letting myself be destroyed by the child who has installed himself in my womb.

Toward midday I stop writing. I take my swimming costume and go down to the sea. I pass in front of the newsagent, who greets me deferentially. I cross the Piazza Santa Caterina walk along the Corso Vittorio Emmanuele cross the Via Liguria and I'm there. I go down some concrete steps onto the crowded dirty beach. I hire a beach umbrella and a deck chair and for a while I sit and read. Then as soon as I start to sweat I go into the water. I swim three hundred strokes as if I were undergoing a penance. I don't enjoy the smooth oily water that's littered with rubber canoes and screaming children and bits of plastic that cling to my body. I swim back to the shore and sit in the sun trying not to listen to other people's transistors. I read for about an hour and then I go home feeling hot and bad-tempered.

I've noticed some newly painted wooden boats that are for hire and tomorrow I think I'll hire one and go right out to sea.

At home I eat lunch listening to *Rigoletto* my eyes gazing vacantly out of the window onto an ancient landscape desecrated by the concrete tower blocks. From the kitchen window I can see white rocks that make sharp patterns on the green water small bushes bent by the wind and the steep coastline with mountains behind dominating the town.

After lunch I lie down for a rest on the big bed that's steeped in the familiar odors of conjugal life: sweet almond oil and urine cleaned over and over again with water and soap and talcum powder that smells of flowers. A huge bed with eighteenth-century brass bedheads a lumpy wool mattress that has witnessed God knows how many acts of copulation and birth and marriage and fights and rapes and deflowerings and abortions and death-agonies.

At four o'clock I start working again. At seven I go down for an ice cream. At nine I have supper and then I read till eleven. Then I go to bed. This is my solitary day which is like all my other days and which I am determined to keep as monotonous and spartan as possible until I've finished this book and have freed myself from all those alien and unacknowledged ghosts from the past.

. . .

Dear Marina

Last night I took sleeping pills and I woke this morning after a short heavy sleep in such a daze that I couldn't recognize things in the market. I stood in front of some lettuces for five minutes thinking, What on earth are those objects? "Chicory endive radishes" I kept repeating the words to myself without being able to associate the object in front of my eyes with the name I had in my mind.

Red mullet whiting trout eels scorpion-fish swordfish. For a moment I become aware that I am looking at the fish through the eyes of a woman who lived centuries ago: a woman whose hands were covered in shining scales and who had all her life been familiar with this dead white fish the smell of entrails and putrescence the faint scent of carnations. I do not actually see the fish I recognize them by touch. They are part of my experience of the world perceived through fingers that open snatch knead dip stuff and baste and through hands impregnated with rich overpowering smells.

I got talking to the old woman in a flowered apron who was

selling fish and shouting rude jokes to the passersby. But she
didn't seem very eager to talk to me. She looked at me suspiciously. What was I doing there chatting away while she was
working? Why wasn't I buying anything? So in order to ingrati-
ate myself with her I filled my shopping basket with fish: squids
that were bruised and slippery "genuine" clams and even an
octopus with long pinkish-gray tentacles.

All at once it dawned on me that this was probably the same
woman through whose eyes I'd just been looking from a distance of a thousand years. I watched her more closely and almost
unawares I felt myself slipping into the greedy exuberance of
her dark wrinkled body. I could tell she lived on her own from
the way she handled money: her fingers closed round the notes
with casual yet voracious haste like the quick graceful cunning
of a fox as it lays hold of a chicken.

The swing of her coral earrings helped me to lose myself in
her: two long narrow pendants widening out at the bottom with
a small flower of tiny yellow petals fastened onto the earlobes.
They swung lightly to and fro as her shoulders rose and fell following the movements of her hefty arms. Her large wrinkled
hands grasped the fish flung it down on the table and took hold
of the knife—less a knife than a hatchet with a massive handle—
letting it fall precisely where the clean flesh meets the backbone.
From time to time she used her wrist to shove back a wisp of
gray hair that had slipped out of her bun.

I sensed the cheerful disdain she felt toward her customers
who came up gave her the once-over sniffed at her fish felt like
having a good snigger behind her back started to make some
comment but were never quite quick enough for her. I sensed
her irritation at the political argument going on between two
market stallholders. I feel as if nothing matters anymore neither
politics nor the market not the fish nor anything at all. All my
attention seems to be concentrated on a few small sensuous

pleasures: the raw taste of homemade grappa which fills me with the burning certainty that I am still alive the sensation of coolness in my genitals as I sit for ages on the lavatory while my eyes follow the image of a fly dying on the wall opposite the feeling of clean sheets against my bare feet the crisp dry consistency of a new thousand-lira note the weight of hundred- and two-hundred-lira coins in the palm of my hand the sour milky smell of my newborn nephew as I secretly offer him my wrinkled breast and he sucks from it a few drops of fluid the last residue of my unfulfilled womanhood.

Dear Marina

Yesterday I came back home with two kilos of fish which I hadn't an idea what to do with. I cleaned them mechanically forcing myself back into some sort of familiar routine. I put them all into an earthenware dish and took it round to my neighbor. Basilia looked at me with astonishment. Suddenly little Mauro climbed on my back pulling himself up by my hair. He and his brother have a habit of attacking the bodies of grownups biting pulling shouting smelling shoving in a way that makes them invincible. One can tell that when they grow up and have money they'll be adored by women and will give them a bad deal just the same as they are robbing their mother now. Big strong and lively with their curly heads acting as cushions they throw themselves against the walls and make them tremble. Woe betide all those who find themselves in the invaders' path! I said this to their mother and she gave me a beatific smile happy to think of her sons growing up to be winners. She has watery eyes and sparse dry hair and when she smiles she shows her black decayed teeth.

She is delighted to see me. She makes me sit down and forces me to eat stale baby rusks and drink some vinegary wine that smells of strawberries. Then in her supple voice so unexpectedly and mysteriously powerful she tells me about herself. How she was raped by her father when she was nine—"I was a woman already. Just imagine! I was having periods so I got pregnant and my mother aborted me with a liter of Epsom salts. That gave me an ulcer and it's still there. When I was twenty-five I got pregnant through the Holy Ghost—that's the only way I can explain it. I didn't want that second child so I went to a neighbor and she lent me a probe and showed me how to push it in. After struggling with it for three days the miscarriage started and I couldn't stand the pain so I said, 'That's it! I'm going to the hospital.' But I never said a word to Toniano I wasn't going to tell him. So I went to hospital and they scraped me out. Then they asked me, 'Who got you an abortion?' I said 'What I don't know anything about that. It just happened.' They said they knew that wasn't true but they'd let it go this time. They kept me in the hospital for three days but they couldn't stop all the blood I was losing not even with all their big pipes and tubes. And so it went on— after Mauro there was an ugly girl who was born dead and then the last."

I tell her about my miscarriage at seven months. She listens attentively and sympathetically. From now on we are friends. We have both suffered the same things: miscarriages hemorrhages unwanted pregnancies. We are equal. But we are also very different and I use the dish of fresh fish to efface these differences created on my side by privilege and on hers by premature aging. She thanks me warmly. Her eyes don't display any envy but even a little compassion. "Poor thing all on her own" is what she is thinking and she sees herself as being luckier than me because she has a husband who screws her every night and sons who eat her alive.

. . .

Dear Marina

I've decided to leave tomorrow. I shall go and see Fiammetta in Sicily where she's rented a house on top of a cliff. "There are three hundred steps to get to it" she told me triumphantly. "There's no electricity or running water but it's a marvelous place. The water's clean and clear and you can catch fish weighing five kilos so why don't you come? But you must arrange it because I've no more money to put in the phone"—and she laughed exultantly as only she can not giving a shit about anyone or anything. I said yes and I felt more lighthearted. I want to leave this place that's overrun with mice and I want to swim in a sea where the water's clean and I want to be touched by Fiammetta's gaiety.

I said good-bye to Margherita who has become miserable and silent. She wished me a good holiday. She made me promise to write to her and in return she will write to me about Damiano. Then she told me the latest about his double and triple love affairs. She kissed me demurely on the cheek and went off tapping her high heels on the pavement.

As it's my last evening Basilia has asked me to go out with her. She seemed anxious about it.

"Aren't you afraid of your husband?"

"He's on night shift."

"And the children?"

"Once they're asleep they don't wake up not even for an earthquake."

Sparkling lights . . . red tablecloths . . . flowers . . . candles. It was a good restaurant I took her to. She hadn't been to a restaurant since her wedding day. She was thrilled and delighted and kept running her hands over her dress.

"Do I look all right?"

"You look lovely."

"You're joking. I'm old."

"Old at thirty-six? You must be crazy! Now—what would you like to eat?"

"I don't know. You tell me."

"What takes your fancy?"

"What I'd really like is cannelloni with cream."

"And after that?"

"A cocktail of scampi with a spicy sauce."

"And then?"

"What about duck with orange? I've never had it. It's on the menu and I'd like to try it."

We both gorged ourselves. Waiters with white gloves bending over us discreet and sly . . . music from the little orchestra mawkish and sentimental . . . wine on ice that had to be taken out of a little silver bucket each time . . . flambé bananas . . . ice cream with brandy. In a moment of euphoria Basilia confessed that it reminded her of the latest photo-comic with Fabio Testi. And just like the people in the comic we were playing our parts—eating and drinking and behaving like ladies. We even danced in the sugary darkness on a floor of blue and yellow glass. Only the dashing young engineer or the elegant gray-haired air pilot was missing and this gave a slightly bitter flavor to our comic strip.

Basilia was dreamy and entranced for a while even forgetting her sons back at home. She half closed her eyes and drank her wine gracefully without getting drunk. By the end of the evening she was laughing like a woman who feels beautiful and confident of herself. And in some way she really had become beautiful: her eyes were shining her cheeks flushed and she moved with slow languorous gestures.

We went home just before midnight. Her husband was due

back at two o'clock in the morning. She went into the flat softly
carrying her shoes so as not to make a noise. She hugged me
dramatically in an anguished farewell in which tears were mixed
with suppressed laughter. I breathed in the scent of her hair that
was usually impregnated with frying oil but tonight smelled of
Parma violets. I promised her I would come and see her from
time to time.

I went and had a shower. I slipped into bed. But I'd eaten and
drunk too much. I couldn't get to sleep. I decided to go for a walk.
I got dressed and went out. The town was deserted. Without
exactly meaning to I went straight to the Neptune Bar. I sat on the
edge of a big tub of oleanders in front of the closed shutters.

Then I went down to the sea. It looked dark and peaceful and
emanated a sickly smell of oil. I walked along the beach my feet
sinking into the dry seaweed stumbling over the rinds of water-
melons and empty plastic cans. A broken bottle cut my heel. I
turned up the Via Garibaldi and stopped in front of the closed
newspaper kiosk. The black outline of a woman with high heels
and a skirt split up to her thighs confronted me from a poster:
"Femininity is fashionable again."

Farther on I came across a cat with five newborn kittens. They
were suckling her hairy stomach. I bent down to look at them.
The mother showed me her teeth but without much conviction.
She returned to licking her kittens still watching me but without
moving. The kittens sucked greedily pushing their paws against
their mother's swollen belly and waggling their deaf heads.

In Sicily I shall be even farther away from you Marina. What
difference will it make though? A hundred kilometers or five
hundred are the same distance when we are not seeing each
other anymore. Yet it seems as if I am distancing myself dangerously from the zone of your love.

Back in the flat I read part of the novel. It seems awful. I drank some wine. I thought, I'm drinking to a colossal failure. I sat down to write this last letter to you before leaving. Then I shall read them all on the train.

In the end I've decided not to go back to bed. I can't stand the smell of the old matrimonial bed and I can't endure yet again the thought of the quarreling voices of the neighbors. And the prospect of being enveloped by that scorching trail of coffee at dawn turns my stomach. I shall take the train to Sicily at five in the morning.

Translated by Dick Kitto and Elspeth Spottiswood

Rosamaría Roffiel

Born in Veracruz in 1945, Rosamaría Roffiel, author of "Forever Lasts Only a Full Moon" (1996), is a pioneer lesbian voice in the literary world of modern Mexico. This story, one of Roffiel's most recent, shows her interest in blending Mexican folklore and history with lesbian romance. Lesbian literature in Mexico may be said to have had its beginnings in the poetry of Sor Juana Inés de la Cruz, a seventeenth-century nun writing to her patroness. After almost four hundred years of silence, Roffiel published Amora, _(1989), the first lesbian novel to appear in her country. In "Forever Lasts Only a Full Moon," translated here for the first time, Roffiel gives lesbian desire an otherworldly dimension, rooted in Mexican imagery._

FOREVER LASTS ONLY A FULL MOON

HE first time that Juliana approached me was at the Museum of Anthropology. The Mexican hall was almost deserted. Outside, a light rain transformed the afternoon into a startling scenario with a ground made of mirrors and inhabited by silences. I was standing in front of the Coatlicue. The monument's magnitude and the ferocity of its attire, full of symbols, made me feel insignificant. Pointing at the monolith, Juliana exclaimed:

"There was a time in the world in which women were goddesses, priestesses, and sorcerers, not these prudish and frivolous beings of today."

I froze in awe and stood with my magazine rolled under my arm and my *morral* from Oaxaca hanging from my shoulder. Juliana went on:

"A time in which only women knew the secrets of plants, of the stars, of life. A time in which the wisest men consulted us even to decide matters of war and state."

She was a thin woman. Her eyes were shifting shades of green, gray, and tawny brown. Her voice was strong and deep. When she spoke, she waved her fine hands, making her reddish hair fly, while a vein pulsed in her forehead. The first time she stared at me, I could have sworn that flames were shooting from her pupils.

"What is your name?" she asked.

"Eleonora."

"Did you know Eleonora is a sorcerer's name?"

"Nnno . . . ," I replied.

"Eleonora, would you care to have some tea with me?"

With a certain amount of fear and a great deal of curiosity, I accepted. We had a chamomile tea at the cafeteria, next to Chapultepec Lake. I told her about my life as if I had always known her, about my unfilled desire to study, my unsatisfying work as a secretary, my hidden vocation as a poet, my lack of self-esteem as a woman.

"You, Eleonora? You, who carry the blue sign of the goddesses between your eyebrows?"

Instinctively, I touched my forehead but didn't feel anything.

Juliana smiled:

"In this world, we, the women who search, the women who dare and don't accept life as it comes are descendants of the goddesses, and as such, we are misunderstood and rejected."

She took my face with both hands, remained silent for a moment, and, in a low voice said:

"Eleonora, you didn't choose. Let this be engraved in your memory, because once you discover your origins you will also find your answers. But I must be honest: the pain is no less because of this."

On my way back home, in the subway, my head was still buzzing. What a peculiar woman! When she spoke with such vehemence she seemed to be in her twenties, like me, but suddenly, she became forty, sixty, or even a hundred years old.

We kept on seeing each other. Juliana waited for me on forgotten benches of parks completely unknown to me, or in cafeterias where they didn't play loud music and where they served exotic teas.

Sometimes, at night, we would go through the city in her wine-colored car. Downtown streets, empty at that hour, were all ours. The main plaza received us with opened arms, on one side its cathedral, on the other the Government Palace. Juliana told familiar stories: the eagle and the *nopal,* Tenochtitlan, the screaming maidens, the prayers, the *copal's* smoke, the bleeding hearts. Like a good student would, I listened very attentively. The priests' *penachos* seemed to graze my nose with their colored feathers. Juliana would laugh at what she described as my unlimited capacity for wonder.

"Have you ever felt the rain in Tepoztlan, my dear?" she asked that Sunday. Before I could answer, she drove her car toward Cuernavaca. At the foot of the sacred mountain Tepozteco, we embraced trees to charge ourselves with energy. I learned to distinguish the pyramid among the stratum of rock, to calculate how many minutes a cloud covers the sun. We drank tequila and beer while the wind blew our hair; the heat and the alcohol made our cheeks turn red.

I never read as much as in those first months after my encounter with Juliana. "Eleonora, did you understand the message behind the written words? Did you, Eleonora?" she would eagerly ask each time I finished a book. If she would notice any doubt on my part, she would settle her green gaze on me:

"Guilt, Eleonora, guilt is the worst! You must learn to control it, because if it controls you, you will be at the mercy of any misfortune."

A film, the rain, a concert, a comment. Juliana would transform even the most insignificant events into a lesson.

"Eleonora, tell me, what do you believe in?"

"In friendship, honor, loyalty . . ."

"Bullshit. These are all clichés, abstractions, ambiguities! Yourself, Eleonora, yourself! Everything is inside you. Nobody can hurt you if you don't allow it. The greatest violence will be the one you inflict upon yourself. Next time, when I ask what do you believe in, you should answer: 'In me.'"

One night, just when I was about to get out of the car, Juliana took my face with both hands, as she did each time she was going to tell me something important.

"Eleonora, you should learn to meditate, to be more in contact with your inner self, to get closer to your poetry."

I don't know if it was mere suggestion, but weird things started to happen. I would menstruate with the full moon and ovulate with the new one. I had dreams in which I saw myself with plumbago-blue wings, flying to wonderful islands inhabited only by Amazons, or, protected by the leaves of a gigantic nest, I would give birth to a shining baby girl, also with blue wings.

My body acquired a different dimension. I started to feel the blood running through my veins, the air filling my lungs, the food entering my stomach. I became extremely perceptive. I learned to read people's emotions. A tense jaw, a veil of tears in the eyes, a different tone in the voice. Behind each face there were codes as clear now to me as the letters on the pages of a newspaper.

"Eleonora, tell me, why do you think that some women condemn themselves to live with a dead heart in their chests?"

"I don't know, Juliana."

Because they have chosen to lead an incomplete life, because they have denied their millennial strength, because they were given imagination and waste it in stupidities, because they are stuck to the outside and don't know how to listen to their inner voice.

Getting closer, she asked:

"Eleonora, are you really living what your essence requires?"

After I met Juliana, I didn't care anymore if men looked at me in the street, if they invited me out, if I was going to get married or not. I began treating them without considering each one as a possible relationship. I didn't need their approval to exist.

When I told Juliana about my unfortunate romances, she would insist:

"Be aware, Eleonora, be aware! You must be alert and discover what things reappear constantly in your life, since that is your karmic lesson in this lifetime."

Through gazes, touches, and words that sometimes were whispers and sometimes cries, Juliana wove a net of magic around me. My weekends and some of my evenings were only for her. Her universe became my space, her space my universe. One afternoon, as we were listening to medieval music while lying on the carpet of her living room, illuminated only by the light of a porcelain oil lamp, she reminded me:

"Eleonora, the full moon is near. That day we will both fast. If you want to reach another realm inside yourself, your body should know how to defeat hunger and thirst, among other things."

When I arrived, she was wearing a blue tunic. We took a crystal container full of water up to the roof of the building; there were several white signs painted on the floor. We burned some *copal* and sat facing each other.

"Tonight, Eleonora, the moon will flow through your blood, you will not need to sleep for hours, and you will know the secrets of past lives. Now, drink this."

It was a bitter, hot tea that made the throat and the stomach burn. Juliana also drank. Immediately, she said: "Undress yourself, Eleonora." I did so very quietly. Juliana rubbed my body with a sandalwood lotion and sprinkled my hair with wet herbs; then, she placed a crown of white flowers on my head and dressed me with a robe, also white. Surrounded by the clarity of the night, we danced with our bodies entwined. Then, we sat again in front of the bowl with the water. She was repeating phrases in another language; so was I, as if we knew them from before. I don't know for how long we stayed like that. I was dizzy from the fast and that revolting brew. Suddenly, we were silent. The moon, round and white, was floating in the very center of the bowl. Juliana dipped in one of her thumbs and traced a half moon between my eyebrows.

"Look, Eleonora, look! Tell me what you see on the water. Concentrate, keep the fear away, use your inner strength, Eleonora, use it!"

On the mirror formed by the water were two faces. There were Juliana and myself, but we were other women as well. The images changed rapidly: two infants, two youths, two older women, two whites, two blacks, two queens, two peasants, two angels, two demons. . . . Juliana and Eleonora. Eleonora and Juliana.

The air was spinning around me. I broke into a cold sweat, feeling very weak. The images of women on the water began to dissolve. I don't know if I fainted. I only remember that I woke up covered with a blanket in Juliana's arms. When I opened my eyes, she smiled. Very softly, I said:

"Juliana, I want to be with you forever."

She placed a finger on my lips.

"Eleonora, be careful with your wishes because they can be granted. Forever doesn't exist . . . not even in the land of the goddesses."

I insisted.

"I would like to know a magic formula, Juliana, a spell, an enchantment so you won't ever leave me."

"Be careful with charms, Eleonora. The enchanter is in the same danger as the enchanted one. Besides, if passion for another human being dominates you, you will be lost and condemned to pay a price as high as your own life. From now on, your only passion must be creativity, Eleonora. Surrender to it."

"But, Juliana . . ."

"Sssh . . . It's enough for today."

In the middle of the night, lying alone on the couch in Juliana's studio, still wandering as in a dream, with my chest full of strange sounds, I felt absurd. I ran through the corridor toward her bedroom and opened the door without calling. Juliana was waiting for me. She pulled the quilt away and embraced me with her body. Delighted, I received her mouth.

Juliana's skin was fair, her flesh was not very firm but quivered with the light touch of my fingers. Her breasts were small and her nipples dark and voluminous. When I sucked them, my tongue filled with a sweet, pleasant taste. Her sex, warm and tender, was to me like a wood of basil and myrrh. I learned a different way of loving, a new language with its own rhythms, secret codes, breathing.

Some nights, while I dozed next to Juliana, images—almost visions—would come to my mind: women raising swords with handles made out of precious stones, large cups full of luminous water, or spheres made of amber-like crystal. Women riding white horses, sailing antique boats with their arms up toward the sky, or walking amidst a fog coming from the earth itself.

One night, I had a dream in which we were surrounded by that mist, each standing at opposite ends of a boat that suddenly broke in half. Juliana stared at me with a mixture of sadness and melancholy. Her lips were repeating my name, though no sound came from them. As we started to move apart from each other, we extended our arms, anxious, until we were completely covered by the fog.

I woke up very disturbed. I tried to calm myself. I breathed deeply and looked around the room. I noticed that Juliana was crying in her sleep. In that moment, I knew: our time was fulfilled.

I placed my face in the hollow of her neck, felt her tears on my own skin, and held her with all my strength. A rare sweetness penetrated me. I fell asleep protected by her embrace while around us, the mist slowly filled the room.

Anna Blaman

The Dutch novel Eenzaam avontuur (Lonely Adventure) by Anna Blaman, first published in 1948, explores the lives of four young women and an unhappily married couple as they try to relate to one another. Viewed as shocking at the time, the novel was nevertheless awarded a major literary prize and is sometimes referred to as the Dutch Well of Loneliness. Anna Blaman (1905–60), the pseudonym of Johanna Petronella Vrugt, lived in Rotterdam her whole life. Her sexual difference, though not often a main theme, is clearly evident in her work. Blaman used her perspective of "outsider" to explore the poverty behind the social façades of relationships.

The following excerpt, translated here into English for the first time, presents Berthe, Yolande, Hilda, and Annie, who—although from quite different worlds—have rented the cottage Mon Plaisir together. Alide, who is staying with her husband, Kosta, in Mon Repos, another cottage, is the source of much fantasy for Berthe, whose romanticism links her in spirit for the moment to mysterious inhabitants of the moonlit forest— elves who live only in the extreme of delirious joy.

from LONELY ADVENTURE

AND it was a sorry sort of pleasure that was to be had in Mon Plaisir. Yolande was provocatively ignoring Berthe and enjoying it too. And Berthe was secretly dreaming of Alide, a dream like a poppy in a wasteland of loneliness. In it, longing became a perverse power struggle that was deeply satisfying. In her fantasy Alide had been deserted and was poor and ill; Berthe reaped a harvest of grateful love. But then she rejected this humiliating harvest again and dreamed that Alide was suddenly seized by an intoxicating obsession. And how did it happen? Quite simply through a kiss, an unexpected kiss in which she felt Berthe very close to her, so that the unknown became powerfully real, warm, young, beautiful, and charming, to be enjoyed again and again, insatiably. She hadn't yet noticed that the boisterous Yolande was ignoring her, that she had a grudge against her. Berthe's mental superiority was just a pretence, a system of defenses. In reality Yolande was the one who was superior, because she represented the majority. The majority may be superficial, but it's still the majority. And it crushed people who were lonely as Berthe was now, wanting to forget that she was a woman and to think about her own sex like a man. No man would look twice at a woman like Berthe; she might be intellectual and have an interesting personality, but in love's garden she was a wallflower. Yolande went on singing, provocative and crude. Her voice was like a tank crashing through the lunar landscape and thundering over human loves and heartbreak: Somebody stole my gal.

Sensible Hilda didn't have any eyes for landscapes nor any ears for tanks. It was a delightful summer evening and Yolande was singing—she thought it was all great fun and it was with a feeling of satisfaction that she set the mugs in a row for tea. In normal life Hilda was in service somewhere. She was the least educated of the four and moreover she was totally uninteresting. She had no problems of any importance. The real world was what she saw with her eyes and she dismissed with scorn anything that was mysterious and unaccountable. The only feelings

she really had were reserved for her bad teeth and the thought-
lessness of her mistress; to compensate for these disagreeable
things there was the comfort she got from her friend, a captain
on the municipal ferry. She was the oldest of the four and in
friendship she was easygoing and motherly. Hard work and a
willingness to help were in her blood. She made things amazingly comfortable for the others, but you did have to ask her
about her teeth and her mistress; she almost never talked about
her captain. As for her teeth, just look at them, how smooth and
even they were. You'd say there was nothing wrong with them.
But the pain they gave her, it was unspeakable! First of all her
back teeth had become infected and she'd had them all taken out
and now the pain had spread to the front ones as well. How
happy she'd be after they'd all been taken out! Oh yes, and her
mistress! She'd stand in the kitchen cooking something fancy,
and a friend of hers, the same sort of woman, stands there just
looking. But Madam is clumsy and drops an egg. It lies there on
the tiled floor with its yolk broken like an oval-shaped omelette.
"Oh lawks!" they say, Madam and her friend, and then they
can't help laughing. Then she points at it with her dainty hand
and says, "Hilda, that's for you." Then they really did start whin-
nying, two ladylike horselaughs, such lively, prissy merriment.
As for her ferryboat captain, she didn't talk about him partly out
of a sort of modesty but also because there was so little to say
about him. He was a little older than her, which she thought
better than the other way round; he had lodgings somewhere.
He would stand there on his ferryboat and without as much as a
thought he'd dump every problem overboard like so much ballast. "Are you crazy or something?" he always used to say. With
typical sailor's directness he looked everyone, man or woman,
straight in the eyes without making any subtle distinctions in his
appraisal; he was calm, cool, and self-composed. "Are you
crazy?" he'd say to Hilda, and no matter how cross she felt about

her mistress it all dwindled into nothing. Hilda was saving money; then she would get married. Lately she'd been living with him, as it's called. It didn't make any difference to her, but she had nothing against it either, only she couldn't understand that there were women who got so excited about it. She could understand however that there were women who did it for money. So by way of frigidity Hilda ended up with a charitable opinion of people. Sometimes she read novels in which the women were beautiful and of noble blood and the men indulged in abstract cravings and passionate kisses on the hand. She herself was much more down-to-earth and so was life. She was fond of Yolande; Annie was sensitive and kindhearted, she was a girl you felt protective toward and wanted to spoil; and Berthe was a bit strange but quite nice all the same. After tea the two latter went for a stroll and Hilda and Yolande had a chat. Yolande said, "You know what I think of Berthe? That she falls for women." Hilda was standing under the lamp, scrutinizing one of her teeth in a pocket mirror. Would this one start playing her up too? If it had to be pulled, it wouldn't look too great. Are you crazy, she said, imitating her sailor. What difference did it make if she still had a few teeth or none at all? "What were you saying?" she asked Yolande and looked at her in the same way as the sailor would have done. "That she falls for women."

For a second Hilda looked unsure of herself, as though she'd been caught off balance. She had heard of this sort of thing, but then it was men with each other. And then there was the question of whether there really was such a thing or whether it was just a perversion, or if you should feel sorry for people like that or just despise them. What a problem! But what was Yolande trying to say by it? She thought of Berthe a moment and then without more ado just like her sailor she dumped the problem overboard like ballast: "Are you crazy?"

Annie with her beautiful curls was walking on Berthe's right-hand side. She looked so timorous and fragile as she walked, like a sister elf who'd forgotten how to feel joy and so had been banished from the company. What was the matter with the girl? Her hair curled transparently round her temples and fell in thick ringlets far down her neck. In profile her nose was small and straight and her mouth had a sorrowful-looking curve. Perhaps Annie really did have the soul of an elf. Goodness and joy might have flourished there, like playful moths freed from a cocoon of timidity by the moonlit charms of a summer night. Not any human goodness or human joy then—no, goodness quite simply as a charming game and joy as a reason for living.

The moon hung there huge and dreamy in the firmament, penetrating the woods with its splendid and perilous light. In moonlight the world is more itself than ever, an eternal and essential world unaffected by everything that had gone on around it age after age. In the wood there were timeless paths with tree roots looking like ancient reptiles and suddenly here and there, like the incarnation of an evil spirit, there was a toad, like a miniature crocodile trapped in the moonbeams. The bushes were motionless and pale in their melancholy splendor; they have a soul, that's for sure, but who sees it in the daytime? And the same is true of trees; during the day they are beautiful, but under the moonlight they are heavy with dreams, full of the knowledge of how badly they miss this paradise at day. The spirit of the elves sails in everyone who surrenders to this world of moonlight. Either they want to die because they feel so unhappy—because elves only live by the grace of heaps of goodness and heaps of joy—or else they're so happy they fancy they're immortal. Eyes become mad or else poetic, mouths are cold with loneliness or else they burn with need, unsatisfied; that is why those who are unhappy are so immensely unhappy while the happy ones are so insatiably happy. And it's this feeling of never enough and never too much that makes the elves dance till they're delirious and makes lunar-minded human children hang themselves from trees that are heavy with dreams or utter stammering invocations that sound like nonsense during the day.

Berthe was unhappy, but not so much so that all that remained for her was to hang herself from some inviting overhanging branch. She was still able to talk about it. She walked beside Annie, who looked very beautiful in the moonlight. Besides, she was the owner of a heart that was rich and languishing. Her dream about Alide had not yet been shattered on the shores of reality, and walking beside her was a girl who was beautiful and delicate and who listened to everything she said, with a gentle passivity. So the spirit of the elves that sailed in Berthe did no more than rouse the unhappy girl to words; melancholy and sorrowful, but only words. She said: "I've such great expectations of life yet it's never given me anything. Why is life so poor when you deserve so much from it? From the moment I realized that I really existed, I prepared myself, because I wanted to think and understand things and to feel love. I deliberately tried to improve myself and to make myself more beautiful. I criticized others too, because I saw how few people took the trouble to do so! I notice that more and more. Soon I'll see through all the masks like a clairvoyant, and I won't even waste my time hoping anymore. Then I won't even dream any longer that there are people who are beautiful. But I could always have known I was condemned to a loneliness that would never end but would only get worse. What's the point of it all? I'm often frightened I won't be able to stand it all my life. Sometimes I also think that I have a destiny that I'm a human being whose situation is particularly difficult, and that this makes me someone special, that I have a destiny. If I put up with it courageously and without complaining, I'll find out what it was all for. But then again I suddenly realize that all I'm doing is wait-

ing, and that I'm just not the type to be a martyr, all I do is look
at every new face, as though it's come specially for me."

The moonlight was more than glorious now. The wood
opened up, becoming what it was completely, a paradise where
elves danced in delirious joy and sang with enraptured voices in
a frequency far higher than that of everyday human joy. A paradise where happiness resounded and anyone who was unhappy
was banished and barbarously invited, in the manner of fairy-
land, to go and hang himself.

. . .

And that's what Annie told her then: "Berthe you know so
much," and she walked next to her, looking delicate and hum-
ble, watching Berthe with her doelike eyes. "If you didn't feel
unhappy," she said, "I'd dare to be happy myself."

"Why?"

"Because I can tell you everything. Everything."

And she looked at Berthe again. Everything, Berthe thought,
oh dear, she doesn't even know what telling is, let alone everything. And Berthe was right: Annie had had so little love in her
life and had been rejected so often that she had no idea of all the
things that could go on in her mind, let alone talk about them.
Berthe however was a free-born traveler in the domain of
desires and reflection. Encouragingly she linked arms with
Annie, as though it was only now that they'd started their walk;
after all, on her own she was like a child gone astray on this road
that was dark and deserted like a dead-end trail, while together
with her she was a happy young woman on the royal road of
fantasy. And that's how the elves saw the two of them as they
walked on. But they didn't go with them, however much they
approved of the timid joy of the one and the tender encourage-

ments of the other. Because what mattered just then was Mon Repos. And in Mon Repos a duel was going on between dream and delusions. Elves are not brave enough for something like that; they play in the eternal woods and are romantic, like children. As long as a battle still has something of a tournament about it, they'll consider it, but when it starts getting serious and people are assassinated they flee the scene frightened and outraged, only returning when the combatants lie still; being corpses means they are innocent once more and belong to eternity. Suddenly then there wasn't an elf to be seen anywhere, not on the road nor in the woodlands around. There was however a light shining in Mon Repos, a light of an ethereal brilliance like a vision. "Alide said she had a headache, but she's still up," Berthe whispered.

She fell silent. They stood there motionless, Berthe and Annie, retreating into the shadow of a tree. No, Alide mustn't see that they were both witnesses. Nor must Kosta. Suddenly Kosta and Alide appeared on the terrace; Alide was running away, as though she couldn't take any more and Kosta followed, imploring her. Kosta went and stood next to her by the balustrade, forcing her to look at him, launching on a passionate whispered plea. It really was Kosta, though he was not supposed to be back till tomorrow. The two girls from Mon Plaisir stood there motionless sunk in darkness. They were watching a theater that was so sad and exciting that they couldn't keep their eyes off it. Later on everything they saw would become even more enormous in their memories; Mon Repos lit up like a mysterious palace, and Kosta and Alide, distraught and despairing like two human children clinging to their fate. As they lurked in the shadow of the tree the two girls from Mon Plaisir felt their hearts pounding and their lips turn cold. In this open duel between Alide's delusions and Kosta's dream they were witnessing the end of a time of happiness. Here were two people who clung to each other in a movement that oscillated between love and murder, two faces that stared at each other hesitating between nostalgia and dread, as though they suddenly saw something hideous in each other's eyes that had once been beautiful and adorable. They saw the passionately whispered conversation, an antiphon of confessions, pleas, and entreaties. And this conversation seemed to make both of them, already separated or estranged from each other by a catastrophe, still more lonesome. And suddenly there was an anguished and furious embrace that at once confirmed and denied the catastrophe. It was an embrace as though to save them both from falling. An embrace where they stood motionless, body to body and cheek to cheek, without however kissing each other. Berthe seized Annie's hand and led her back into the woods. Tentatively they looked for a path without noticing whether it led back to Mon Plaisir. Tentatively they fled, Annie holding Berthe's hand, like children who all unaware had accidentally seen inside of the palace of the terrible giant who ate human beings. Annie's hand was chill and Berthe's clasped hers firmly as though saving her life. Their escape was both riotous and light-footed like the elves a minute ago. Only when they were safe did they come to a halt. And now they were no longer children who had just seen the terrible giant, or elves in flight, but were once again two girls trying to find their way back home, one of them timid, the other with a somber languishing look on her face.

Translated by Donald Gardner

Christa Winsloe

The Child Manuela *(1934) by the German author Christa Winsloe prefigures the death of the spirit that would ensue with the victory of Nazism. Winsloe (1888–1944), born in Darmstadt, Germany, into a military family, rebelled against a harsh repressive education, going on to live a life of social and sexual nonconformity. In this novel, her most well known, a young girl suffering the loss of her mother and neglected by her militaristic and self-indulgent father refuses the soul-numbing constraints of a Prussian boarding school.*

This selection presents Manuela, or Lela as she is called, triumphant on the school stage as a male hero. Success, however, can only have meaning if it is ratified by Fräulein von Bernburg, a compassionate, responsive teacher who also finds herself caught in the school's determination to cleanse itself of such "hysterical devotion."

from THE CHILD MANUELA

XII

UNREMARKED, Fräulein von Bernburg slipped into her place again among the audience. People were laughing at poor Marga, who had had to take the part of Orosman at a moment's notice and was finding it far from easy to balance the turban on her head and read Voltaire's none too simple lines at the same time. Everybody was giggling. But then Lela appeared upon the stage. The girl was as if transformed. The moment she appeared the stage seemed to shrink. She more than filled it; she filled the hall; she seemed to fill the entire building. Profound silence settled on the audience. Her somber voice carried far, without apparent strain, even when she spoke low—perhaps then most of all. Her force, her sincerity, her warmth, gripped every person in the darkened auditorium. The Head was already uneasy. Even Bunny was twisting in her seat as if something were happening in defiance of the regulations. But what could have gone wrong? Should Mademoiselle perhaps have chosen a different play?

The children followed Manuela's slightest movement; their eyes hung on her as if spellbound. Secretly they squeezed one another's hands. Manuela was surpassing herself. One believed every word she said, one suffered with her, one sacrificed oneself when she did, rose to her heights of nobility and courage . . . and finally burst into tears with her because poor Edelgard lay dead on the stage, pierced by the sword of the jealous Orosman.

When the curtain fell a ripple ran through the hall. Forgetting all their good manners the children rioted. The Headmistress applauded benevolently. Mademoiselle Oeuillet bowed modestly. But from the audience there came a roar: "Manuela, Manuela! Brava! Brava! . . . ." and chairs scraped and hands clapped—and Lela, tottering on her feet, with one arm round Edelgard and the other round Marga, made her bow, very grave and very pale. Anxiously she sought Fräulein von Bernburg's eye . . . and caught it. Unlike the others, Fräulein von Bernburg did not send her a smile. As if she were thinking of something very serious, her gaze met and rested in Lela's.

The classes waited until the Head and her guests had left the hall, then they stormed out. Everybody was clutching at Lela. Everybody wanted a hand, a kiss, a word. Lela was pining to be left alone. But that was out of the question. Everybody was pushing to get near her. She had become unreal to the other children: they all wanted to touch her and speak to her as if to reassure themselves that it was really Manuela. Mademoiselle Oeuillet, too, after acknowledging endless compliments on the excellent performance of her pupils, felt a need to address a few words of appreciation to Manuela. She was indeed amazed at the child's powers of acting, flowing elegance, and musical enunciation, which had never been displayed at rehearsals to such a degree as tonight.

Manuela had first to be disentangled from a mass of girls.

"Eh bien—you did very well, Manuela."

"Do you really think so, Mademoiselle? Now that it's all over I have a feeling that I ought to have done it much better. Don't you think so?"

Mademoiselle was unwilling to let herself in for a serious discussion.

"Mais non, mais non, que pensez-vous? It was very good as it was—we're not a dramatic school—we're not actors here— much better?—but that wouldn't have been the thing at all—not ladylike—mais Manuela—quelle idée—you're not thinking of becoming a professional, surely?"

"No, I would never dare to try that. I haven't enough talent for that. I was only thinking. . . ."

"Tut, tut . . . never mind that . . . go off with the others and enjoy yourselves. . . ."

Obviously there was nothing to be gained from her. But now Manuela thought of something else. Without paying the slightest attention to the fact that both "shouting" and "running" were forbidden in the large corridor, she did both and ran calling for Ilse. Ilse came into sight. Manuela put an arm about her and bestowed a kiss on her, which Ilse accepted, unaccustomed as she was to kisses from Lela.

"I'm all right again, Lel. I'm not needing any more comfort. At the first go-off I was simply bursting with rage, but then—then the Bernburger turned up. . . ."

"Ye-es?" asked Manuela, lingering on the word. "And then?"

"Oh—well—then I just went down among the others."

"Where were you sitting?"

"Just behind the ladies."

"I say"—Manuela dragged Ilse into a window bay—"what did they say? . . ."

"Oh, Gaerschner thought you had learned your part very well, but your costume wasn't quite respectable. . . ."

Manuela was hardly listening.

"And Evans?"

"Evans, she said: 'Oh, sweet! Isn't she a darling?' But of course she didn't understand a word of it."

"And . . . the other ladies?"

"The Head went so far as to say that you had a very nice pair of legs."

Manuela stamped her foot.

"Oh, leave my legs alone. . . ."

"But nice legs aren't to be despised. I never really knew that you had nice legs!" and Ilse circled round Manuela, who irritably aimed a kick into the air.

Then Lela seized Ilse by both arms, and half laughing, half imploring, gazed into her face.

"Ilse, darling, please . . . what . . . ?"

Ilse screwed her eyes up.

"What did *she* say?"

Manuela nodded energetically, and Ilse replied, looking her steadily in the eye:

"Well, this is just the remarkable thing: Fräulein von Bernburg didn't say a single word."

Manuela blenched. Deep dejection was visible all over her face. Then Ilse grabbed her.

"But you should have seen what *eyes* she made! Such *eyes,* I tell you. . . ."

At this moment Marga appeared.

"Girls, what are you doing? We've all been in the dining room for ages, waiting for Manuela. . . ."

XIII

. . . Marga warned her.

"Manuela, we're supposed to have only one glass apiece. . . ."

"Oho!" came an indignant chorus from the others.

"Leave Manuela alone—let her, if she wants to," and Marga felt herself outvoted.

Manuela thrust her arm under Marga's.

"Come on, Marga, I'll drink this glass all by myself to the health of my foster mother and forgive you this day all the good you have ever done me. Here's to you!"

Everybody laughed, and Marga, protesting still but no spoil-sport, returned:

"All right then, do it, you mad goose!"

"Oh!" and Manuela threw out both her arms. "Why shouldn't I be a little mad?" And then, thoughtfully: "I think I'm really a bit off my nut, for I'm feeling amazingly happy—gloriously happy!"

"Well, we'll have to mark this as a red-letter day in our calendars."

This time it was Oda who had interpolated the remark. Since her last encounter with Manuela Oda had avoided her, but when she now sent a glance over the table Manuela lifted her glass again.

"Prosit, Oda—let's make it up, shall we?"

At any price Manuela wanted to be reconciled with all her fellow creatures that evening. Oda stood up, ceremoniously carried her glass round the table, and begged in a low voice:

"Lela, tell me one thing: can't you really like me a little bit?"

Manuela recoiled slightly but then cried aloud so that everybody could hear it:

"Yes, of course I like you—I like you all, without a single exception. . . ."

She turned and embraced Edelgard.

"Doesn't Edelgard look sweet?"

Edelgard's hair was very fair, and, indeed, the light veil and flowing white robe suited her admirably.

"She looks marvelous. But she's not nearly such a good actress as you are. She didn't speak loud enough." That came from Oda, who had returned to her seat.

"Oh, Oda, she had to speak low. She was a girl."

"And you, Lela, I suppose, were a man? Your voice was quite deep, and you suddenly had all the right movements. . . . We were inclined to believe tonight that you—that you're really half a boy. . . ."

"Here's to Oda!" and they both emptied their glasses. Lela was standing upright by the table, while all the others were sitting down.

"Oh, it was lovely, anyhow, to be able for once to yell out one's feelings. . . ."

"How's that? They weren't really your feelings," remarked Mia.

"Yes, they were. . . ."

"Go on with you. Edelgard wasn't your sweetheart at all; it came out that she was only your sister. . . ."

Manuela smiled.

"Yes, my sister—but that's lovely too, isn't it?". . .

"Oh, girls, there's something I simply *must* tell you. . . ."

"What is it?" They all came crowding about her.

Manuela bent to steady herself on Oda's and Edelgard's shoulders, for they were standing nearest her.

"She made me a present of something. . . ." The words came tumbling out.

Single voices called:

"Who? What? . . ."

They were all beginning to feel interested.

"She gave it to *me*," and Lela stood upright again. "To *me*. A chemise, and I have it on at this minute. I can feel it here on my breast, on my body, cool—pleasant. . . ." And since she still encountered nothing but incomprehension and questioning looks, she shouted it aloud: "Fräulein von Bernburg's chemise . . . she gave it to me. . . ."

At that moment Bunny's small gray figure appeared behind the backs of the children. Nobody remarked it. All eyes were turned toward Manuela, who stood high above them with flying hair, glittering in her silver sequins.

"Yes, to me . . ." and then, in a lower voice, very rapidly: "She went to her wardrobe and took out a chemise and gave it to me, I was to wear it, to wear it and think of her. . . . No, she didn't say that, but I know all the same. . . ."

"What? What do you know?" came in agitated voices from the crowd.

Fräulein von Kesten vanished again. But Manuela spread her arms wide.

"That she loves me . . . that's what I know." Shaking her head in humility, she went on: "She laid her hand on my head, her lovely white hand. That thrills through and through you and is so solemn that you want to kneel and . . ."

Now the Headmistress came in, followed by Fräulein von Kesten. A few of the girls caught sight of them and stood as if turned to stone.

Lela laid both hands on her breast. "To feel it here makes one good. From now on I want to have only good and pure thoughts. I want to be good," and louder and louder: "There's nothing can touch me now—she, she is there—she . . ." For a moment Lela faltered, and then, as if recalling the original purpose of her speech, she hastily snatched up a glass. "To her we all love, to our holy, our good, our one and only Fräulein von Bernburg. . . ."

Then at last she observed an uneasy agitation among the children. The Headmistress was thrusting aside those who were barring her progress until she came to a halt close beside Manuela, who, summoning her last strength, gazed fearlessly into her face.

"The whole world must know it—*she*, she is the miracle—she is the love that passeth all understanding. . . ." With that her glass fell from her hand and splintered. She herself shut her eyes and swayed into the arms of Edelgard and Oda, who caught her.

An uncanny hush spread in the room. Horrified, the girls cowered away from the Head. Fräulein von Kesten ran bustling around.

"Water . . . lift her up . . . carry her away. . . ."

Loudly the Head's stick beat on the floor.

"A scandal . . . a scandal . . ."

XIX

"The girl must be made an example of."

The Head's stick thumped on the floor. The Headmistress was stumping up and down the room. Fräulein von Bernburg, pale and composed, was standing by the lamp.

"That girl's a pest. She'll infect all the others. That kind of thing sets fashions. She's a danger to the house, to the reputation of the school."

Fräulein von Bernburg did not flinch.

"Reputation?" she repeated, with a faintly questioning inflection.

"Our reputation is more important than anything else."

"May I ask what you have decided?"

"Decided! What is there to decide? . . . Decide!"

Fräulein von Bernburg remained waiting. In a correct posture she stood before her superior, waiting to hear her sentence—her sentence, for whatever verdict was decided on would strike at her too. . . .

"You, my lady, are responsible for all this. If you can take the trouble to remember, I mentioned it to you before. You are encouraging for your own ends an hysterical devotion."

"Ma'am . . ."

But Fräulein von Bernburg was not to be allowed to speak.

"You should have nipped that kind of hysteria in the bud. There's a limit to everything. You see now what it leads to." And then, as if speaking to herself: "An unhealthy business. . . . Decide?" She sat down and stared at the motionless face of the young woman before her.

"Above all things, of course, she must be separated from you. Full stop. Finish. The end. Do you understand?"

"Yes." The answer came like a breath.

"And from the other children too. Isolated. Locked up. Not to make the other children as bad as herself. I'd like best of all to write to her father and tell him to take her away. But how could I explain such an unusual step to Her Royal Highness? That's the difficulty. The affair must be hushed up. The servants are gossiping too much already."

"The servants!" said Fräulein von Bernburg, and in spite of herself her tone was bitter.

"Certainly, that kind of gossip can have the most unpleasant consequences. Scandal. Rumors . . . Well, to stick to our point: Manuela must be isolated. . . ."

"But even so, ma'am, I beg you to consider—what if the child has a nervous breakdown? She's a very nervous child—sensitive—she. . . ."

Fräulein von Bernburg twisted her slim hands together.

"That means nothing to me. Nervous breakdown—what kind of expression is that to use? When I was a child no such thing was ever heard of. Fräulein von Bernburg, we are here to educate soldiers' children."

"I'm afraid for Manuela, ma'am; she is not strong. She'll take terribly to heart a separation from me and from the other children."

"And that will be her punishment. Fräulein von Bernburg, I expect you to obey me."

"I know my duty. But, ma'am, I beg of you, let me wean the child gradually from her devotion to me. . . ."

"Gradually? Devotion? Are you aware what we are really dealing with? Manuela is sexually abnormal." The Head took a step toward Fräulein von Bernburg. "And perhaps you know what the world thinks of such women—our world, Fräulein von Bernburg?"

Fräulein von Bernburg did not evade the look that was fixed upon her. Her mouth was closely compressed. Firmly she looked the old woman in the eye.

"I do know, ma'am."

And then, in a low voice, as if she were speaking only to herself: "Manuela's not a bad child. But she has to grow into a free and independent woman . . . and therefore I want to detach her from myself."

"I'm glad you're able to see it. I think there's nothing more for us to say to each other tonight."

Fräulein von Bernburg remained standing as if she had not heard her dismissal; it was only the continued silence that told her the Head was waiting.

Still as if she were meditating on something, she walked slowly to the door.

"Good night, ma'am."

"Good night, Fräulein von Bernburg."

But in the very doorway fear clutched again at the heart of the departing woman—dreadful fear.

"Ma'am, suppose Manuela . . . suppose she can't bear it. . . . I mean, if the child falls ill . . ."

"Then we'll make that an excuse for sending her home."

And as if this were the final solution, the Head laid her stick on the table to intimate that she wished to be alone.

Translated by Agnes Neill Scott

Achy Obejas

The Cuban-born Achy Obejas gives a complex portrait of an emigrée's return to her homeland in her story "Waters" (1996). Born in Havana, Obejas came to the United States by boat as an exile when she was six years old. Both this early experience and its resulting dislocations have provided the basis for a rich literary exploration of loss and reconstitution. For Obejas, as for many other writers in this collection, the power of memory shapes personal history into fiction. This search to find meaning both in a cultural past and a present lesbian self is represented by the narrator of "Waters" as she encounters current-day Cuba.

WATERS

THE moon burns. I had imagined it would dance across the water in Cuba, swing gently from one wave to the other, but instead it simmers, pale yellow flames blistering on the water.

I pull the black cotton T-shirt I have on away from my body. It's still dry. I can feel the soothing talc on my skin after my shower but I know this feeling of release will be short-lived. In an hour or so, I will be damp and glowing. Unlike some other travelers—who wring the sweat out of their shirts after an afternoon walk and wheeze and worry about their hearts—I am comfortable in this state of humidity, as at home as if it were amniotic fluid.

It's steaming here but I still welcomed the hot water for my shower—my first in Cuba. Until I got to Isabel's house in Varadero, every shower had been more of the theoretical sort: little bursts of icy liquid from rusty showerheads in tourist hotels in Havana, or cupfuls of cold water drawn from a bucket while standing chicken-skinned in otherwise dry tubs. These experiences only added to my admiration for the Cubans who live on the island; when I rub against them on the old, tired buses or in crowded streets, they always smell sweet and fresh.

Here at Isabel's, as soon as I spied the tiny water heater in the bathroom, I begged her to light it for me. She shook her head but smiled. "All right," she said, telling me without words how unnecessary and excessive it is to take a hot shower in Cuba. "But it won't last very long anyway," she warned me, a precious match trying to catch the heater's hissing gas. Its flickering seemed to pump up the temperature. Even Isabel's brow grew moist.

In the shower, I exercised my privilege: I luxuriated under a mass of lather on my hair, felt the streams of soap running between and down my newly browned legs. I imagined the salt of the ocean water from the afternoon's playful bath on the shore racing alongside the salt of my own sweat as it drained through flaky pipes and back into the land of my birth.

The day before the hot shower at Isabel's, I was invited for coffee to the home of one of Cuba's leading poets, a large, impressively built man with a long and thin, perfectly manicured mustache in the style of the patriots from the early twentieth century. As he talked to me in his Havana apartment—a magnificent place with a view of the Malecón and the broad boulevards that make Havana seem so French sometimes—I imagined him a man in a time warp, caught between his real existence, in which he whispered profundities with José Martí in a café, and ours, looking down at the crumbling revolutionary city, its baroque façades raked by the wind and the constant onslaught of sea salt.

The poet leaned against the windowsill. "I believe that you, of course, are a Cuban poet, a poet of the nation," he assured me, "although I do think the issue of language is very important."

We were talking in Spanish. He handed me a recent edition of one of the periodicals put out by the Cuban writers' union. Like all the other publications on the island, the pages were thin and limp, as if wilted by the heat and humidity. The front page featured an essay in which the poet, contrary to everything he was saying now, drew a definitive line between Cuban writers on the island and those living abroad, regardless of whatever language they used. I thought immediately of Martí, who wrote in a New York tenement not far from my own home.

"We must create a place for poets like you, who write in English," he said, "a Cuban place, of course, but *different*."

"But," I said, "sometimes I write in Spanish as well."

He smiled indulgently. "Yes, I've seen what you bilingual poets do. It started with the Chicanos, didn't it?" He paused. " 'Chicanos' is right, no? Or should I say 'Mexican-Americans'?" He looked about and giggled, as if we were sharing a terribly mischievous secret. Then he sipped noisily on his coffee.

"No," I said, "I'm not that type of bilingual poet. I write in English and Spanish, but not in the same poem."

He smiled, his fingers twisting the thin ends of his long mustache. The wind, whipping up from the streets and the ocean through the open windows, ignored his work and scattered the hair above his lip, making him look like a ferret or a mouse. "You mean, of course, that you translate into Spanish what you write in English."

I squinted and shook my head. "No, no," I said. The light was falling. "Some things come to me in English, others in Spanish. I write in whatever language it comes to me."

He nodded, as if he understood. "Yes, I write some things in English too. I even have a few things in Russian, from my youth, when I spent some time studying in Moscow. That was a beautiful time."

I looked out one of the huge windows and down to the street. I spied Isabel, who had refused to come up to see the poet. "He's overrated," she'd said. "But he is well connected. You should see him." She was waiting for me. Her body was spread out on the hood of her gray Lada, looking like someone who'd thrown herself down in an attempt at suicide. The street was deserted, otherwise she'd have drawn a crowd. The wind made her long, golden hair dance on the windshield.

"The poet's true language is the one in which he thinks," my host announced abruptly. "And you? In what language do you think?" He moistened his fingers and pressed down on his mustache, as if trying to hold it in place.

"It depends," I said. "Right now, I was thinking in Spanish, maybe because we were talking in Spanish. I don't know. I go back and forth, depending on who I'm with, what I'm doing."

The poet's eyebrows, pencil-thin black lines above his eyes, squiggled like an electrocardiogram. "Yes, yes, but what language do you dream in?" he demanded.

"Well," I said, "it depends. I don't always recognize the language in my dreams."

After my shower, I sit on the porch at Isabel's house trying to compose my thoughts into something coherent on the page. I've told myself I need to write every day I'm in Cuba, no matter how tired I am, how much activity there is around me. Above my head, shirts and towels flutter on a clothesline.

In the United States, I'd heard about Isabel's house mostly from friends. They told me it was on the beach, on the water at Varadero, and I had imagined something pastoral and pleasing, where I might feel the breeze off the ocean and smell the salt in the air. What no one mentioned was that there is a great expanse, a vacant lot, really, between Isabel's house and the sea, and that between the lot and the water there is a highway with trucks and buses and rented cars full of Argentinean and Spanish tourists coughing fumes and throwing litter out the windows. The lot, which is apparently no one's concern, is thick with aloe, brambles, and garbage, unpassable unless you're wearing long pants and hiking boots.

In the morning, we'd gone to the beach. We drove there in the Lada, fifteen minutes of maneuvering through narrow streets lined with prostitutes and illegal vendors.

"I always thought you lived *on* the beach," I said to Isabel.

She seemed confused. "I do," she said, her head nodding, as if I had somehow missed the fact that, yes, her house is right there, only a matter of yards from sand and sea.

"Well, yes," I said. I was going to go on, to explain what I meant, when someone tapped my arm through the car window. I turned to see a young man holding a lightbulb. He looked newly scrubbed, his hair combed back and still wet, his clothing perfectly pressed.

"Oh, we need one of those," Isabel said, reaching into the pockets of her shorts for some money.

"Here, I'll get it," I said, beating her to my bills.

I handed the young man a damp American dollar and though all he'd heard us speak was Spanish, he responded in English. "Thank you," he said with just the slightest accent and dropped the lightbulb into my hand. He smiled broadly, showing a pair of missing teeth, and backed away from us and into the crowds. Isabel took the lightbulb and shook it, seemingly satisfied with it. The whole exchange seemed odd to me, out of sync.

We piloted the Lada through the streets and onto a driveway leading up to one of the newer tourist hotels. It sat on a hill, its architecture hinting of the Bahamas, with sparkling white-washed walls, red-tiled roofs, and cozy verandas. As we drove through the resort, I spied a sign in English that read MINI-MARKET. There was no Spanish translation. Another, in the shape of a small arrow pointed to a glistening lawn and read (also in English and without translation) GOLF COURSE.

"It's not completed yet," Isabel said, as if reading my mind. In contrast to the jammed, sweaty streets of Varadero, it was cool and empty up here.

Isabel pulled up to a designated parking space. A uniformed security guard waved at her from a distance. "He's a friend," she said, gathering her beach towel and a pair of goggles from the backseat. "He and I went to school together."

We entered the ocean slowly, almost cautiously. Isabel had dropped her shorts on the shore but she kept her T-shirt on and now it expanded and became transparent. She wore brilliant tropical colors underneath that came alive when wet. It was low tide so I dropped to my knees to immerse myself in the water. There was nothing refreshing about it, though. It was as warm as bathwater, thick with salt and something vaguely oily on the surface. When I asked Isabel about it, she shrugged, put her goggles on, and dove into the sea. She swam about for a minute or so, emerging with a small rock in her hand. She examined it carefully then tossed it back. I watched as she glided underwater, a ribbon of color against the sandy bottom. As she explored, I hovered, my arms outstretched, sitting in the shallow water, searching out the shore for signs that this was, in fact, Varadero and not an abandoned St. Croix.

"Hey," Isabel said, coming from behind me and putting her arms around my neck. "I'm glad you're here," she said, and kissed me.

"Me too," I said, holding hands with her underwater.

We are just friends but, at different times, we have been involved with the same woman, a rather reckless Don Juanita who now lives in the U.S. and who recently dumped Isabel in favor of a former Olympian. Isabel knows about her own breakup with Don Juanita mostly through friends; our mutual ex has managed to communicate only indirectly.

"I'm not angry at her," she said, "but the Olympian, yes, I'm mad at her." She shrugged, took her goggles off, and dunked them in the oily water. She rubbed the lenses as if it mattered. "It's circumstances," she said.

"You ready?" Isabel asks. She pokes her head out from the house, car keys in hand.

"Absolutely," I say, and close my journal.

She turns off the porch light, bright with its new bulb. A truck drives by on the highway, its groaning muffled somewhat by the ocean. Smoke rises from its exhaust pipe and trails up to the low-hanging moon, a big yellow ball rising on the horizon.

We are on our way back to Havana for a party. I am well aware that if it weren't for me, Isabel would probably not go. She'd stay at home and read or watch American movies with Spanish subtitles on TV. But she wants me to see Havana, her city although she lives in Varadero, and she wants me to have a few good stories to tell when I return to the States.

In the car, we listen to Marta Valdes and Sara Gonzales on a tape player I sent her for her birthday last year. The music is soft and sad, its lyrics remarkably gender-free. The car rattles, but it's soothing in its own way. As we drive along, we pass a handful of other noisy cars, a couple of closed roadside snack shops, and the huge, aviarian shadows of oil cranes on the shores. They silently dip and rise, one after the other, for miles and miles. The car window's wide open, my elbow sticking out Cuban style, and my black T-shirt flaps like wings on my shoulders as we enter the city. The moon floats over the sea.

At one of the first stoplights in Havana, we're examined from a distance by a small crowd of male and female prostitutes. The Lada, with its fading paint, is clearly local, but both Isabel and I mystify them: though her clothes and body language correspond to the languorous way of the island, she is blond and wears too-fashionable-for-Cuba yellow and black frames for glasses (a gift from another New York friend); there's too much burnt red under my tanned skin, and my clothes—all dark colors—do not correspond to the logic of Cuba's heat and humidity.

At the stoplight, I lift my camera to my eye and focus and, as if on cue, the prostitutes descend. The first is a sinewy boy in his late teens, chocolate-skinned and perfect but for the gold tooth that appears when he smiles.

"*Señorita,*" he says, doing his best Latin Romeo imitation, "perhaps you would like a little company tonight, no?" He affects an Iberian accent, taking a chance that I'm a Spanish tourist and might be amused by his attempt to sound like a compatriot. He leans into the car window and with him comes a waft of soap and cologne.

"She's already got company for tonight," Isabel says a bit too quickly, too protectively, in her own open-mouthed Cuban Spanish.

"Ah," he says, still holding onto the car, but waving over two much-too-young girls with his other arm. "Then perhaps you'd like to make it a party, eh?" He's looking at me but talking to

Isabel, unsure where I'm from or whether I understand. His gold tooth seems to spark. "This is Nena," he says, pushing one of the girls up to the window. She's no more than fourteen, her eyes encircled with heavy black liner and fatigue. "And this is Pilar," he says, grabbing the other girl by the arm. This one is caramel-colored and resentful, her lips curling.

"*Encantada,*" I say.

Isabel rolls her eyes in disgust. The light has changed. The other cars are involved in their own transactions or going around us, the drivers indifferent to the scene.

"Ah, you're from Miami," says the boy, understanding my accent as native but my demeanor as foreign. (I'm too amused to be local.)

"No, from New York," I say, smiling at them.

"Pilar has a cousin in New York," he says, yanking her up closer.

She shakes him off. "*Ya coño,*" she says, resisting. She's not much older than Nena, her face still round and babyish under all the makeup.

"We can show you Havana," the boy says, "a private Havana, a Havana especially for you."

An exasperated Isabel shakes her head, tells him no. He leans in, his whole head inside the Lada now. I'm blinded by his gold tooth so I push myself back, giving him room to continue his sales pitch to Isabel, who I know won't be moved.

I look out the car window to Pilar, who's standing out on the street, her arms folded stubbornly across her chest. She stares back at me, full of pride and hate.

The party's in an old, majestic but dilapidated mansion in the Vedado neighborhood. It's a colorless, muddy shade but I can see its former elegance in the chipped Roman columns at the front, the scalloped borders on the doors. A young girl sits in

front with a metal cashbox on her lap. She asks for ten pesos—
not even a dollar's worth. I give her a few American bills and
Isabel and I enter through the large wooden doors that seem to
open just for us.

Inside there is a crush of bodies, revolving disco balls, and a
suffocating humidity. It's wall-to-wall flesh, all of it drenched
and alive and yearning. I smell talcum and blood, sex and perfume. It takes a minute for me to adjust my senses. There is a
dizzying disco song blasting from the speakers—large, coffin-
size boxes hung from chains on the ceiling; paint flakes down
like confetti.

As the partygoers come into view, I see men and women
pressed up against each other, men rubbing their naked nipples
against other men, women gyrating between pairs of men who
encourage them with grins and long snaky tongues that dart in
and out of their purple mouths. Shirts and blouses are translucent, second skins sticking to breasts and bones. Everything's
gauzy.

In one corner, I see a black figure separate into two silhou-
ettes, long dark hair soaked and fused to their naked shoulders.
"I want their picture," I shout to Isabel above the noise, pointing
to the two women breathing in the corner. She has her finger
around a loop in my jeans, making sure we don't lose each other.
She follows me as I approach the lovers.

"*Con permiso,*" I say in my loudest voice, although I can tell
from the way they're looking at my mouth that they are lip-
reading. "Listen, I'm a writer—a poet—from New York and I
wonder if you'd mind if I took your picture?" I lift my camera
for them to see.

They are both gorgeous, olive-hued, with dark, wounded
eyes and creamy skin. The smaller one turns away and folds into
her lover, who looks at me with a sober and unforgiving expres-

sion. "We would mind very much," she says. And I hear her slightly accented English through the crunching sounds of some German industrial dance song.

"*Aaaayyyyyyyy*, take my picture, take my picture!" shouts an excited young queen dripping with faux pearls who drags his drunken lover into my face.

I laugh and nod, bring the camera up and push the button. The flash explodes, freezing everyone for a split second. Faces turn toward us, some excited, some enraged. The beautiful women are gone.

"*Mi amor*, photograph us!" says a boy in a sailor's suit, pushing his companion, a soldier in full military drag, at me.

Isabel puts her hands squarely on my hips and drives me away, through the labyrinth of flesh out to a patio, where the air is suddenly cool and refreshing. We pass a small table, where greasy paper plates are piled up, and a cart full of rapidly melting ice from which a couple of lithe young men are selling beer and soda. We settle under a low hanging tree on which the leaves are ripe and aromatic. The moon is somewhere high above us.

"Jesus," I say, laughing, "what is it about gay men, huh? It doesn't matter where in the world I go, they're always listening to disco, they always want their picture taken."

Isabel pulls a handkerchief from her pocket. She wipes her face and sighs. "Good party?" she asks.

I nod. "Yeah, and an amazing place," I say, surveying the mansion. The owners have cleared the front room of all furniture and blocked access to all the other rooms. There are meaty men standing guard in front of the doors leading to the bedrooms and kitchen. Some of the windows that look out to the patio are boarded up, nailed shut, but we can see the glow of a light inside one of them and a solitary shadow in a rocking chair, reading a newspaper.

"That must be the mother," Isabel says. "Listen," she says, coming closer to me. Her breath is hot on my face. "No more pictures here, okay?"

"Yeah?"

She shrugs. "Yeah, you know . . . the flash." I know it's more than that, but it's okay.

Then a short, brown-skinned woman comes over to us. She's wearing a red suit, with a lacy red shirt and a red ribbon holding her hair in a curly, wet ponytail. Her apparel is sort of corporate femmy, but her demeanor is entirely butch. As she crosses the patio, she's practically marching.

"*Tú—mujer linda*," she says, pointing to me. Her smile is sly, cocky. "*¿Quieres bailar?*"

There's an unintelligible rap song booming through the speakers now, which seem nearly as powerful out here as inside the house. I see Isabel in my peripheral vision, smirking at my little admirer. I tower over this girl.

"Maybe later," I say, "something slower." Isabel smiles, nods approvingly at my discretion.

But suddenly, the music shifts. The beat is tropical and lazy. "*J'imanijé . . .*" sings an indolent, Caribbean voice.

"*Ay, mamita, si es una canción francesa*," says the little butch, imploring.

Isabel laughs. "That's not French," she tells her, "it's some kind of Creole."

"You're not together, are you?" the girl asks, as if it just occurred to her.

Instinctively, we both shake our heads. The red-dressed butch grabs my hand with her moist, slippery fingers and pulls. "*Vamos*," she says, and I obey, laughing over my shoulder at Isabel, who seems entertained by the turn of events.

On the dance floor, we are overwhelmed by the long, gangly bodies that sway dreamily around us. Their features come in and out of shadow, sweat running from their temples unabated. A few women wrap themselves around each other, their bodies encased in shiny perspiration.

My dancing partner pulls me toward her with one swift, hard tug but I resist. I feel my T-shirt molding to my back, as soaked as if I'd been standing out in the rain. We struggle wordlessly back and forth until we come to a compromise: I nail my elbows to the inside of hers and her hand goes to the small of my back and works from there. All the while, she sings, *"J'imanijé...."* In my head, I make it French: *"J'imaginais."* As we turn, I catch Isabel's eye. She's leaning up against a wall, watching us and smiling. She's drinking a beer I don't remember her buying.

When the song ends, my partner doesn't give me a chance. As soon as the notes of the new tune begin—something even slower, even more drippily romantic—she takes advantage of the instant I relax to smash me into her. My breasts squish up against her chest, hers slide around under mine. My nose is in her hair, which smells of sweat and roses. She sings, and I know it's for me. Her voice is raspy but strong, directed at my ear. I feel her flushed breath on my lobe and neck. I think I recognize the song—something by Marta Valdes?—but I can't make out the words.

And now she seems more convincing, leading me, turning us in small, tight circles. The room spins, like a ride at an amusement park. I look for Isabel but all the faces have smudged together. I try to pull away but I can't. It's as if all the air has been sucked out of the space between our bodies and we're being held together by suction. The little butch continues to sing, her tone rising with the song's crescendo, her throat full of emotion. I feel as if I could drown.

It's then I look up and see Pilar, the girl from the intersection. She's framed by a pair of couples whose deliberate moves make them look as if they're orgasming in slow motion on the dance floor. She is across the room, standing in a thin funnel of light, her shirt loose around her candied shoulders, barely damp, but her full lips glisten, even at a distance. Her eyes are bright and she's smiling, free and open. She waves at me, as if we're old friends. I feel something loosen and drop inside me.

I jerk away from my dancing partner, who falls back, disoriented by my sudden determination. The disco ball spins aquamarine, like water or bile.

Pilar's eyes open widely; she's laughing now, her head tossed back languidly against the wall. She mouths something to me. I have no idea what language she's speaking. But, wet and feverish, I slowly begin to make my way toward her.

Nicole Brossard

In her novel Mauve Desert *(1987)—the first pages of which are included here—the Quebecois writer Nicole Brossard uses the voice of a sexually aware fifteen-year-old girl to explore the arid and dangerous world of the nuclear-haunted 1950s, represented here by the shadowy form of Long-man—Robert Oppenheimer, a leading figure in nuclear development. The novel, written in three sections, is structured to explore the relationship between a text and its reader. One of the founders of the theories of* l'écriture féminine *(writing in the feminine), Brossard combines both feminism and literary innovations, interweaving detailed storytelling and poetic language to achieve a provocatively playful mix of experience and ideas.*

from MAUVE DESERT

THE desert is indescribable. Reality rushes into it, rapid light. The gaze melts. Yet this morning. Very young, I was already crying over humanity. With every new year I could see it dissolving in hope and in violence. Very young, I would take my mother's Meteor and drive into the desert. There I spent entire days, nights, dawns. Driving fast and then slowly, spinning out the light in its mauve and small lines that like veins mapped a great tree of life in my eyes.

I was wide awake in the questioning but inside me was a desire that free of obstacles frightened me like a certitude. Then would come the pink, the rust, and the gray among the stones, the mauve and the light of dawn. In the distance, the flashing wings of a tourist helicopter.

Very young I had no future like the shack on the corner which one day was set on fire by some guys who "came from far away," said my mother who had served them drinks. Only one of them was armed, she had sworn to me. Only one among them. All the others were blond. My mother always talked about men as if they had seen the day in a book. She would say no more and go back to her television set. I could see her profile and the reflection of the little silver comb she always wore in her hair and to which I attributed magical powers. Her apron was yellow with little flowers. I never saw her wearing a dress.

I was moving forward in life, wild-eyed with arrogance. I was fifteen. This was a delight like the power of dying or of driving into the night with circles under my eyes, absolutely delirious spaces edging the gaze.

I was well-acquainted with the desert and the roads running through it. Lorna, this friend of my mother's, had introduced me to erosion, to all the ghosts living in the stone and the dust. She had described landscapes, some familiar, some absolutely incompatible with the vegetation and barren soil of my child-hood. Lorna was inventing. I knew she was because even I knew how to distinguish between a Western diamondback and a rat-tlesnake, between a troglodyte and a mourning turtledove. Lorna was inventing. Sometimes she seemed to be barking, so rough and unthinkable were her words. Lorna had not known childhood, only young girls after school whom she would ostentatiously arrange to meet at noon. The girls loved kissing her on the mouth. She loved girls who let themselves be kissed on the mouth.

The first time I saw Lorna I found her beautiful and said the word "bitch." I was five years old. At supper my mother was smiling at her. They would look at each other and when they spoke their voices were full of intonations. I obstinately observed their mouths. Whenever they pronounced words starting with *m*, their lips would disappear for a moment then, swollen, reanimate with incredible speed. Lorna said she liked molly and salmon mousse. I spilled my glass of milk and the tablecloth changed into America with Florida seeping under the saltshaker. My mother mopped up America. My mother always pretended not to notice when things were dirtied.

I often took to the road. Long before I got my driver's license. At high noon, at dusk, even at night, I would leave with my mother yelling sharp words at me that would get lost in the parking lot dust. I always headed for the desert because very young I wanted to know why in books they forget to mention the desert. I knew my mother would be alone like a woman can be but I was fleeing the magical reflection of the comb in her hair, seeking the burning reflections of the blinding sun, seeking the night in the dazzled eyes of hares, a ray of life. "Let me confront aridity," and I would floor the accelerator, wild with the damned energy of my fifteen years. Some day I would reach the right age and time as necessary as a birth date to get life over with. Some day I would be fast so fast, sharp so sharp, some day, faced with the necessity of dawn, I would have forgotten the civilization of men who came to the desert to watch their equations explode like a humanity. I was driving fast, alone like a character cut out of history. Saying "so many times I have sunk into the future."

At night there was the desert, the shining eyes of antelope jackrabbits, *senita* flowers that bloom only in the night. Lying under the Meteor's headlights was the body of a humanity that did not know Arizona. Humanity was fragile because it did not suspect Arizona's existence. So fragile. I was fifteen and hungered for everything to be as in my body's fragility, that impatient tolerance making the body necessary. I was an expert driver, wild-eyed in mid-night, capable of going forward in the dark. I knew all that like a despair capable of setting me free of everything. Eternity was a shadow cast in music, a fever of the brain making it topple over into the tracings of highways. Humanity was fragile, a gigantic hope suspended over cities. Everything was fragile, I knew it, I had always known it. At fifteen I pretended I had forgotten mediocrity. Like my mother, I pretended that nothing was dirtied.

Shadows on the road devour hope. There are no shadows at night, at noon, there is only certitude traversing reality. But reality is a little trap, little shadow grave welcoming desire. Reality is a little passion fire that pretexts. I was fifteen and with every ounce of my strength I was leaning into my thoughts to make them slant reality toward the light.

And now to park the car in front of the Red Arrow Motel. Heat, the Bar. The bar's entire surface resembles a television image: elbows everywhere leaning like shadows and humanity's trash repeating themselves. I have a beer and nobody notices I exist.

CHAPTER ONE

Longman puts his briefcase on the bed. He has been hot, he loosens his tie. He heads for the bathroom. He thinks about the explosion, he thinks about it and it's not enough. Something. He knows some lovely little footpaths, delicately shaded areas. He hesitates in front of the mirror. He washes his hands. He thinks about the explosion, he thinks about it and nothing happens in his head. He removes his jacket, throws it on the bed. A ballpoint pen falls to the floor. He does not bend down. He lights a cigarette. He fingers the brim of his felt hat, which he almost never takes off. He thinks about the explosion. For the pleasure of sounds he recites a few sentences in Sanskrit, the same ones that earlier delighted his colleagues. He paces the floor. His cigarette smoke follows him about like a spectral presence. Longman knows the magic value of formulas. He thinks about the explosion. The slightest error could have disastrous consequences. Longman stretches out with white visions then orange ones then the ground beneath his feet turns to jade—I / am / become / Death—now we are all sons of bitches. Longman rests his head on the equation.

I had the power over my mother to take her car from her at the most unexpected moment. My mother had the unsuspected power to arouse in me a terrible solitude which, when I saw her in such closeness to Lorna, devastated me for then there was between them just enough silence for the thought of their commingled flesh to infiltrate me. One night unexpectedly in the obscurity of their room I came upon my mother, her shoulders and the nape of her neck braced like an existence toward Lorna's nakedness.

I'm driving. Howling, rock-jaw'd, mouth full of lyrics I sing to the same beat as the woman's voice exploding the radio. A voice of doom interrupts the song. I howl. I lean on the announcer interrupting the music until the earthquake ebbs into the distance, tidal wave, resorbs into the Pacific blue. The desert is civilization. I don't like leaving my mother at night. I fear for her. Mothers are as fragile as civilization. They must not be forgotten in front of their television sets. Mothers are spaces. I love driving fast in my mother's Meteor. I love the road, the vanishing horizon, feeling dawn's fresh emptiness. I never panic in the desert. In the middle of the night or even in the midst of a sandstorm as the windshield slowly covers up, I know how to be iso-

lated from everything, concrete and unreal like a character con-
fined to the steering wheel of an old Meteor. In the dark of the
dust I know how to exist. I listen to the dreadful sound, the roar
of wind and sand against the car's metal body. I yield totally to
blindness. I lightly press two fingers against each eyelid and look
inside the intimate *species,* at time going by in the back of my
mind. I see seconds, small silvery scars, moving along like creatures. I recognize the trace of creatures who have passed through
there where seconds form pyramids, spirals among the remains,
beautiful sandstone chevrons. Only once words I was unable to
read. And their form soon faded as if it were a partial transcrip-
tion of light deep in the mind.

I was driving avidly. Choosing the night the desert to thus
expose myself to the violence of the moment which propels
consciousness. I was fifteen and before me space, space far off
tapering me down like a civilization in reverse, city lost in the
trembling air. In my mother's Meteor I was exemplary solitude
with, at the tip of my toes, a brake to avoid all disasters and to
remind me of the insignificance of despair amid snakes and cacti
in the bluest night of all ravings.

I am my mother's laughter when I pale in the face of humanity's distress. Never did my mother cry. I never saw her cry. My
mother was unable to imagine that solitude could be like an
exactness of being. She trembled when faced with humanity's
noises but no solitude really reached her. In the worst moments of
her existence my mother would conclude: "This is a man, we
need a bed; this is a woman, we need a room." My mother was as
obstinate as a man struggling with the desert. She did not like men
but she defended the desert like a feeling leaguing her with men.
She was a woman without expression and this frightened me.

Every time I think of my mother I see girls in swimsuits lying
by the motel pool. This motel, purchased in 1950, my mother
renovated it and spent fifteen years paying it off with polite ges-

tures, discipline, and energy repeated in the heat of Tucson afternoons. But before Lorna's arrival, everything is vague. Vague and noisy like the to-and-fro of travelers, of suppliers, of the chambermaid.

Lorna's presence will always be linked in my memory with my first years of school and especially with learning to read and write. I liked to read but don't remember reading otherwise than in Lorna's presence. She would watch me, static watcher, monitoring every blink of my eyelids, spying any flutter of sensation, the slightest sign upon my face liable to betray an emotion. I would follow her little game with a discrete eye but when I happened to look up, it was my turn to follow upon her lips the strange alphabet that seemed to constitute a dream in her gaze. I would then invariably ask the question: "What are we eating?" as if this could keep her at bay or protect the intimate nature of what I had experienced while reading.

One day when looking for some blank paper to draw on I saw, at the far end of the kitchen, Lorna and my mother sitting on the same chair. My mother was on Lorna's lap, who was holding her by the waist with her right arm. With her left hand Lorna was scribbling. Their legs were all entwined and my mother's apron was folded over Lorna's thigh. I asked Lorna what she was writing. She hesitated then spun out some sentence to the effect that she was unable to read the marks her hand had drawn. I was about to exclaim, to say that . . . it made no sense when I noticed the ease of Lorna's hand in my mother's hair.

Yet that night. Very young I learned to love the fire from the sky, torrential lightning branched out over the city like thinking flowing in the mind. On dry storm nights I would become tremors, detonations, total discharge. Then surrender to all the illuminations, those fissures that like so many wounds lined my virtual body, linking me to the vastness. And so the body melts like a glimmer of light in the abstract of words. Eyes, existence give in before that which comes forth inside us, certitude. The desert drinks everything in. Furor, solitude.

In the desert there is the pursuit of breaks clouds sometimes make. Sometimes they are like little lead pellets the sun shoots toward the horizon to signify tomorrow's coming future. I am well acquainted with lead, copper, cartridges, and all weapons. I know weapons. Any desert girl learns at a very young age how to hold a weapon and to drive a car. Any young girl learns that what glitters under the sun can also hurt or excite feeling so utterly that shadow itself turns to crimson.

Translated by Suzanne de Lotbinière-Harwood and the author

Gila Svirsky

Gila Svirsky, an Israeli author and peace activist who lives in Jerusalem, creates a political and emotional triangle in her story "Meeting Natalia" (1996). This triangle, composed of two women and the city of Jerusalem, symbolizes the challenge of historical loyalties. The narrator in the story finds herself drawn to a German non-Jewish woman, a desire that leads her into unexpected territories. Even though Jerusalem is a fragmented world, the city becomes a familiar and comforting lover whom she refuses to betray. Svirsky, like many Israeli feminists, is searching for a land in which differences can find a home. In this story, the search is historical, immediate, and sexual.

MEETING NATALIA

I did not invite her: I would never have brought a German-accented guest into my home. But Natalia needed a place to stay in Jerusalem and had been sent by a mutual friend. So, like a true, hospitable Jerusalemite, I opened to her my home, but not my heart. I would sculpt and she would sit writing as I studiously ignored her, letting my fingers capture in form and substance the dense texture of these evenings together.

One night I came home late and found Natalia tending the fire. No, my house is not warm in the normal course of winter.

My fireplace is beautiful but holds only the promise of thaw to numb limbs. So I feed it and stoke it, carry in fresh wood, and carry out old ashes—small flickers of hope in a world where small flickers of hope are all that keep one warm sometimes. But this evening, Natalia was taking care of the fire.

"You do that well," I said, watching her move the logs around.

"It is something we must learn to do where I come from," she replied. "In my village the snow lies on the ground all winter long, like a quiet carpet."

In Malha, my section of Jerusalem, fallen almond blossoms form a quiet carpet of their own in spring.

I sat down and watched her turn the logs. Perhaps it was her reticence that finally caused me to speak, a reticence that proclaimed indifference to my hostility.

"Tell me about your village," I said at last. Natalia continued to shift the wood. When she was finished, she carefully hung the tools and then sat down.

"I did not come to talk about Germany," she said. "You tell me about Jerusalem."

I looked across at her curled into the couch, her expression expectant, and considered talking to her about this place/presence that is Jerusalem. We inhabitants of Jerusalem do not easily share our thoughts with outsiders. But something in her compelled me to answer.

"Jerusalem is not just a city, it's a state of mind." Could she grasp this at all? "Jerusalem is an attitude of intense religiosity garbed in modern clothing. It's a spiritual outlook on all matters, even those not ordinarily in the realm of the spiritual."

The words sounded stilted. Natalia waited for me to continue.

"The spiritual can be very primitive sometimes. In the center of town there's a building under construction—near the *shuk*—that came under the curse of a kabbalist rabbi. People were so afraid of the curse that workers didn't show up, suppliers stopped deliveries, the apartments couldn't be rented. And why did the rabbi curse it? Because the height of the building cast a shadow on his courtyard."

"You do not mind if I interrupt while you are speaking?" she asked.

"No, I don't mind," I said, thinking that I had started the wrong way.

"I make hot wine so that we can be more easy on the subject." She smiled. "Is this all right?"

Her smile disarmed me. I watched her as she stood up, no longer quite so aloof as she prepared the wine. Her dark hair fell onto her thin shoulders. She brought two mugs to the table and set them down gently, as if afraid of breaking the fragile thread between us.

"Tell me more," she said.

I sipped the wine and tried not to concentrate on her eyes as they watched me over the rim of her cup. I looked into the fire and began to tell her about Jerusalemites—a people set apart. The old men who live their lives as ascetics—in sackcloth and ashes, still mourning the destruction of the ancient Temple. The women who shave their heads once they have married, to prevent themselves from being attractive to other men. Adolescent girls who swaddle their bodies to conceal the biological life beneath. Young men who spend all their waking hours in tiny yeshivas: memorizing, interpreting, chanting the archaic arguments of the Talmud.

"But that's not all," I said, overwhelmed by the thought of describing a modern world suffused with medieval rites and superstitions. "There are Jerusalemites who attend the university, who travel to foreign lands, who study science and technology—and who still ritually kiss the doorpost when they enter and leave a room; they still weep bitterly at the remnant wall of the ancient Temple; they still have their life partners chosen for them by a matchmaker and a rabbi. They live their lives with one foot planted in a dark age and the other in a mystical present."

"And this is wrong to you?" asked Natalia.

I heard in her question an implied criticism of my modern position. Perhaps it was the wine that led me to this conclusion. Perhaps it was my own guilt at having broken away from the ancient traditions.

"It's complicated," I said.

We were quiet then. I had wanted to hear from Natalia that this is a wonderful city, a city set somewhere between heaven and earth. We who live here—having full faith that this is true—always long for others to confirm it. But Natalia did not. I sipped my wine to the last drop and found my head spinning chaotically, unloosing thoughts that should have remained unuttered.

"You are German. You would not understand this."

"But I . . . ," began Natalia.

"Germans are not welcome here," I said, the memory of my gassed grandparents suddenly flooding my mind. "Your interest in Jerusalem is an ugly curiosity, a cynicism, a monstrous, sadistic, necrophilic fascination with the dead!"

I put down my cup and stood up. Too much wine and history were running through my mind, and I could no longer bear this conversation.

"No, it's not that at all!" said Natalia. "My grandparents . . ."

"Were Nazis," I hissed at her, and slammed the door as I left.

I walked down the narrow path from my house and found myself alone in a dark Malha, hemmed in by the houses that push out against the narrow lanes. I walked through the alleys until I reached the hill behind the village and climbed down the other side, entering the mouth of the valley, walking to the light of the moon, past gnarled olive trees and young almond trees about to give winter blossom, sometimes losing the path and tripping over stones and thorny brambles, making my way deep into the valley, feeling my rage slowly subside as the night wrapped itself around me. Finally I reached a small glen, a place I sometimes go to when I need silence. I sat down on the soft patch of grass, hugged my knees against the cold, and cried. I didn't know what had come over me.

I went back to the house later that night, but Natalia was gone. She had taken her things and left. I went searching through the rooms, opening every door in hope of seeing something of hers, a sign that she would be back, but there was none. The two mugs and pot were washed and put away. An empty wine bottle stood at attention on the counter.

I didn't expect to see Natalia ever again. I didn't know how to contact her or find her address. I spent many days thinking through that evening—what had been said, what had not been said—and I could not excuse my outburst. It pained me, but I gradually forced it out of my mind, suppressing the thought of her and of that night.

Months later, I found myself once again walking through the darkened city, the streets, now deserted, leading me east. The night air was crisp, invigorating. I walked until I came to the wall of the Old City.

It was late and the buses were no longer running. I passed through Jaffa Gate and entered the walled city, turning toward the Armenian Quarter. I continued along the road and then cut across the Jewish Quarter to the broad stairs leading down to the Western Wall. I do not go to the Wall for solace, but I do sometimes go there to gaze at its sculpted beauty. The light and shadows playing on the stones stirred in me feelings long buried.

I stood behind the prayer area and watched the few who were keeping an all-night vigil sway back and forth in their prayers. As I watched, I tried to recall some of the prayers that I had learned as a child. The words were coming to me: "Thou shalt love the

Lord thy God with all thy heart and with all thy soul and with all thy might. These words which I command thee today shall be in thy heart. Thou shalt instill them diligently in thy children. . . ."

"The stones do not listen."

The words came through the night, soft and direct. I looked up and was shocked to see her there.

"Natalia!"

She smiled, and, remembering how I had left her, I felt that I did not deserve such a lovely smile.

"We meet again," she said, "this time on ground that is holy and casts its own spell. Do I stand a chance to speak to you in such a place? If now you run away, I will not interrupt your prayers next time."

"I'm so glad to see you, Natalia, so glad to find you again, so long wanting to talk to you after that evening." The words were rushing out unsorted. "How inconsiderate I was that night— unfair and bigoted. Please forgive me. It was so rude. . . ."

"Now you come to my home and drink some of my wine," she said, "and I decide if I forgive you."

We walked back together through the large deserted plaza. I wondered what she was doing out at this hour, and at the Western Wall, no less. In fact, what was she doing in Jerusalem? All these were questions I held in my heart as we walked silently through the restored quarter. Reaching a gate, we entered a courtyard, passed several homes, and then stopped at one low, wooden door, set apart from the others by a sign: "N. Koenig-Strauss, Therapist. By appointment only."

She led me inside to a sparsely furnished apartment, and I looked around while she went to bring the wine. The room was simple and warm—oriental carpets, two overstuffed armchairs, a low table between them on which a book in German lay open. One wall was lined with shelves of books, another carried diplomas from a Berlin institute. She surprised me with this profession. And I was surprised at myself for never having inquired while she was staying in my home.

"I didn't know that you're a therapist," I said, "and I surely didn't know that you stayed on in Jerusalem."

"You talked me into staying," said Natalia, and I could not tell if she meant it.

"But what's your life like here? Do you have family? What's it like for a German to live in Jerusalem, in the heart of the Jewish Quarter, a short walk from the Temple site?"

"You come to the point quickly," she laughed.

"I spoke too much—and too little—when we were together last. Now you speak and tell me as much as you can bear to tell someone who once insulted you unfairly, but feels great remorse and is sincerely interested."

Natalia sat back and sipped her wine. I watched her dark eyes study me.

"Yes, I will share with you some of these thoughts. You are a careful listener, and you begin to view me through your heart."

Natalia then told me about some of her life that had preceded her coming to Jerusalem. Her father had died when she was seven, and she never got along with her mother.

"Mother's boyfriends were her first priority," she said, "and my brothers and I had to help each other cope with that." It was a difficult childhood, but Natalia had done well in her studies, had found friendship, and had even been married—very young, very briefly—to a volatile Jewish playwright. Perhaps this was part of a fascination she felt for things Jewish: "Not to become a Jew, but to learn about this people and its history." Several years after her divorce, she came to Israel.

"And, yes, my grandparents were Nazis," she concluded, "but I am not."

Her words coursed through my system, slowly sinking in. "And I had the arrogance to treat you like the enemy," I said.

"That is no longer important," Natalia responded. "It is now part of our common history. Even confrontation becomes a bond between two people."

Yes, a bond between us. There had been a bond ever since that outburst of mine at her. Now she was sitting opposite me in her home in Jerusalem. What was to become of this bond now? Once I left this room, would our chance encounter have broken my tie of remorse to her, freeing me of any further connection?

"So, will we have anything to say to each other after all the apologies and explanations are over?" she asked.

I laughed. "You're good at reading thoughts."

"Sometimes," said Natalia.

We sipped our wine in the late night, the quiet lying between us.

"And I suppose there are one or two little facts in the stories of our lives that still bear some clarification," she said, a smile just hovering behind her eyes and mouth.

I looked directly into her eyes and wondered. And she looked directly back into mine. These looks are sometimes unequivocal, but still I felt uncertain.

"So, does this call for another meeting at a more reasonable hour?" I asked.

"It might. Or for an invitation to stay the night."

I looked at her. "It's complicated," I said.

She didn't reply.

"But I'd like to," I continued. "Another time. If I may."

"You may," she said softly.

I stepped outside and felt the brooding darkness enclose me, but it did not reach a small light that had turned on inside me. The church spires rose above the rooftops of the Old City, looking more dark and intriguing than I remembered them. Yes, yes, I'd like to. I began the long walk home. And she said I may.

Maureen Duffy

A portrait of a 1950s British working-class lesbian bar community, The Microcosm *(1966) by Maureen Duffy was a ground-breaking novel, intriguing both for its content and its style. In the following excerpt, the author challenges narrative structure by using shifting points of view to reveal the complexities of this community of women. Prefiguring contemporary discussion of gender representation, Duffy allows her characters to speak in a gender-breaking language that expresses their "butch-fem" identities. Duffy, born in Sussex, England, in 1933, started her long publishing career in 1962; her works include biography, fiction, poetry, and plays. In this passage, the reader overhears Judy's thoughts as she endures her shift in the factory and anticipates rejoining Jonnie, her lover.*

from THE MICROCOSM

So it better be time and a half too, dragging us in here like this on a Saturday morning, dragging us out of our nice warm beds, making us do without our little bit of Sat'day lie in and the only time we do get a little bit of the old how's-your-father these days with Jonnie always so tired working her guts out till all hours every night just so's we can live a bit near the mark, a bit like normal people, all them Joneses we're supposed to be so hot on keeping up with like they're always stuffing us with on the screen, the goggle-box like Matt says. And what was it she said now, she said we love it and hate it, love it and hate it sitting there night after night with only Mitzi for company the little darling, must bathe her tomorrow when Jonnie's home to help me cos she struggles like a little demon for all she's only a scrap, nothing of her at all when you come to pick her up but she does her little best snuggling up to me so's I won't be too lonely as if she knew somehow and we sit there hour after hour loving it and hating it because there's so many things I could be doing about the flat if only I could tear meself away but I seem so tired somehow so gawd knows how Jonnie must feel and it's wrong of me I know to take it out of her when she comes in, but I can't help it, making up to her, smooching round her for a little bit of the old you-know and feeling all aggrieved when she turns away only wanting a cup of tea and a sit by the fire and I can see it going through her head what have I been doing all evening but she's too tired to come out straight with it so it's never brought out in the open for an airing, only I see her looking round at the dust you could write your name in on every flat top and thick enough to grow carrots along the ledges and me still sitting there in me old slacks like I just come in from work, with me hair a mess of tangles and me face gone all blotchy from the fire. Oh I see when I go out to put the kettle on, catch a sight of meself in the glass and think what a fright to come home to. You watch it my girl as mum would say or one day she may not be so keen to come home.

Look at her down there now working away so all I can see really is her curly black hair with not a gray one in it yet and I'll make her touch it up as soon as they start showing cos I'm not having my Jonnie looking old even if it is supposed to be distinguished. All the filmstars dye their hair men as well as women so why shouldn't others and it does you good makes you feel younger if you look it and she's got such a slim figure still, looks real handsome in her best suit not like some of them fleshy butches you see about and even Matt's starting to put it on a bit though maybe that's the winter like that program on bears I saw where they put on pounds to see them through hibernation and there's a big word for something I wouldn't have known except for the box so it's not all rubbish they put on there though I should have known it from school I suppose if I'd paid any attention or had any brains. And that was something they didn't teach us in nature study only about the birds and the bees and only then how to get a baby and what happens to it inside of you though we knew all the rest anyway from each other and who had seen their mum and dad having it away and whose big sister was expecting but what I've needed to know since they never told us, don't suppose they knew theirselves some of them though looking back there was one or two of the teachers I wouldn't be so sure about knowing what I do now with that Steve and the others who come down the club, still if they were they never let on to us. That's why I didn't know when the girls started calling me names and just because me and Sheila was friends and didn't run after the boys like all the rest. After all we was only kids of thirteen and how the others knew there were such things I don't know cos I'd never heard the word before and even when I did I went running home to ask mum what it meant and even she a married woman and dad was never finicky with his language still she didn't know.

"What's that bloke doing in among all them girls?" that man in the blue suit wanted to know when the foreman showed him our shop. Laugh though I went a bit hot and cold at first wondering if the others had heard and what they'd say but funny they never said nothing cos they seem as if they take Jonnie for granted. Being in the army so long I suppose they think makes

her a bit different, a bit strange and the foreman he never says
nothing neither cos he knows she's the best worker in the shop
and don't waste no time chinwagging with the others and always
keen to do a bit of overtime. Gawd knows how we'd manage
otherwise with the lousy wages they give you here, and the rent
of the flat, but she would have it we must have a decent home
although now I've got it I hardly know what to do with it being
dragged up to newspaper on the table and hardly a stick of furniture cos he'd never give her anything toward it, food money
that was all and not much of that and the few chattels we had
were chuckouts from the neighbors like the clothes to our backs
was handmedowns. Still we had a bit of fun in them days when
he was out of the house till he come home knocking our heads
together and clouting her round the earhole till she fell against
the scullery wall and her face was the color of dirty sheets not so
much because of the pain, no not so much that though he hurt
her we could all see more than he hurt us but for the hurt inside
and the foul language that seemed to stick to you and thick the
air like an open sewer. Seven colors of shit that's what he used to
say he'd knock out of us. Played on me mind as a kid so I was
always imagining it and making me stomach throw up and I
imagined other people could see it too, the kids and the teachers
at school so they'd turn their noses up at me and point. "That
girl's . . ." Oh it doesn't do to think about it too much even now
how we lived from poverty to poverty in them days.

Maybe that's why Jonnie's so good to me now, gives me
everything I could ask for, cos she knows what it's like. She's
seen hard times too but she's come out different being more like
a man I suppose and not so easy upset though I reckon she
understands better'n any bloke could. Only one ever understood. "What do they mean by it Larry?" "It's hard to put it
Sadie. I mean I don't know what to say." "Go on tell us. I want
to know." "Well they mean you, you'll never get married. Yeah

that's it, that's what they mean, you'll never get married."
"Gawd is that all—what's so terrible about that. Lots of people
don't get married. My cousin never has. He's always stayed with
his mother. He's not lonely or miserable. He has his mates come
round the house. And our Georgie's not married either though
it's different for him I suppose being in the army. Still he might
when he comes out." "Oh I don't reckon. It runs in your family
by the sound of it." And that was all there was to it then. We
went on being friends, going out together but he never touched
me except sometimes to put his arm round me and I liked it like
that. Then it was his turn to go away and I was so lost without
him I thought hell why not. After all I'm going to work now
and everyone else does at my age. What you think you know at
fifteen. So knowall I thought meself all tarted up for me first real
date with a boy. He said would I come to the pictures and now I
can't even remember his name. Wouldn't have been a bad picture *The Old Man and the Sea* but he never let me see it in peace,
had to be all the time messing about and then when we got outside and we was walking home he said could he kiss me good
night and I said yes thinking it'd be like me and Larry used to be
sort of nice and gentle, friendly and suddenly there he was feeling me in the hatshop doorway and his mouth open on mine
with his wet tongue I could feel poking between me teeth till I
thought I'd be sick all over him and serve him right the dirty little devil at his age.

There now I've done it, gone and made a mistake, made me
hand shake even after all this time and there's one'll have to go in
the can unless I can rub it down a little on the other edge to
even it up. Funny how you can bring it all back and what happened, nothing really, just what's normal for kids that age but it
wasn't normal for me and I sat on my bed and cried when I got
in, rubbing me mouth with me hanky till it was sore, half afraid
I'd get a dose or something just from a kiss. Silly little bitch I was

then. That's better. The numbers are coming up right now. Slip
it in with the rest and no one'll know the difference. Now you
try to keep your mind on your work my girl stead of rambling
on through what's over and done with and no good crying over
unspilt milk. If that was what you wanted you could have had it,
still could now come to that so where's the need to get so
worked up. Funny how you can get excited just thinking about
sex, any sort of sex, but when it comes to the pushover then
something doesn't click as it should and stead of going all weak
at the knees you feel sick, sick as a dog right down through you,
a real griping gutsache if it's a man. A woman's different though.
That Matt now that time in them leather pants with that little
purse slung from her belt in front. When we danced and she
held me I could feel it hard pressing and the leather like another
skin and I could have, right there on the floor I could have, if
she'd asked me. And she knew it too. Don't tell me she didn't
know and strong that one, all butch not like some of these half-
time change ends and wanting you to kiss their fanny and things
no real butch should want a girl to do. And that's another thing I
like about my Jonnie. When she wants you it's a woman she
wants not a little boy; playing winkles together in the boys' lava-
tories and all the girls giggling round the door. "I'm telling sir of
you." "Go on, only jealous cos you haven't got one.". . . .

Oh the time drags; think it was running backward when you
weren't looking. Seems like hours gone and gawd the morning's
hardly under way yet. They'll be swinging down the rise now to
the market. Not too many yet, just enough to make a bustle and
give you a feeling of, oh I don't know, what would you call it? A
sort of excitement as if you was all going to a big party. I miss
my Saturday morning. If it wasn't that we need the extra, that
you got to take every chance when it's offered cos what they pay
you come the end of a normal week ent enough to keep little

Mitzi in biscuits hardly, let alone pay for Jonnie's new suit and paper and paint for doing up the sitting room. Then there's the holidays coming along and nothing in the kitty for that. No holiday at all last year just kept on from day to day cos we wanted to move so bad from that basement with the walls all running water and all the work she put into it, those hours every evening when she come in just so much you might as well have gone out in the gutter and poured down the drain. It wearies her I know it does, not so much the actual work but the coming to nothing and the starting all over again.

Going shopping now, that's what I'd be doing with a pocket full of money and Jonnie egging me on. "Go on, get it if you want it." And then back home with the bags stuffed to bursting and we'd stand emptying it all out on the kitchen table and gloating over what we've bought. Oh I'm an extravagant bitch I know but it does you good a treat of a weekend and I love looking in all the windows like when we was kids me and Georgie only we couldn't buy then. Wonder how he's getting on and who his latest affair is. They're not like us though the boys, don't seem to stick for long most of them though when I get down the House sometimes and you don't know who's going with who this week cos you missed a couple of Saturdays I start to wonder about us and how long we can last. Four years this June which is pretty good going. And think I might never have got started if I hadn't decided to leave home and take that job at that holiday camp in St. Brigid's Bay. Still, as I said to Matt, if it's in you it's got to come out and if it isn't it won't. Look how I fought it for months, saying to Larry, "I'm not like that, no I'm not," but even with him and I was fonder of him than anyone I was trembling before we even got to his bedroom door. And then he just turned and said he couldn't. Couldn't force me he meant cos he was fond of me too.

All because of them two I saw in the pictures, never forget it.

Give me their tickets she did and as I was showing them down
the center gangway with me little torch she asked if they could
sit in the back row. That was it; asked if they could sit in the
back row so I found them a couple of seats. Then I'm swinging
me torchlight along a bit later to see if there's any seats going
spare and I catch them in it for a second and I see they're holding
hands. I can see it now; their two hands joined and I flicked the
torch off them quick and leant against the wall at the back shaking and ill with shock I suppose. I felt I couldn't go past them
again I was so frightened. I opened the door and went out into
the light. Just stood there a minute taking deep breaths when up
come the manager and asked me if I was alright. It all come out
in a rush, always does with me, just like me dad. He laughed.
"So what. They won't hurt you. Just a couple of leses." And it
hit me he was using the same word the kids had shouted after
me at school. Was that what it meant? No not me. I wasn't like
that. Yeah that was it and how I come to ask Larry. I have to
laugh when I think of it now. . . .

The next evening I'm there on time and she doesn't come. It's
raining and wind that blows through you like a knife. I walk up
and down to try and keep from freezing to death and I'm just
giving her up and deciding it's a damn good job I haven't built
nothing on it and how they're all the same people not to be
trusted when I see her hurrying along toward me and I'm so
glad to be getting out of that perishing street that I hardly bother
with what she's saying about how come she's so late. We go in
and she's not like some she lets you watch the picture and she
never makes a move to hold your hand even. I like her better for
that cos she's treating me as a human being with feelings not just
a lump of meat in the butcher's window, something to be gob-
bled up to satisfy your appetite. When the pictures come out we
go to a coffee bar and have coffee and them Danish pastries cos

she says I look half starved. I tell her about losing me job and having to get out of me room and how I've got this job but the money isn't brilliant and I'm trying to get enough together for a week's rent in advance before I look for a place of me own.

Then there's a misunderstanding cos she thinks I've been living with this butch and I'm just looking for out so I have to tell her all about that night and she goes very quiet so I'm frightened she thinks I'm just a tart and she won't have no more to do with me but it seems she's only picking her words careful. "You can't stay there," she says. "You can come and stay with me for a bit if you like. No strings attached and I won't lay a finger on you till you really want me to. That's a promise and I don't break my word." I didn't know what to say. I looked at her all dark and serious sitting there opposite me and I thought I'll risk it cos I can't be much worse off. "I'll go back and get me things," I said and she said she'd come too and wait for me outside because she didn't want to see that other one for fear she might get wild knowing what she'd done to me and she'd learnt one or two tricks in the army that could hurt so it wasn't worth the risk.

She didn't want me to go the other one when I got inside and she said again she was sorry and couldn't we give it another try. I said there never had been nothing so how could we give it another try. I put me few clothes back in me case and away we went. I never speak when I see her down the House cos I know Jon'd go wild. It wasn't a bad room with a bed and a couch and she slept on the couch so it was just like she'd said. I kept it up for a fortnight and every day I loved her more and I wanted her to want me till I couldn't stand it no longer and thought if she didn't I'd have to go cos it was making me ill. At last she come back from the House one night when I'd been egging her on to get us quite a few drinks to screw me courage up and when it's time for bed I say, "You can come in here if you want." "You sure?" she says. "Oh yes, I'm sure," and I put the light out quick

and lie there waiting me heart going crazy till I think I'll choke
and I feel her get in beside me and then I put me arms round her
and . . .

God make it soon. God let it be alright. Not too late. Don't let
there be anyone else. Never too late to mend, mum'd say. All his
fault the old bastard, never give any of us a chance, but mine too
for not knowing when I'm well off. How could she go with a
woman like that after the things she's told me, things it makes
you sick to think about, my Jonnie? Swears she never had her
but how could she be in the room while she was doing all them
things for them men all standing round watching and afterward
not do nothing? But I mustn't say it, must keep me big trap shut
or we'll be rowing and the evening spoilt since she won't hear a
word against her as if she was the bloody queen or Lady Muck
herself. Gawd help me to keep me mouth to meself and hang on
to what I've got with both hands till I know I been crossed, hear
it from her own lips. Move round the hands of the damn clock
the last five minutes. Some of 'em sitting back already, packing it
in. Poor old Edna looks as white as a ghost. Be lucky to see her
in on Monday morning. Well that's one thing we're spared, and
all this about what'll happen when you're old and alone, I don't
reckon we're any worse off than anyone else. I mean how much
will her kids care for her then? Besides who makes their life as if
they was laying up for their old age? It's enough just trying to get
by from day to day for most of these so where's the difference?
See you soon, Jonnie, meet you outside and we'll walk to the
bus stop together. Can you hear me Jon? Soon be home with
Mitzi jumping all over you, glad to see us back. And I'll try, I
will try to keep me and the place looking decent so you need
never be ashamed of us, never let you down. She lifted her head
up then just as if she could hear. Laying her things neat like she
always does. Nearly time. Wonder what's on this afternoon
while we're having our dinner. Nothing but sport I suppose. A

lot of silly schoolboys chasing a ball about. It's films I like best. Old films though all them lovely women do spoil you for yourself. Have to find something to cheer meself up after sitting here all morning. Maybe there'll be something later while we're getting ready to go out before Rick comes with the car. Unless there's anything more interesting going on. But I won't think about that, won't bank on it and then I can't be disappointed. Hallo Nan's had enough, jacking it in, first on her feet. Now the others all following suit, all standing up, pushing their chairs under the benches, stretching, the tongues unloosed starting to wag. Who's for home then eh? Open the cage man, we're coming out.

Jeanne d'Arc Jutras

In Georgie *(1978), the French-Canadian author Jeanne d'Arc Jutras depicts the dramas of daily life when material survival is both difficult and monotonous. Jutras, who died in 1993, was a working-class Quebecois lesbian writer—author of three novels—whose work is known for its originality and directness. As is evidenced in* Georgie, *Jutras focused on those women marginalized not only by their sexuality but by their place in society. In her writing, Jutras showed particular concern with the interplay of violence and tenderness in the lives of women "on the edge."*

from GEORGIE

insert the key into the cash register. The drawer opens. I break open the rolls of coins and let them fall into their respective compartments. I let out a long sigh. A busy day is ahead because of all the sales. My headache is still there; I rub my hands over my eyes. In spite of a strong, cold shower, I can feel myself getting older. Too much older. I realize that I can't always keep up the pace. At times, it's really too fast, swallowing up energy that I don't always have in reserve. There's a time for screwing like rabbits. The day hasn't even begun and I already want it to be over. As I break open the rolls of coins, my mind stays hooked on last night's adventure. . . .

Longing for love, swept up in a violent fit of discouragement, I had headed out looking for someone. It was still pretty early when I went into the bar Au Champ de Velours. There was a small blond woman sitting near the piano. She looked vaguely familiar. I waved. She answered with a smile. The jukebox exploded with a new song. I took a chance and went over to ask her to dance. The dance over, she agreed to go back to my table with me.

At first, I found her kind of colorless. After a few drinks, she was less and less colorless, more and more to my taste. Once again, I signaled to the waiter. Looking into the blonde's eyes, I asked if her name was Brigitte Bardot. She leaned toward me and confessed that, just between the two of us, it was. I congratulated myself. What an extraordinary meeting! I never would have believed that luck would shine on me to such an extent.

I invited her home. After some hesitation, Brigitte accepted.

Euphoric, we leave the bar arm in arm, promising ourselves the delights of Seventh Heaven. In the cab, Brigitte, also hungry for love, leans her head on my shoulder. I kiss her. The driver, all eyes, adjusts his mirror, blows his nose, and turns the radio up louder. Frank Sinatra is singing "Strangers in the Night."

But this morning, I'm sober. So is she. *Geez, she's sure no Brigitte Bardot!* Politely, we promised to see each other again. I took a Bromo Seltzer to calm the butterflies doing acrobatics in my stomach along with a couple of aspirins to give the thoughts in my head—which was about to explode—a chance to line up. The little blonde got dressed after a quick morning pick-me-up. She left regretfully. Her lover works nights. She has to be home when he gets in to cook his bacon and eggs. Her darling boyfriend certainly doesn't know about her little love games. I'm convinced that if he caught the beautiful Brigitte at it, she'd have some serious financial problems, not to mention a possible solid beating. It's no joke to play hide-and-seek.

I remember the story of Claudia, who made a cuckold of a well-known lawyer from Montreal. The lawyer went hunting for his wife. He found her in Claudia's arms, on the seventh floor of the Château Champlain. Jealous and furious, he made a terrible scene. *How dare you do this to me!* The lawyer tried to bury the whole business—along with his wife—not wanting to appear the fool.

Claudia doesn't work, her exceptional talents in bed free her from it. Claudia is "in-love available," like thousands of others throughout the world. I am more and more surprised and delighted by the number of women who look for lesbian love.

There are young women who want to be initiated and try for a first experience with an experienced and tender lesbian, others who swing on the side, those who dream, who go to movies, read magazines, newspapers, answer personals, eye the neighbor, the sister-in-law, the cousin, the mothers of their friends, trip out on women stars; others who, at least once in their lives, dare to sleep in the arms of another woman and find themselves confronting the confusion of the male/female choice.

Knocked around by life, fashioned like the hammer shapes a nail on the anvil . . . All those years of personal struggle. Guts mixed with aggression. My savage desire to live free, my desire for independence . . . Discriminated against as a woman, colonized, labeled in every possible way as a lesbian . . . Always rules, definitions, social classes, ranks . . . To be a woman, what does it mean? To live one's life just surviving? And for a lesbian, what does living mean?

To refuse shackles in theory is easy. But in practice?

To live, maybe that will be the day when the pain will stop in the pit of my stomach, when I'll give up getting drunk the days that I'm at the end of my rope. Maybe that will be the day that people stop giving me icy stares. To live is maybe when people give us a look that's just a look, a look of understanding, a look of love. . . . Oh yes, the look of love! Maybe that's what it will be like to live, or something like that. But when? In what era? I wonder. From tolerance to acceptance, there is deliverance and liberation.

The thoughts spin in my head while I stare at the coins. Already, a client is in front of me. A steady customer. He's a shriveled old guy who has laid claims on me. He has adopted my cash register. Hands shaking, he pulls a bottle of mineral water out of his cart, a small package of soda crackers, two cans of chicken noodle soup, three packages of cherry-flavored Jell-O, and a small bottle of Sanka, along with his *Playboy* and *Penthouse*. This afternoon, he'll come back to buy two or three things. He'll say to me, with his vocal cords stiffened by trembling sexual obsessions, devouring my breasts with his little squinting eyes,

"You sure got beautiful peepers, Georgie!"

I'm fuming, fighting my daily dose of nausea, feeling myself turned into an object. I stab hard at the button that lets the conveyer belt roll. The old guy's items wobble along. One day, though . . . Yes, one of these days, I'll lose my patience. I'm disgusted watching him lick his chops. In the meantime, I keep punching in the price of each article. I know what he'll do when he pays: he always tries to squeeze my hand. He'll do the same thing when I give him his change. A round-trip ticket. A drooling old geezer, as Thérèse would say.

Translated by Naomi Holoch

Suzana Tratnik

"Under the Ironwood Trees," by the Slovenian writer and lesbian-rights pioneer Suzana Tratnik, is a contemporary prose poem that uses a dark, feverish language to express a time of loss. Marked by severe images of disintegration, Tratnik's story creates a Gothic atmosphere to depict the narrator's rendezvous with a long-dead lover. In the context of a war-torn region, these images take on new levels of meaning. Tratnik, a writer and sociologist, was born in the small Slovenian town of Murska Sobota in 1963 but now lives in the much larger Ljubljana, a center of feminist and gay organizing. Since 1984, Tratnik has been the most outspoken lesbian voice in her country.

UNDER THE IRONWOOD TREES

still remember how it once was, dancing under the ironwood trees. Magical, with you. Now I walk alone into the steely silence of the cemetery. In the darkness I grope for the door hidden in the tall grass and then . . . No, I can't forget so easily! Three more steps to the left, when the cemetery gate has squeaked three times, and then straight forward till the patch of violets. The smell is heavy, of you. Then four steps to the left and four steps back. I turn around on my heel and now feel the hard edge of the grave marker at my right foot. I walk onto the grave and jump up onto the highest marble column. This is the tradition: whoever, in the third new moon of the year, with breath held, jumps upright onto the highest column will sink into the new moon and look down from afar on the radiant woods. Thus I sink in timeless time into the black new moon, in which the living are blinded and the dead can hear the salt of their tears.

And indeed I do see a level field, and behind it woods going up in flames, and there is the smell of fire in my deepest night. I see the dark outlines of shapes that, unused to nights full of life, dance awkwardly to the rhythm of the young flames. When the fire begins to sing its tireless melody, I imagine that you are there, singing beneath the ironwood trees, in the embrace of delicate flames.

If I silently slip down from the column in the quiet dawn and kiss the left side of the grave marker, I'll find my way to the ironwood trees through all the tall grass. That is what you told me: "Come when it's the third new moon in the seventh year, when the graves open, but only at the time of the black new moon, and I'll lead you to the ironwood trees. You are the only one to know this. Then you walk down the stone path three, four, or five steps to the black violet patch; don't worry about the darkness, for you know about the light under the ironwood trees."

Now I'm the only one who knows this. I walk along the stone path in the midst of tall poplar trees—do you still remember how they were cut down during the last autumn of your life? Now I slither past motionless, familiar faces. You didn't tell me about these lost seekers for the black new moon. How these blind eyes beneath the ironwood trees turn back, ignorant that their seventh year is past. The wild flame should have reached their eyes.

Why then do I have this sense of strangeness, of not knowing, when the stone path, bordered with poplars, brings me before the familiar woods? The branches of the old ironwood trees are so densely intertwined that they could silence birds by strangling their beaks. The steel eagle on the gate latch pecks at the cold from my numb fingers. Where has your call brought me? Where then is the dance during the black new moon, where are the musicians, the singers with their hoarse throats? I know about the light under the ironwood trees. I cry out these untrue words into the cold. And at that moment I hear a warm crackling, and a swirling wind drives the branches and the foliage into the tight clutch of the fire. The iron gate gives way and I am embraced by the passionate rustling of the brown-yellow leaves. Now I also hear the smothered song, the disorderly clatter of dancing shoes and the clanging of gold goblets. Perhaps it only seems so to me because of the seductive odor of the juices pressed out through thin spigots from the overripe fruit of the trees. I am intoxicated. This certainly cannot be a productive night.

Still, I manage to reach the ruins beneath the ironwood trees, to dance on the floor of the old castle. Now I can dance into the old memories, alive, trembling in the fire of dead names. Who will make me dance, who will rest hands on my breast if I do not catch sight of you? See their deformed hands that grasp me in the wild dance. So it is said: Bitter are the hands of the dead names. They touch one and then full of fear startle away, and their black tongues crawl into one's face, because the warm blood of one's skin burns on them. But their eyes remain unmoving: they gaze far, far back into one, back to the time when one was still a child and without shame burrowed into the earth with one's teeth. "Don't look at me in the name of Death!" Thus one yells out to them but in vain. One remains small for them, even when one is no longer small, and perhaps never was. Are you blind, combing all the spiderwebs from their hair?—they are still asking this, before their hands heavily sink down the length of the body.

But I am not concerned about them, where after all young women with bared breasts dance, and the dancers become ever more lively and offer sweet wine from heavy trays. Should one take wine from these dead hands and drink to these dead eyes? Or should one be shattered from within, beneath these empty gazes? The young women offer wine to me too; it seems as if I were drinking from their breasts; is the magic of this intoxicating wine my fate, will I perhaps see you now?

The skeletal girls and boys—I drink to them, while I gaze at your face mirrored in the gold goblet.

But how blameless this wine is, this wine born of violets from your weary grave! Burning blood again and again shoots into my veins, my legs, and already I dance, surrounded by the mutilated dancers. I perceive all the madness of their percussive rhythms and hum the seductive song of the fire. The flames burn, they burn deep into the horror of my heart. They are many times too hot for me but can hardly warm the white limbs, the magic, and the blood of the unskilled dancers.

How goes the dancing beneath the ironwood trees? Why am I blinded by your look? You yourself gave me violet wine to drink and sent me bare-breasted girls, so that they might steal the sword from my head. Perhaps here where I am bewitched I can now give myself up to the dead-limbed pleasures; blindly and wildly I touch the open flesh wounds and with bony fingers lift the gold goblet to my ashen lips. Surely you don't believe that I, like the others, will stuff dry earth into my joints in order to be able to dance into the dawn? I do not forget it, I can never forget it. The temptation of wine cannot keep me far away from the rosy drops.

Now horror overwhelms me. I am afraid of the dead hands and the stinking mouths that, toothless, have wedged themselves into the young trees. I want almost not to see them, your wedding guests, who throng onto the dance floor. Through their torn clothing I recognize their crooked bones and their mangled flesh. You don't know how you can reach them, to grasp them, to crush these decaying beehives, to cut through their wrinkled necks until the yellow death-juice brims over the madness in their eyes. Now I am not allowed to curse you.

Not here, not amid the dead-limbed ones. The heavy wine flows from my mouth and eyes. Who knows, perhaps I am already crushed to pieces or tired of life and already have lain for many new moons on the gold-yellow foliage near the castle floor. Not far from what once existed. And already mouth and eyes brim over with yellow juice. But I never open my eyes. What if I really see you only as a mirror image in the gold goblets? If I should go blind, then let it be only on your wine. I want never to rub it from my eyes.

Now I cry. Bitterly. A heavy smell surrounds me, and it cannot be the wine, I am already lying next to your violet grave. It will be a morning of horror, a dawn of powerlessness. Let my body collapse to the ground. But when I wake and look into the white pain, I will make the sign of the cross on my face, in the morning of the new moon; I will pour the pitch of black trees into my mouth and will burn out my eyes with glowing coals. Because you no longer hear the salt of my tears.

Translated from the Slovenian into German by
Elisabeth Vospernik;
translated from the German by Nora Reed

Elena Georgiou

Cyprus is the land of origin for Elena Georgiou, a poet and teacher who after many years in London is now living in New York City. In writing about her story "Aphrodite's Vision" (1996), Georgiou said, "The Cypriot part of my consciousness seemed to take control of my creativity." In this story, Georgiou, capturing the experience of her blind narrator, creates a strong sense of place through character and action, rather than through visual description. The poet has written a story where language becomes a form of sight and a direct entry into a sensual world.

APHRODITE'S VISION

WHEN the flames leapt out of the oven door and burned my eyes many women came to console me by telling me their bad-luck stories. I was twenty-two and unmarried. Before the accident my parents began putting the word about that they were ready to find me a husband. But when the accident left me blind, all three of us knew this would make arranging a marriage almost impossible. We had no land or money to make up for what my parents and the families of the single men saw as a liability.

And I was pleased to be a *liability*. The word fell off my tongue with a lilt that meant I had the freedom to sit with my legs open like a man and not have to wonder if marriage was going to come along to close them. I began to sit for hours. My legs, open. My ears, open. But my mouth, shut.

Losing my eyesight kept me quiet for at least six years. During this time I sat outside my father's store and listened to conversations. I listened to the sounds of people's sentences and their choice of words. I listened to the silences in between their words, and the silences after their words stopped. I listened to the footsteps of the people who had been conversing. I felt how quickly or slowly the air moved when they walked away from one another. Eventually, I was able to tell by the sound of the footsteps, and the touch of the air, if these people would meet to talk again. How their conversation would sound the next time they met. What kind of words they would choose. What kind of sentences they'd make. And what kind of silences they'd leave. It was as though someone had taken the eyes from my face and relocated them inside my body. My feelings now had the eyes my face could no longer use. It was with these inside-eyes that I saw Efthalia.

Efthalia didn't come to console me or tell me a bad-luck story. In fact, she hadn't come to tell me anything. She came to ask my father if he would put new soles on the bottoms of her shoes. I could feel she knew at the time that she didn't have the money to pay for the new soles, so I watched with my inside-eyes to see how she was going to get her shoes back once my father had finished working on them.

My father was the kind of man who always asked people for a fair amount of money for the work he put into his repairs. He didn't raise the prices when he saw someone walking to his store in shop-bought clothes and he didn't drop the price when he saw someone walk away from his store barefoot.

Efthalia came to pick up her shoes when my father was eating his lunch and I was taking care of the store. She read the numbers on her ticket to me and I walked toward the third box on the left, behind the counter. I gave her the shoes and held out my hand to receive the money. In silence, she used her finger to draw a heart in the palm of my hand and then I felt the air move as she rushed out the door.

"Efthalia came for her shoes," I said before my father had time to notice they were missing. "I gave them back to her for free."

"Why, Aphrodite? Why would you do such a thing?"

"Because I could feel the skin in the palm of her hand had cracked."

"And?" my father said, waiting to hear the rest of my explanation.

"And what?" I said, trying to avoid the sharpness in the sound of his voice.

"What have the shoes she wears on her feet got to do with the cracked skin in the palm of her hand?" His voice pleaded for an explanation he could understand. I spelled it out word for word, trying to accommodate his plea.

"I gave her the shoes for free so she could use the money to pay for olive oil to soften her skin." It frustrated me to have to explain myself as much as it frustrated my parents that I didn't explain enough. I was sorry I had to be bad to my father in order to be good to Efthalia, but today I could feel she needed my goodness more than he did. I had no regrets.

My inside-eyes followed his eyes following me as I went to sit outside. I could feel every nail he hammered into the sole of the shoe he was working on, which is why I shouted back into the coolness of his workspace, "I know how to find the way to her house." He pretended not to hear me. "I can go and ask her for the money, if you want." He said nothing. "I'm going," I said, holding on to the wall to steady myself down the two steps that took me to the pavement. I could feel the air change as he walked quickly to catch me.

"Where are you going, all by yourself?"

"I can do it."

"Come back and sit down. Please. Sometimes, Aphrodite, I think you do what's good for strangers even if it means you're not going to be good to yourself. And that's not being good. That's being foolish."

"I'm not being foolish. Just because I don't have sight doesn't mean I don't have sense. And Efthalia is not a stranger. I'm going to her house to ask her to bring you the money, when she has it. That way, I can be good to her and I can be good to you."

"Come back and sit down."

"No. I'm going."

"Sit down." There was a sound in his voice I found hard to argue with. I sat on the pavement and felt the afternoon sun on the back of my neck. My father returned to his hammering and the sound faded into a quiet silence allowing me the space to daydream. I turned my body around so the sun could shine on my face and started to trace the heart Efthalia had left in my hand. I repeated the shape for a little while and then used my fingers to explore. I realized this was the first time I'd used my hands to feel my body. It surprised me that I could have sat still for six years and not touched myself. I wondered why I hadn't used the time to feel the shape of my neck, or the width of my wrists, or measure how much of my breasts my hands could hold. I sat by the roadside and measured my wrist by making a circle around its circumference with my thumb and forefinger. I felt under my chin and down my breastbone. And, instead of going inside the house to cup my breasts in my hands, I walked away from the store to Efthalia's house.

Efthalia was the kind of woman who enjoyed the feel of words so much that even when she couldn't turn a one-syllabled word into a two-syllabled one my ears felt as though she had. So when she asked me onto her veranda with the word *welcome*, I felt as though she'd said much more.

"I haven't come for the money," I said as I sat outside the doorway to her house.

"Would you like some almond cordial?" she said, ignoring my words but acknowledging my presence. I listened to her meander through the rooms that led to the kitchen and then shouted, "I said, I haven't come for the money."

"And I said, would you like some almond cordial," she called back in a sing-song voice.

At school, Efthalia was the only girl in my class who didn't say nice things to the twins who had a piano in their house so they could invite her home to play. I thought it was because she didn't like pianos or didn't like music, but I was wrong. Not only did she like music, but it was so connected to her body that if she walked along the street it was impossible for her to hear a radio pouring out of someone's house without stepping in time to the music. Efthalia found another way to be invited to play the piano. She waited until the twins came to her. And that was how life was for Efthalia: a series of waiting times linked to a series of getting times. That's how I knew she was waiting for me to tell her what I was doing at her house if it wasn't to ask for the money. And because I knew she was going to wait for me to explain, I promised myself I'd wait for her explanation first.

Making promises to myself and taking risks were two things I didn't do when I had sight. But, now, I feel I can take risks without having to fear losing anything. Life will make the loss into a change. And the change will be an *in*, or an *out*, an *up*, or a *down*, or even a circle, but the important thing is life goes on and there's nothing I can do to stop it, or predict it.

Yes, on occasion, life can leave me feeling as if I can direct it, but this feeling is always fleeting. For example, when I woke up this morning I said to myself, Today I am going to begin writing songs in my head. I want to make songs that tell a story so that the people who listen to them will have something to do with their minds. And I want to fill these songs with music that will flood into peoples' bodies until they have no choice but to move. But when I left my bedroom and walked into the front of the house, life took the straight line in my head and threw all my plans out the window. Why? Because Efthalia came into our parlor-turned-storefront and drew a heart in the palm of my hand. What's more, my inside-eyes couldn't find an explanation for why she had.

I know, I know, you're probably asking, but what about the cracked skin and what about money for the olive oil. I made that up, of course. That's how I know it's not true when my father says that sometimes I'm good to others at the expense of being good to myself. My father thinks he knows everything about me, but he doesn't.

Thinking you know everything about your child is a mistake that many parents make, but I can understand how the mistake is made. What I don't understand, though, is how people can think they know everything about someone else's child. For instance, I've heard many people from our town talk about Efthalia. They feel sorry for her. "It's a shame," they say. "A young girl like that with no one left alive to arrange a marriage for her."

I was never told directly how Efthalia's parents died, but I recall catching the end of one of my mother's arguments with my father, on a Sunday morning. She was using their death as a way to get my father to go to church with her.

"You know, if Maria and Demetri had spent less time drinking together and more time praying together then perhaps they wouldn't have met their end by slamming their bicycle into the rear end of a truck. Twenty-two years old, they were. Both of them. Maria had just given birth. Her forty days weren't even up yet. I don't even know what she was doing out of the house!"

"Saturday night is the one night I get to myself and you're going to take that away from me?" My father always responded to my mother's goading with words that created feelings of guilt. In fact, both of my parents argued by using words that created guilt rather than raising their voices at one another.

"Sunday is the one day I get to stay in my bed and snore to my heart's delight without having to feel your fingers digging me in the ribs." My father usually won the arguments simply because, for my father, guilt was just a tactic he used to get his own way, whereas feeling guilty was something my mother took seriously.

"Do what you want," my mother said. "You always do." She punctuated her words by yanking my arm and pulling me out the front door, in the direction of the church, mumbling something about not wanting me to grow up godless like my father.

But me, I'm much better at winning arguments with my father than my mother is. All I have to do is pretend I'm telling the truth and then stay silent until he has shouted, or talked, or hammered himself out of the bad mood I've put him in. It's so simple that, sometimes, it's hard for me to believe I can keep winning without him noticing my tactics. I live in dread of the day he wakes up to me.

I knew my father would be angry when I gave back Efthalia's shoes for free, but I also knew that all I had to do was sit still and wait until he hammered the anger out of himself. Waiting for his anger to dissipate was a small price to pay for adventure. *Adventure?* you're saying to yourselves. *What adventure?* I suppose that's what people mean when they say *"Get to the point, Aphrodite."* And I suppose that's what *I* mean when I say I tell stories in a roundabout way. Roundabouts are important. For example, while I stopped to tell you about my plans to write songs, my inside-eyes blinked into a wide-open expression of recognition;

they gave me the reason I'm on Efthalia's veranda. Who better to teach me how to write songs that will make a body move than Efthalia?

Efthalia returned with our drinks. I focused on the mix of soap and jasmine that drifted from Efthalia's body while she began a new conversation.

"Once, when my grandmother was still alive, she asked me to make her some almond cordial. My mind was thinking of other things. I hadn't noticed that I'd put the almond concentrate in one glass and poured the water into another." Efthalia inched closer to me on the step and wrapped my hand around the glass without taking a break from her story. "My grandmother was a quiet woman, used her gestures and her words carefully. I remember her looking into the two glasses and saying, 'You must need a few more years at school so you learn that the concentrate is supposed to go in the *same* glass as the water.' She had a way of telling me about myself that made me laugh. We really didn't speak to each other much. We didn't have long conversations, but we did have long periods of laughter. Do you remember laughing together at school, Aphrodite? Do you remember the time we followed the twins home—"

"And locked them in their outside toilet—," I interrupted.

"And turned the hose on them." She finished off the sentence and stopped to drink the cordial. The retelling of this story didn't make us laugh, so I filled the silence by listening to a series of her gulps until I heard the sound of an empty glass.

One of the odd things I missed about having sight was watching someone's throat bounce up and down while they drank. I decided to tell her that. After all, she had told me about her grandmother.

"Put your hand on my throat," she said, taking my hand and putting it there for me. "I wonder why the lump on a man's throat is called an Adam's apple. Wasn't it Eve's apple?" I knew she wasn't expecting me to answer so I listened to her silence, knowing she was thinking. "Maybe it's because the bite Adam took got stuck in his throat. I've never read the Bible. Have you?"

I gave her a one-syllable *No* so I could quickly return to the feel of her skin next to mine. Today was a big day. Not only did I have to understand sounds and silences, but I also had to understand touch. The feel of me. And, now, the feel of her.

"I don't think I've ever touched someone else's throat before," I said as I removed my hand from her neck. Continuing with words that backtracked over the earlier part of the day I said, "I touched my own throat, today. Actually, I was feeling the area from under my chin to my breastbone."

"Oh," she said with one syllable that sounded like nine. I had let my guard down. The nine were *oh-did-you-and-why-were-you-doing-that?* Just how was I going to respond to this *oh?* Was I going to be safe and ignore it? Was I going to take a risk and exaggerate? Or was I going to be Aphrodite and elaborate? I decided to be me.

"I was feeling my neck because I realized I'd never felt my body before. I wanted to explore it, to see how well I knew myself. It seemed strange to me to walk around with a body for so many years and not know it. So I decided to feel my neck, and my wrists, and my breasts."

Have you ever noticed how some words seem to go on much longer than the time it takes to say them? *Breasts* is one of those words. My inside-eyes showed me Efthalia felt that way, too. But, instead of giving the word the time it needed to drift between us, Efthalia caught the sound of *breasts* in her mouth and repeated it in a way that told me more.

"Ba-reasts," she said, making it into two syllables.

"Why do you do that?" I asked.

"Do what?"

"Make one-syllable words into two."

"Do I? I hadn't noticed." My inside-eyes told me she knew she was lying. I decided to take a risk and tell her what I could see, but she beat me to it. "I suppose I do, don't I? I guess I do it for the same reason you decided to feel your body. I like to explore the feel of a word in my mouth." She stopped for a second and in my head I pictured her sucking the ends of her wavy hair as her eyes drifted into her feelings. "If you take a word that has one sound and turn it into two you can hold on to the word that much longer. Not only can you hold on to it, but you can say it in a way that makes it yours."

"It's important to you to do things in a way that's yours, isn't it?" The words flew out of my mouth. I tried to understand where the intimacy of this question came from. The only explanation I could find was that it sprang from the awkwardness and the emptiness my hand had felt lying in my lap ever since it left her throat. It was as if I could hear my hand saying, Okay, so we've done necks and wrists, but what about feet, or calves, or thighs. The word *thigh* joined the word *breasts* in my head. They were dancing together. My inside-eyes were dizzied by the image of disconnected human body parts waltzing. "Yes. It is important to me," she said. "When my grandmother died I could feel everyone feeling sorry for me. It didn't bother me that I washed rich peoples' clothes to feed myself. And I know people feel sorry for me because I haven't got a husband, but the truth is I wouldn't know what to do with one if I had one. For me, the important thing is that I have no one telling me what to do. I like to walk around barefoot. People call me gypsy when they think I'm not listening. They think I'll be insulted. But I think it's a compliment. I don't want anyone in my life who'll tell me to put my shoes on. I only leave my house to buy food, what do I need shoes for? The radio brings me music. There's a song on the radio that says,

All I want is a room somewhere
Far away from the cold night air
With one enormous chair
Oh, wouldn't it be love-er-ly

When I heard that song I thought, I'm so lucky, I have everything this woman wants. I have warm air, an enormous chair,
and a home of my own. I even understand why she makes *lovely*
into *love-er-ly*. She wants to keep the word in her mouth longer.
She wants to make it hers. All *I* want is someone I can talk to
who won't feel sorry for me. And if I'm really going to dream I
want someone who will, sometimes, choose to talk to me with
words and, sometimes, without words."

"Is that why you drew the heart in my hand?" I clicked.

"Yes," she said and then I felt the air stir as her face moved
closer.

"I wondered why you were bringing in your shoes to be
repaired."

"So who dresses you?" she whispered.

"Pardon?" I said, while my inside-eyes searched to find the
part of Efthalia's body that her question came from.

"Who dresses you?" she repeated. "You look like you've been
wearing the same clothes for six years."

"I have," I admitted. I ran both hands down my thigh, over
my knee, down to my ankle. The more Efthalia spoke to me the
more my hands felt disconnected from my body. "I don't trust
my mother to pick out clothes for me," I continued. "She thinks
clothes should be loose and hair should be pulled back and tied
tight."

"You know your mother has everything backward, don't
you?" I waited for Efthalia to elaborate, but she didn't. Continuing, she said, "Well, seeing as how you've spent your day touch-

ing things you've never touched before, why don't you come
inside? I have a silk dress for you to feel."

"A silk dress! Where did you get that?"

"One of the women I work for gave it to me."

"Rich women give away silk dresses?"

"This one did. She said it was a gift for my hard work. But *I*
think it's because she hasn't always had money and watching me
work reminds her of where she came from. She feels sorry for
me, but in a different way. I don't mind that as much." Efthalia
paused for a second. I could feel her mind flying backward.

"When I was young I collected silkworms. I made a home for
them in a shoebox. I think watching a worm change into a
cocoon and then into a butterfly is like watching a miracle. I love
the word *butterfly*. You can play with it. You can rearrange the
letters and it will tell you more. My word for butterfly is *flutterby*.
It's a much better word. Because butterflies are not always the
color of butter, but they do always flutter by." My inside-eyes
watched Efthalia's body unfold. In the music of her sentences
and her silences I could hear she had accepted me as someone
who didn't feel sorry for her. "Do you have favorite words?" she
asked, wanting me to move into her feeling.

"Well, there's a song I heard on the radio. . . . I don't like the
song for the words, I like the song for the things it makes me
think about touching. The first time I heard the song it made
me want to touch raindrops resting on the petals of flowers. The
second time, it made me want to touch the whiskers on my cat.
And the third time I heard the song my ears rested on the line
that said, 'Snowflakes that fall on my nose and eyelashes.' I'd love
to feel snow on my eyelashes, but it doesn't snow here."

"It does snow. In the mountains. I'll take you."

"Two women going into the mountains on their own? My
parents would never allow it."

"Oh yes, your parents. I forgot." I heard melancholy seep into her voice, but it didn't stay there for long. "Well, let's start with something you can feel. Come feel the silk dress and if you like we can share it. But there's one condition. I'll only share it if you promise me that every time you wear it you'll come and drink something with me."

We both laughed. I had no idea why *she* was laughing. My inside-eyes were failing me. But I did know why *I* was laughing. It was a sound to fill up the silence while I tried to work out what to think of her offer. I didn't say anything. When the laughter stopped I knew that neither of us could fill the silence because it was already full.

"Please. Will you come?"

As she pleaded I felt a certain kind of victory because this was the first time I had witnessed Efthalia waiting without being sure she would be getting. But my victory was fleeting because I wasn't very good at waiting, either. I wanted to feel silk. She took my hand and gave me a gentle tug to bring me up to standing. I didn't make it difficult for her. I let out an eighteen-syllabled sigh that spelled *I-suppose-this-is-going-to-be-another-one-of-her-getting-times.*

"Please?" she repeated.

I had a vision of her unbraiding my hair.

"Yes," I said.

She took my hand and led me through the meandering maze of her stone-floored house until we reached her bedroom.

"Just a second," Efthalia said, making subtle changes in the air as she moved away from me. The sound of her voice rang around the room while my mind searched for the next sentence.

"Do you have the dress hanging or folded?" I asked.

"The dress is hanging now," she said, letting her words trail off until the *now* was almost inaudible.

I dropped my voice to a whisper. "Can I feel it?"

She moved her body closer and said, "Yes."

Etel Adnan

No one asked you to be an angel of fear
    or even death

We only wanted your skin to be
    as smooth
    as the sea
    an October afternoon
    in Beirut, Lebanon
Between two civil wars.

    You came
With a handful of pain
    and a smile
which broke the ground under my feet
    as the earthquake does
when two people
    meet.

    —From Love Poems (1978)

Etel Adnan, born in 1925, came to the United States from Beirut thirty
years ago, but as this excerpt from her prose poem "In the Heart of the
Heart of Another Country" (1977) shows, Adnan lives with both the

horrors *of her war-torn country and the wondrous persistence of the will to love. In writing about her work and its place in the Arab literary tradition, Adnan noted, "I could say that I was for a while the first and only woman in Arab literature, past and present, to publish love poems addressed to a woman." A writer, poet, painter, and tapestry designer, Adnan has always kept a poet's notebook in her pocket. The piece we have chosen reflects that concern with details, details overwhelmed by a city's suffering and a writer's exile.*

from IN THE HEART OF THE HEART OF ANOTHER COUNTRY

Place

So I have sailed the seas and come. . .

                to B. . .

a town by the sea, in Lebanon. It is seventeen years later. My absence has been an exile from an exile. I'm of those people who are always doing what somebody else is doing . . . but a few weeks earlier. A fish in a warm sea. No house for shelter, but a bed, from house to house, and clothes crumpled on a single shelf. I am searching for love.

Weather

In Beirut there is one season and a half. Often, the air is still. I get up in the morning and breathe heavily. The winter is damp. My bones ache. I have a neighbor who spits blood when at last it rains.

My House

My father built a house when I was a child near the German
school so I could go to it. The school moved out as he finished
the roof. Ever since, my property has been rented for the
cheapest rent in town. The laws are such that I can't push out
the tenants. Anyway, I am afraid of houses as of tombs.

A Person

My other neighbor (from neighbor to neighbor I shall cover
the world) sells birds. And cats. A Siamese cat was born to him
and was really Siamese: it had two heads, four ears, two bodies,
two pairs of four legs, two tails. And boy, were they glued! He
has on sale a little monkey that has been growing for the last
seventeen and half years. The store is in front of a newspaper
that went broke. All the windows are since blind.

Wires

They are few, and, as there are no trees in Beirut, the wire
poles are dead, geometric semblances for trees. Dead
archetypes. As for the birds, Lebanese hunters have killed them
all. Now they are killing the Syrian birds, too.

The Church

We have churches, mosques, and synagogues. All equally
empty at night. On weekends, many flies desert their gardens.
People come in.

My House

I should say my side of the bed. Half a bed makes a big house
at night. My dreams have the power to extend space and make

me live in the greatest mansions. During the day it doesn't matter. There are many streets, a few remaining sidewalks, and, yes, the café "Express," in which I move, hunted by memories.

Politics

Oh, it's too much, too much. Once I dreamed of becoming the new Ibn Khaldoun of America or the de Tocqueville of the Arabs. Now I work for a newspaper and cover the most menial things. So I don't understand how it is that there are kings without kingdoms and Palestinians without a Palestine. As for the different scandals, they do not matter to me. Why should I care that some thieves steal from other thieves. Should I?

People

The Lebanese go on two feet, like the Chinese, for example; sometimes on four, to pick up a dime under the table. Their country is small, the desires too, and their love affairs. Only their cars are big. Detroit-made Chevys and Buicks. All the unsold Buicks of America are on our roads. So, in this country, you only see the heads of the people. Their bodies are carefully washed and stored away. As for the women, there aren't any. They all consider themselves as being the other half of their men. With one exception.

Vital Data

The most interesting things in Beirut are the absent ones. The absence of an opera house, of a football field, of a bridge, of a subway, and, I was going to say, of the people and of the government. And, of course, the absence of absence of garbage.

Education

Everybody speaks Arabic, French, English, Armenian, Greek,
and Kurdish. Sometimes one language at a time, sometimes all
of them together. And even the children are financiers.

Business

Merchants sell to other merchants and buy from them. Men
sell women to other men and buy women from them. Women
sell women to women. And everybody sells a child: for vanity,
for money, for pleasure. In the tall buildings of Hamra children
get assaulted under the eyes of their parents. Parents thank God
when they get the money.

My House, This Place and Body

There was a house in a eucalyptus grove. My father and I
sneaked in, and in the middle of the night a guard came to
awaken us. I advised my father to offer him money and he did:
he gave him nine hundred pounds. "I didn't ask for that
much," said the guard. My father, then, disappeared.

Don't talk to me about my body. It has been battered, cut
open; discs, nerves, and tissues have been removed. My belly, a
zoological garden. My eyes, poor lighthouses, and my mind a
rocky and barren garden, exactly like this place and the
unexisting house.

The Same Person

I went to the store, and, feeling sorry for the caged birds, I told
the guy: "How can you sell animals?" He replied: "Aren't you
an animal too?" So I lowered my eyes and admired him.

Weather

I used to love the heat and, even now, the sweat. My sheets
used to get wet and I, rolling on them, my body in ecstasy.
I was then sixteen, or a bit more. I kissed the air of this
town with passion and carried it in my arms. I couldn't love
a man because I loved the sea. Then, I went away, and the
spell broke. The weather aged, got wrinkles, its bones and
marrow became soft. It is nowadays like breathing mud. When
it rains, I can't feel happy for the trees. They do not exist. So I
feel happy for the buildings. They get an imperfect bath. As for
me, the eternal sun has worked like a siren on my brain.

It has eaten up my intelligence. The dust has filed my nails.
Cockroaches run over my paintings, and I get up at night to
kill them and to keep them away at the edge of my dream. But
the dampness is constant, and invisible amoebae constantly
dance in the air. One feels always a bit swollen in Beirut. It is a
pregnancy of bad omen. You have to go to a village called
Sannine to start breathing properly. But you never stay too long
up there. You miss the weather of Beirut.

Place

I left this place by running all the way to California. An
exile that lasted for years. I came back on a stretcher and felt
here a stranger, exiled from my former exile. I am always
away from something and somewhere. My senses left me one
by one to have a life of their own. If you meet me in the
street, don't be sure it is me. My center is not in the solar
system.

People

This is the cruellest place. A man in a motorboat hit a
swimmer and sped away. The skull was broken. A large space of
blood covered the sea. Painters rushed to the scene to make a
painting for sale. A girl was killed by her brother because she
smiled to her lover. A house in the city was set on fire because
they wanted the tenants out. A rebellion has started, the
rebellion of the rich against the poor. Yes, to make sure that
the latter do not multiply, and rather be dead, the sooner the
better.

My House My Cat My Company

From every drawer, the blood of my spirit is spilled. My eyes,
anguished by the light, have cruel particles of dust covering
them. Noises come in as demons. No crime in the newspaper
is as gory as the noises that surround my bed. It is an eternal
beat.

MAO is the name of my cat, who has been rescued from a
friend. He sleeps on my left side, watches my heartbeats. At
night, when he sometimes runs away, I have to go out and
look for him. Most often, he runs out at about four in the
morning, when the Koranic prayer fills the air and when its
lamentation seems endless and fills me with sacred terror. That
terror is communicated somehow to MAO, whose hair stands
up. He shivers against me when we come home.

One morning my breast was bare and he put his paw on it. It
was a moment of perfection.

So I gave him away, but he came back.

I live with a woman who shares with me my passion for ants, from the day I told her that my father had taught me to watch them attentively in order to imitate them later in life. This was my education. I was told that ants had all the necessary qualities. They were tiny and carried weights bigger than their size. They never slept. Industrious, they stuck together, never doing anything alone. And when you killed them, they multiplied. So my friend fell in love with my father for having been so right. But he is dead. The ants keep me company, coming from under the flowerpots all the way into the closets, glasses, spoons. They stop at the door of the refrigerator. Their brain is tinier than the head of a pin. So angels must exist.

I am a species all by myself. That's why no fish comes to swim in my territorial waters. I have no enemies.

I live with a woman who has a recurring dream: each night she goes to unearth Akhenaton and carries his coffin all over the house. The young king has a nocturnal journey on her arms. His solar boat had been shattered by his murderers. She weeps for him, sometimes, during the day too, but she does not go around like the women from America in pink slippers and bobby pins to the supermarket. No. She uses silverware, puts salt and pepper on her meat, and she tells me that she does not proceed from a source of light but from a source of shadows.

As for me, I told her that I find my reason to be in the configurations of matter.

I love the different objects I encounter with violence. I have a passion for cars. My spoon is to me what the angel used to be to Jacob: my moment of truth. People throw their fingernails away, and I look at these pieces of matter with awe: transparent like alabaster, tiny like African ants, pale as erased memories. I throw them away with a tremendous melancholy. I would like to be buried with "St. James Infirmary" playing. Or something like that, maybe a song by Oum Kalsoum.

Then I would like to resurrect. Death would appear as short as the time for the batting of an eyelash. I am of those who like resurrection, and I am not alone in that; I hear people saying it, when I walk, and mostly in New York.

. . .

Weather

Spring is deadly, like red roses.

The weather always awakens in me the fear of death. I am of those animals who have a strong life instinct, but the forces of death, like huge tides, beat against me. I go from country to country and each time, the earth, under my feet, becomes an ocean. So I move on. Chasing each place's weather.

At noon, I visit buildings under construction, I look at the Syrian workers while they eat. There is always some cement on their bread. When they cut a watermelon, they count the black seeds in order to know how many days separate them from their own death. They don't know what they are doing. It is for them like playing chess.

Spring starts, here, in February. We faint on our desks. In classrooms. In rooms. A thin veil of sweat covers my face and my neck, runs between my shoulders, all along my spine. My nerves quiver. The heat grows. In June, July, August, I resemble a flat tire. Then, all kinds of amoebae stir in my belly. The heat is a culture bed, my body works like marshes, and in the green foliage of my insides flowers of some anti-paradise grow. Airplanes zoom above, and, because I am a four-footed animal, I stay on the ground, and even below. October in Beirut is the end of the road to hell. Dampness has reached its saturation point. By then one can hardly move. Tired bones, tired eyes, tired fingers. One by one my nerves go. The harbor is cluttered. So are the streets. In a dark and polluted air I act as if I were breathing. The year is almost gone, and the very short rains are waiting. . . .

Place

My place is at the center of things. I am writing from within the nucleus of an atom. Blood beating under my ears. Some dry heat radiating from my nerves. A pressure trying to push my eyes ahead of me; they want to travel on their own. My place: highways, trains, cars. One road after another, from ocean shore to ocean shore. From Beirut to the Red Sea. From Aden to Algiers. From Oregon to La Paz. I keep going, prisoner of a body, and my brain is just a radio station emitting messages to outer space. Angels, astronauts all dressed in white, I would like some strange being to take me somewhere where no disease blurs my perception. I will grow wings and fly.

Gina Schien

The Australian writer Gina Schien represents a new generation of open and irreverent lesbian writers. In "Minnie Gets Married" (1993), the Sydney-born writer unabashedly carries the reader through a spirited disruption of a conventional social ritual. Schien's playful use of dialogue and internal asides pokes fun at the absurdities of "normal" behavior. The author, who has written extensively for Sydney's gay and lesbian press, nevertheless undercuts the heavy drama that usually surrounds the absence of heterosexual privilege. While not denying the seriousness of social struggles, this story's humor promises new vitality and unrepentant victories.

MINNIE GETS MARRIED

ANN sat in the back of the car next to little Deb and Katie. Her dress creaked. Her nasal passages were clogged with the perfume that weddings are drenched with. Or maybe it was some cheap stuff that the twins had on. She breathed, quick and shallow, trying to clear her head.

"You right?" The chauffeur turned his head and little Deb and Katie looked at her.

"Yep. Sorry. Ha."

Little Deb looked up at her. "Will there be food soon?"

"I hope so."

"Why are you so tall?"

"Why are you so nosy?"

"Just askin'."

The limousine purred on in silence. Ann examined her hands, which were nested in her lap, until the car stopped outside the RSL club. The driver stood at her window, opening the door, helping them out. The three bridesmaids looked beautiful out in the sunlight. Minnie's parents, Mrs. Bellini and Mr. Bellini, stood and smiled at the two little cuties (Steve's kid sisters) with the little rings of flowers around their heads. That tall Ann, little Minnie's friend (it had to be said now that she was closer), actually looked the worse for wear after the service. Minnie's brother Peter peered into her face, concerned. His face was raw from shaving.

"You don't look too hot," he said.

"I don't feel it either."

He put a hand on her shoulder. "I'm amazed you did this."

"From this point on, I'm here for the alcohol."

Just as she was getting the hang of walking in those shoes over the grass, Mrs. Bellini scooped up Ann's hand and placed it gingerly in her own.

"Ann, in case I don't get to you later." *Wait till I get to you, you little pervert!* "I just want to say thank you because we do appreciate it."

"That's fine, Mrs. Bellini." Her hand was dropped.

And then the MC positioned them in a subdued V shape at the club door. Her and the two littlies, their tiny hands thrust into hers.

"Stand here until I call you."

He disappeared. Where was Minnie? They stood rustling in hot silk. Rooted to the spot, wavering uncertainly like three pulsating blue lilies.

"Bridesmaids, Ann and little Deb and Katie!"

The twins had to lead this huge lumbering woman, who clearly had no idea how to walk (how embarrassing for them), into an important event. Ann was expecting, hoping for semi-darkness, but it was incredibly, rudely bright. There was the Bellini family. Her own seat was next to Minnie's tiny Aunt Luisa and her own partner Ian, who was Minnie's cousin. Aunt Luisa craned to kiss Ann on the cheek and patted her down like a willful dog.

"Well, Annie, sit sit sit. . . ."

Even when she had sat obediently, Ann towered over the diners like a mournful crane among merry-making, chattering sparrows. Aunt Luisa poured her some champagne.

"Yuk. Soup!" the twins said.

"And now can we please welcome. . . ," the MC boomed. "For the first time, Mr. and Mrs. Nikkaleiedes!"

Minnie and Steve swept into the room. Clear across the room, Ann could see the snail trail of tears on Minnie's cheeks.

My Minnie, my sweetie pie. Careful kid.

Aunt Luisa patted her hand. "They look wonderful, don't they?"

"One more kiss for the cameras," the MC boomed. It was an order.

Minnie stood with Steve at the door. Steve ran his hand over the back of his head again and again as though wondering where all his hair had gone. There was a storm of flashes while he kissed Minnie once, again, and then again, on damp cheeks. "That enough?" he asked.

"The church kiss was longer," teased the MC. "And more on target."

He was a devil! He'd always found that ignoring the tears was the best shot and so Minnie was led gently to a seat, a freshly crowned but bewildered princess. She was six places away from

Ann. The littlies ran up and down behind the tables for the rest of the courses, too excited to eat. The soup was good. Little Deb and Katie had stored their bowls under the table but were playing a game with the croutons.

For one moment or maybe two, Minnie caught Ann's eye and smiled. Ann raised an eyebrow and smiled back, showing what she hoped was an elegant irony, as if to say "Look at this hand that fate has dealt us." Then it was time for the telegrams. As in wartime, the arrival of a telegram could mean life or death.

"Could we have a bit of shoosh please?" The awful MC handed over the microphone to the best man. The hand that held the telegrams shook.

"To Steve, roses are red, violets are blue . . ." The mike was adjusted but the shaking hand couldn't be helped. ". . . if you don't get some tonight, then what good are you?"

Har har! Steve's dad was nodding in approval while a line of Bellini relatives pfffed and snorted into the hands and glasses.

"To Steve and Minnie, best wishes from the class of seventy-nine."

So tame! Ann closed her eyes.

To dearest Minnie, I love and lust after you but I don't forgive you. I miss sex with you. What a team we were! Your loss, honey. Hot kisses from your bridesmaid, Annie.

"More champagne, Ann?"

"Thanks, Aunt Luisa."

After the cake was cut, symbolizing their first action taken together, Steve and Minnie danced the bridal waltz. The wedding party watched in polite silence as they shuffled back and forth. An unerringly flicked crouton from little Deb crunched under Minnie's heels.

Aunt Luisa felt that something was wrong. Her smile faded. She frowned. A sensitive radar seemed to emanate from her. Her head moved back and forth as though she were a psychic sniffing out the scent of the future. She gave a low questioning moan. She was tracking down a very clear signal.

"What's wrong, Aunt Luisa?"

Ann looked at Luisa just as the same thought occurred to both of them: Minnie would not end up with this man, this Steve. And should not. Not at all! Aunt Luisa studied her plate, her dark brows knitted together. Ann smiled into her warm champagne. So all was not lost.

"Good food eh?" Ian, who was adjusting his bow tie, belched. "We're next." He drained his glass because this was going to be tough, dancing with this girl Ann.

"And the bridesmaid and partner, Ann and Ian!"

Ann nearly jerked him off his feet in her hurry to get the dance floor and her little Minnie.

"Take it easy!" Ian said. The girl was huge and gawky.

"And little DebnKatie!" The MC could have been calling raffle winners.

So now there were six of them in this circus. The little twins clutched each other, their flowers skew-whiff over their ears, and swayed in a parody of Steve and Minnie. Ian and Ann did a neat, precise lap of the floor. Ian had started to relax a bit when they approached the happy couple for the second time.

"Minnie!" It was a restrained but urgent whisper that Ian could hear coming from right next to his head. Bloody Ann. Maybe she'd dropped something. He looked at the floor.

"Minnie Min!"

"Shut up!"

"No!"

Minnie was looking at Ann over Steve's shoulder. Ian tried to dance Ann away from them but that made it worse. The next whisper was louder.

"Are you sure, Minnie?"

Minnie was whimpering, for God's sake.

"Are you?!"

The MC had never seen anything like this stringbean girl who was whirling her partner around like a dervish. She seemed to be hissing at the poor little bride.

"And now, ladies and gentlemen. When you're ready to join these lovely couples, get up and have a spin!"

Ian was about to suggest sitting down, now that there were plenty of other couples up, thank Christ, when he felt Ann melt away from him. Ann tapped Steve on the shoulder.

"Excuse me. May I?" Quicker than a wink she scooped up Minnie, her little Min, around the waist. Steve and Ian stood and watched.

"For fuck's sake." But Steve was as nothing next to her. A mere speck.

She was dancing with his wife.

Steve looked at Ian. "She's dancing with my wife, mate."

Ian nodded. "Maybe that's what you're supposed to do. Do you want a drink?"

Minnie tried to look at Ann, but the overwhelming familiar smell of her, the feel of her body, was enough.

"Jesus, Ann. Jesus!"

"You signed my dance card, remember?"

The stringbean and the crowned princess swirled around the floor, scattering little Deb's croutons. Minnie was half laughing, half groaning with embarrassment. Ann was in full stride, now that action had been taken.

"Remember when we came home from that party? Remember when we fell asleep on the lawn and your mother found us in the morning?"

"Is this supposed to make me feel wistful?"

"Yes. I want you to remember. Remember everything."

"Mum said we were perverted."

"No. She said I was perverted. You are still her baby daughter."

Other couples, looking and then looking again, were laughing. Little Deb and Kate waltzed past professionally.

"When do we get cake?"

Minnie smiled down at them. "Soon."

Little Deb watched them a bit more. "Why are youse dancing together? You shouldn't be dancing together."

"It's the tradition for women to dance together at weddings."

"Oh sure."

"Anyway, look at you two."

Ann turned back to Minnie.

"Remember when we danced together for the first time?"

"Whah yayes!"

Minnie and her southern accent! It was a good sign. Inside herself, Ann crowed. Quick! More!

"Remember when your mother found us kissing in the garden?"

"Why did everything happen in the garden?"

"The smell of hot lawn and your gardenias. There was something . . . labial about them. To put it quite frankly, they smelt of fanny."

"They didn't!"

"Yes, Min, I'm afraid they brought out the butch in me."

"Not in that dress, mate."

"See what I do for you? I cross-dress for you. Would Steve do that? I'll even kiss you if you like."

"If we kiss, then this wedding is finished. My marriage is a sham."

"Then I will, definitely."

Ann pressed her body closer to Minnie's and kissed her cheek. Mrs. Bellini, her eyes narrowed, was watching from her seat.

"I love you, Min."

"I love you."

"Even better, marry me! I have a limousine waiting."

"My mother's looking a bit strange."

"Well well well, are we surprised?"

Mrs. Bellini was standing, walking, brushing away Mr. Bellini's hand. Aunt Luisa watched her sister approach, then turned and watched the stringbean Annie with her little niece.

Mrs. Bellini was nearly upon them. Aunt Luisa, sitting nearest the dance floor, was able to reach up and with much force pull her sister into a seat. With one hand, Aunt Luisa waved at Ann and Minnie, still smiling.

"Yoo hoo! You girls!"

Her other hand, under the table, had a firm grip on her sister.

"Luisa! Stop it. Let me up!"

Luisa continued to beam. Her champagne glass was lifted high, frothing and full. Ann turned back to Minnie and grinned.

"Somehow I don't think we've got the full story on your aunt."

Aunt Luisa's glass spilled over just as Minnie reached up and kissed Ann quite expertly on the lips.

VIII

My hand on your hand
    both
In the hollow of
    a tree
one sky chasing another
    sky
    both
devouring atoms
    and
going to the moon.
Green is the color of
    space.

Two lips tasting mushrooms
and the Colorado River
    haunting
    the village . . .
from the persistent Mediterranean
to the persistent
    Pacific
we cut roads with our feet
    share baggage and
    food
running always one second
    ahead of the running of
    Time

we are traveling at some
infinite speed

we are not scared.

—Etel Adnan
from *The Indian Never Had a Horse*

Bibliography

Most of the books on this list—as well as all the correspondence and manuscripts growing out of this collection—will be housed at the Lesbian Herstory Archives (LHA) in Brooklyn, New York.

Adnan, Etel. "In the Heart of the Heart of Another Country." *Mundus Artium.* 10:1, 1977. Dallas: University of Texas.

———. *The Indian Never Had a Horse.* Sausalito, CA: Post Apollo Press, 1985.

Best, Mireille. *Les Mots de hasard.* Paris: Gallimard, 1980. Translated by Janine Ricouart.

Blaman, Anna. *Eenzaam Avontuur.* Amsterdam: J. M. Meulenhoff, 1948. Translated by Donald Gardner.

Brand, Dionne. *Sans Souci.* Ithaca, New York: Firebrand Books, 1989.

Brantenberg, Gerd. *The Four Winds.* Seattle: Women in Translation, 1996.

Brossard, Nicole. *Mauve Desert.* Toronto: Coach House Press, 1990. Translated by Susanne de Lotbinière-Harwood.

Dorcey, Mary. *A Noise from the Woodshed: Short Stories.* London: Onlywoman Press, 1989.

Duffy, Maureen. *The Microcosm.* London: Virago Press, Ltd., 1966.

Jutras, Jeanne d'Arc. *Georgie.* Montreal: Editions Pleine Lune, 1978. Translated by Naomi Holoch.

Leduc, Violette. *L'Asphyxie.* Paris: Editions Gallimard, 1948. Translated by Naomi Holoch.

Maraini, Dacia. *Letters to Marina*. London: Camden Press, 1987. Translated by Dick Kitto and Elspeth Spottiswood.

Min, Anchee. *Red Azalea*. New York: Pantheon Books, 1994.

Molloy, Sylvia. *Certificate of Absence*. Austin: University of Texas Press, 1989. Translated by Daniel Balderson and the author.

Peri Rossi, Cristina. *A Forbidden Passion*. San Francisco: Cleis Press, 1993. Translated by Mary Jane Treacy.

Mootoo, Shani. *Out on Main Street*. Vancouver: Press Gang Publishers, 1993.

Rifaat, Alifa. *Distant View of a Minaret and Other Stories*. London: Quartet Books, Ltd., 1983.

Silvera, Makeda. *Her Head a Village and Other Stories*. Vancouver: Press Gang Publishers, 1994.

Te Awekotuku, Ngahuia. *Tahuri*. Auckland, Aotearoa/New Zealand: New Women's Press, 1989.

Tusquets, Esther. *The Same Sea as Every Summer*. Lincoln: The University of Nebraska Press, 1990. Translated by Margaret E. W. Jones.

Winsloe, Christa. *The Child Manuela*. London: Virago Press Ltd., 1994. Translated by Agnes Neill Scott.

Yourcenar, Marguerite. *Fires*. New York: Farrar, Straus and Giroux, Inc., 1981. Translated by Dori Katz.

Suggested Additional Reading

Anderson, Shelley, ed. *Lesbian Rights are Human Rights*. Amsterdam: International Lesbian Information Services, 1995. Can be ordered from ILIS, Nieuwezijdo Voorburgwal 68.70 NL.1012 SE Amsterdam, the Netherlands.

———. *Out in the World: International Lesbian Organizing*. Firebrand Sparks #4. Ithaca: Firebrand Books.

Arguelles, Lourdes, and Ruby B. Rich. "Homosexuality, Homophobia and Revolution: Notes Toward an Understanding of the Cuban Lesbian and Gay Male Experience." *Hidden from History: Reclaiming the Gay and Lesbian Past,* edited by M. Duberman, M. Vicinus, and G. Chauncey. New York: New American Library, 1989.

Bergmann, E. L., and P. J. Smith, eds. *Entiendes: Queer Reading, Hispanic Writing*. Durham, N.C.: Duke University Press, 1995.

Dorf, Julie. "A History of Homosexuality in Russia and the USSR." Unpublished paper, nd. Lesbian Herstory Archives, P.O. Box 1258, New York, N.Y. 10116.

Gevisser, Mark, and Edwin Cameron. *Defiant Desire: Gay and Lesbian Lives in South Africa*. New York: Routledge, 1995.

Healey, Emma, and Angela Mason, eds. *Stonewall 25: The Making of the Lesbian and Gay Community in Britain*. London: Virago Press, 1994.

Krouse, Matthew, ed. *The Invisible Ghetto: Lesbian and Gay Writing from South Africa*. London: Gay Men's Press, 1995.

Likosky, S. *Coming Out: An Anthology of International Gay and Lesbian Writings*. New York: Pantheon Books, 1992.

Lim-Hing, Sharon, ed. *The Very Inside: An Anthology of Writing by Asian and Pacific Island Bisexual Women.* Toronto: Sister Vision Press, 1994.

Martinez, Elena M. *Lesbian Voices from Latin America.* New York: Garland Publishers, 1996.

McLeod, Donald W. *Lesbian and Gay Liberation in Canada: A Selected Annotated Chronology, 1964–1975.* Toronto: ECW Press and Homewood Books, 1996.

O'Carroll, Ide, and Eoin Collins. *Lesbian and Gay Visions of Ireland: Towards the Twenty-First Century.* London: Cassell, 1995.

Parikas, U. and T. Veispak, eds. "Sexual Minorities and Society: The Changing Attitudes Toward Homosexuality in 20th Century Europe." Paper presented to the international conference in Tallinn, May 28–30, 1990.

Randall, Margaret, and Lynda Yana, eds. " 'Coming Out as a Lesbian Is What Brought Me to Social Consciousness': Rita Arauz." In *Sandino's Daughters Revisited: Feminism in Nicaragua.* New Brunswick, N.J.: Rutgers University Press, 1994.

———. "To Change Our Own Reality and the World: A Conversation with Lesbians in Nicaragua." *Signs* 18 (Summer, 1993): 907–925.

Rosenbloom, Rachel, ed. *Unspoken Rules: Sexual Orientation and Women's Human Rights.* London: Cassell and the International Gay and Lesbian Human Rights Commission, 1996.

Silvera, Makeda, ed. *Piece of My Heart: A Lesbian of Colour Anthology.* Toronto: Sister Vision Press, 1991.

Tuller, David. *Cracks in the Iron Closet: Travels in Gay and Lesbian Russia.* Boston: Faber and Faber, 1996.

Acknowledgments

First of all, we wish to thank Sydelle Kramer, our agent, from the Frances Golden Agency, and LuAnn Walther, our editor, and Diana Secker Larson at Vintage, for their patience and perseverance during this long process.

We are deeply indebted to the following individuals who supported our vision, taught us the technological ropes of online communication, put us in contact with writers and their work, and did translations: Huey-Min Chuang, Janine Ricouart, Francesca Sautman, M. Katherine Cirsena, Maria Gagliardo, Sylvia Molloy, Ginu Kamani, Sonja Franeta, Marilyn Hacker, Achy Obejas, Margaret Randall, Naomi Replansky, Elena Madrigal Rodriguez, Saskia Scheffer, Lisa Davis, Maike van Haskamp, Joke Peters, Nerina Milletti, Jared Becker, Ruth Siegel, Carolyn Gammon, Elspeth Spottiswood, Karin X. Tulchinsky, James Johnston, Karla Jay, Helga Pankratz, Gail Phederson, Claire Maree, Junkio Yoshiawa, and Masha Gessen.

We want to thank all the activists and authors who wrote background essays for us on the legal, social, and political realities facing lesbians in their countries: Yasmin V. Tambiah (Sri Lanka), Sharon Lim-Hing (China), Giti Thadani (India), Claire Maree (Japan), Odette Alonso (Cuba), Makeda Silvera (Jamaica), Karen X. Tulchinsky (Canada), Karen Williams (South Africa), Alison J. Laurie (New Zealand), Barbara Farrelly (Australia), Nerina Milletti (Italy), Suzanne Triton Robichon (France), Dorothee Winded (Germany), Marike van Harskamp and Joke Peters (Holland), Karin Lutzen (Denmark), Suzana Tratnik (Slovenia), Sonja Franeta and Mash Gessen (Russia), Ide O'Carroll (Ireland), Constantia Constantinou (Cyprus), Gila Svirsky (Israel), Etel Adnan (Lebanon), and Shelley Anderson (International Lesbian Information Service). All of these essays are available at the Lesbian Herstory Archives, P.O. Box 1258, New York, N.Y. 10116.

We also want to thank the independent and feminist press and publishers who have brought to print so many of the authors included here: Cleis Press, Aunt Lute Books, Seal Press, Women in Translation, Firebrand Books, Gay Men's Press, Cassell Press, and Talon Books. A special thank you to J. M. Meulenhoff Publishers of Amsterdam.

We want to thank the following individuals who helped the anxiety-provoking permission process reach a happy conclusion: Richard Abbate of Pantheon Books, Patricia James of Little, Brown, Barbara Tolley representing Gallimard, Dana Wooley of Cleis Press, Christine Scudder of Aunt Lute, Claire Maruhn of the University of Nebraska Press, Barbara Kuhne of Press Gang Publishers, and Barbara Wilson of Women in Translation.

Permissions Acknowledgments

About the Editors

Naomi Holoch is co-editor, with Joan Nestle, of the *Women on Women* series of anthologies of American lesbian short fiction and the author of short stories and a novel, *Offseason*. She teaches French language and literature, lesbian and gay fiction, and fiction writing at SUNY-Purchase.

Joan Nestle, author of the award-winning *A Restricted Country* and *A Fragile Union* and editor of *The Persistent Desire: A Femme-Butch Reader,* is also co-founder of the New York–based Lesbian Herstory Archives. Along with Naomi Holoch, she has edited three volumes of *Women on Women* anthologies. She also had the honor of working with John Preston on *Sister and Brother: Lesbians and Gay Men Talk about Their Lives Together.* In 1996 she was awarded the Bill Whitehead Award for Lifetime Achievement in Lesbian and Gay Literature by the Publishing Triangle. For close to thirty years, she taught writing in the SEEK Program at Queens College, CUNY.

Printed in the United States
by Baker & Taylor Publisher Services